From Pasta

to Pigfoot:

Second

Helpings

Praise for From *Pasta to Pigfoot*

'The storyline is beautiful and I enjoyed reading about Faye and her experiences... This book educated me on Ghanaian culture, I felt like packing my bags and going on holiday to Ghana.'
Motunrayo Akande, Tunrayo's Thoughts

'This delightful romantic adventure captures, with stark realism, the journey of cultural awakening, self discovery, love and familial relationships experienced by the main character Faye Bonsu... Frances Mensah Williams's portrays her likeable characters with great skill. (...) One to pack for the beach.'
Barbara Grant, Words of Colour

'*From Pasta to Pigfoot* presents a youthful narrative that grants deep questions of identity and self discovery a universal resonance. [The novel] possesses a lightness of language crafted with lyrical finesse.'
Afrikult.com

'(...) Mensah Williams continues a trend evident in the works and outlook of other writers of the African diaspora: to delink themselves and their characters from received cultural knowledge, literary practices, and classification tags; to distinguish themselves by their individual aesthetic choices and practices, and, in that process, reveal the social usefulness of literature in its search for or construction of the universal.'
Pede Hollist, author of *So the Path Does Not Die*

First published in this edition in Great Britain 2016 by
Jacaranda Books Art Music Ltd
Unit 304 Metal Box Factory
30 Great Guildford Street,
London SE1 0HS
www.jacarandabooksartmusic.co.uk

A CIP catalogue record for this book is available
from the British Library

ISBN is 978-1-909762-27-5
eISBN is 978-1-909762-28-2

Typeset by Head & Heart Publishing Services
www.headandheartpublishingservices.com

Printed and bound in Great Britain
by CPI Group (UK) Ltd, Croydon, CR0 4YY

From Pasta
to Pigfoot:
Second Helpings

Frances Mensah Williams

JACARANDA

For my brothers and sisters: Pete, Nana, Akwasi, Ophelia, Emma and Victor. And for Thomas. Love always.

1

Baby Love

Lying on her back propped up on her elbows, Faye chewed thoughtfully on a blade of grass and surveyed her surroundings in wonder. The combination of sun and a Saturday afternoon had seemingly brought all the yummy mummies in Hampstead out to the Heath, a huge expanse of park and woodland a few minutes' walk away from her house.

Looking around, all she could see spread out across the dry, springy grass were children of different sizes, colourful blankets, picnic mats and shiny buggies. Ridiculously slim mothers in uniforms of strappy vest tops, cropped cargo pants and brightly coloured flip-flops coaxed freshly pureed vegetable mush into their babies' mouths while simultaneously shrieking at the older versions running around tripping over mats, dogs and clumps of grass. From where it was parked on the gravelled car park by the entrance to the Heath, the ice-cream van's occasional chimes tinkled above the cacophony of well-bred voices.

It really is true that what you focus on is what you see. *When the hell did there get to be so many children in the world?*

A few metres away from where Faye was stretched out, a frisky puppy dashed back and forth between a just-fed toddler in a floppy white hat sitting up on a blanket, his chubby cheeks smeared with generous dollops of sunscreen, and a boy of about four years old who was energetically flinging a red Frisbee into the air, presumably intended for the puppy to fetch.

Faye spat out the grass stalk and turned her attention back to the baby right in front of her who had spotted the dog and was quietly crawling off her colourful straw mat and heading purposefully in its direction. Coco's latest trick was to hug anyone or anything within sight as tightly as she could. With an endearing smile, she would tightly wind her chubby and surprisingly strong arms around her victim. For such a small child, her embrace was overpowering and Faye briskly hauled her back, alarmed at the sudden vision of Coco hugging the poor puppy to death. Ignoring the child's indignant yelp, she plonked her firmly back onto the mat and looked across to where Caroline lay flat on her back, a huge pair of sunglasses wedged onto her face, too exhausted to notice – or care – what her child was up to.

She had arrived unexpectedly at Faye's, just before lunch, clutching a protesting Coco under one arm and the mat under the other. She insisted that they take a picnic up to Hampstead Heath and instantly dismissed Faye's objections that she had to finish some work for her boss with terse instructions to bring her work with her. Taking pity on her friend whom she had to admit really did look shattered, Faye put Lottie in charge of the baby and assembled an impromptu lunch of pasta salad, pitta bread and some leftover cold-cuts from the fridge. Loading up the picnic basket, the three of them had strolled down to the edge of the Heath to soak up the sunshine.

Faye stretched her long legs out across the mat, effectively corralling Coco between them, putting paid to her renewed efforts to sneak across to play with the puppy. Although her feet were bare and she had rolled her black jeans up to her calves, Faye still felt oppressed by the summer heat. Her scalp prickled and she fanned the air in an effort to cool down. When that didn't work, she flapped her arms up and down, causing the wide sleeves of her caftan-style cotton top to waft gracefully about, creating a short-lived cooling breeze through the still, warm air.

'Hey, are you awake under there? Your daughter was just about to inflict one of her deathly hugs on some poor dog!'

'This is such bliss...' Caroline murmured drowsily, turning her face up towards the sunshine. 'It's so nice not to hear anyone asking me to do anything. I've made so many decisions this week, I'm exhausted!'

'Jeez, Caro, it's really hot out here! I hope you've put on some sunscreen. You redheads don't do tanning very well – remember what happened that time you fell asleep sunbathing?'

''Course I've got sunscreen on,' Caroline muttered irritably. 'SPF 50 on both me and Coco, for your information. Anyway, it's not that bad out here. For someone who comes from Africa, it's really weird how you can't cope with a bit of sunshine.'

Faye flapped her arms again, much to Coco's delight. Burbling happily at this new game, she stood up and tottered over to Faye, collapsing against her chest as she tried to force her arms up and down. Chortling with laughter, Faye seized Coco in a warm embrace and nuzzled her lips against her neck.

'You are so gorgeous, my little angel!' she exclaimed. 'I want one – no, a hundred, just like you!'

Caroline sat bolt upright and snatched her sunglasses off her face, her blue eyes round and wide and her expression a combination of incredulity and triumph. Without warning, she shrieked. 'I knew it! Faye Elizabeth Anastasia Bonsu, you do want babies!'

Raising her head, Faye looked around in horror but no-one appeared to be staring at her. 'Why don't you say it a bit louder just in case there's someone in London that didn't hear you? And go easy on the whole full name thing; you know it makes me feel like I've done something wrong.'

'When, when did you decide you want babies? It's been years since you've actually said the words! I can't believe it.' Caroline was practically babbling in her excitement.

'I've never said I didn't want them,' Faye muttered defensively, putting the wriggling child back on the mat. 'I just said I wasn't sure I was ready for them. It's not like I'm married yet or even living with the guy, although thanks to my beloved dad, that's not about to happen any time soon. Of course I want to settle down and have kids, even if I haven't exactly spelled it out.'

She sighed and distractedly ran her fingers through her hair. 'Look, Caro, I don't know. For ages I've been fine

4

about me and Rocky just being boyfriend and girlfriend, but lately it's really been getting to me that we're not moving forward. If anything, I'm seeing less of him than ever. I mean, you take today. It's the weekend, but he's in New York yet again and won't be back until next week. So, you know, maybe it's just not the right time. I mean, things are still really busy for me and Rocky—'

Caroline had heard enough and cut decisively into Faye's stream of consciousness. 'Rocky, nothing! If you're ready to make things official and have kids, it's time he took your relationship more seriously. I mean, really, how long are you two going to go on just dating? You're not getting any younger, and neither is he. Anyway, I'm really glad you've come to your senses. I can't wait for us to be mums together like we always planned!'

She flopped back down onto the grass and replaced her sunglasses, a wide grin taking up the lower half of her face.

'Stop looking so smug and watch your child while I get my work finished. Matt wants to pick this up today.' Faye reached for the large portfolio case she had dragged along to the Heath and pulled out a big square cork board covered in pieces of fabric and clippings.

Caroline raised her glasses and looked at the object curiously. 'What is that?'

'It's a mood board for my pig of a client's new gallery. He wants a different theme in each of the main halls but the rooms have to have an organic flow. We've built up boards for each space to give him a feel of the design flow.'

'Is he still being a pain in the you-know-where with

you?' Caroline glanced quickly at her daughter who was developed an alarming habit of randomly repeating any words that took her fancy.

Faye secured a loose magazine clipping with a small pin and began re-arranging the fabric swatches into colour groups. 'That's putting it mildly. I try and keep my distance and let Matt do the talking. As far as I'm concerned, the less I see of him, the better for both of us.'

She tucked a loose strand of hair behind her ears and concentrated on the task at hand while Caroline lifted up her daughter and blew loud raspberries on the little rounded belly under the cotton sundress. She turned back to Faye who was holding the board at arms length and squinting at the pattern through her long-lashed, almond-shaped eyes which looked more Asian than African.

'Why do you have to do this today, anyway? It's Saturday, for God's sake. You're getting as bad as Rocky!'

Faye grinned and lowered the board, making a few adjustments to the layout. 'This is a big project for the firm and we really need to deliver. Justin wants to open the new gallery in October and it takes time to order all the furnishings. He's still dithering about the design concept Matt and the team put together so the mood boards will help him get a sense of the colour palette and the feel of the different spaces without us having to spend an arm and a leg on materials which he then decides he hates.'

Faye held the board out again and scrutinised it for a few moments and then nodded in satisfaction. She pulled out a second cork board and carefully placed the first one back into the case. Ripping off a couple of the magazine clippings, she carefully re-arranged the swatches and added a couple of scraps of paper with sketches of light fixtures.

'I thought you did all this stuff on computers these days?' Caroline looked at the board dubiously.

'We've done all the drawings on computer but sometimes it helps to have some hand-drawn sketches and boards like this. Matt insists that the boards always get the sales. Doing it this way also helps us to understand what the client sees, and it makes it easier and more intimate for them than doing it robotically on a CAD piece of software—'

'Faye?'

She paused at the sound of her name and turned in surprise. Walking towards them from the direction of the car park was Matt, his long legs bounding across the springy grass as he weaved his way through the blankets and buggies. He was dressed casually in a dark green sports shirt and jeans and had a red baseball cap perched backwards on his mop of curly hair. Even more surprising than seeing her boss suddenly appear on the Heath was the fact that he was walking hand-in-hand with a young boy who was practically skipping to keep up with the older man's long strides.

'Matt!' Faye hastily raked her fingers through her hair, conscious that it was desperately in need of washing. Under pressure from Caroline to get a move on, she had left home without a scrap of make-up and was now feeling scruffy and distinctly "boho un-chic", not to mention hot and sweaty. Caroline watched Matt advance towards them and her eyes narrowed speculatively as she took in her friend's feeble attempts to tidy herself up.

'You've never mentioned that your boss is so hot,' she murmured, her eyes returning to the tall figure almost upon them.

'Shhh!' Faye hissed, mortified at the idea of Matt overhearing. 'I told you he was picking up the mood boards this afternoon. Lottie must have told him where we were.'

'Faye!' Matt's booming voice drowned out the shrieks of the yummy mummies as he bore down upon them. Caroline sat up straight and pushed her sunglasses back on her head, craning her neck upwards to inspect the new arrival. Coco, never backwards in coming forward, tottered a few steps over to him and placed her small palms on his trousers as she tried to keep her balance on the soft turf. Clearly enchanted by her, Matt released the hand of the boy at his side and reached down to pick her up and swing her into his arms. She promptly wound her chubby arms around his neck and Faye winced as she watched his face suddenly turn a deep shade of pink.

'Hi, Matt, I'm so sorry! My demon goddaughter is a lot stronger than she looks.' She jumped up and hastily pried Coco out of his arms. The child reluctantly let go and then, ready for her next victim, looked eagerly at the young boy.

Matt roared with laughter and then turned to greet Caroline who had been watching the scene with a smile of approval.

'Hi, I'm Faye's friend, Caroline.' She stretched out her hand and Matt shook it firmly before turning and gesturing to the boy who had dropped down onto his knees to play with Coco.

'This is my nephew, Charlie,' he said, his voice was warm with pride. Charlie's dark purple *Transformers* T-shirt hung loosely on his small frame and covered the top of his jeans. His black trainers were fastened with fluorescent purple laces and when he smiled shyly up at the two women, identical little dimples appeared in the centre of each rosy cheek.

'Sorry to barge in on you like this, Faye. I stopped at your house to pick up the boards. The lady there said we would find you here.' Matt looked apologetically at Faye who smiled as she watched Charlie gently extricate his blond curls from Coco's grip. He took the little girl's hands in his own and walked her along for a few steps while she gave him a wide, flirtatious grin, displaying her pink gums and tiny white teeth.

'Just like her mother,' Faye murmured, pretending not to hear her friend's indignant snort.

A group of yummy mummies sitting a few feet away and who had studiously ignored them earlier were now openly ogling the new arrival. *To be fair, he's probably the only man on the Heath this afternoon*, Faye mused. She watched, fascinated, as one of them, a brunette with a whippet-thin body wearing microscopic white shorts revealing toned bronze legs, stared hungrily at Matt. She sat up straight, clearly willing him to look at her, patting her carefully-styled-to-look-casual topknot, while fixing an inviting smile on her pearly glossed lips. It felt strange to see Matt being gawked at by other women. Although Faye was well aware that he was an attractive man, for the past year he had simply been Matt 'the boss.' Yet, judging by the effect he was having after only two minutes on the Heath, he was apparently also Matt 'the hottie.' She dragged her mind away from that particular train of thought and smiled at him cheerfully.

'It's no problem at all. I brought the boards with me and actually, I'm glad you're here – I could use your feedback on this one.' She gestured to Matt to sit down and dropping back down onto the grass, she picked up the second mood board and explained her ideas. After a few minutes of discussion, having made a number of tweaks to the clippings on the board Matt stood up and brushed down his trousers. Charlie and Coco had wandered a few feet away and, under Caroline's watchful gaze, were playing with Elsa, Coco's long-suffering stuffed grey bunny that accompanied her everywhere.

Faye followed Matt's gaze. 'It looks like Coco has commandeered poor Charlie. She's a strong-willed little one; we're all putty in her hands.'

He smiled, and little laughter lines deepened at the corners of his dark blue eyes. 'He's great with kids. An only child, you know, so always happy to have someone to play with. Luckily, he hasn't yet reached the age where they wouldn't be seen dead playing with toys.'

Although his speech was as choppy and staccato as usual, Faye was struck by how much more relaxed he appeared than when he was at work.

She watched him swing Charlie up and round and deposit him gently back onto the grass with a playful ruffling of his blond curls, a far cry from the usual pacing, restless energy that she always associated with him. He bent down to pick up the portfolio case and beckoned to his nephew.

'We'll leave you to enjoy your picnic, ladies. Caroline, a pleasure to meet you. Lovely daughter. Faye, thanks for finishing these off and I'll see you in the office on Monday.'

The dark-haired woman sitting nearby gave a moue of disappointment and let her back slump back into its normal position as she watched Matt walk back towards the car park, Charlie practically jogging alongside him.

Caroline looked sideways at Faye, who turned and stared at her suspiciously.

'What? Why are you looking at me like that? Do I look even more of a hot mess than I thought?'

Her friend examined her critically. 'No, you look fine. Your nose is a bit shiny- not that he seemed to notice,' she added.

Faye frowned. 'What do you mean?'

'Well, let's just say he seemed very happy to see you. Did he really need to get those boards today or was it just a good excuse to pay you a visit?'

'Caroline, he's my boss! There's absolutely nothing going on there and, yes, he did need to get the boards. He's got a meeting with Justin Parker, our client from hell, on Monday.' Faye looked outraged at the implication but Caroline just shrugged.

'Well, I'm just saying what I saw...' She broke off and sighed with impatience. 'Coco – come here, darling! Leave that poor puppy alone!'

Later that afternoon, after her friend had departed with a now exhausted Coco to prepare for dinner with her dreaded mother-in-law, Faye lay slumped across the sofa at home, relieved to be out of the relentless sunshine. The spacious living room was light and airy and with the French doors as well as the windows thrown wide open, she could just about feel a faint cool breeze from where she lay.

She closed her eyes and tried to block out the muffled sounds coming from the direction of the kitchen where Lottie, their housekeeper, seemed intent on using every saucepan available for a practice run on the lamb recipe she was planning to tackle at her next cookery evening class. Her thoughts turned back to the earlier conversation with Caroline, and Faye racked her brains trying to understand what could have put any ideas into Caroline's head about her boss's intentions. Try as she might, she couldn't pinpoint anything less than professional in the way Matt behaved around her. As far as she knew, he was unmarried but the office gossip was silent on whether he had a girlfriend or significant other. Probably because he's at work so much, no-one even thinks of him as having a private life, she reasoned.

Faye felt a sudden pang as she realised that her own private life wasn't up to much these days either. Impulsively, she picked up her mobile and tried Rocky's number, groaning in annoyance when it went to voice-mail. She glanced at her watch, calculating that it would be just after eleven in the morning in New York.

She vaguely remembered from their phone call the night before that he had mentioned something about calling a team meeting today, but as usual she found it difficult to pay attention when he talked about his work, resenting that it took up so much of his time. She also knew from experience that getting hold of him when he was on a business trip was always a gamble.

She tried once more and his voice-mail clicked into operation. With an irritated sigh, she typed out a short text and tossed her phone aside.

2

Perfect Stranger

Faye looked at her watch for what felt like the hundredth time, almost grinding her teeth in frustration. *Where the hell is Rocky? He should have been here over an hour ago!* She squashed her intense desire to strangle him and instead reached down to lift Coco out of the travel cot. It wasn't Coco's fault that she had been left literally holding the baby while, as usual, Rocky was nowhere to be found. Coco burbled loudly in her own private language and Faye nuzzled her face into the space between the child's head and neck, inhaling the heady scent of warm baby mixed with talcum powder.

'Aren't you just the most beautiful thing ever,' she cooed. Her silky black hair tickled the baby's face and Coco giggled uncontrollably. Encouraged by the chuckles, Faye hoisted the child high above her head with a loud 'Weee...!'

Seconds later, she watched in fascinated horror at the line of drool heading straight down towards her cheek.

'Urgh! Coco, no!' She ducked her head to dodge the liquid coming at her and hastily lowered her arms. Coco chuckled with pleasure, causing even more drool to emerge from her little mouth.

'I thought we were friends. You can mess up my jeans all you want, but do you know how much money I spent on this top?'

Dabbing at the child's mouth with a damp bib, Faye's brown eyes looked sorrowfully into the unrepentant blue eyes of the one-year old. Changing tactics, Coco opened her chubby arms and flung them around Faye as far as they would go, nestling her soft red-blonde curls into the crook of Faye's neck.

Faye's reproachful expression melted into a beatific smile, which lasted for at least thirty seconds before another glance at her watch transformed it into a heavy frown. She put Coco down and paced up and down the polished wooden floor of Caroline's living room, her eyes darting restlessly between the toddler and the silent phone on the side table.

Seriously, where was Rocky? While he wasn't the best at being punctual; okay, correction, he was the worst, this time she would have bet real money that he would show up as promised. Even if babysitting Faye's best friend's daughter wasn't exactly her boyfriend's idea of a romantic night in, Rocky had sounded fine about it when she had spoken to him earlier.

It had been unusually warm, even for June, and the breeze blowing through the car window brought a welcome relief from the bright sunshine. She had been driving for almost twenty minutes before she remembered that she had yet to tell Rocky about the change of plan. Rummaging under her discarded jacket and the pile of fabric samples and scribbled notes detailing quantities and prices on the passenger seat, she retrieved her phone and stuck it in the holder, all the while keeping one eye out for speed cameras. Turning down the music reverberating around the car, she flicked on her hands-free and after two rings, heard the familiar deep voice that never failed to make her heart beat faster.

'Hey, I was just about to call you. Where are you?' Rocky's low drawl sent familiar shivers juddering straight through her body. From her first encounter with Rocky Asante, his height, perfectly sculpted face and close cropped hair combined with light copper coloured eyes slightly at odds with his chocolate brown skin, had thrown her into a state of utter confusion. Faye still had trouble understanding how one man could be quite so gorgeous and be her boyfriend.

'I'm in the car heading home to change,' she said. 'I'm really sorry, but Caroline's got a mini crisis on and needs me to babysit Coco this evening.'

'Oka-ay,' he said, sounding wary. She smiled, instantly picturing the furrowed brow that always appeared when he had a decision to make.

'I take it that means that our dinner plans are off, then?'

'I know; I'm so sorry. I was really looking forward to going to Barzini's. They've got some brilliant reviews and apparently their head chef trained in Italy with some of the best-' She broke off apologetically, not wanting Rocky to think she had been critiquing his choice of restaurant.

He laughed, no trace of offence in the warm, deep voice coming through the speaker. 'Trust me, I checked before I booked. Picking an Italian restaurant for a pasta addict isn't something you do lightly.'

Faye grinned and navigated a sharp bend in the road. Her love of pasta was legendary and to her mind, there was no occasion too sad, too happy, too humble or too grand that didn't warrant a dish of Italian magic. From a plate of her favourite corkscrew-shaped cavatappi to a steaming bowl of heavily garlic infused tagliatelle, as far as Faye was concerned, every situation demanded a pasta dish of its own.

'You know... you could meet me at Caro's and help me with Coco?' Instead of the immediate 'No, thanks' she had been expecting, Rocky's reply caught her off-guard.

'Okay, why not? She's a cute kid, and at least I'll get to spend some time with you. It seems like forever since I've kissed those beautiful lips of yours.' His chuckle reverberated around the car and she flushed as the shivers returned in full force.

'What time do you want me there?'

Still distracted by his last comment, she just made it through the traffic lights before the amber light changed to red. 'I'll be at Caroline's by five. Why don't you come over at six o'clock and we can order a pizza or something?' she suggested, still shocked that Rocky had agreed to anything that resembled domesticity.

Even after four years together, Rocky had yet to say or do anything that smacked of wanting to settle down. At almost thirty-five, her ambitious boyfriend was the ultimate career professional. His job as an investment banker meant long hours and constant travel and even if he had shown any interest in domestic bliss, it was hard to see how his punishing schedule would have allowed it.

Six o'clock had been and gone and it was now seven-thirty. Faye stared at the phone willing it to ring; all her attempts to reach Rocky had sent her straight to his voice-mail and she resisted the temptation to check the battery.

Instead, she leant back against the sofa watching Coco play and tried to calm her mind. There were still some vestiges of light creeping in through the French doors leading to the patio and private garden, and the small open window above the doors allowed a cooling breeze to circulate around the room. With big, squashy sofas lining the walls and stylish chrome floor lamps at each corner of the room casting a gentle glow against the soft cream of the walls, the living room was both spacious and cosy. A large television screen – a basic necessity as far as Caroline was concerned – hung on the wall and the tall bookcases built into the chimney nooks were filled with her extensive collection of bestsellers. Marcus's prized stereo and scores of photos of Coco at different stages of her development sat on sleek rosewood sideboards that ran along the length of the room.

Coco scuttled off the shag pile rug to retrieve Elsa from the pile of toys scattered across the floor, and Faye's thoughts turned back to her absent boyfriend. Rocky was so unlike anyone she had ever dated that even after four years, she sometimes still wondered if she really knew him. When it came to his job, she knew he could be as tough and flinty as his name. She had seen and heard enough to realise that he could be ruthless in business and that he was able to negotiate tough deals for his bank and manage mind-boggling sums of money for his clients without batting an eyelid. But the Rocky she knew was lovable and playful and also extremely generous, buying her gifts for no particular reason and remembering special occasions without prompting. He had a warm, easy manner that charmed and reassured people initially intimidated by his height and muscular frame and had immediately impressed her African father's traditional sensibilities with his courteous good manners. Even William had quickly dropped his over-protective older brother attitude after their first meeting.

So where the hell was he? The ping of a text message broke into her thoughts and she grabbed the handset, her sense of relief quickly fading when she saw that the message was from Rocky's younger sister, Amma. Since meeting Rocky and his family in Ghana, Faye and Amma had become close friends, cementing their friendship when Faye returned to Ghana a year later for Amma's traditional engagement ceremony to her boyfriend, Edwin. With Edwin now back at home from America, he and Amma was busy planning their wedding.

Momentarily distracted from thoughts of Rocky, Faye scrolled down the text and couldn't help smiling. She could almost hear Amma's typically breathless voice as she read through the long, rambling message. The smile turned to an annoyed frown as she read on. '...I hope Rocky has told you that we've finally settled on October 28th for the wedding, and that you've booked your flights.'

Chance would be a fine thing, was Faye's first thought. Honestly, where were Rocky's priorities? She had been nagging him for weeks about their travel plans for Ghana. It was all right for him with a PA on hand to sort out his diary and organise his flights. As a lowly assistant designer way down in the pecking order at Cayhill's, she still had to beg her boss for the time off and make sure there was cover for her projects.

Fuming, she snatched up Coco, ignoring her wail of protest at being pulled off the rug she had been quietly chewing, and marched to the kitchen.

'Come on, trouble. It's time for your milk so stop glaring at me!' Quickly warming the bottle in the microwave, she watched as Coco's grumpy expression transformed itself into a sunny smile.

'Let's get this down you and then I think it's probably time for a nappy change.' She popped the bottle into Coco's eager mouth and smiled at the deep frown of concentration creasing her forehead as she drank. Faye sniffed cautiously in the direction of the baby's bottom and earned a glare of annoyance.

'Okay, I'm sorry! You smell delicious, as usual.' Faye smoothed down Coco's yellow summer dress and went back to sit with her on the sofa while she swiftly drained the bottle. With a loud burp of satisfaction Coco dropped the empty bottle and clambered down from Faye's lap ready to play.

Ten minutes later, there was still no word from Rocky.

Frustration and irritation had now morphed into anxiety and a sneaky feeling of unease. Handing Elsa back to an impatient Coco, she sat up and crossed her legs, the soft rug cushioning her bottom against the hardwood floor. Not showing up for a date was one thing; but it really wasn't like Rocky not to have at least called her. Try as she might, she couldn't stop her fertile imagination from running riot. Something bad must have happened to him. Maybe he'd been in an accident. What if she was sitting here seething while his car had crashed into a ditch somewhere, leaving him bloodied and bruised and unable to reach her? Panicked by the scenes swirling around her head, she pinned Coco between her legs and was reaching for her phone to try his number again when Caroline's house phone rang, the shrill tones causing them both to jump.

Faye cursed and shot a guilty look at the baby. Praying that Coco hadn't heard, she leapt to her feet and seized the handset with a muttered hello, all the while keeping a cautious eye on the toddler.

'Caroline, is that you?'

Faye groaned silently, recognising the genteel accent of Rose O'Neill, and cursed again for not having left the call to go straight to answer phone.

'Hi, Mrs O'Neill. No, it's Faye speaking.'

When there was no immediate response, Faye forced a friendly tone she was far from feeling and added helpfully, 'You know, Caroline's friend?'

I know you know exactly who I am, you silly cow. She rolled her eyes in exasperation and when Rose still didn't speak, she continued. 'Caroline had to leave for an urgent appointment this evening.'

After a short pause Rose finally answered. Her voice was distinctly frosty and almost quivered with offence.

'Oh, I see. Well, I wish I had known that she needed someone to mind the baby. She should have called me to help her – I've told her countless times that it's never a problem. I can always come down and stay at our pied-à-terre in London for a night or two if she needs a hand with the little one. She is my only grandchild, after all!'

'It was a last-minute work thing; I just happened to be here when she got the call, so I offered to babysit.' Faye tried to sound both apologetic and diplomatic but from the sound of Rose's indignant sniff, her efforts at appeasement clearly hadn't worked.

'So it's just you and little Camilla there?' Rose made no attempt to disguise the alarm in her voice.

'Erm, yes, but she's fine. I've looked after her loads of times and after all, I am Co- I mean Camilla's godmother.' Faye rolled her eyes again and tried not to sound defensive. She was beginning to understand Caroline's attitude towards her mother-in-law and she tried to curb her rising irritation. For heaven's sake, what does she think I'm going to do to the baby and where is the sense in coming all the way to London to watch a child for a couple of hours?

As luck would have it, Coco had been trying to crawl under the sofa and finding herself trapped, emitted a loud wail, giving Faye the excuse to ring off hastily. A quick sniff confirmed her suspicions and she whisked her god-daughter upstairs for a nappy change before coming back down to the living room to retrieve her phone.

She deposited Coco on the rug and was again about to dial Rocky's number when the house phone shrilled. With an impatient sigh, she dropped her mobile and hurried over to answer it.

'Faye, it's me.' Caroline sounded harassed. 'We've just taken a short break – Paul's calling his wife again. They're going on holiday tomorrow and she's really pissed off that he's not home yet. How's everything going? Is Coco alright? I'm sorry this is all taking so long; I thought we'd be finished by now.'

'How's it going so far?

'It's looking good – I'm just glad that we got Paul to agree to meet us this late in the day. He's not happy about it but he is the Marketing Director. By the time he gets back from holiday, it will be too late to sign up sponsors in time to get the series on air this year.'

Caroline and her production team had spent countless hours developing the idea of a television series on modern-day role models and this meeting to pitch the programme was her last-ditch gambit to save the show. Having slogged ferociously to reach the ranks of senior producer, Caroline was determined to prove that she hadn't lost her skills or her edge, particularly after the extended maternity leave she had taken when Coco was born.

'I'm so sorry you had to cancel your plans tonight. I feel so bad that you didn't get to go to that swanky Italian restaurant.'

'Hey, it's okay. I've already said it's not a problem,' Faye protested. 'I know how important this project is to you!

Look, Caro, relax. Coco's fine. She's had a nappy change and is wearing that ridiculous elephant onesie she loves so much. She's finished her bottle and we're playing – or at least we would be, if you and your mother-in-law didn't keep interrupting.'

'Oh God, don't tell me Rose called!'

Faye laughed. 'Don't worry about it. She sounded a bit fed-up that she wasn't asked to babysit – and she obviously thinks I can't be trusted with her precious granddaughter.'

'Just ignore her; I keep telling you the woman is a nightmare. How's Rocky getting on with being a surrogate dad? Did you get him to help you change Coco's nappy?' Caroline sounded more relaxed and a teasing note crept into her voice.

'He hasn't shown up! I've tried his number but I just keep getting his voice-mail and I'm bloody well not leaving any more messages.'

Despite her spirited words, Faye felt the nagging sense of anxiety rear its head again. What if none of this was Rocky's fault? In her mind his car was now not only in a ditch, but had become part of a seven car pile-up. But any concerns about her boyfriend's safety were clearly hers alone.

'What do you mean he hasn't shown up?' Caroline demanded. 'And why hasn't he let you know where he is? That's outrageous!'

'I know, but I'm getting really worried now,' Faye muttered. 'He normally calls me when he can't make it to something, but I haven't heard a peep out of him. Not even a text.'

'I'm sure he's absolutely fine and doing his own thing,

as usual. Forget about being worried; what you should be is pissed off that he's stood you up again. I can't believe you think it's normal! I don't care how gorgeous he is – that's just not on! Where has that lovely, romantic man that swept you off your feet gone?'

Where indeed? With no answer on offer, Faye bit her lip in misery.

'Sorry, Faye, Paul's calling us back in. I've got to go. Look, we should be finished going over the numbers and schedules in an hour or so. I'd call Marcus to take over from you but right now, when it comes to work, my husband's even worse than Rocky! I'll see you in a bit; give Coco a kiss for me.'

Faye picked up Coco to dutifully deliver the kiss, and then snuggled into the soft cushions of the sofa and cuddled the warm, wriggling child, breathing in her talcum-powder scented freshness. Nudging the soft elephant trunk attached to the onesie out of the way, she rested her chin gently on Coco's head, wondering if Caroline had a point about her attitude towards Rocky. *Am I letting him off the hook too lightly? What has happened to the Rocky I first fell in love with*, she mused. While the physical side when they did actually manage to get together was as strong as ever, to describe the other aspects of their relationship as being in the doldrums would be an understatement. Lost in a haze of work, her high-flying investment banker boyfriend was fast becoming a stranger. The demands of his job had Rocky dashing off to meetings in different countries as frequently and as casually as she went to Sainsbury's. Parties, film and theatre plans were all apologetically jettisoned at a moment's notice to attend to the whims of his über-wealthy clients in places as far flung as Abu Dhabi, Turkey and Johannesburg.

Over the past few months, his hectic travel schedule had worsened as he and his team worked frantically to conclude a major deal between an American technology start-up and a huge global corporation. Working like a crazy person was one thing; his casual attitude to the problems it was creating was quite another.

Lately, his response to her grumbling about seeing so little of him had fallen into a pattern of him pointing out that their time together was about quality, not quantity, reassuring her that the markets were 'manic', but that things would soon change, and then kissing her until she forgot what she had been complaining about. Notwithstanding his formidable kissing skills, she was increasingly growing resentful of being sidelined and forced into playing a supporting role to the star act of Rocky's seemingly never-ending ambitions. If she were honest, Faye thought, her patience with her once-perfect boyfriend was fading fast.

And, yet, what if today was not just another case of Rocky leaving her in the lurch without warning. She sighed and shook her head. *Why are you making excuses for him, Faye? Don't you deserve to have someone who's there for you?*

Despite the breeze wafting in through the window, the living room was warm. After a few minutes, Coco's restless squirming subsided and her body relaxed into sleep. Faye carried her back to the cot and draped a light muslin cover over her before once again picking up her phone.

This time, instead of the clipped voice-mail recording, the phone rang several times. Her heart lifted with relief and she waited anxiously to hear Rocky's voice. But the strongly accented voice that answered was certainly not Rocky's, and definitely not male.

Her eyes wide with shock, Faye quickly checked the name displayed on her phone, but there was no mistaking the number she had dialled. Briefly wondering if her car-in-the-ditch scenario might not be preferable, her voice echoed her disbelief as she blurted out, 'Who is this?'

'This is Yvette. To whom am I speaking?' The unmistakable French accent made the lilting, slightly husky voice sound even sexier.

Momentarily speechless at the audacity of another woman holding her boyfriend's mobile and asking who she was, Faye felt her skin prickle with anger. Conscious of Coco sleeping nearby, she forced herself to whisper.

'This is Faye. Rocky's girlfriend.' The words emerged like little stone pebbles popping out from behind her gritted teeth.

'Oh yes, Faye.' Yvette laughed lightly.

Does she think this is funny? Faye stared indignantly at the handset for a moment before clamping it back against her ear.

Yvette was speaking. '...and Rocky asked me to let you know. I would have called sooner but it's been so 'ectic here, I did not get the chance. In fact, we are still at the office – Rocky is on a call with our New York team at the moment. Perhaps I can give him a message?'

Faye frowned in bewilderment. Rocky going to the

office at the weekend was a regular occurrence, so why hadn't he just called to let her know? And who the hell was this Yvette anyway? She was damned if she was going to ask and let this woman, whom she had already decided she hated, believe that she felt insecure about her man.

The silence on the line stretched out for a few moments.

'Just ask him to call me when he's finished, please,' Faye said curtly and cut off the call, taking deep breaths in a futile attempt to calm down. Caroline was right, she fumed, now ready to drive Rocky into a ditch herself. This is not okay.

She checked on the sleeping baby and returned to the comfort of the sofa. Clutching one of the over-stuffed throw cushions to her chest, she stared at the huge TV screen flickering on the wall and tried to calm the tide of emotions washing over her. Between her work and his travel schedule, she hadn't seen Rocky in almost two weeks and for him to delegate the job of cancelling their plans to sexy-voiced Yvette rankled bitterly. Since when had she become someone he could dismiss with a phone call from one of his team members as if she were some awkward client he wanted to put off?

Her phone buzzed and she stared at the screen for a few moments, suddenly reluctant to answer the call she had been waiting for all evening.

'Faye?' His deep voice rumbled through the phone line.

'Rocky?' She echoed evenly. If she launched into her litany of complaints now, she didn't quite know how she would stop herself.

'Yvette just told me that you called. Are you okay?' Without waiting for an answer, he continued. 'I'm sorry I couldn't make it this evening but everything kicked off without any warning a few hours ago, which is why I asked her to call you to let you know I'd been held up. We've had a problem with a threatened strike at the firm we're doing a deal with and it's...' She stopped listening as he continued to give a detailed rundown of the latest impediment to their merger project. The intricacies of investment banking left her cold and she could still hear Yvette's smug voice with its proprietary overtones in her ear.

Rocky had stopped speaking and before she could help herself, she rushed in. 'Rocky, do you realise how long it's been since we've spent any time together?'

The sound of a deep sigh coming over the phone suggested he did. 'Look, I know it's been manic lately, but—'

She cut in abruptly. '—but the markets will calm down soon and things will get better. How long have you been saying that? Okay, I get that something came up unexpectedly, but since when do you delegate calling me to someone else?' *Particularly a woman with a ridiculously sexy voice.*

'Faye, I was stuck on a long call and I wanted to let you know I couldn't make it. How is that a problem?' His patient tone sounded like a parent dealing with a fractious two-year-old and she bristled with irritation. 'Besides, you were the one that changed our plans in the first place and since we weren't going to be doing anything, I thought you would understand.'

That's the problem, isn't it, she thought in frustration. *I'm always the one that has to understand. And looking after Coco isn't 'not doing anything'. It's supposed to make you see what having a baby can be like.*

'Faye?' He sounded troubled and it was her turn to sigh as the fight drained out of her. It was glaringly obvious that his agenda didn't include parenting, surrogate or otherwise, and she could hear voices in the background demanding his attention.

'It's fine, Rocky. It sounds like you need to get back to whatever you were doing, so let's talk tomorrow.' Without waiting for a reply, she ended the call.

When she heard the front door slam an hour later, Faye jumped up with relief. 'Hey, Coco, you woke up just in time! Guess who's back?'

She scooped up the child and walked out into the hallway. Caroline slipped off her jacket and reached out to hug her daughter, squeezing her hard despite the baby's protests.

'I'm gasping for a cup of tea! Here, take her.' Handing Coco back, Caroline smoothed down her linen dress and headed into the kitchen.

'So, how did it go?' Faye demanded, leaning against the door frame.

'Well, we got the sign-off on the show, thank God. Quite honestly, after her third phone call, I think Paul was so desperate to pacify his wife that he'd have agreed to a documentary about baby monkeys!'

Coco blew loud, wet kisses against Faye's smooth brown cheek and Caroline laughed. 'Honestly, the two of you are as bad as each other!' She tucked an errant curl back into the red-gold bun on top of her head and reached for the kettle.

She paused and a sly smile crept onto her face. 'You're so good with her, Faye. We're best friends and our children should be growing up together so they can be best friends too. At this rate, we're never going to hear those wedding bells and get you sorted out with a brat of your own!'

Faye grimaced and hoisted Coco onto her slender hip, smoothing the hair swinging across her face back behind her ear. 'Don't even get me started, Caro. It's hard enough getting that man to have a normal conversation these days, let alone one that includes the 'm' word.'

Caroline switched on the kettle and studied her friend thoughtfully. 'So what on earth are you going to do about Rocky?'

3

A Touch of Haven

The sound of voices in the corridor and the slam of the heavy front door had Faye sitting up and seconds later William and Lucinda strolled in. They both looked so fresh and buoyant with energy that she groaned and fell back against the cushions.

'What's wrong with you?' Her brother grinned as he approached the sofa. Tall and lean, his chocolate colouring was a darker shade than her mocha complexion. Although they were similar in build, in contrast to William's sharply angled features, Faye's oval shaped face and high cheekbones were softened by her rounded cheeks and full lips.

Lucinda, eyes sparkling and almost jumping up and down in her excitement, cut in before she could reply.

'Oh my God, you are not going to believe it! We just saw Sam Molloy coming out of his house! Faye, don't look at me like that – you know how much I love *Getting Back with Bridget*. I saw him walking a woman out to her car when we were driving past and he's even better-looking in real life. Lottie's going to die!'

She sounded exactly like a star-struck teenager who'd just spotted her favourite boy-band member and William sighed and rolled his eyes, while Faye just stared at her incredulously.

'What is it with you and Lottie and this actor? And isn't that the second time you've seen him since he moved into our road? God, I hope the poor guy doesn't think he's being stalked!'

'Don't be daft; he probably didn't even notice me.'

'Lucinda, you're gorgeous; everyone notices you. Even when you're nearly three months pregnant.'

Suddenly energised, Faye jumped up to hug her sister-in-law, grinning in excitement. 'Oh my gosh, twins! I still can't believe it.'

William cleared his throat and rubbed his chin with a look that Faye could only describe as nervous. It wasn't a characteristic she usually associated with her barrister brother whose supreme sense of self-confidence often teetered dangerously close to the border with arrogance. Amused that he was finding the prospect of twins more daunting than the hardened criminals he faced in court without turning a hair, she couldn't resist teasing him.

'What's wrong, Will? You looked a bit weird just then; I thought you were up for having two babies at once.'

He threw a sheepish glance in the direction of his wife, who shot a warning glare in his direction as if challenging him to disagree.

'Of course I am. Anyway, we're still not a hundred percent sure it's twins; we'll get confirmation with the next scan.'

He quickly changed the subject. 'What are you doing at home on a Saturday afternoon? Where's the boyfriend?'

Faye's face fell and she dropped back onto the sofa with a grimace. 'New York. Again. He left yesterday and he's not back until Thursday, so here I am.'

Lucinda perched on the edge of the sofa and scrunched her nose, her eyes full of sympathy. 'You poor thing! Is he ever around anymore? He always seems to be jetting off to one place or another.'

'Hey, give the guy a break!' William protested. 'Rocky's a good man with a tough job and it's not easy when there's so much money riding on these deals. It takes a lot to make it in that industry; believe me. I once thought about going into investment banking, but I had zero interest in working every weekend and sleeping under my desk for a few nights a week! Look, Faye, do you remember Daniel Stein – the guy I was at school with?'

Faye nodded, and he continued. 'Well, after he graduated, he joined one of the big American investment banks and he's done very well; front office role on a Sales desk, mega bonuses, you name it. Anyway, I bumped into him a couple of weeks ago and the man was not looking good. He says it's absolutely insane in the City these days with banks laying off people en masse and that no-one feels safe. Dan's already on his second wife – according to him the long hours wrecked his first marriage – and they've just had a son. Get this – the pressure is so bad that he actually missed being at the birth because he was in a meeting with their top client and didn't dare ask to be excused!'

Lucinda glared at her husband. 'Well, don't even think about trying that with me when the babies are due!'

William shook his head impatiently. 'The point I'm trying to make is that Rocky doesn't like having to work eighteen hours a day or spend half his life on a plane, but it's a very competitive environment and a man's got to do what a man's got to do. If you don't play the game, you'll just end up sitting on the sidelines!'

'Of course you're taking his side,' his wife scoffed, patently unimpressed. 'You men always stick together, even when you're in the wrong. He should be here with Faye, not constantly running off around the world for one meeting or another What's wrong with phones – or using conference calls or Skype?'

'Honestly, we can never get it right with you women, can we? When we're not working, we're idle and shiftless and not taking care of our responsibilities; and when we're trying to do the best we can, we're not putting you first!'

'No-one's accusing Rocky of being idle,' Lucinda retorted indignantly. The tip of her perfectly shaped nose turned pink and she smoothed back a stray tendril from the blonde French braid hanging down her back and scowled at her husband. 'I just don't think it's fair that she has to put up with all the absences and going to social events on her own because her boyfriend is always somewhere else. Yes, Rocky's got a tough job, but who hasn't? That's no excuse for being a perpetual bachelor.'

William groaned and dropped into the armchair next to the sofa. 'Jeez, really? Now he's in the wrong because they're not married yet? Faye's my sister, so of course I'm not just taking his side. But the man needs some space to sort his life out. Let's face it, he hasn't exactly had a smooth ride with his job – he's had to prove himself as a black MD in a pretty conservative British bank, and that's not easy.'

'Maybe so, but he's also been doing very well at the bank. Aren't you the one always saying that he's pretty young to be at his level?' Lucinda's response echoed Faye's thoughts.

'He is, but in that environment you're only as good as your last transaction, and the higher profile you get, the more people are ready to take a pot shot at you.' William retorted. 'There's a lot riding on this particular deal he's working on and if he's able to pull it off, it's going to parachute him into the big leagues. From what he's told me, with this kind of deal behind him he'll be able to write his own ticket for what he does next.'

Faye looked at her brother, both surprised and annoyed by his revelations. How come he knew so much about what Rocky was going through and why would her boyfriend talk to her brother rather than to her? She suppressed a momentary twinge of guilt as she remembered how her mind always seemed to drift off when Rocky tried to talk about his work. But then if he didn't spend so much time at the office instead of with her, she might be more inclined to pay more attention to what he did instead of resenting it. Nevertheless, whatever the rights and wrongs of the matter, it was her problem to resolve and not up for general discussion. She frowned at the squabbling couple who were still speaking as if she wasn't sitting there right in front of them.

'Yes, that's all very well, but Faye deserves to have someone who's there for her. She has needs as well.' Lucinda persisted. She stroked the gentle swell of tummy covered by her blue cotton dress as she said the words, making her meaning crystal clear. 'It's not fair on her if he's always away. Look, I love Rocky, but—' she broke off as she took in Faye's mortified expression. 'Okay, sorry, I'll shut up. You don't need me making you feel worse.'

Then, in typical Lucinda fashion, she immediately changed the subject. Hauling herself up from the sofa, she flashed a mischievous grin. 'I'm going to find Lottie and tell her about Sam Molloy – she will just die!'

With that, she practically ran out of the room leaving Faye and William looking at each other with near identical expressions of disgust.

'That's the top female defender that has the CPS quaking in its boots when she's in court?' Faye broke the short silence, her gaze back on the doorway through which Lucinda had just vanished.

William laughed. 'Scary, isn't it? I don't know what it is about that grey-haired, middle-aged actor that's got her and Lottie in such a state. Lucinda's pregnant, so maybe we can put it down to hormones. But Lottie...?' The incredulity in his voice had Faye laughing in turn.

Her brother was sprawled across the chair, his long legs hanging over the side, and his eyes narrowed as he took in her rumpled appearance.

'You look shattered. It's probably just as well Rocky's away, so you can actually get some sleep.' He ducked as she aimed a throw cushion at him and rubbed at his fast receding hairline where the cushion had glanced harmlessly off his head.

Chuckling in protest, he raised his hand in surrender. 'How's work going? Is that client still giving you a hard time?'

Faye sighed, noting that sighing had become her body's default reaction whenever Justin Parker's name came up in conversation. She propped another cushion under her head and stretched her legs along the length of the sofa, wriggling her bare toes in an effort to release the tension in her tired feet.

'Let's just say I've managed to stay out of his way for the past few days, which has helped me remember how much I really love what I do. It's a world away from the work I was doing at Fiske, Fiske and Partners.'

William raised an eyebrow in derision but before he could launch into yet another of his 'I-don't-know-what-took-you-so-long' tirades on the subject of her former employers, she sat up, a note of excitement creeping into her voice.

'You'll never guess whose business we're pitching for and who's on the pitch team?' Not giving him a chance to speak, she continued rapidly. 'Harriet Woollaston! Can you imagine?'

Her brother swung his legs round and sat up with a low whistle of appreciation. 'What, the cosmetics woman? That's incredible! What would you be doing for her?'

'She's pregnant and wants a really cool, eco-friendly crèche for her company – although Matt reckons it's really just for her own benefit.'

'Well, it's fantastic that they're giving you a chance to work with someone like that when you're still quite junior. Your boss must really like you.'

She winced, trying not to read anything more into her brother's words after Caroline's earlier insinuations. Since joining the company, she had worked really hard at Cayhill's and she knew that she had fully earned her spot on the team. There was no other reason why she would have been put on such a high-profile project and besides, she reasoned, it had been Ruth's idea, not Matt's, that she should help on the project.

'What did Rocky say when you told him?' William's eyes were alight with amusement. 'I bet he would kill to have Harriet Woollaston as a client!'

She smiled, remembering Rocky's enthusiastic response when she had confided her news to him before he left. Feeling more than a touch of remorse at the contrast between the interest her boyfriend always showed in her career and her attitude towards his, she changed the subject by asking William about the case he had just won – a subject she knew her brother was only too happy to talk about.

Four days later and back at work in her rabbit hutch of an office, Faye gathered her papers together and nervously smoothed down the moss green linen skirt she had chosen to wear for the project team's pitch meeting with Harriet Woollaston.

She quickly checked the small mirror in her handbag and, satisfied that her make-up hadn't smudged, her cream silk blouse was still spotless and her favourite nude court shoes were clean, she took a deep breath and hurried towards the meeting room.

As she walked passed Reception, she noticed Chelsea sitting bolt upright behind the reception desk in what looked like a new jacket. Her eyes were fixed on the lift doors and her hair had been gelled back into a smooth blonde cap which flowed into the high waterfall of her customary ponytail. Someone's been told to stay off the phone and look efficient, Faye thought, flashing Chelsea a reassuring smile before hastening to join the group waiting in the glass-fronted conference room.

The project team meeting the week before had left Faye more nervous than ever about meeting the famous cosmetics titan. Ruth Wendell was Matt's business partner and a co-founder of Cayhill's. Although she was a gifted graphic designer, she had opted to spend less time on creative design and instead was usually out and about chasing after new business. A tiny, heavyset woman, she was a ferocious networker who had become a sought-after speaker at industry events and was single-minded in her vision to make Cayhill's the top design consultancy in the city. Faye had often heard talk around the company about Ruth's phenomenal network, but she had been amazed to hear that it included Harriet Woollaston. Ruth had made it clear that Harriet didn't suffer fools gladly and was spoilt for choice when it came to designers for her proposed crèche. Without mincing her words, Ruth rammed it home to her hand-picked team of five designers and the assistants that she expected thoughtful, creative suggestions and that there was no way Cayhill's was going to lose the account except over her – or whoever messed it up's – dead body. Ruth's normally pleasant demeanour had been fierce as she marched up and down her office, her authority undiminished by the fact that she was barely five feet tall. Faye, who was still faced with a long list of items on her to-do list for the Parker gallery, had gulped at the brief from Harriet that Ruth had read out.

'Eco-friendly natural materials, serene but intelligence enhancing palettes, nurturing but robust furnishings...' *What is this woman on?* Faye had listened incredulously to the long list of commands, wondering how someone with such a widespread reputation as a hard-nosed savvy business woman could come up with such new age-y demands.

'Wood's a natural material, isn't it?'

'What?' Lost in her thoughts, Faye jumped as Ruth barked the question in her direction. 'Er... I mean, yes. Yes, it is,' she stammered, hoping she didn't sound as stupid as she suddenly felt. "But it would need to be responsibly sourced."

'Right, then. My thoughts are that we should aim for a light, bright palette with lots of colourful soft furnishings – oh, and maybe a theme wall that can feature characters from one of the popular children's stories. We'll have to find sustainably sourced tables and chairs for the smaller children – the crèche will take them up to the age of five apparently. We'll need to consider materials for changing tables and an area for the staff and the minders. Don't forget to factor in loos for the little ones, some kind of kitchenette for heating milk and kids' food, high chairs, toys, toy boxes, changing mats in organic cotton, cots for naps with organic mattress covers and anything else kids need.'

The team scribbled frantically while Ruth reeled off her ideas and then dismissed them with strict instructions to come up with at least three concepts for discussion by the next morning. The client pitch would take place at Cayhill's on Thursday as Harriet had apparently decided to stop by on her way from her doctor's appointment.

'Ok, you lot, get on with it,' was Ruth's parting shot. 'The woman wants a baby haven and we're going to give her one if it kills us!'

The second project design meeting was again held in Ruth's office and after a near sleepless night during which Faye had spent hours sketching out some rough ideas, her head now felt like cotton wool. Looking round at the tired faces of the rest of the team, every single one of whom was clutching a mug of coffee, none of them looked any better than she felt.

Ruth's bite was only marginally less scary than her bark and after quizzing each of them relentlessly, she pulled together some of the more promising ideas into three distinctive proposals.

It was well into the afternoon before she finally dismissed the exhausted group with a stern warning to get a decent night's sleep and look smart for the pitch. The last instruction was accompanied by a meaningful glare at Jojo Haines, a talented designer who had been at Cayhill's for four years, and whose standard uniform was skinny jeans, a black sweatshirt (for winter) or T-shirt (for summer) and at least five piercings in each ear, every one of them decorated with a silver earring.

Almost collapsing with exhaustion, Fay stopped at her office long enough to pick up her bag before heading for the Underground. She managed to stay awake until the tube pulled into Hampstead station and she dragged herself into the lift and down the road for the short walk home, where she headed straight to her bed and slept for five hours without stirring.

The next day, hurrying into the conference room to join the rest of the team, it was immediately apparent that Ruth's edict to dress smartly had been taken to heart. The normally laid back creative design team, more at home in leggings, jeans and T-shirts adorned with questionable slogans, practically stood to attention, looking as uncomfortable as they felt in their smart jackets and belted dresses. Harvey Johnson, one of Cayhill's most experienced creatives, had abandoned his usual uniform of ripped jeans and rock band T-shirts. Instead he wore a shirt with a collar, clearly a novel experience judging from the finger he was continuously running around the inside of the neck as if he was suffocating. When she spotted Jojo, Faye gasped and bit her lip in an effort not to laugh. Gone were the skinny jeans, black T-shirt and multiple earrings, and in their place was a navy shirt dress that would have looked more at home on a nun than a rising design star.

Jojo grimaced as she caught Faye's expression and she seized her arm, pulling her over to stand next to her so she could whisper without being overheard. 'This project had better bloody be worth it. I've had to borrow my sister's dress for this stupid meeting. She's slapped a ton of make-up on me and I look like a prize dork!'

'It's not that bad,' Faye whispered, stifling a giggle. Up close, she could see quite clearly the results of Jojo's sister's efforts. Instead of the cosmetics enhancing her natural prettiness, a rosy blusher sat heavily on Jojo's delicate cheekbones. A black eye pencil had made her brows look fierce and the slash of a dark plum lipstick with an even deeper lip liner did nothing for her pale colouring. Faye squeezed Jojo's hand reassuringly and then jumped to attention as the conference door flew open and Ruth marched in, closely followed by a tall, slim and unmistakably pregnant woman.

Faye stared in fascination at their prospective client and a jolt of nervous excitement shot through her. Since hearing about the project, she had pored through Wikipedia and trawled through endless links from Google to find out all she could about Harriet's phenomenal career, and it was hard to believe that she was actually in the same room as the business legend. From her research, she knew that Harriet was thirty-eight and had recently split up with her husband, a much older man who, despite his wife's wealth, still held onto his job as a university professor.

Dressed in a loosely cut silk aquamarine dress and a cream jacket, Harriet's strawberry blond hair was cut into a shoulder length bob, the bluntly cut ends flicking out perfectly. Her face was expertly made up and her jewellery was confined to a pair of pearl stud earrings and, Faye noted with interest, a plain gold band on her wedding

44

finger. Even in her low-heeled cream sling backs, Harriet towered over Ruth.

Ruth introduced the team and Harriet's heavily-lashed hazel eyes quickly scanned the room, resting for a moment on Jojo. If she was appalled by the cosmetics hatchet job on display, she didn't show it, and instead complied with Ruth's murmured invitation to take a seat at the other end of the long conference table.

At Ruth's command, each member of the team said a few words about their background and the part they would be playing if they won the pitch. Faye was the last to speak and couldn't quite suppress the tremor in her voice as Harriet coolly appraised her. There was a brief silence while their client took a sip of the water that Ruth had solicitously placed in front of her, and when she finally spoke, her voice was clear and almost girlish with excitement. She leaned forward and clapped her hands together – a gesture that she repeated several times – and directed a wide smile at them.

'It's lovely to meet you all and thank you so much for agreeing to present me with some ideas. I know it's all been very short notice but you can see that I don't have a lot of time to play with.'

She glanced down at her bump and gave a self-deprecating laugh which the assembled team nervously echoed. 'I'm very grateful to Ruth for agreeing to this meeting and I'd love to hear what your thoughts are.'

Harvey had been picked to lead on the pitch and he stood up and walked to the screen at the end of the boardroom, his finger nervously tugging at the unfamiliar collar.

'Right, so we thought we would give you an overview of three possible ways we could go with the design. We've taken all the dimensions for the ground floor space in your building that you've allocated to the crèche – erm, I mean, baby haven – and I'll just go through the key concepts now. Of course, we can make any adjustments you like; it's just to give you a sense of our thinking and to see how close we are to what you're looking for.'

Harriet nodded without comment and Ruth dimmed the lights, giving Harvey the nod to start the presentation. Faye kept her eyes on the screen as he clicked on each slide and gave an overview of the theme, concept and the suggested materials. At one point during Harvey's pitch, she couldn't resist taking a sly peek at Harriet, but the cosmetics queen would have made a superb poker player and her face gave no clue as to what she thought of their efforts.

Harvey finished his spiel and turned up the lights, once more taking his seat at the long conference table. All eyes turned towards Harriet who coolly took a few more sips of water before clearing her throat.

'How many of you have children?' She scanned the table, starting from her left as she posed the question.

The blank stares of the twenty and thirty-something year olds around the table appeared to answer her question. Ruth recovered first and glared around at her team, her coal black eyes accusatory as if she couldn't understand why any of her employees could possibly be childless. Jojo fidgeted awkwardly, although whether from the question or her dress, it was hard to tell. Harvey gave up the struggle and opened the top button of his collar, the pressure of the moment and a formal shirt all too much to take in one go.

Mindful of Ruth's death threats if they lost the account, Faye tentatively raised a hand. Emboldened by the look of relief on the senior partner's face, she spoke up hesitantly.

'She's not my daughter, but I do have an eighteen month-old god-daughter who I spend a lot of time with,' she offered.

Harriet nodded, her flicked-up bob bouncing lightly with the movement, and the bright smile appeared once again.

'Remind me of your name again?'

'It's Faye.'

'Great. So Faye, you know what has to be taken into account when you are designing a safe haven for little people, don't you?'

For a moment, Faye's mind jumped to Rocky's sterile steel-and-glass apartment before she gathered her thoughts together and said with more confidence than she felt, 'Yes, I do. At Cayhill's we've worked on a number of child-friendly projects in the past. We're all very mindful of health and safety concerns as well as sourcing with sustainability as a criteria when it comes to fabrics, lighting and materials. I'm confident that with your instructions, our team will be able to put together something very special.'

Wow! Where did that come from? She blinked at her own temerity but Ruth's satisfied smile and the look of relief on her colleagues' faces seemed to suggest that she had said the right thing.

Harriet fixed her thickly-lashed eyes on Faye for a moment and then nodded and gave another of her little claps.

'Okay, then. Here's what I think. I'm not sold on the first two concepts, but I think that last one has got possibilities.'

She spoke for several minutes, pausing only to take an occasional sip of water. Under Ruth's watchful glare, the team kept their heads bent low over their notepads, noting down every word of Harriet's critique. She came to an abrupt stop, finished the water in her glass and stood up, making it clear that the meeting was over.

Taking the hint, the others scrambled to their feet and mumbled their farewells as Ruth escorted Harriet out to the lift. Harvey rapidly undid a further two buttons on his shirt while Jojo scrubbed at her ruby lips with a scrunched up tissue.

'Thank God that's over,' she said with relief, giving her cheeks a quick swipe before tossing the tissue in the bin. 'Nice save, Faye. For a moment there, I thought she was just going to get up and walk out!'

Nathan Forrester, a quiet bespectacled designer who looked ten years older than his biological age of twenty-nine, chimed in. 'Yes, well done, Faye. She's terrifying, isn't she?'

Before anyone could answer, Ruth swept back in, her face a mask of inscrutability. The team stood meekly to attention, no-one daring to ask what she thought. But whatever Harriet had said on her way out was clearly good news as Ruth's stern face suddenly broke into a wide smile.

'Okay, you lot, it looks like we've got it!'

The team looked at each other with relief and a cheer of excitement went up. Jojo seized Faye in a fierce embrace.

'Yes! Thank God you spoke up!'

Ruth laughed, and her dark eyes were suddenly far less fierce than they had been only moments earlier.

'Yes, Faye, well done. I want you to work closely with Harvey and Nathan on this one. Harriet wants to see how you interpret her feedback since apparently you're the only one here who knows what a baby is!'

Embarrassed by the unexpected attention, Faye flushed with pleasure, and sat through the next hour as they went through the pitch feedback in detail, feeling a lot more confident about offering her suggestions to the considerably more experienced members of the team.

Back in her office, she checked her phone for any message from Rocky. He was due back in London that evening and she couldn't wait to see him. Feeling euphoric at winning the Woollaston account, she pushed to one side her concerns about the state of their relationship and rushed home to change, suddenly desperately anxious to be with him and to recapture the closeness that seemed to be in increasing danger of dissipating.

She decided not to phone, but instead to go over to his flat and surprise him. His flight was scheduled to land at six o'clock and it was past nine when she arrived at his building. *He is going to be so psyched when I tell him that I actually spoke to Harriet Woollaston!*

Brimming with excitement and longing to feel his arms around her, she scooted up the stairs. But, as soon as she pushed open the door to his flat, it was evident from the darkness and the silence that greeted her that once again she was on her own.

4

Conundrums

'Welcome to my world, honey.' Caroline splashed water into the jug and snapped the lid firmly back into place. 'Getting involved with someone who works in banking and finance is not a smart idea. It's like they're from another planet. You need to have read the small print that comes with these guys, because they certainly don't tell you all the terms and conditions you have to put up with when you get involved with them. They might be bringing home the bacon, but that's about all that ever does come home!'

She spooned some instant coffee into two pink mugs and unearthed a carton of milk from the cavernous fridge that took up almost an entire corner of the roomy kitchen.

'Is Marcus still working stupid hours?' Faye asked curiously. Caroline's husband was a highly successful hedge fund manager and he and Rocky had become close friends since her boyfriend had moved to London.

Caroline sighed as she stirred sugar and milk into one of the mugs and pushed the other one in Faye's direction. She took a tentative sip of her drink, then put it down and hoisted herself up onto one of the chrome and black bar stools arranged alongside the kitchen counter.

'Beyond stupid. Coco and I have barely seen him over the past few weeks. I know things are tough in the City these days but at this rate I'm going to have to make him a name badge so we know who he is when he comes in! And when he does get home, he spends half his time parked in front of his laptop on a conference call. He's never around to help with Coco. It's bad enough that she's in nursery all day, but the whole point about not getting a nanny was so that we would spend weekends together as a family. I really thought things would be better when Marcus set up his own firm and could be his own boss...'

Abandoning her attempts to pick some stray bits of fluff off her black T-shirt, she crossed her legs and took another sip of coffee. 'Anyway, enough moaning from me; we were talking about you – or rather, Rocky. I know things are pretty tough right now and from what I can glean from my phantom husband, a lot of banks are cutting back on staff. Do you think his job's safe?'

The baby seemed to be getting heavier by the second and Faye concentrated on adjusting Coco's positioning on her hip before replying. 'I've got absolutely no idea. I do know that he only has a few months left on his current contract but I can't get a straight answer from him about what happens next. I don't know whether they'll extend it or if he even wants to stay on. Lately, he's just so stressed all the time. I used to think people were exaggerating when they talked about the pressures of investment banking, but it really is no joke. He's always working at the weekend; half the time he doesn't get home before midnight – if he isn't jumping on a plane at a moment's notice. I just wonder if it's all worth it.'

'I suppose there's no question that you could just move in together at least?' Caroline sounded doubtful even as she asked the question.

Faye spluttered with laughter. 'Are you kidding? Don't act like you don't know my traditional African and very Catholic father! Don't you remember how long it took for William to finally move out and live with Lucinda? My poor brother had to stay at home practically until the day he said 'I do!"

Caroline giggled. 'I remember how scandalised your dad was when they moved in together, even though their wedding was only a couple of months later!'

'Every time I bring up the idea of moving out, all I get is "Faye, on your salary it really makes very little sense for you to pay rent when you have a perfectly good home to live in."'

'But come on, you're almost thirty! Surely he would understand if...' Caroline's voice trailed off as her friend shook her head firmly.

'Trust me; I'll still be living at home when I'm fifty if I don't get married! I suppose I shouldn't complain, really. How many people get free accommodation in a mansion in Hampstead? Besides, Dad's away so often that it's almost like living on my own. And to answer your question, even if I did move in with Rocky, he travels so much that I still wouldn't see much of him.'

She picked up the other mug of coffee and leaned back

against the counter, allowing her gaze to sweep around the spacious room.

'I really like this kitchen.' A mischievous smile curled across her full lips and Caroline smiled in response.

'Well, that's hardly surprising since you designed the place. But you did a really good job of it; I love the colours – and putting that little nook over there for Coco was pure genius!'

Faye eyed the décor speculatively, remembering the weeks of planning and hunting around to source fabrics and materials for her first commission at Cayhill Designs.

Finding an entry level interior design job after three years as a mature student at the College of Art had been anything but easy. After wasting years working as a PA in a quiet backwater law firm, she had found herself in competition with her much younger fellow graduates for coveted trainee interior design roles. A chance meeting at an exhibition had led to an interview with Matt, an alumnus of the College and a rising star in the world of interior design. The interview had been gruelling; Matt had probed every area of Faye's history, scrutinised her design portfolio, and grilled her about her design philosophy and what drove her choice of themes, colours and textures.

'If you work with us, you need to be commercial,' was his stark warning. 'We're all involved in business development as well as design, so you need to be up for finding new clients as well as getting the job done.'

Blithely confident that she would have no trouble finding commissions, Faye had gratefully accepted the job offer. But after two months with the company and having failed miserably to source even a single piece of new business, she had literally begged Caroline and Marcus who were in the process of moving to give Cayhill's the redesign job for their three-storey townhouse. This room was her particular pride and joy and she had worked hard to make sure that the hi-tech appliances and giant fridge blended in with the warm apricot walls and the cosy niche she had created as a play area for Coco.

'By the way, I'm sorry you had to deal with Rose when you were here with Coco the other time. I don't know how Marcus has managed to restrain himself from strangling the old bat over the years. Oh wait, maybe it's because he's never around and I'm the one who's always stuck having to take her annoying phone calls!'

'Caro, I know she's not the easiest of people, but she is Marcus's mother. You need to find a way to get on with her.' Even as she said it, Faye felt a stab of sympathy for her friend. Rose O'Neill was the very model of a difficult mother-in-law. Conveniently ignoring her own husband's working-class Irish ancestry, she had looked askance at her only child's choice of girlfriend and had reluctantly accepted that Caroline wasn't going anywhere only when the wedding day loomed and Marcus still showed no sign of changing his mind. It was only after the baby arrived that Rose had made a dramatic switch from being distant to suddenly wanting to be ever-present. Caroline, who had actually welcomed the years of being ignored by Marcus's mother, now found herself in a constant battle to fend her off.

Caroline's blue eyes were mutinous and the precarious bun on her head threatened to tumble down with the ferocity of the head shaking that accompanied her response. 'You try dealing with a woman who thinks she has the answer to everything, even when she hasn't been asked! She is the most opinionated human being I have ever met.'

She mimicked Rose's carefully genteel voice. 'It would be so much better for little Camilla if you and Marcus would move out to where we are. I could spend so much more time with the baby and the schools here are absolutely splendid compared with those appalling inner-city schools one hears about.'

'I keep forgetting that Coco's real name is Camilla,' Faye laughed.

'Yes, well, I wouldn't go jumping to that woman's defence too fast if I were you,' Caroline retorted. 'She was really chuffed that Marcus named Coco after her late mother, and then you had to go and ruin it all by saying the baby looked like a little clown! Forget Rose – try some of this amazing lemon cake I got from M&S yesterday.'

Caroline ripped the wrapper off the cake and cut two generous pieces, and then sighed with pleasure as she tasted the sweet lemony sponge.

Faye set Coco down on the play mat in the alcove and moved across to stand by the kitchen window, chewing slowly on tiny forkfuls of cake. She watched as Caroline coaxed a rusk into Coco's hands, pondering on how they had remained best friends since they were eleven in spite of their differences. At school they had both struggled to fit in; Caroline, because life with her nouveau-riche working class Irish family had been no preparation for the upper class children, and Faye, because she was one of only a handful of black students. Faye's reluctance to engage in conflict was in stark contrast to Caroline's quick temper and her readiness to take on 'the snooties', as they had called the band of stuck-up, students with their latest designer clothes and brutal put-downs, and had set up the dynamics of their relationship. After school, and even after Caroline had moved to south London and into TV production while Faye continued to live at home, Caroline had remained the protective half of the pair, ever ready to fight her friend's battles, while Faye provided the listening ear and the calming intervention when Caroline's volatility threatened to erupt.

Caroline finished her cake and absently fingered the stray cake crumbs on her empty plate, her expression thoughtful. 'How did we end up like this? I thought when we moved to this house, we'd be living our dream of being a real family. Now I hardly ever see Marcus and I'm acting as mother and father to the baby.'

She looked straight at Faye. 'I know you love Rocky but I also know you want to settle down. Faye, you love babies; how long are you going to wait for him to stop working every hour God sends and put your needs first?'

Faye shifted uncomfortably at the direct question. That was one of the downsides of having such a close friend, she thought. Not only did Caroline know all her secret hopes and dreams, but she had no qualms about using that knowledge when it came to proving her point. Caroline wasn't known for her diplomatic skills and her direct, take-no-prisoners approach made it difficult to dodge her truth seeking missiles. Recognising the irony of trying to defend Rocky against exactly the same complaints she had been making, Faye nevertheless gave it a try.

'Caro, I don't know; I've been asking myself the same question. Yes, his job is really demanding and yes, he's always been ambitious and a workaholic. But Rocky is really successful now, especially for someone of his age. He earns a ton of money that he spends on everyone else but himself – I know for a fact that he's paying for most, if not all, of Amma's wedding – so it's not about money. It's almost as if he still feels he has to prove himself in some way, I don't know...' Her voice tailed off and she sighed deeply.

'So it's all about what Rocky wants?'

'Look, it's not as if I'm sitting around waiting for him to propose! How could I fit in kids anyway? Working at Cayhill's isn't a piece of cake and I've got a long way to go to prove myself at work.'

Caroline's shrugged. 'My point is that it's taken you years to figure out what you wanted to do with your career. How many more years are you going to waste before you get the life you want?'

5

Blond Ambition

Faye was five minutes from home when her phone buzzed. A quick glance at the caller ID showed her boss's name displayed and she smiled as she flicked on the speaker.

'Hi, Matt. I'm driving, but I'll be home in a couple of minutes.'

Matthew Cayhill answered in his usual slightly staccato style – a bit like a one-fingered typist jabbing on a keyboard, had been Faye's first thought on meeting him. Matt radiated energy and paced around restlessly even during a normal conversation. Whenever he was deeply into sharing an idea, he would automatically tap urgently on any available surface as if providing a background beat to his words. He also never used two words where one would do, and although his choppy, abbreviated speech took some getting used to, it didn't hide his dry wit and good nature.

Typically skipping the obligatory 'hello', he launched straight into the reason for his call.

'Faye. Yeah, look, I've picked up a message from Justin.

59

Just checking in with you on the final designs. I'm in late tomorrow. I'd rather get back to him before he decides to show up at the office.'

Faye groaned in frustration and pushed her sunglasses up onto the top of her head. The Parker account was proving to be the most difficult assignment she had taken on since joining Cayhill's, not least because of the supercilious attitude their client displayed towards her. Faye rarely worried about whether her skin colour was the reason behind any antagonism she encountered, but lately she had started to conclude that it had to be a factor in explaining Justin's curtness whenever he spoke to her and his constant needling criticism of her work. Unwilling to give Matt any cause to take her off what was both a huge account for the company and a fantastic opportunity to work with her boss; she forced herself to grit her teeth whenever she encountered Justin and instead focus on her contribution to the design project for the new Parker art gallery.

'I've finished with the changes he asked for, Matt, if that's what he's chasing about.' She swung the car into the wide avenue leading up to her house. 'The drawings are on my desk if you need to see them today. If not, you can go through and sign off on the changes when you get in tomorrow. Once you've personally approved them, there'll be less chance of Justin implying that I'm completely incompetent.'

She pulled into the carriage driveway in front of her house and parked next to Lucinda's sleek Mercedes. Matt's voice squawked through the speaker and his bark of laughter spilled into the car.

'He's a tough one. But you'll come across worse than him in this business.'

'Maybe so,' she retorted, 'but I really think he hates me.'

'Probably fancies you. You know, playground stuff. He'll be pulling your hair next.'

She couldn't help smiling as she said goodbye. Matt's good humour was infectious and temporarily lifted the cloud of the Parker account from her horizon. He's right, she thought as she stepped out of her car and locked it, you don't get to where he is today without growing a thick skin and learning how to deal with awkward clients.

She hurried into the house and dumped her bag on the hall table, eager to see Lucinda. She followed the sound of voices into the kitchen and her high heels clicked on the white ceramic floor tiles as she rushed in and seized her sister-in-law in a warm hug.

'Hi, Luce! What a nice surprise. When did you get here?'

'About an hour ago. Lottie's been catching me up with all the goings-on in the street. She saw him Sam Malloy outside his house again yesterday. He's getting on a bit, but he has the sexiest Irish accent. For an older guy, he is really hot!'

Faye dismissed the reference to the sitcom actor with an impatient wave of her hand and smiled affectionately at her friend. 'You look amazing, although it's hard to imagine that you could be any prettier. Pregnancy really suits you.'

She turned to hug Lottie and ruffled her short, wiry chestnut curls affectionately. Although technically their housekeeper, Lottie Cameron had lived with the Bonsu family since Faye was five and had been more of a mother – and father, given Dr Bonsu's extensive travelling schedule – than employee. Originally from Glasgow, Lottie had come to London to work as a teacher before deciding on a career in nursing. A traumatic love affair had led to her abandoning her training and she had eventually applied to work as a housekeeper and nanny for Faye and her brother, William. Never one to suffer fools gladly, her disastrous past encounter with the opposite sex had left Lottie deeply cynical about men.

Faye turned back to Lucinda. 'I'd love to stay and have a good chat but I've got to get some work finished for tomorrow. I should have done it this morning but I was shattered after three hours of playing with Coco yesterday.'

Lottie chuckled and returned to the potatoes she had been peeling when Faye walked in.

'That child is such an adorable wee thing; I'm not surprised you've taken to her so much.'

Lucinda shook back her long mane of blonde hair and stroked her tummy. 'Yeah, well, just bear in mind that you've got another two to babysit for in a few months.'

Lucinda rummaged in her handbag and triumphantly pulled out a grainy picture, her sparkling blue eyes flashing with mischief. 'This is what I came to tell you. It's definitely twins! Take a look at the first pictures of your nephews or nieces... or whatever they are!'

'Wow,' Faye sat down, staring at the picture intently. 'I still can't believe it! Seriously, Luce, two babies? And at the same time? How are you going to cope?'

Lucinda laughed and raised her hand to fend off the barrage of questions. 'I'm still in complete shock, to be honest with you. William's putting on a brave face but I know he still hasn't got his head around the idea of two children appearing at once. He gets this glazed look in his eyes whenever I bring it up. You should have seen him the other morning – he left for work and had to come back when he got to the tube station because he'd forgotten his briefcase.'

Both William and Lucinda were barristers and had carved out successful careers in their respective specialties. Her brother was the archetypal conventional lawyer and Faye could easily imagine how the unexpected bombshell of twins had destroyed his highly structured and well-planned approach to life.

Faye handed back the ultrasound photo with a wry smile. 'He'll get over it. If I know Will, he'll have sorted out schools for them by the time the babies get here.'

Lottie snorted with laughter and rinsed the peeled potatoes under the sink. 'That sounds about right.' She looked across at Faye, a gentle smile playing on her lips. 'And when can we expect to hear some news from you, Faye? You're not getting any younger, you know,' she teased.

'Oh, please! Not you as well – you sound just like Caroline!' Faye snapped, then immediately felt remorseful. 'Sorry, Lottie, I didn't mean to bite your head off. Look, I'd better go up and get this work finished or I'll be up working all night. Luce, it's brilliant news about the babies; I'll come over soon to spend some time with you and Will.'

She raced up to her room, still trying to process Lucinda's news. She tried to picture what the babies would look like and felt a pang of longing which she suppressed as quickly as it came. Marriage and babies didn't appear to be on Rocky's to-do list and she had more than enough on her own plate with clients like Justin Parker to deal with.

The next day, in her tiny cubbyhole of an office, too small to swing an under-sized kitten, never mind the proverbial cat, Faye tapped moodily on her keyboard, smarting from her latest encounter with Justin Parker. Just as Matt had predicted, their client had turned up early and unannounced and had demanded to see the changes in the gallery designs. Ignoring Faye's protests that Matt would be in later in the morning and would double-check the revisions, he had insisted on going through the drawings and as she had feared, had found new faults to complain about. Refusing her invitation to take their discussion into a meeting room, he had insisted on examining the designs while standing in the Reception area which, to Faye's relief, had been empty of any waiting clients, although well within earshot of Chelsea the receptionist.

'Why hasn't the hardwood flooring section been extended? I thought we had agreed that you would make provision for the expanded café area.' His eyes were like frozen chips of blue ice as they raked across Faye's frustrated features. She resisted the urge to snatch the drawings from between his long thin fingers and instead leaned in and pointed to the diagram as she spoke.

'Well, yes, we will. If you would let me explain, the carpet area will be cut back from this side to allow for the extra seating in—'

'Look, where's Matt?' He interrupted brusquely, pushing the drawings back into her hands. 'This is hopeless! This gallery is going to be the biggest investment Parker's will have made for years and I can't afford to have some rank amateur messing things up.'

Faye glared at him and willed herself not to give voice to the words trembling on her lips. *Don't say it*, she thought as she literally clamped her teeth together. *If you say it, he wins. Don't let him get to you!*

Justin Parker was one of Cayhill's oldest clients and head of the exclusive chain of art galleries located in London, Bristol and Manchester. With their original London lease coming to an end, the company had acquired a new building and Parker had naturally turned to Cayhill's to undertake the design. The new gallery would be almost double the size of the existing one and Justin's ambitions to outdo his father in growing the family business had made him even more difficult to deal with than usual.

When it was clear that Faye wasn't going to rise to his comment, Justin smoothed back his gleaming dark blond hair and pointedly adjusted his cuffs. Angry though she was, Faye couldn't help noting the elegant fit of his dark navy suit, his pristine white shirt with thin navy pinstripes and the flawlessly knotted pale pink tie, although uppermost in her mind was the growing desire to strangle him with it.

She took a deep breath and tried again, keeping her voice as even as she could.

'Justin... Mr Parker, as I said, I have taken note of all your comments and the changes are clearly shown. Matt will be here shortly and he will check what I've done and we will get the revised drawings back to you today.'

She had barely finished her sentence when he turned

on his heel and strode towards the lift. After a couple of steps, he wheeled around, his voice dripping with sarcasm.

'Well, Faye… Ms Bonsu, let's hope you're right. I have a lot riding on this job and I expect the best that this company has to offer. Is that clear?'

Chelsea had been watching the exchange with wide eyes and as soon as the lift doors closed behind Justin, she exploded in all her East End glory.

'Bloody hell! Who the heck does he think he is to talk to you like that! I'd have given him a right kicking if he'd said that to me!'

Faye stared miserably at the lift doors, almost willing Justin to come back so Chelsea could get to work on him. She sighed and turned to the indignant receptionist, biting back a reluctant smile as she took in the outrage in her heavily kohl-lined brown eyes.

'He'd never have dared say that if Matt was here!' Chelsea shook her head angrily and her highlighted blonde pony tail swished from side to side in annoyance.

With a loud ping, the lift doors opened again and Matt Cayhill strode out, his briefcase in one hand and a takeaway coffee cup in the other. He stopped short when he saw Faye and glancing quickly from her to the indignant receptionist, immediately picked up on their heightened emotions.

He sighed. 'Justin?'

Faye nodded and concentrated on carefully folding the offending drawing, not trusting herself to speak without swearing at their client. Chelsea, on the other hand, didn't suffer from the same levels of self-restraint.

'Matt, you should have heard him. Bloody cheek – he actually had the nerve to call her an amateur!' The pony tail bounced in indignation as she ranted on, only stopping when an incoming call to the switchboard forced her to pick up her headset and deal with the enquiry.

Matt moved over to where Faye stood taking in deep breaths in an attempt to calm down, his long legs easily crossing the short distance. His thick, wavy brown hair, swept back from an angular face with almost perpetual stubble, cascaded over the collar of his navy linen jacket. Up close, his dark blue eyes looked at her with sympathy tinged with a hint of concern at the anxiety clearly etched on her face. Then he broke into a wry smile and shrugged in a don't-let-it-bother-you way.

'Just caught a quick glimpse of him downstairs. He didn't look happy so I didn't stop him. Don't worry about it – grab a coffee and let's go through the changes.'

With a silent sigh of relief that her boss didn't seem concerned about his prize client's tantrum, Faye hurried over to the coffee machine in the reception area before following Matt into his large, airy office. Cayhill's was on the sixteenth floor of a towering glass building in the heart of Chiswick and Matt's signature look was evident in the spartan décor of his office. His desk, a chrome-edged angular glass affair set against the back wall, was almost entirely clear of papers and with only a solitary laptop looking lost in the surrounding expansive desk space. A tall brushed-steel lamp presided over a large easel set up beside the floor-to-ceiling picture window that revealed a stunning aerial view of West London.

Matt took a seat at the round table in the middle of his office and gestured to Faye to sit down. Moving his coffee aside, he unfolded the plan she had deposited in front of him and listened patiently while she talked him through the changes they had agreed with Justin, and outlined the new concerns he had just raised.

When she finished, Matt leaned back in his seat and sipped thoughtfully on his coffee, now considerably cooler after having sat for fifteen minutes in his heavily air-conditioned office. Faye tried not to shiver; she had dressed for the summer warmth of a lovely June day and her sleeveless blue silk dress was proving no match against the semi-arctic settings of Matt's thermostat.

Pushing his coffee cup aside, her boss stood up and paced around his office, one hand in his pocket jangling a few loose coins, and the other scratching at the low stubble on his jaw.

'Well, it looks like you'd covered everything he asked for. I don't understand his problem.' Matt sounded pensive and his usual smile was absent. He came to a stop and fixed a thoughtful gaze on her, his thick eyebrows almost touching.

Faye shrugged, reluctant to voice her suspicions. 'Maybe he hates women...?' she proffered weakly.

Matt grunted with scepticism and then grinned. 'Justin Parker? You must be kidding. Biggest skirt-chaser ever at school.'

'Oh, yes, I forgot you were at school together. Was he always such a pain in the arse?'

'Faye, he's one of our biggest clients!' Matt said sternly

and then laughed as she flushed and muttered an apology.

'Just kidding. Yes; huge pain in the arse. Trying to outdo Daddy and prove he's the dogs' bollocks makes him even worse.'

Grinning at Matt's breezy dismissal of their tricky client, she stood up and gathered the papers together. 'I'll re-do the café flooring area and get these back to you by lunchtime.'

She turned towards the door, ready to leave his office when Matt called her back, his words rapping along in a quick flow.

'Talking of lunch, if you're free, let's go to The Hungry Duck. One o'clock suit you?'

She nodded, trying to hide her surprise. Unless it was in an effort to schmooze a client, Matt rarely went to lunch, usually preferring his endless cups of coffee to real food.

Back in her office after completing the revisions to the drawings, Faye stared distractedly at her keyboard, re-reading yet again the e-mail to the soft furnishings factory that she had been trying to finish for twenty minutes.

She briefly considered phoning Rocky and then thought better of it, both because he was more than likely to be in yet another meeting and because she was still annoyed that she had made a wasted journey to his apartment and had yet to see him since his return from America.

A light knock at her door brought her back into the present and she sat up as Matt hovered in the doorway.

'Ready to go?' His smile eased the tension that had built up as she simmered over the encounter with Justin and her frustration at the situation with Rocky, and she up and seized her black leather tote, grateful for the chance to get out of her shoebox of an office and clear her head.

'I'll meet you at the lift in two minutes.' She brushed past her boss and headed for the Ladies to freshen up. Five minutes later, and with a quick wave at Chelsea who was deep in a conversation that clearly had nothing to do with work, she and Matt were in the lift heading down.

The Hungry Duck was about ten minutes from the office and a popular lunch spot for Cayhill's staff. As they walked in, Faye spotted a couple of her colleagues and waved a hand in greeting. Feeling more than a little self-conscious about their curious looks at Matt who was gesturing towards the waitress for a table for two, and hoping they weren't drawing the wrong conclusions about her being out with their attractive boss, Faye followed the waitress to an empty booth and shuffled across the padded bench to sit at the far side by the wall. Matt slid in across from her and picked up the menu stuck between a chrome napkin holder and matching fat pots of mustard and ketchup.

After a quick glance, he pushed the laminated card towards her. 'What do you fancy?'

Faye glanced down the short lunch menu. She looked longingly at the description of the deep dish spinach and ricotta lasagne but decided to stick to the tuna salad; with so much work to get through, she couldn't afford to feel sleepy during the afternoon.

The waitress appeared with her notebook in one hand and a bottle of still mineral water in the other. She dropped the bottle onto the table and flipped over the two glasses resting on white frilled paper coasters before taking their orders. After another cursory glance at the menu, Matt opted for a club sandwich with fries.

Faye took a cautious sip of water, trying not to spill any of the liquid on her silk dress which was on its first outing. After a few minutes spent discussing the Parker gallery project, she couldn't contain her curiosity any longer.

'So what's this lunch in aid of?' she asked.

'Just thought you might like to get out of the office for a bit after that little scene this morning.' Matt took a long swallow of his water and set the glass down, his fingers drumming impatiently on the table.

Faye's eyes widened in surprise. Matt hadn't taken her to lunch since her first week at the firm, and both he and Ruth were notoriously tight about expenses not directly chargeable to clients.

Matt grinned and his fingers temporarily stopped their beat. 'I know, shocking, right? Well, we might not provide a free crèche, but we do try and take care of our people. Talking of which, how are you getting on with Harriet's project? I know the woman says she's putting in a crèche to help her staff with their childcare but I bet it's really just so they work longer bloody hours.'

Faye laughed in protest. 'That's really cynical, Matt! From what I've heard about her, she's really into supporting women at work.'

His shrug told her that he had little interest in their client's feminist credentials. 'Anyway, I shouldn't complain if it means that instead of just getting the painters in, she's spending good money with our lovely design firm to create a – what did Ruth say she calls it? Oh yeah, "a baby haven."'

He pulled his phone out of his pocket and scrolled down. 'This should cheer you up. In the e-mail she sent me and Ruth, she said she was looking for a firm to create "an eco-friendly, nurturing space for young minds so my team can relax while they are at work." I'm just glad that Ruth's handling this one!'

Faye's response was cut off by the arrival of the waitress with their food and for a few minutes they both ate in silence. Stabbing her fork into the colourful lettuce leaves on her plate, Faye pondered on her boss's statement. Dubbed by the press as 'the new Anita Roddick', Harriet had built a highly successful organic cosmetics brand with the slogan 'Created by concerned women for concerned women'. Despite Matt's teasing, the prospect of working for such a high-profile client was both an exciting and a daunting challenge, particularly at a time when Justin Parker seemed to be on a personal mission to shoot her down.

In between a detailed discussion of how Faye could balance the demands of working on two major projects, Matt wolfed down his sandwich and picked at his fries, dabbing each individual chip into a generous pool of ketchup, much to Faye's amusement. He looked up to catch her smiling and he paused in mid-dab looking slightly sheepish.

'That's what comes of spending too much time around kids,' he said with a shrug, resuming his efforts to bathe each chip in the gloopy red sauce on his plate.

Faye frowned in bewilderment; as far as she knew Matt was single and didn't have any children. He chuckled at the expression on her face and popped the last chip into his mouth, chewing it decisively.

'Not my kid; my sister's. You remember Charlie?' He leaned back and took a long sip of his water.

'Do you spend a lot of time with him, then?' Faye tried not to sound as curious as she felt. Matt was friendly and approachable enough, but he spent so much time at the office that she had never really given much thought to what his life outside it was like.

'Yes, he's a great kid. His father died two years ago. Very sudden. My sister's still on her own, so I help out with Charlie whenever I can. You know, take him for weekends or the odd day? I was out with him all day yesterday which is why I couldn't pick up those plans for Justin any earlier.'

Matt's staccato voice had softened considerably when he mentioned his nephew and Faye looked at him in surprise, intrigued by this side to her energetic, workaholic boss.

'Do you like kids?' His unexpected question threw her into a momentary spin and she took a sip of water before answering.

'Yes, I do. I love children. You've met my goddaughter, Coco. She's only one and a half, but she's amazing and already a real person.'

'Any thoughts about having some of your own?'

For a brief moment, Faye's eyes narrowed in suspicion at Matt's question, but the warmth and interest in his voice didn't sound like someone who was attempting to trap her into admitting whether she would be angling for maternity leave soon. Without realising it, she sighed deeply, wondering why everyone suddenly seemed interested in asking her this question and how she was expected to reply.

'I would love to have kids, eventually,' she said carefully, hoping he had caught her emphasis on the last word. She traced the moisture on the outside of her glass with her index finger, struck by the fact that the only person who hadn't put that particular question to her was Rocky.

Matt's voice broke into her thoughts, his eyes taking in the disquiet on her expressive features.

'God, I'm sorry, Faye. I shouldn't be asking you such personal questions!' He sounded so appalled that she rushed to reassure him.

'No, really, it's okay, I don't mind. It's just–' She flushed in embarrassment at the question she was about to ask as it suddenly occurred to her that that this was the most intimate conversation she had ever had with Matt since coming to work for him. On the other hand, it wasn't often that she came across a man who so obviously loved kids and she was desperate to resolve her own dilemma.

'My boyfriend isn't exactly Mr. Domestic and all the men I know seem to be more obsessed with their work than anything else.' She hesitated since he was one of the men she would have placed in that category, but he didn't seem offended so she plunged on.

'Don't laugh – I know it sounds stupid, but... is there some particular point that men get to when they feel like they're ready to start a family?'

His fingers drummed lightly on the table as he carefully considered her question. He ran a hand through his silky hair, leaving a few curls standing to attention, and absently gestured to the waitress to bring the bill.

'It's not a stupid question but I wish I could tell you that I knew the answer,' he said finally. 'I don't think there's any one thing. It's a tough time in this economy and kids aren't cheap, as my sister keeps telling me. I suppose for us guys, we want to know that we can afford to look after a family, whereas women just kind of get on with it. But if it's important to you to have kids, you should tell your boyfriend. No point wasting time if he's not going to give you what you want.'

She sat silently and watched him pay the bill. She turned his words over in her mind, idly wondering if there was any chance that her boss had been speaking to Caroline, and then slid out of the booth and accompanied him out into the sunshine and back to the office.

6

Sole Mate

Later that evening as she changed out of her office clothes to head over to Rocky's flat, Faye tried unsuccessfully to get Matt's words out of her head. Was she wasting her time with Rocky? If anyone had suggested to her even a few months ago that she would find herself questioning her relationship with the man she had come to think of as her soul mate, she would have laughed in their faces.

From the first moment she had laid eyes on him, Rocky had consumed her thoughts and when, after a shaky start, they had finally got together, being with him had been such a rollercoaster of spontaneity, fun and new experiences that she had never looked back. But the days of surprise concert tickets to watch her favourite bands, impromptu trips to Paris, Barcelona or New York, or exotic holidays like the trip to Thailand that he had planned for her birthday a couple of years before, now felt like eons ago. The only surprises on offer these days were limited to finding him at home and without a telephone glued to his ear.

She slipped her feet into a pair of pale blue wedged sandals and sprayed a liberal blast of Miss Dior over herself. Waiting for the perfumed mist to subside, Faye tried to pinpoint when things had started to change. While she had been at the College of Art and trying to handle an ever increasing workload of research projects, practical assignments and essays, there had definitely been no question in her mind about taking things with Rocky on to the next level; even after starting work at Cayhill's, she couldn't say she had immediately felt any real desire for a more settled and domesticated life. The long hours she worked to justify Matt's hiring of her had coincided with Rocky's own heavy work schedule and she had actually been relieved that she didn't have to feel guilty about spending so much time at work instead of with her boyfriend. It was only in recent months as she had settled into a routine at work – and suddenly found babies coming out of every corner of her life – that she had really noticed her increasing disenchantment with a relationship that didn't seem to be going anywhere.

Faye loved children and had always dreamed of having some of her own. She thought back to when she and Caroline used to spend hours lolling on the twin beds in her best friend's enormous bedroom looking through Argos catalogues to choose their favourite engagement rings – Caroline always insisting on a ruby, while Faye wanted nothing but a square cut diamond – and agreeing on their baby names and how they would make sure that their children were born at exactly the same time so they could experience all their key moments together. Even as a teenager, when admitting to wanting a husband and babies was as far from being cool as you could get, Faye had continued to harbour her secret dreams of a big family of boisterous, noisy children, a far cry from the small family unit she had grown up with.

She stared into the full-length mirror, smoothing down the maxi length black T-shirt dress, perfect for the warm summer evening. She turned around to check the back and smiled at the silhouette of her bottom revealed by the clingy fabric. Her self-described 'African bottom' was high and round and gave her some welcome curves in what was otherwise a long and very slim physique.

She picked up a set of thin silver bangles held together with a diamante band and slid them over her slim wrist. Applying a light layer of mascara to emphasis her unusual oval shaped eyes, she gave her hair a quick brush, then picked up her tote and a small overnight bag and left her bedroom, consciously averting her eyes from the pile of clothes strewn across her bed, and shutting the door firmly behind her. One major disadvantage of still living at home was the rare but potential chance of her fanatically tidy father wandering into her room.

Lottie was in the living room, engrossed in the latest episode of *Getting Back with Bridget* and she glanced up as Faye put her head around the door.

'Are you off, then?' Her eyes were back on the TV screen before she finished her sentence and Faye gave a short laugh of disbelief.

'I can't get over the idea that you, of all people, are so taken with that actor? What's his name again?'

'Sam Molloy,' Lottie muttered impatiently. Her eyes were glued to the TV and focused on the silver-haired actor in the middle of a love scene with his on-screen estranged wife.

'Is that woman Bridget?'

'Yes. Shouldn't you be heading off if you want to avoid the traffic?'

Faye giggled at Lottie's undisguised impatience. 'Fine, I'll take the hint. I'm staying at Rocky's tonight, so I'll see you tomorrow evening. Have fun with Sam!'

Still laughing, she shook her head as she walked out to her car. Would wonders never cease? Lottie, who never had a good word to say about any man she wasn't related to, was actually taking an interest in a member of the opposite sex, even if it was only a fictional version. She steered her car out of the narrow driveway and down into Hampstead, turning left at the traffic lights to head to Rocky's flat in St John's Wood. Not for the first time, she was thankful that he had moved from his original location south of the river to a mansion flat less than twenty minutes from her home. At the time, she had seen this as a first step to when they would eventually live together but, ironically, she had seen far less of him since he had moved to her neighbourhood than when he lived over an hour's drive away.

The air was balmy and she rolled down the car window and sang along to the Ed Sheeran tracks she had downloaded onto her phone and which were now blaring through the speakers. It was almost eight o'clock and with only a little traffic on the roads, she was soon in front of the imposing building that housed Rocky's third-floor apartment. Parking the car, she walked up the short flight of stairs to the front door and punched in the security code to enter the building. She clutched her overnight bag in one hand and climbed carefully up the wide staircase, taking care not to trip on the carpet strip draped over the flagstone steps, her mind flashing back to the day they had finally found the flat. After weeks of online searches and house-hunting, Rocky had liked the traditional façade immediately and for once the estate agent's description had matched the real thing.

Puffing a little from the climb, she rummaged in her handbag to find her set of keys. Just after the removal men had left, and while they were collapsed in exhaustion on the black leather sofa that had moved in with him, Rocky had handed them to her, his face serious for once.

'Are you giving these to me in case you lose yours and need a spare?' Although she had joked about it at the time, she had been surprised and touched at the gesture. She had also wondered whether he was finally going to say what she had been waiting so long to hear.

But Rocky hadn't remained serious for long. 'No, I just want you to know that you are free to come over whenever you want, whether I'm here or not. And, of course, if you do ever feel like cooking for your man, the good news is that you'll be able to let yourself in.'

She pushed the front door open and walked into the hallway; it was dark and she turned on the light, disappointed but not altogether surprised that Rocky was not yet home. She kicked off her shoes and dropped her bag on the floor next to them before making her way to the kitchen. The near silence in the flat was unnerving and the only noise came from the quiet murmur of the fridge, which was probably the only appliance he ever used in the kitchen. She pulled open the fridge and extracted a bottle of white wine, pouring herself a large glass before retracing her footsteps across the hallway and into the lounge.

The flat had two large bedrooms, one of which Rocky had turned into a study with a fitness bench and a few loose weights stowed in one corner. The living room was spacious with pristine cream carpets and equally pale curtains over traditional iron-lattice windows. Concealed lighting subtly highlighted the dark furnishings and the discreet stereo and speakers emphasised the apartment's clean, uncluttered style.

Paulina, Rocky's Spanish cleaning lady, laboured to keep the dark oak bookcase and sideboard scrupulously clear of dust, making sure his prized collection of CDs was carefully stacked in the brushed steel racks. The TV screen on the wall, while not quite as huge as Caroline's, was designed to give him the best view of his favourite sports programmes.

To counteract the sombre masculine colour scheme and at Faye's insistence, a large watercolour of an African beach scene hung on the wall in the alcove at the far end that passed for a dining room. The painting's vivid cobalt blue sky, white sands and scorching yellow sun provided colourful relief to the subdued tones of the room and the hard-edged chrome and glass dining table. Two striking sculptures – one male, the other female – about three feet in height, souvenirs from their trip to Ghana for Amma's engagement, stood in silhouette at each end of the alcove.

Faye settled herself onto the leather sofa and flicked idly through the copy of the Economist magazine lying on the coffee table. A few seconds later, she tossed it back where she had found it and sat back, taking in the sophisticated décor of the room and the spotless deep pile carpet. She thought back to the meeting with Harriet Woollaston and idly imagined bringing Coco here, instantly shuddering at the havoc her goddaughter could wreak in Rocky's home. This is definitely not a room for someone who has babies or children in mind. Despite herself, the depressing thought entered her mind and seemed to take root. She shook her head in an effort to shake off the mood that threatened to engulf her and glanced at her watch with an impatient sigh. She was just reaching for her phone to call him when she heard the sound of the front door opening.

'Faye? Are you in there?' The sound of Rocky's deep voice was followed soon afterwards by his entrance into the room.

She scrambled to her feet and, for a moment, she just stared at him, struck yet again by how utterly beautiful he was. At six feet and two inches, Rocky's muscular physique was emphasised by his fitted charcoal-grey suit. His complexion was a striking dark copper and his eyes – a colour Faye always likened to melted caramel – crinkled at the corners as he smiled at her. His dark hair was cut very low, emphasising high cheekbones and a square jaw that would have had any modelling agency salivating with joy.

He loosened the grey tie around his neck as he walked in and unbuttoned the neck of a white shirt that even after a day's work still looked freshly laundered. Striding towards her with a huge grin on his face, he opened his arms wide and seized her in a suffocating embrace. Ignoring her squeal of protest, he dragged her back down onto the sofa without loosening his hold.

'I have missed you!' he exclaimed after kissing her hard for several minutes. Pushing against the arms still firmly locked around her, Faye pulled back slightly to look up into his eyes.

'I've missed you too,' she said, gasping for breath. She stroked his face lovingly and feeling the roughness of the light stubble coming through on her fingertips. She noted the deep shadows under his eyes and frowned.

'You look exhausted. Have you been getting any sleep?'

He kissed her again before releasing her from his hold. He smoothed out the frown on her face with a gentle forefinger and stood up to shrug off his suit jacket. Spotting her wine glass, he took a quick sip of her drink.

'Not really. It's all a bit mad at the moment. I've got everyone on my team working round the clock to lock down this deal and every time we think we're almost there, something else comes up.'

The very faint transatlantic twang, a legacy from his years in America, sounded more pronounced.

'Why, what's happened now?' She braced herself for the barrage of acronyms and complicated explanations that always seemed to go with his job, but he just grinned knowingly at her.

'I think you're about as interested in my answer to that question as I am in talking about work when I finally have you to myself.'

She flushed guiltily but knew better than to protest since they both knew she could never quite get her head around what he did at his bank. She prudently changed the subject.

'I just got here a few minutes ago. What do you want to do for dinner? I'd offer to cook but I bet you don't have anything in the cupboard.'

He laughed. 'You know me so well. Let's stay in – I could do with a quiet night. Do you fancy a pizza? I'm going to have a quick shower and change. Why don't you call? Order what you want.' He picked up his jacket, extricated some notes from his wallet and dropped them onto the table before leaving the room.

Faye took another sip of her wine and made her way to the kitchen. She rifled impatiently through the pile of takeaway menus on the shelf next to the door, yet more evidence of Rocky's entrenched bachelor lifestyle. Pulling out the flyer for the local pizzeria, she placed the order and topped up her wine glass, filling another glass for Rocky.

Two hours later, and deep into a second bottle of wine with the now empty pizza carton open on the dining table, Faye relaxed against him on the sofa. With her back against his chest, she could feel the beat of his heart and the warmth of his body through the thin cotton of her dress. She sighed with pleasure as his hands slowly stroked her hair while they talked and for what seemed like the first time in weeks, she felt totally connected to him.

After emerging from his shower dressed only in a pair of khaki shorts and a white cotton T-shirt, they had devoured the large pepperoni and cheese pizza from Rossetti's, laughing and chatting like old times. As she had predicted, Rocky was suitably impressed by the news that Cayhill's had won the pitch for Harriet Woollaston's project, and he frowned in sympathy when she related her encounter with Justin Parker. Knowing her boyfriend as she did, she had prudently skipped telling him Matt's theory about the motives behind their client's behaviour.

Now, as the TV screen flickered soundlessly on the wall, the football match that would normally have captured his attention was the last thing on his mind as he listened to her biggest news and the bombshell about William and Lucinda's babies had him almost upright in shock.

'Bloody hell – twins? Are you serious? Those guys are going to have an even harder time of it.'

He sounded horrified and although Faye had been stunned by the news when she first heard it, she was stung by the obvious dismay in his voice.

'It's not exactly the end of the world,' she said, trying not to sound as irritated with him as she suddenly felt. 'Two babies will definitely be more work than one, but it's a lovely surprise and they're both over the moon about it.'

She could feel him shrug behind her and he sounded unconvinced. 'Faye, twins are a big deal. It's twice the expense at the same time – think of the costs of food, childcare, school fees. William and Lucinda are both busy lawyers, and I don't see her giving up work.'

'She doesn't have to!' Faye protested. 'You said it

yourself; childcare. I'm sure they'll get a nanny to help them. For God's sake, they're not the first couple to have kids!'

Moving from the shelter of his arms, she turned around and glared at him and he raised a startled eyebrow in enquiry.

'Hey, why are you getting so worked up about this? I'm not saying I'm not happy for them. If that's what they want, it's great news. But you can't deny that it's not exactly what William would have planned; you know your brother doesn't do the unconventional very well.'

Clearly still in shock at the news, Rocky shook his head slowly. 'Well, I don't envy them the next eighteen years of their lives, that's for sure.'

Feeling like he had taken a knife and was nicking off little parts of her heart with each word he spoke, Faye swung her legs off the sofa and sat up, pushing back her dishevelled hair. She resisted his efforts to pull her back against him, feeling the intimacy between them only a few moments ago fast dissipating. She searched for something to say to break the brewing tension but the only other thing that came to mind didn't help matters.

'Why didn't you tell me that Amma and Edwin have set the date for their wedding?' She didn't need to look at him to picture the puzzled expression that would follow the unexpected change of subject.

For a moment Rocky didn't reply. She looked over her shoulder and her heart sank when she saw his surprise and bewilderment at her abrupt change in demeanour. Squashing her guilt at being the cause of the sudden coolness in the air, she repeated her question defiantly.

'I didn't intend to not tell you; it just slipped my mind.' He spoke slowly and sounded wary, clearly not sure which direction the conversation was now taking.

She turned her back on him again, her guilt resurfacing as she felt the closeness of the past couple of hours tear at the seams. But, having started, she couldn't help herself.

'Rocky, you know I've been asking you for ages about whether they had set a date. I have to get Matt and Harriet to agree to me taking time off their projects, not to mention having to book flights and plan my clothes for the wedding. The least you could have done was to let me know the date as soon as Amma told you!'

Taken aback by the vehemence of her tone, he sat up and turned her to face him. 'Faye, what's wrong? What's going on? Have I done something to upset you?'

No, she thought miserably. *That's the trouble – you haven't done anything – or at least anything that I want.* She stared helplessly into his troubled brown eyes and even in her dejected state she couldn't help noting the length of his lashes and how totally wasted they were on a man.

'Hey, sweetheart, what's the matter?' The genuine concern in his voice only served to make her feel sad, and she turned her head away. She remembered Matt's words and wondered if she had the courage to broach the subject of how he saw their future together. *Go on, say it!* But another voice, much surer of its ground, argued back. *What if you say it and he gives you that look? You know, the look that comes over his face whenever someone tries to push him after he's made a decision. The look where his eyes go blank and his faces closes in and you know, you just know that he's not about to change his mind.* Faye shuddered inwardly at the thought of having that look directed at her and her fragile hopes and plans.

He was still waiting for her to reply and she bit her lip anxiously. The trouble with asking a question, she realised, was that you had to deal with the answer and she knew instinctively that if he reacted negatively to the idea of settling down, if she saw that look when she told him how she felt, she wouldn't be able to look at him in the same way again. And if that was the case, it meant she would have to walk away. A shot of panic jolted her as she tried to imagine how life without Rocky would feel. Was she really ready to take that step – and for a baby that didn't even exist? She loved Rocky and if he wasn't ready to take the next step, she reasoned, she was being an idiot to push him and almost certainly jeopardise their relationship. And with so much going on with him at work, was this really the time to bring up the issue of marriage and babies?

Frightened by the possible consequences of what she was doing and suddenly overwhelmed with a desire for things to return to how they were, she shook her head and pinned a determined, if slightly shaky, smile on her face.

'It's nothing. I'm just tired and a bit grumpy.'

He didn't look convinced. 'You were fine a few minutes ago, so what's changed?' Rocky's stare was piercing and direct as he urged her to look at him. 'Faye, talk to me.'

She shifted uncomfortably on the sofa, her resolution to stay silent swinging back again in the face of his insistence. If he really wanted to know how she was feeling, she argued against the voice, surely she owed him the truth? *Okay, then, but don't say you weren't warned.* She took a deep decisive breath, but just as she opened her mouth to speak, he pulled her towards him and kissed her, at first gently, and then with greater insistence, and she felt the unspoken words dissolve as the passion that always overwhelmed her at his touch flooded through her. Like a blowtorch applied to a snowflake, his touch obliterated her resolution. *It doesn't matter, this isn't the time...* the words hammered a chorus in her brain as she moved against him and he started to stroke her insistently. Their bodies were welded together as they fell back onto the sofa and she gave herself up willingly to his questing hands.

The piercing ringtone of his phone abruptly shattered the intensity of the moment. Rocky's hands stilled and she groaned in frustration.

'Don't answer it...' she whispered urgently. But it was too late. With an apologetic kiss, he sat up and reached for the handset lying on the coffee table.

Faye thumped the sofa in frustration as he stood up and took a step away, his voice betraying no sign of unsteadiness when he answered the call. She rolled over onto her side and her gaze fell onto his bare toes a few inches away, almost hidden by the thickness of the pale carpet. Unbidden, the thought of spilt food and crayons came to mind and she groaned silently. This fixation with babies needs to stop; this really isn't the time.

Her attention was caught by the word 'Yvette' and she looked up at him sharply. He was pacing up and down and there was no trace of the passionate lover from a few minutes ago in the crisp, business-like instructions he was barking down the phone. Relieved that she wasn't the person at the other end, Faye studied him thoughtfully, marvelling at his effortless transformation into efficient executive. His hand gripped his phone in concentration and his well-defined muscles strained against the short sleeves of his white T-shirt. Trailing her fingers through the thick shaggy carpet as she watched him pace up and down, she wondered yet again how he managed to keep so fit despite only occasional trips to the gym and the odd workout on the fitness equipment that would be gathering dust in his study if Paulina had allowed it.

With a sigh, she turned to stare instead at the silently flickering TV screen, trying to work out which teams were playing, and then yawned widely as the effects of the wine and a long day at work combined to bring on her sudden fatigue. Rocky showed no signs of returning to carry on from where the call had interrupted them. Having thrown a few silent 'Sorrys' and a couple of ostentatious 'what-can-I-do?' shrugs in her direction after he had answered the phone, his attention was now totally focused on his conversation. Yvette of the annoyingly sexy voice clearly had his undivided attention as he sat at the dining table scribbling notes and spelling out instructions to resolve what sounded like yet another crisis.

Twenty minutes later, finding it increasingly difficult to keep her eyes open, Faye reluctantly dragged herself off the sofa and walked over to where Rocky, still engrossed in his call, was crossing through a list of points he had written on a notepad. Seeing her approach, he paused in mid-sentence and looked up at her enquiringly, his mind obviously still on the scribbled notes in front of him. Suddenly too tired to even urge him to hurry up, Faye just shook her head and gestured in the direction of the bedroom. He gave a quick nod of understanding and another I'm-sorry-but-what-can-I-do shrug, and then went back to his conversation.

Smoothing down her crumpled dress, she looked down at him for a long moment before leaving the room and going to bed alone.

7

Hard Talk

The builder removed his hard hat and scratched his head as he took in the mess in front of them. Replacing the hat, he looked at Faye and shrugged in helpless apology.

'It wasn't our fault, love – that wall should have been reinforced. Whoever owned this place before must have had some real cowboys do the work because there's no way it should have collapsed like that!'

Taking a deep breath and, when that didn't work, another deep breath, Faye surveyed the rubble in the middle of the gallery space. The deep breathing was not a good idea as the swirling dust went straight into her lungs and provoked a fit of coughing.

Covering her mouth with one hand and trying to wipe her suddenly streaming eyes with the other, she stared helplessly at the heavy-set construction worker. With an already tight project timeline for the new Parker gallery, this latest development was nothing short of a disaster. Stopping by the site to nudge the builders along, she had been just in time to see the dust rising from a pile of bricks and concrete in the room which should have been almost ready for the interior decorators to start work.

She looked anxiously at the debris scattered in front of her, frantically trying to work out how to turn this situation around. Justin Parker was due to arrive for what was becoming an almost daily progress inspection and there was simply no way he was going to miss the pile of rubble sitting in the middle of the elegantly constructed space. Whilst the collapse of a shoddily-built partition wall couldn't be laid at her feet, such a minor detail wouldn't stop Justin from launching into another rant at her lack of competence.

It had been almost a month since the incident in the reception area of Cayhill's and Faye had just about managed to keep their volatile client in check. The fact that this came at the cost of sleepless nights spent working to near impossible deadlines to cope with his ever-changing demands was just something she had learned to live with. Even with Matt doing his best to shield her from Justin's cutting tongue, it was pretty obvious that she was definitely not on their client's Christmas card list, and she had gone out of her way to forestall another blow-up.

Her eyes mirrored the turmoil raging through her mind and the builder waved away the dust in front of him and cleared his throat discreetly as if by pretending that the dust wasn't that thick, it would help minimise the problem.

'Look, love, we can get this mess cleared up quickly and I can get the boys to put up another partition. It might take a couple of days, but it's not as bad as it looks.'

Her coughing fit over, Faye found her voice. 'I'm glad to hear that, Barry, but the boss will be here soon and he's going to go ballistic – you've seen him in action! How long will it take your guys to clear this up?'

He shrugged. 'I can pull Costas and Polish Boy off the job on the other room and get them to help out. We've still got space in the skip out front and if the other lads pitch in, we can get a new partition up before you know it.'

'It's not me I'm worried about,' she said gloomily. 'The boss is going to have a field day with this one.'

'Well, it's not your fault, love. You shouldn't even be in here.' He looked reprovingly at her bare head. 'Health and Safety would have a fit if they saw you in here without a hard hat.'

This wasn't the right time to point out that she wouldn't even be here if he and his boys had finished the work when they were supposed to, and Faye sighed and pulled her mobile out of her shoulder bag, tapping on Matt's contact.

'I know it's not my fault, Barry, and you know that. But, believe me, that's not going to change anything as far as the big boss is concerned.' She held up the phone to her ear and moved towards the window where the signal was stronger. The sooner she shared the bad news, the better. Hopefully Matt could reach Justin before he turned up and prepare him for what had happened.

Unfortunately, Matt's voice-mail was the only response and she reluctantly left him a message to call her urgently. In the meantime Barry, his heavy boots caked with building dust, had dragged two men in grubby overalls – Costas and Polish Boy, she assumed – from the back room and was yelling instructions at them in slow English, obviously convinced that the louder he spoke, the better they would understand him. Costas was burly, with a heavy-set build that looked made for the job. Polish Boy, on the other hand, was reed-thin with a pale face peppered with acne. After staring at the debris for a moment, they dragged in a mud-encrusted wheelbarrow and began tossing in the broken pieces of plasterboard and cement, swirling even more dust into the hot air. With a cautious sigh of relief, Faye watched the pile of rubble slowly subside.

Her reprieve was short-lived as the sound of Justin Parker's cut-glass vowels came from behind her, his voice raised in annoyed disbelief. 'What the hell is going on here?'

She whirled round in dismay. Costas and Polish Boy – surely Barry could make the effort to pronounce his real name, Faye thought distractedly – kept their heads down and steered the loaded wheelbarrow outside, studiously avoiding any eye contact with the irate new arrival. She suppressed her instinctive desire to join them in making her escape and instead looked steadily at Justin, straining to keep her voice even.

'I just got here a few minutes ago. Apparently the display wall wasn't properly reinforced and all the building work going on cracked the foundation. It had literally just collapsed when I walked in.'

She watched in fascination as his face flushed deeper with each word she spoke, his eyes like blue lagoons in an expanse of desert – in his case, a deep pink and highly outraged desert.

As usual, Justin was dressed impeccably, although

his grey pinstriped suit looked even more out of place in the dusty space than her tailored black Zara trousers, embroidered white smock top and open-toed sandals. Health and Safety would probably also take a dim view of his highly polished wing-tipped shoes and unprotected head, Faye mused, bracing herself for the inevitable explosion.

'That makes no sense! That wall was fine yesterday; there was absolutely nothing wrong here. What did you make them do to it?' He glared at her, the accusation in his voice unmistakeable.

'Justin! Stop being such a bully.'

Faye gaped as a pretty woman in her thirties strode in, dodging skilfully past Costas on his return trip with the wheelbarrow.

Amazed that anyone could dismiss Justin so casually, Faye tore her eyes away from her fuming client and eyed her saviour with interest. She was immediately struck by her eyes, which were identical in shape and colour to Justin's. But where the gallery owner's were – at least when directed at her – an icy, cold blue, the newcomer's were warmed by a wide smile that caused little lines to form at the outer corners. She was several inches shorter than Justin and her sun- streaked brown hair hung in a straight curtain to her back and covered her forehead with a deep fringe. Her sleeveless cream dress emphasised her deep tan, narrow waist and long toned legs.

Thrusting a hand towards Faye, the woman's smile grew even wider. 'Hi, I'm Amanda – Mandy. Justin's sister', she said. 'Take no notice of him. Unless you actually pushed down that wall yourself—' she eyed Faye's slim figure appraisingly, '—and looking at you, it would be pretty awesome if you had – I don't see how it's your fault.'

She directed a stern gaze at her brother, daring him to argue. Impressed that someone actually had the ability to shut Justin Parker up, Faye shook Mandy's proffered hand with a smile.

'It's a pleasure to meet you. I'm Faye, I work with Cayhill's – we're the interior designers for the gallery.'

'At this rate, there isn't going to be a gallery,' Justin said sourly. He stepped carefully around the now considerably reduced pile of rubble. 'How long is it going to take to put this back up again? We're already running behind schedule!'

He ran his hands through his hair, leaving his usually well-groomed locks slightly dishevelled. He puffed his cheeks out, clearly making an effort not to lose his cool and Faye sent up a silent thankful prayer for his sister's timely intervention.

Mandy looked thoughtfully at the space where the wall had been. 'Well, it doesn't look like it was that big – surely they can put up another partition fairly quickly?'

'Barry, the contractor, reckons they can get a strong, reinforced –' Faye emphasised the word to underline her point, '—wall up in a day or two. All things considered, it's probably just as well it happened now rather than when we had actually started to mount the pictures.'

Her helpful observation clearly cut no ice with Justin and he didn't bother to hide his sarcasm. 'I would have thought that it was something you and Matt would have picked up when you did your initial assessment.'

Refraining from pointing out that she wasn't a builder and that he should have had a proper surveyor's report undertaken when he bought the premises, she maintained a brooding silence, only broken when Mandy spoke again.

'Speaking of Matt, where is he? I thought he'd be here today.' She sounded casual, but Faye picked up an undercurrent of something else she couldn't quite place.

'I just tried calling to let him know what's happened, but I couldn't reach him. I can try again, if you like?' she offered.

Mandy shook her head, the movement setting off silky ripples in the curtain of hair flowing down past her shoulders. 'No, no, it's fine. I just thought it would be nice to say hello; it's been a while since I've seen him.'

She laughed at Faye's openly curious expression. 'I've been living in France for the past three years and just moved back to London. Matt and I are old friends and I was hoping I'd catch him here today and surprise him.'

'Oh, right. Well, I left him a message to call me urgently, so I expect he'll get back to me shortly.'

Mandy shrugged. 'Hey, it really doesn't matter. I'm back now, so I'm sure we'll run into each other at some point.'

'I hate to interrupt your conversation but if it's not too much trouble, do you think I could actually get an update on where we are with this project? I have a business to run,' Justin snarled, giving Faye a ferocious glare.

Suppressing the heavy sigh that threatened to emerge, she pulled out her notebook and dutifully ran through the most recent developments in the project and delivery timescales. From the corner of her eye, she could see Barry the foreman whispering fiercely to his workers, the clear message being to remove the remaining rubble at top speed.

The dust in the air was clearly irritating Justin and after a few more minutes of constant interruptions and 'Excuse me, boss!' from the builders noisily hauling out the debris, he gave up.

'There's obviously no point hanging around here with all this commotion going on. I'll be back tomorrow to see what progress they've made. Make sure they get moving on this!'

With that, he turned on his heel and walked out. Faye glared at his retreating back, itching to shout after him, 'I am not your building supervisor, just a lowly designer trying to do her job!'

As if she had read her thoughts, Mandy smiled apologetically, making no attempt to follow her brother. 'Take no notice of him; he's always cranky when things don't go his way.'

Cranky wasn't the word Faye would have used, but she bit her tongue.

'To be fair, he's desperately keen to get this gallery up and running; he's the only one of us that works in the family business and he's really feeling the pressure with this expansion.'

'How many of you are there?' Faye couldn't help asking, intrigued by the idea that Justin was actually human and not just some client from hell created for the specific purpose of torturing her.

'Four of us, I'm afraid. Justin is the only one who decided to make Dad happy by joining the family firm. For years we all thought that Jeremy – he's the oldest – would go into the business and eventually take over when Dad retired, but Jez decided he wanted to be an artist himself rather than sell other people's work, and took himself off to live in some god-forsaken part of Greece. Dad was absolutely heartbroken and I suppose Justin's been trying to make up for it ever since. Between you and me, Jez would have been hopeless anyway; he's got no head for business whatsoever, but–'

The sharp sound of a car horn pierced through the racket from the loud hammering by Barry's team, now back at work.

Mandy looked slightly guilty, as if realising that she had said more than she should.

'Oops! Sounds like someone's in a hurry – I'd better go. It was lovely to meet you, Faye, and please tell Matt I'm back and would love to hear from him.'

She dashed out of the shop, almost colliding with Costas who was dragging in an open sack of cement which narrowly missed being tipped onto her cream shoes.

Faye stood for a moment absorbing the new information about Justin Parker. Matt's comment about him trying to impress his father made more sense in the light of Mandy's explanation. But while she could understand Justin's anxiety about completing the new gallery and making the business successful, it still didn't explain his obvious antipathy towards her.

'Excuse me, boss-lady.' Polish Boy, wheelbarrow in hand, stood in front of her, intent on picking up the final pieces of rubble lying by her feet.

There was nothing to be gained by staying in the dusty

gallery and after a final plea to Barry to speed up things up, Faye left the building site to head back to the office.

Coming out of Chiswick Park tube station into the warm July sunshine, she was enjoying the short walk to the office when she heard the familiar ping of a text coming through. She stopped to retrieve her phone and scrolled down to read the message.

Amma's text was so long that after skimming through the first few lines about fittings, dress sizes and flight reservations, Faye rolled her eyes and closed the text. Feeling slightly guilty that as a bridesmaid she had paid so little attention to Amma's upcoming wedding plans, she made a mental note to read the text later and to call Amma in the evening. Although the date for the wedding was getting closer, she had been so busy on the Parker and Woollaston projects that despite her best intentions she had still not put in her request for holiday, let alone booked her flights. She felt even guiltier for haranguing Rocky for not sharing the wedding date when, weeks later, she had done nothing with the information.

Amma, on the other hand, appeared to have planned every element of her wedding down to the last detail and each day sent forth a new set of instructions. She had personally vetted every family member's outfit for the day, and even ordered her father onto a 'healthy eating plan' to make sure that the suit she had commissioned against his protests fitted his stocky frame. Amma had insisted that Faye's bridesmaid's dress would be made in Ghana and finished only when she showed up in person 'just in case you've put on weight.'

Faye cut through the tiny patch of green near the office, breathing in the scent of the colourful flowers in full bloom. She smiled, remembering her last conversation with Amma's exasperated mother.

'Faye, you have to speak to Amma – she's driving us all crazy! I don't know whether I should feel relieved that Edwin is taking her away or warn the poor man that he should run for his life.'

Faye had long since lost track of the number of arguments she had witnessed – and refereed – between mother and daughter and the stress of the upcoming wedding had increased the frequency and intensity of their disagreements.

'What's she done now?' Having made the phone call in the hope of getting some words of wisdom about her own romantic dilemma, it was obvious that this wasn't the best time to bring up Rocky.

'Well, you know I told you that she didn't like the boubou I planned to wear for the wedding? Can you believe that after I had my dressmaker sew another one, the girl now has the nerve to tell me that the gold thread might clash with the colour of her father's waistcoat, so I should think about making something else!'

'What did you say?' Faye choked back the laugh threatening to spill out. She could just imagine the look of indignation on Mrs Asante's face.

'I told her in no uncertain terms that I was wearing that boubou and only that boubou and if she has any problem with that, it's her problem, not mine! I know she's the bride but...'

102

'I'll give her a call – I need to check on a few things she's asked me to get from here. I've been so busy that I haven't done it yet and I didn't want to call her until I had.'

'Yes, well, good luck is all I can say. We're really excited that she's getting married, but I can't wait to see the back of that wedding folder she carries round everywhere!'

'Thanks for the warning. I'd better sort out our flights as well – I haven't dared tell her that we haven't booked them yet. I need to check with Rocky on his dates first, and he's not the easiest person to get hold of at the moment.'

'Well, don't leave it too late – and as for that son of mine, I'm still waiting for the phone call he promised me. Something tells me I shouldn't hold my breath!'

Walking into the coolness of her office building, she waved her pass at the security officer on the front desk and punched the lift button for the 18th floor.

Her smile dimmed as she reflected on Auntie Amelia's parting comment. Life with Rocky was going from bad to worse as he practically ate, slept and breathed work. She had been over to his flat countless times only to end up sitting in front of the TV while he made endless phone calls into the early hours to his team members scattered across various parts of the world. On more than one occasion, when he did finally put the phone down and pay attention to her, he had promptly fallen asleep, leaving her both furious and frustrated. It was becoming increasingly obvious to her that any thoughts of marriage or settling down were light years away from his thinking. Despite Matt's advice to talk to her boyfriend about their future, she alternated between determination to know exactly where she stood with him, and fear that she wouldn't like where that turned out to be.

Consequently, as the weeks went by and Rocky's attention became almost exclusively focused on the deal now set to close, she had found herself becoming increasingly distant towards him. To her intense irritation, he didn't seem to notice that she no longer called him every day or that she rarely bothered to wait for him any more before heading to bed on the few occasions that she went to his flat. The more unavailable he became the more time she spent with Caroline and Lucinda; a mixed blessing as both women had made it their mission to see her married with children and talked about little else.

It wasn't as if she needed other people weighing in with their opinions when she already had her own doubts about her relationship. Going out with her friends and their partners, she couldn't help but notice how different a life they led and how normal it seemed for them to do things together. It was becoming harder for her to defend Rocky's constant absences and to explain why she put up with it when, in truth, she no idea if he had any serious intentions towards her. And if after four years together he wasn't ready to make a commitment or even say the one thing that she wanted to hear, she had to wonder if he would ever be ready.

She stepped out of the lift into Cayhill's Reception. Chelsea was chattering excitedly on her headset, her blonde pony tail bouncing with each nod of her head. As Faye walked past, she gave her a wide smile and a thumbs-up without breaking off her conversation.

I seriously doubt that's a client she's speaking to, Faye thought wryly, as the words 'I dunno, Leanne, but 'e was bloody gorgeous! He's got my number though...' floated over to her. Chelsea was notorious for the diversity of her boyfriends, none of whom seemed to last longer than a month. Her usual pattern was to fall madly in love for the first two weeks, start finding fault in week three, meet a potential replacement – usually different in every possible way to the current incumbent – in week four, and be ready to start the whole cycle again. At times Faye envied Chelsea's uncomplicated approach to relationships, but finding one good man had been tough enough without deliberately putting herself back into the dating wilderness.

Matt still hadn't responded to her voice message and she walked over to his office, anxious to fill him in on the latest setback with Justin. She knocked at his door and walked in when she heard a voice. Stopping short, she stared in astonishment at the young boy sitting at the easel by the window, his legs dangling from the high stool and his blonde curls in disarray. He looked up from a drawing he was painstakingly colouring in.

'Charlie! What are you doing here?' Faye walked over to him and glanced down at the picture on the easel. The puppy he had drawn was recognisable enough, if a little shaky on perspective. The small stick figure holding the dog's lead was, she guessed, a self-portrait. The tall figure with long brown hair standing to one side of the boy and the female figure on his other side she assumed to be his uncle and his mother.

'That's a great picture, Charlie,' she said softly, unable

to resist ruffling his soft curls. He smiled at her, his dimples even more adorable than she remembered. It was almost four o'clock and judging from Charlie's grey trousers and his rather grubby white sports shirt with a green embroidered crest, Faye guessed that Matt had brought Charlie from school.

Before she could ask the boy any questions, Matt strode into his office, stopping short when he saw her.

'Sorry, Faye. Saw your missed call but haven't had time to listen to your message yet. Lizzie called with some emergency at work and asked if I'd pick Charlie up from school. Just went to get him a cold drink.'

With that, he placed a chilled can of Coke on the table in front of Charlie and watched the boy take a long sip of the drink. With a satisfied burp, Charlie deposited the can back onto the table and looked from his uncle to Faye with a cheeky smile.

'Is Faye your girlfriend, Uncle Matt?'

Dumbfounded, Matt turned scarlet and stared at his nephew, while Faye's jaw dropped in astonishment. Matt was the first to recover.

'Don't be silly, Charlie! Where on earth did you get hold of that idea? Faye works with me – why do you think she's here at the office?'

'She wasn't at the office when we went to see her at the park, though, was she?' Charlie looked triumphantly at his uncle, daring him to argue with his logic. Obviously stumped for a reply, Matt raked his hands through his long curls and looked at Faye in confused apology. She suddenly noticed just how dark the blue of his eyes were, standing out as they did against the deepened colour of his skin.

'Please forgive my nephew – obviously the sun's got to him and he doesn't know what he's saying.'

Although Faye was still shocked by Charlie's innocent question, she fixed a bright smile on her face and shook her head in easy dismissal, keen to change the subject. 'Don't worry about it. Have you seen Charlie's drawing? He's very talented.'

With a grateful glance, Matt picked up her cue and stared down at his nephew's handiwork. 'Absolute genius! Great work, kid. I like that puppy. Is that Mum standing next to you?'

Charlie nodded and started to draw another figure, this time standing next to Matt. 'Yes, and this one's Faye, 'cos she's nice, and I like her. And I think she should be your girlfriend. I heard Mum telling Auntie Jackie that you need to find a good woman 'cos you spend all your time at work.'

Speechless and now almost puce, Matt looked everywhere but at Faye. 'Okay, young man, that's enough from you. You're embarrassing Faye – and me! Finish your Coke and I'll take you home. Your mum should be back by now.'

Faye bit back a smile as Charlie reluctantly finished drawing the new stick figure and quickly scribbled some dark brown hair around the out-of-proportion head. While the child concentrated on finishing his drink, she turned to Matt and briskly updated him on the collapsed wall saga at the gallery.

Her boss stared at her in dismay. 'You're kidding! And Justin walked in just as it happened?' He groaned and moved away to sit behind his desk. Faye followed and sank into the chair opposite him. She crossed her long legs and sat back, idly brushing off the traces of grey dust visible on her black trousers.

'Well, as I pointed out – although he didn't seem to appreciate it – it's probably better that it happened now rather than when we've actually started hanging the pictures. Barry reckons they can get a strong wall up in a couple of days but we really don't need this delay. The fabrics are being delivered next week and now we've got even less time than we thought to finish up the measurements.'

Matt pursed his lips in thought, letting his fingers drum restlessly on his desk. For a moment there was silence, broken only by the sound of his blunt nails tapping out a staccato rhythm on the thick glass.

'Okay, let's see what we can get done in the meantime. I'll get Britt to go over tomorrow and start measuring up the windows and flooring – at least that way we can get started on the curtains and soft furnishings. Once the builders have finished, we'll know the dimensions for the new wall. On second thoughts, I'll go with Britt and make sure none of this has an impact on the signed-off plans – the last thing we need is Justin using this as an excuse to demand yet another change.'

'Oh yes, I forgot to mention it earlier. I have a message for you.'

He frowned, puzzled. 'What message?'

'From Justin's sister... Mandy? She came with him to the gallery and was hoping to see you. She said to let you know that she's back from France and would love to catch up.'

Faye watched curiously as her boss flushed for the third time in ten minutes. His fingers stopped drumming and instead threaded through his curls in a gesture that Faye was beginning to find rather endearing. For a moment he looked about the same age as Charlie and she wondered why Mandy's name was having such a powerful effect on him.

'I've finished my drink, Uncle Matt!' Charlie jumped down from his stool and shook the empty can in case confirmation was needed. Matt immediately sprang up from his chair and seized his keys.

'Right, let's get you home, then. Thanks for the update, Faye; we can follow up in the morning. Could you let Britt know what's happened? I'll brief her in more detail tomorrow before we go to the site.'

She nodded and followed them out of his office before heading to her cubicle. Punching out Britt's extension number on her office phone, she quickly updated her and relayed Matt's instructions. Britt was one of Cayhill's stars and was a genius at designing beautiful soft furnishings. Already under enormous pressure to meet the deadline for the gallery opening, Britt took the news in her stride and Faye hung up, relieved.

Logging on to check her e-mails, she chuckled softly as she remembered Charlie's guileless question. The thought of her stick figure standing next to Matt and Charlie sent an unexpected surge of warmth flooding through her. Seeing Matt as a surrogate father had radically changed her impression of him as just another work-obsessed man. Why couldn't Rocky combine a busy career with helping to take care of a child in the way Matt seemed able to do? She sighed and pushed the thought aside, her mind returning to the pile of work in front of her.

8

Designing Women

It was late by the time an exhausted Faye decided to make her way home. Closing down her computer, she picked up her bag and briefcase and left the building. The faint remnants of the day's sunshine had almost disappeared as she strolled across the tiny park, a brief oasis from the snarl of honking traffic caught up in the road works by the station. She inhaled deeply, the fragrance of the flowers and the pungent scent of newly turned earth helping to ease the tension in her shoulders after hours hunched over her desk.

Her thoughts returned to the curious scene in Matt's office and her heart gave an unaccustomed wobble at the memory of the look Matt had given her when Charlie dropped his bombshell. Was she imagining it or had there been a tinge of guilt in his dark blue eyes? Did Matt really have feelings for her? Uncomfortable at the direction her mind was taking, she quickened her steps and walked into the Underground station, navigating her way through the late rush-hour crowd heading for the platform.

Once on the tube, she clutched onto the strap as the train jerked from one station to the next, escaping with relief when they pulled into Embankment. As she walked along the connecting corridors towards the platform for the train to Hampstead, her mind once again strayed back to her boss. Between Charlie's words and Caroline's insinuations, she couldn't help wondering whether there was any truth to the idea that Matt liked her any more than his other employees. But, try as she might, she couldn't recall a single thing that would make her think that her boss saw her any differently to Chelsea, Britt or anyone else at Cayhill's. True, he had brought her onto the Parker account team, the firm's biggest client until the recent Woollaston coup, but Faye knew she was a hard worker and that she had more than pulled her weight on the gallery design project. Whatever his feelings might be, no-one could accuse Matt of showing her undue favouritism.

She jumped as the approaching tube shrieked its way into the station and stepped in, grateful for the empty seat by the door as she tried to figure out why Matt had suddenly become so intriguing. She couldn't deny that her boss's obvious devotion to family played a large part in her sudden interest – not interest, she corrected herself hastily, awareness of Matt Cayhill. It had been years since she had given any serious thought to dating other men and even if, unlikely as it seemed, Matt did harbour any feelings for her, what difference would it make unless she felt something in return? Remembering Caroline's comment about Matt's looks and recalling the reaction of the woman on Hampstead Heath, it struck Faye that she was the only one who hadn't been paying attention. With a sudden jolt, she also remembered Mandy Parker's almost too casual enquiry about Matt and his deep blush and flustered expression when she delivered Mandy's message. *I wonder what the story is there.*

Lost in thought as she left Hampstead tube station and walked down the avenue towards her house, she nearly missed the man sitting on the doorstep of a red brick mansion a few doors from her home. She walked past, hesitated, and then retraced her steps. Sure enough, sitting on the steps of number 27 Heathfield Drive, his head in his hands and groaning very loudly, was the unmistakable figure of Sam Molloy.

Fighting her instinctive urge to keep walking, Faye turned into the actor's driveway and walked up, stopping a couple of feet away from him. If he heard her footsteps on the gravel, he gave no indication of it and continued to issue anguished groans from where he sat on his doorstep. She looked apprehensively at his crouching figure, struck by the sheen of his thick silver hair.

Approaching famous actors wasn't something she was used to doing and she hoped he wouldn't think she was some star-struck, psychotic fan. His head was now tucked between his knees and his muffled groans suggested that a deranged autograph hunter was the last thing on his mind. Emboldened by the pain in his voice, she cleared her throat loudly. The groans stopped but the head stayed down. Slightly encouraged, she tried again.

'Sorry to bother you, but are you okay?' Even as she spoke, she realised how ridiculous her question sounded.

A nationally famous actor who just happened to be sitting on his doorstep groaning out loud? Of course he wasn't okay. Just as she was beginning to reconsider the wisdom of her intervention, he raised his head and she stood transfixed by the piercing blue eyes peering at her through thick black lashes. Starting to appreciate Lucinda and Lottie's reaction to the man in front of her, she hesitated before repeating the question.

'Did Phoebe send you?' His voice was rich and deep with a beguiling Irish brogue that perfectly matched his soulful blue eyes.

'Erm... no. I live a few doors down the road. You sounded like you were in pain and I just...' She stopped as he dropped his head again and resumed the moaning. She reached out and tentatively touched his shoulder. He looked up again, naked despair in his eyes.

'It's okay, darlin'. You can't help me – I've just buggered things up royally.' The thought flitted through her mind that even in despair, his voice was extremely sexy.

'I'm sure whatever's wrong can't be that bad.' Mentally kicking herself again for making stupid comments – how the hell would she know what he'd done or how bad things were? – Faye looked at him anxiously.

Grateful that she had at least put a stop to the heart-rending groans, she crouched down next to him, tucking her hair firmly behind her ear, and tried to sound reassuring.

'Look, obviously I don't know what the problem is, but is there anything I can do or anyone I can call? This Phoebe... is she your wife?'

'No, she's my agent. She always knows when there's something wrong; I've been out here for an hour – I thought she'd sent you. Oh, bloody hell, this is impossible!'

Hastily butting in before he reverted to groan-mode, Faye tried again. 'Would you like me to help you inside?'

'I can't get inside, darlin' – I've bloody locked myself out!'

'Oh!' She sat down heavily on the step next to him, trying to take in his words. Is that what all this fuss was about – he was locked out? He's a bloody actor, she reasoned; of course he'd make a drama out of something that happened to most people at some point.

Trying not to sound as irritated as she now felt, she pulled her phone from her bag and said briskly, 'Okay, why don't you use my phone to call a locksmith? They'll be able to sort you out, although...' She broke off and looked dubiously at the solid double front doors and the three sets of locks visible from the outside. '... they might charge you a pretty penny to replace all those keys.'

'Phoebe's got a spare set if I can get hold of her. I don't know her number, though. I'd have to look it up and my phone's inside the house!'

Faye sighed. 'Okay, let me make a suggestion. I live a few doors away. You're welcome to come to ours and I'll help you contact her. At least that way you can wait indoors until she's able to bring your spare keys.'

She felt like Father Christmas handing out gifts to an orphan child as Sam turned his brilliant blue eyes on her in abject gratitude.

'Would that really be okay? You're an angel!' He sat up straight and held up a sheaf of papers. 'I thought it would be grand to sit outside and rehearse my lines for tomorrow's filming – I didn't realise it was so breezy until the bloody wind blew the door shut!'

Trying not to roll her eyes at the plaintive note in his voice, she scrambled to her feet and brushed down her trousers; between the dust from the gallery and Sam's stone steps, their next port of call was definitely the drycleaners.

He stood up, his towering height an unexpected surprise; Caroline was always insisting that actors were much shorter than they appeared on TV. She surreptitiously glanced at him as he tucked his faded denim shirt into crumpled grey chinos, and she couldn't help noticing his lean, muscled torso. They set off down the road and she grinned in anticipation of Lottie's reaction to the unlikely guest she was bringing home. Whatever she had imagined as she ushered Sam inside and slammed the door was nothing compared to the stunned surprise on Lottie's face as she came out of the kitchen into the hallway.

'Faye, I'm glad you're here! I need you to taste this recipe for my class...' Her voice faltered to a stop and her eyes widened in shock as she took in the tall, silver-haired man standing in her hallway. 'What the...?'

Lottie stood dumbstruck, while Sam's downcast expression immediately brightened. Unable to help herself, Faye burst into laughter, heedless of the glare Lottie shot in her direction.

'I'm sorry, I'm forgetting my manners,' Faye said, biting her lip to suppress the giggles still threatening to erupt. 'Mr Molloy, this is Lottie. Lottie, this is...'

'I know who he is, Faye, for heaven's sake!' Lottie had found her voice and the rich Scottish burr that was always particularly pronounced when she was under stress. Her expression clearly asked 'But what's he doing here?' and Faye hastened to explain.

'Mr Molloy—'

'Call me Sam,' he interjected helpfully.

Faye took a deep breath. 'Sam has locked himself out of his house. I'm going to call his agent who has his spare keys and in the meantime, he has to learn his lines for filming tomorrow. Have I got that right?'

She raised an enquiring eyebrow at the actor and he nodded without comment. She held out her phone. 'Here, use this. Does Phoebe have a website or a number we can look up or do you want to check your e-mails?'

He seized the phone gratefully and to her surprise he seemed to know what he was doing as he tapped rapidly on the screen and eventually brought up a web page. With a shout of triumph, he tapped out a telephone number and was soon connected to his agent.

Lottie stood motionless with her eyes fixed on the actor as they listened to him explaining his dilemma to Phoebe. Handing the phone back to Faye, Sam sighed with relief.

'She's just finished a meeting in town, so she'll head back to her house shortly to pick up my spare keys. She reckons she'll get here by about nine o'clock. Is it really okay with you if I wait here? I don't want to put you out or get in your way?'

Despite the fact that it was to Faye that he was passing the phone, his eyes were on Lottie and Faye watched curiously as her usually no-nonsense housekeeper flushed a deep red. It was obvious that Lottie wasn't in any fit state to answer and Faye hastily jumped in. 'Of course it's no problem. Look, I've got dinner plans with my boyfriend this evening, so I need to go and get ready. Lottie – why don't you get Sam to try out your recipe? And maybe you can help him with his lines,' she added helpfully.

If it were possible, Sam's blue eyes brightened even more while Lottie looked in danger of keeling over. Feeling like a mother hen, Faye put a gentle arm around Lottie and propelled her back into the kitchen, gesturing to Sam to follow them. Back on home turf, Lottie visibly shook off her stupor and moved over to the cooker to stir a pot of heavily wine-infused stew. Faye ushered Sam to a seat at the kitchen table and opened the huge double-sided fridge that was Lottie's pride and joy.

'Would you like a drink, Sam? We've got fruit juice, wine – or would you prefer a beer?'

'A beer would be grand, darlin'.'

His rich voice caused Lottie to visibly quiver and Faye struggled to keep a straight face. She pulled a chilled bottle of Becks from the top rack and rummaged in the drawer for the bottle opener. She deposited the open bottle and a large glass on the table in front of him and watched him fill the glass and take a deep, appreciative sip.

'Ah... That's just magic!' He grin was more naughty boy than middle-aged silver fox and Faye was beginning to appreciate why at least three women had earned the title of Mrs Molloy. And if the drama she had already witnessed was anything to go by, she thought ruefully, Sam had probably contributed his fair share to the departure of all three of them. From the little she had seen of him so far, the man seemed extremely high maintenance. Hoping she hadn't made a mistake in bringing him home to Lottie, Faye returned his smile with touch of trepidation.

'Right, then. I'd better get on and sort myself out.' With a quick glance at Lottie who was intently stirring her stew and had yet to utter a word, Faye shook her head in resignation and raced up the stairs to change for a rare night out with Rocky.

A little later, at dinner with Rocky, she was still giggling as she relayed the story of Sam's rescue. Almost choking at her description of Lottie's near catatonic state, Rocky wiped the corners of his eyes with his napkin.

'I wish I'd been a fly on the wall. Seeing Lottie actually speechless would have been a first. That woman is fierce!' His early encounters with Lottie were still painfully etched in his mind.

Faye grinned; it was so good to see him smiling and relaxed for a change. Rocky reached across the table to take her hand and his unusually light brown eyes reflected the flickering flame from the candle between them.

'Hello, beautiful,' he said simply. His deep voice sent a shiver down her spine. Even after four years together, Rocky could still make her feel as excited as she had on their first date. With the preliminary deal document signed, he had finally been able to take a break from the frantic pace while the two companies finalised the due diligence and compliance requirements. Or, at least that was what she thought he said. She had been so relieved to hear him sound like the Rocky she knew and loved that when he suggested dinner, she had focused only on the fact that they were actually going to spend an evening together without work coming between them. As far as Faye was concerned, Rocky's company combined with the mouth-watering pasta from the well-known Italian restaurant they were now sitting in had all the makings for a perfect evening. Pushing aside all thoughts of wedding rings and babies, she was determined to enjoy their first proper evening out together in weeks. As they ate, she kept him in stitches with stories about work, the most recent highlight being the unfortunate incident with Chelsea's most recent ex-boyfriend who, in a last-ditch attempt to recapture her waning interest, had made the mistake of sending a singing gorilla-gram to the office.

'How's your Mousseline of Sole?' She grinned and gestured towards the heavily garnished fish on his plate.

Rocky pulled a face. 'I'm still struggling to find the hint of essential truffle oil.'

Faye giggled; she loved Rocky's lack of pretension which no amount of frequenting fancy restaurants and hanging out with wealthy billionaires had changed. She forked up the last of her ravioli and savoured the flavourful wild boar ragu sauce with a sigh of pleasure. It felt good to be back to their usual joking banter and like shedding a heavy coat once inside a warm house, she felt the tensions of the past weeks fall away.

She finished her pasta with a loud 'Mmm...' of sheer joy and looked up to find him grinning at her.

'What's so funny?'

'I love watching you eat,' he said softly, his eyes fixed on her full lips as she licked away the last of the sauce. 'I've missed this. You always make food look like the best thing on earth – especially when you're eating pasta. I honestly don't know anyone who loves pasta more than you.'

'It is a terrible fixation, I know,' Faye sighed happily. 'I've loved pasta ever since I was a kid. It's just so... I don't know, amazing and versatile and just has this...' She broke off and laughed. 'Okay, I know I'm not making much sense but, trust me, pasta is seriously the best food ever.'

'Yeah, well don't forget you're talking to an African man. We just need to have our meat and we're fine.'

As they shared a creamy tiramisu, with Rocky teasingly feeding her the occasional mouthful, Faye remembered her conversation with Mrs Asante.

'Rocky?'

'Hmm...?'

'You do realise that we should need to book our flights for Amma's wedding, don't you? She keeps asking me about it and I'm running out of ways to duck the question.'

She put down her cutlery and looked at Rocky who was still spooning the last of the dessert into his mouth. For a man who had always refused dessert when they first started going out, insisting it was 'un-African', it was now rare for him not to order dessert.

He frowned and a tiny crease furrowed its way between his eyebrows.

'Haven't you booked your flights yet? Yvette sorted mine out some time ago.'

She stared at him in horror. 'What do you mean

Yvette booked your flight? This isn't a business trip; we're supposed to be going to Ghana together!

'Faye, I thought you'd taken care of your travel ages ago. In fact, I distinctly remember you getting pretty annoyed at me for not telling you the date sooner because you wanted to sort out your arrangements.'

'Yes, but you could have at least mentioned that you were planning to book your flights. If you had bothered to let me know, I would have told you that I hadn't done anything yet.'

Rocky shrugged helplessly, clearly at a loss as to what to say without inflaming the situation. He reached for the hand she had pulled away and lowered his voice to an apologetic near-whisper.

'Sweetheart, I'm sorry. You're right – I should have thought to ask you first. It's been such a crazy few months that after you brought the subject up, I was worried that it would slip my mind again. You know Amma would flay me alive if I missed any of the wedding stuff.' He kissed the hand he was holding and smiled penitently.

She was not mollified. 'I can't believe that you actually went ahead and booked without me. We're supposed to be going on holiday together and—'

It suddenly dawned on her what else was wrong with his sentence and she yanked her hand away.

'—and why on earth was Yvette booking your flight, anyway? I thought she was a Director, not your PA!'

He raised an eyebrow at the sharpness of her tone. 'She is a Director – and a very good one – but she's also a friend. Rhonda was off sick at the time; I mentioned it to Yvette and she offered to help. Faye, I'm sorry, I really didn't think it would be a problem.'

His wary expression suggested that he was rapidly rethinking his assumptions and she took a deep breath, not wanting to ruin what had been, up until now at least, a wonderful evening.

'So which date did you-?' She broke off, her attention caught by a woman who had just walked through the door of the restaurant, scanned the room and was now marching purposefully in the direction of their table. Puzzled by her expression, Rocky turned his head to follow her gaze.

'Yvette!'

Faye stared in disbelief as the woman practically scurried over to where they sat. As she approached, Faye just had time to make out a curvy figure in a sleeveless black dress, spiky black heels and a huge black and silver statement necklace – *more of a speech than a statement*, Faye thought sourly. Her jewellery was the only thing large about the new arrival. With a small, shapely frame combined with huge dark eyes, pointed chin and a short, jet black foxy bob, she looked like a tiny and very sexy Betty Boop cartoon come to life.

Rocky's initial astonishment turned into a concerned frown as he took in Yvette's grim expression.

'What is it – what's wrong?' As if suddenly conscious of Faye's presence, he brusquely made the introductions before impatiently repeating his question.

With a brief nod of acknowledgement in Faye's direction, Yvette seized a chair from the adjoining table and sat down, pulling out a sheaf of papers from a mustard-coloured handbag.

'I overheard you making the reservations earlier and I am so pleased you are still here because I didn't want to tell you this on the phone. We need to contact Marshall urgently.'

Her French accented voice was as husky and sexy as Faye remembered from the phone call, but this time there was also a note of panic. 'I've been going through the numbers the Americans gave us and their analysts have messed up on the valuation of the pension fund. I've gone through the figures several times and they don't add up to what we agreed. I think that what they have sent does not take into account all the liabilities for the old scheme and...'

Is she serious? Faye stared open-mouthed as Yvette rattled on at speed, pushing various sheets of figures under Rocky's nose as she raced through her commentary. Outraged by the interruption to her long-awaited dinner date, she fumed silently as the other woman and her boyfriend debated the latest crisis, their voices lowered in urgent discussion. Picking up her discarded dessert fork, she trawled it through the sticky chocolate sauce decorating the plate, wishing it was Yvette's face she was scraping. This was definitely a first! Taking phone calls during their dates was one thing; actually sharing a date with his colleague was quite another. She peeked up through her lashes and covertly studied Yvette, watching her ruby red lips move animatedly when she spoke and purse thoughtfully as she paused to listen to Rocky. For someone in a panic, she had certainly found the time to dress up, Faye noted moodily, her eyes on the dramatic necklace around Yvette's neck. And, if she's so great at her job, how come she let this mistake get by her?

Rocky raised his hand and gestured to the waiter to bring their bill and then returned to his discussion with Yvette. It was clear that their date was over and from Rocky's worried expression it was highly likely that her man, having arrived with one woman, would be leaving with another. Burning with anger at the unwelcome intrusion and feeling humiliated at being ignored, Faye reached down for her silver evening purse and pushed her chair back from the table, snatching her shawl from the back of her chair

Rocky looked up in surprise. 'Where are you going?'

She shrugged. 'You've obviously got a crisis to sort out, so it's probably best if I leave you to it. I'll get a cab home.'

'There's no need; this won't take much longer. Yvette's got a good handle on how we can resolve this. We need to adjust the numbers that were sent to the deal partners and get the revised figures out to all the parties. Just give me a few minutes, okay?'

He could have been speaking Greek as far as Faye was concerned, and she was in mood for a lecture on investment banking. She tightened her lips and shook her head, making no attempt to take her seat or to hide the sarcasm in her voice.

'No, Rocky, it's fine; do what you need to do. I actually thought that we could have a night to ourselves for a change – but clearly not.'

Yvette looked up from her papers and their eyes met. Faye saw a look of unmistakable scorn and a hot flush of anger surged through her; this was her private time with her boyfriend and this bitch had the nerve to gatecrash it and then look at her as if she was being a diva.

Rocky stared up at her, visibly torn between letting her go and dealing with the unexpected crisis. Her heart ached at the sudden and unwelcome turn of events and even more at the hurt and disappointment she could see in his eyes. Without another word, Rocky stood up and kissed her cheek and Yvette nodded when Faye muttered a 'goodbye' in her direction, her dark hair swinging forward against her narrow face.

'It's good to meet you, Faye.' She looked pointedly at the papers on the table. 'I must apologise for interrupting your evening. If this wasn't urgent, I wouldn't have come here. But there is really no need for you to go. As Rocky says, we should be able to resolve this quite soon, and—'

'No, really, it's okay,' Faye interjected quickly. She looked at Rocky. 'I'll call you later.'

For a moment he looked ready to argue with her. Then his expression changed and he nodded slowly, his eyes inscrutable.

Feeling unaccountably guilty and a bit like a sailor deserting a sinking ship, she turned and walked out of the restaurant without looking back.

9

Meltdown

The ping of the e-mail cut through her concentration and Faye sucked her teeth in irritation. She picked up her phone and her heart sank as she saw yet another message from Amma. She reluctantly opened the message and immediately wished she hadn't; much as she loved her friend, she would have cheerfully throttled her if she had been within arm's reach.

With the wedding now only weeks away, it had become all Amma could think or talk about. Amma had started yet another diet in a bid to look as skinny as her naturally curvy figure would allow and her low-carb regime was making her highly irritable and even more prone to turning every setback into a major crisis. As the wedding date loomed, the Ghanaian bridezilla bombarded Faye with a constant barrage of e-mails and every day brought a fresh avalanche of instructions and demands for her opinion on everything; who to add or to leave off the guest list, the catastrophic last-minute change of catering company, her mother's intransigence about almost every issue and, most recently, the wedding photographer who had the nerve to leave town without telling her. Although with the last, even Amma had grudgingly conceded that attending his mother's funeral had to be considered an acceptable excuse.

Faye skimmed through Amma's latest complaint – an argument with her best friend and maid of honour, Baaba, about her dress – and tapped out a short reply to the e-mail, tossing her phone back onto the desk as she tried to refocus on her notes for the meeting with Harriet Woollaston later that afternoon. Harriet had approved the final designs and now that the reconfiguration of the areas designated for the staff kitchen and the crèche was almost complete, the Cayhill's team was on standby to start work on the interiors. Ruth had managed the project with all the tenderness of a military commander, driving her staff relentlessly and negotiating ruthlessly with suppliers to get the best deals on the high-end eco-friendly fabrics and soft furnishings that were going to adorn the Woollaston baby haven. With recycled rubber for the flooring, toxic-free paint for the walls and murals, and biodegradable fittings for the play areas, the baby haven project would have taxed the most ecologically minded expert, and had proved a real challenge to the young designers who found it a struggle to recycle their empty Starbucks cups.

Although Ruth remained the main point of contact with their client, Faye, along with the team, had met Harriet several times since the initial pitch and it was clear that while Harriet was a warm and approachable boss, she did not suffer fools gladly.

Now officially tagged as the baby guru of the design team, Faye was increasingly called upon by Harriet for personal updates on the project and her initial awe had settled into a healthy respect for the cosmetics titan. As Harriet's pregnancy advanced, she showed little sign of slowing down. A single morning spent scurrying after her for feedback on their design ideas in between her tightly packed schedule had left Faye stunned by the woman's sheer capacity for hard work.

It wasn't until that afternoon when she dutifully reported to Harriet's office with a progress report that Faye witnessed the first crack in her client's superwoman façade.

Jessica Allen, Harriet's PA, was at her desk outside Harriet's office when Faye walked into the executive suite. An elegant and capable woman, Jessica kept track of every minute of Harriet's day and had gate-keeping skills that would have been the envy of security at Fort Knox. Without breaking off from her phone conversation, she smiled and gestured to Faye to go straight through. Faye knocked softly and cautiously pushed opened the door to the CEO's plush office. She stood in the doorway, staggered by the sheer size of the vast room with huge windows that offered a clear view of St Paul's Cathedral. She hesitated as Harriet made no move to acknowledge her presence. For once not ensconced in the winged-back chair behind her ornate oak desk, the cosmetics queen was stretched out on the cream sofa by the window, her eyes closed as she gently massaged the rounded bump of her stomach. From where she stood, Faye could see Harriet's face clearly and her heart contracted at the desperate sadness etched on the other woman's features. Uncomfortable at intruding on Harriet's privacy, even though she had been summoned, Faye settled for clearing her throat loudly.

Harriet's eyes flew open and she struggled up into a seating position. Strands of blonde hair stuck out at all angles as she swung her legs down to rest her feet on the thick pile carpet. Smoothing down her dress, she flushed, clearly embarrassed at being caught unawares.

'Faye, I'm so sorry! I'm afraid I didn't hear you come in; I was just putting my feet up for a few moments. The baby was kicking like a trooper and I thought I'd give him a massage to calm him down.'

'You must be exhausted – I can't imagine what it must be like to carry around a little person all day long. Particularly if they're so ungrateful as to kick you at every turn.' Faye smiled gently, suddenly struck by the irony that it was she who was trying to reassure the famous Harriet Woollaston.

Harriet grinned and relaxed against the sofa, gesturing to Faye to take the seat across from her. Walking across the plush beige carpet, Faye settled herself into one of the matching cream armchairs and looked around in appreciation. It must be amazing to work in this space, she thought enviously, comparing the luxurious surroundings with her pigeon hole of an office.

Harriet's desk at the far end of the room was a large and very solid affair. On its gleaming surface sat a razor slim computer monitor along with several neatly stacked piles of paper. An array of brightly coloured products in clear plastic cases, colour charts and a rack of marked–up vials of fragrances covered the remaining space.

130

Harriet followed Faye's gaze and sighed. 'I should be reviewing and approving the new colours for our spring collection. Not to mention signing off the perfume samples for the product development team. But I'm afraid they'll have to wait; Junior here gets priority.' She rubbed her bump with a wry smile.

'Is it a boy, then?' Faye asked curiously before she could stop herself. Now it was her turn to look embarrassed, but Harriet didn't appear to mind.

'Yes, he definitely is. Just as well, I suppose, given his kicking skills. When he gets going, I usually calm him down by talking to him; it's as if he can understand what I'm saying. Does that sound crazy?'

She sounded anxious as she looked at Faye, and suddenly she was no longer the super successful business-woman, but simply an expectant mother in need of reassurance.

'Not at all. My sister-in-law is expecting twins and she's always talking and singing to them. Mind you, my brother does think she's crazy; but then he thought that before she was pregnant.'

Harriet's smile was wistful. 'She's lucky to have him around. Being pregnant is not easy, and it's even tougher if you're doing it on your own.' As she spoke, she twisted the gold band on her finger and Faye was struck once again by the sadness in her eyes. Knowing it was none of her business and aghast at her own temerity, she nonetheless asked the question that had nagged at her since their first meeting.

'You still wear your wedding ring?'

Harriet looked at her sharply and Faye's heart sank. *You silly cow, you can't ask questions like that; she's not your friend, she's a client!*

Without any warning, Harriet's eyes brimmed over with tears and she started to sob. Horrified at upsetting a pregnant woman, Faye scrambled out of her chair and knelt in front of her.

'I'm really sorry! Please don't cry. I've got such a big mouth and it's absolutely none of my business...'

As suddenly as she had started, Harriet stopped crying. She wiped her eyes carefully as though she was well practiced in how to erase unexpected tears.

'It's not your fault.' She smiled shakily and waved Faye back to her seat. 'It's just my hormones.'

Faye reluctantly returned to the armchair, not buying Harriet's explanation for a minute. Apparently Harriet didn't buy her own story either and after a moment's silence, she spoke again.

'Yes, I am still wearing my ring.'

Faye said nothing, noting the dark circles under Harriet's eyes where her tears had wiped away the thickly applied concealer. *Don't say another word*, she warned herself sternly. *If she wants to talk, she will.*

And Harriet, it seemed, did. She looked hard at Faye for a moment and apparently satisfied with what she saw; she spoke softly, her voice almost a whisper. 'I'm sure you've heard that my husband and I are no longer together?' She didn't wait for a response and carried on. 'What you don't know is that he walked out because he thinks I'm a controlling bitch who's unable to let anyone else make any decisions.'

She smiled grimly at the look of shock on Faye's face. 'Yes, it's not pretty, is it? The great Harriet Woollaston, cosmetics queen, global export award winner, superwoman, blah, blah, blah, can't even keep her own husband!'

Her eyes welled up again, but this time she took a deep breath and composed herself. 'So here I am, a total superwoman, just as my publicity says. I'm even having my baby by myself because obviously I don't need a man. That's exactly what my husband said to me, you know? "You don't need a man; you don't need me, you don't need anyone, do you, Harriet?"'

Faye bit her lip, her own eyes moistening in sympathy. 'I'm so sorry. But surely you can talk to him and work things out? If you love him...' she tailed off as Harriet gave a snort of derision.

'Talk to him? I've tried until I'm blue in the face. No, James Woollaston is absolutely convinced that he has no place in my life.'

She gave a short, mirthless laugh and leaned back against the sofa. 'It's ironic, really. When I was just a struggling entrepreneur with an idea for a different type of cosmetics line, Jamie was my soul mate, my confidant – hell, he was a much better business adviser than the two idiots the bank dumped on me to keep an eye on their loan! And now, when I've finally made it and we have more money than we can spend and a baby on the way, he's turned into a cold, unfeeling stranger.'

'So, what are you going to do?' Faye asked carefully. Although she had sworn to keep silent, she was no longer worried about Harriet the client. The person in front of her was just another woman going through a tough time and she wished desperately that she could help her.

Harriet shrugged. 'What can I do? Our little boy will arrive in a couple of months and then Jamie will probably divorce me. I can't bear the idea of just sitting around on my own at home waiting for it to happen – which is why I need your team to have a gorgeous, safe haven ready for my baby. At least at work I'll be doing something useful.'

Thinking back to Coco's early months and Caroline's perpetual state of exhaustion, Faye somehow doubted that any baby haven – no matter how gorgeous or eco-friendly – was going to save Harriet from the realities of motherhood or the pain of heartbreak.

The reference to the nursery project had reminded Harriet of the purpose of Faye's visit and she sat up and reached for the briefing notes. Within seconds she had reverted to the archetypal businesswoman, her face revealing no trace of the tears she had shed moments earlier. A few minutes later, Jessica came in to remind Harriet of her next appointment and Faye took her leave.

She walked slowly back to the tube, her mind in a whirl after Harriet's revelations. Being a millionaire didn't appear to protect you from experiencing the same pain and heartache as other people, she reflected. Having all the money in the world wasn't making Harriet content or providing a happy home into which her unborn baby could emerge. Indeed, if a baby wasn't enough to solve the problems between Harriet and her husband, Faye wondered again why she was so sure that getting Rocky to commit to starting a family with her would resolve their issues in their fast deteriorating relationship.

The night at the restaurant had marked a turning point between her and Rocky. Since that evening, the intervals between them seeing each other had grown longer and the desire on her part to talk things through had begun to fade. The more distant Rocky grew, the more Faye found herself resenting him for not doing more to put her first and as time went on, she appeared no closer to ever hearing the words she had been waiting for Rocky to say.

Yvette's quick thinking that fateful evening had apparently saved the day and much to everyone's relief, the deal had successfully closed two weeks later. Rocky was now not only the darling of his own company, but the newest hero in the City for having pulled off a transaction that nobody had apparently given any hope of success. The takeover engineered by Rocky's bank had created an innovative partnership between Alexander Electronics, founded by the legendary Marshall Alexander who had long resisted efforts by more established financiers to restructure his business, and LaserTech, a young, fast-growing technology company. The agreement offered both parties a path to developing and manufacturing lucrative new technological platforms for the electronics sector and had resulted in a major boost to Alexander's share price as well as a massive injection of new finance into the joint business.

As Faye had learned from Caroline who had it on good authority from Marcus, the deal was regarded as a major business coup and the rash of interviews by City journalists and investment pundits looking for a new story had dramatically raised Rocky's profile. Suddenly everybody was interested in setting up a meeting – and doing business – with the handsome African banker who had guided LaserTech's multi-million-dollar sale to Alexander Electronics.

With her focus off her boyfriend, Faye had thrown herself into her work, spending long days and sleepless nights on her two major projects. Her life had become a treadmill between Harriet's office and the new Parker gallery, now set to open in a week. Working closely with the exhibition specialists commissioned by Parker's, the Cayhill's team had completed the interiors of the new showroom and Britt's dramatic window drapes had proved the perfect backdrop to the modern art and ceramic collections going on display.

The flooring for the gallery's café and lounge areas had caused Faye untold headaches, as had the late delivery of the plush leather cubes to be used as seating for visitors. Thankfully for Faye, Justin's time had been taken up with cataloguing the new exhibits for the sales brochure and planning the opening party, keeping him far too busy to complain.

When they did have to interact, relations between Faye and their client remained distinctly frosty, sorely testing even Matt's easygoing attitude to Justin. Still at a loss to understand why their second most important client seemed to so obviously have it in for Faye and yet needing her input to meet the tight project deadline, Matt and the rest of the team took it in turns to shield Faye from direct contact with Justin, not an easy task as he would deliberately direct questions at her during briefing meetings, whether or not the job in question was her responsibility. For her part, Faye kept her head down and concentrated on getting to the end of the assignment unscathed. Along with the other team members, she had been invited to the opening night party and as far as she was concerned, that would be the last time she planned to set eyes on Justin Parker. When it came time to design the next Parker gallery, Matt would just have to keep her off the team.

Faye was a few metres away from the office when she heard the muffled ring of her mobile. To her relief it wasn't Amma and she grinned cheerfully as she answered.

'Hi, Caro – I haven't heard from you in days!'

Her relief was short-lived as the only reply was silence followed by a loud sniff. Despite the noise from the busy afternoon Chiswick traffic, there was no denying what she heard next and Faye came to an abrupt halt, perplexed by the sound of a sob. Caroline didn't cry. Not ever. Not when she was eleven and teased mercilessly at school for her flame red hair. Not when she had been forced to run 800 metres on Sports Day, anathema to Caroline who loathed any form of exercise. She had moaned and whimpered all the way round, but she hadn't cried. Even when she had endured sixteen hours of agonising labour with Coco, only to go through an emergency caesarean, she hadn't shed a single tear. Yet, here she was, doing what sounded very much like sobbing down the phone.

'Caro, what's happened? Tell me! Is something wrong with Coco?'

'No'. The sobbing stopped and although her voice was hoarse, Caroline spoke with conviction. Faye sent up a silent prayer of gratitude.

'So, what's happened? Why are you crying?' she asked gently. She moved off the uneven tarmac footpath to sit on a deserted bench in the middle of the tiny park, dumping her expensive lavender tote bag carelessly on the rain-warped slats of wood.

'I'm not "crying" crying – I'm just furious,' was the defiant response, accompanied by another sniff. 'I've just had the most god-awful row with Rose and I'm so angry I could spit!'

Faye bit her lip anxiously. Caroline's relationship with her mother-in-law had been steadily going from bad to worse, a situation not helped by Rose O'Neill's extraordinary gift for saying exactly the wrong thing at the wrong time.

'What happened?' Faye held her breath in trepidation. Although she could be forthright in her opinions and never shied away from a fight, Caroline was generally pretty easy going and not inclined to spend any energy arguing if she could help it. She would have had to be severely provoked to actually shed tears.

'The bitch had the nerve to call me a bad mother – can you imagine?'

Faye couldn't. Tactless; yes, that was Marcus's mother all over. But surely even Rose wouldn't be foolish enough to accuse Caroline of bad parenting.

'Are you sure that's what she said? I know she can be difficult but—'

'Difficult! The woman is a witch. You know how hard I've been working on this TV series, right? Well, Eliza Henry has agreed to present the show, which is a real coup.'

She brushed aside Faye's attempt to congratulate her.

'I know... It's amazing. Having her on board will really get us the ratings. But Eliza's in the middle of filming some documentary or other about cathedrals, which means I'll have to go up to Bristol to meet with her and talk through the programme and schedule dates and stuff.'

'Okay,' Faye said cautiously. So far, so good. She shifted slightly on the bench, hoping the thin layer of dried moss wouldn't attach itself to the pale lilac dress she was wearing.

Caroline's voice rose as her outrage intensified. 'So I thought it would be a good idea to ask Rose if she wanted to have Coco for the weekend. Marcus has been going on and on about how his mother feels so left out and how I should let her do more with the baby.'

'So you asked her, and...?' Faye felt a pang of guilt at prodding her friend along but a quick glance at her watch confirmed that she had only a few minutes to get to the team meeting for the Parker project.

'So, like an idiot, I asked her and she then goes off into this whole spiel about how ridiculous it is that I spend so much time at work instead of with my child, and that she would be delighted to help out but I really should – get this – 'reassess my priorities.' Can you imagine the nerve of the woman?'

Sadly, Faye could, and she winced in sympathy. 'That's awful! I know she can be a pain, but that's really uncalled for. What did you say to her?'

'I just lost it.' Caroline suddenly sounded deflated. 'I told her that if she thought I was such a terrible mother then I didn't want her around my baby poisoning her against me. She said I'd got the wrong end of the stick and she wasn't saying I was a bad mother but that I needed to realise that Coco was more important than 'some job' and that I should be at home more and supporting Marcus instead of running myself into the ground when I don't even need to work!'

'Sweet Jesus, she didn't go there?' Faye groaned, the reason for the tears now apparent. Caroline was incredibly sensitive about Marcus's wealth and had made no bones from the beginning about her need to keep her financial independence. Although her husband earned a fortune, Caroline had sworn to never ever turn into one of the archetypal Hampstead snooties she and Faye had grown up hating, and she despised the trophy wives desperate to cling onto their golden goose husbands and whose biggest concern was where to shop, how to find the best Botox miracle worker, and which restaurant to choose for the obligatory salad lunch.

'Yes, she did! I should probably have slammed the phone down at that point. As it was, I just said that it was obvious that we have different ideas about parenting and that until she learns to respect me and my choices, then I don't want her around my daughter. Then I hung up before she could say another word!'

Faye was silent for a moment, wondering how to tackle the situation. Another glance at her watch told her that she had only a few minutes left to get up to Matt's office. But reluctant to leave her friend in such a state, she suppressed her frustration and tried to sound reassuring.

'Look, Caro, I'm sure she didn't mean it the way it

sounded; no-one could accuse you of being anything but a wonderful mum. I know Rose can be difficult, but she does love Coco and she'll be devastated if she's not allowed to see her. I know the two of you have your differences but for Marcus and Coco's sake you're going to have to find a way to get along.'

The response was a defiant sniff. 'Right now, I don't care. I don't want that woman anywhere near my child, and that's that! There's a woman, Anastasia – well, she's more of a girl really – who used to help out at Coco's nursery. She gave me her number when she left the nursery and said she's always available to do some babysitting. She lives quite near us and I've decided to ask her to help out at weekends and when I've got to work late.'

'But I thought you and Marcus had agreed not to have an au pair?'

'Yes, well we also agreed that he would spend more time at home and be of some use. Faye, I can't do it all! My job is really important to me and this TV series is taking up a lot of time. There's no way I'm going to let Marcus or his wretched mother make my life more difficult!'

Faye could just picture the stubborn expression on Caroline's face, probably now a deeper shade of red than her hair. It was going to take a lot more persuasion to get her to make her peace with Rose than she had time for at this moment.

Feeling as guilty as she sounded, she cleared her throat apologetically, 'Caro, I'm really sorry and I know you're upset, but I've got to get to a team meeting and I'm running late. I'll give you a call when it's over, but please don't do anything rash, okay? If Rose phones you back, just don't take the call for now.'

Caroline didn't reply for a moment and when she did, her voice sounded subdued. 'Okay, it's fine, hon. We'll talk later.'

She rang off immediately and Faye sighed, feeling uncomfortably like a mother who had abandoned her baby on the side of a busy motorway. She brushed down her dress and scrabbled in her bag for her security pass. Hurrying into her office building, she was almost at Matt's door when her phone rang again. She groaned in exasperation and checked the screen quickly. It was Marcus and she hesitated, torn between ignoring the call and her gnawing anxiety about Caroline. After the third ring, she gave in and punched the green button.

'Marcus?'

'Faye, I'm sorry to bother you.' Instead of the teasing banter she usually exchanged with her best friend's husband, Marcus sounded tense. 'Have you spoken to Caroline?'

'Yes, a few minutes ago. She was pretty upset.'

Marcus sighed heavily. 'I've just had my mother on the phone in tears. Apparently Caro said she's not allowed to see the baby? I've tried ringing her but she's not picking up. What's going on?'

Faye gave an agonised look at her watch. Why did everyone need her attention at exactly the same time? She quickly explained what Caroline had told her and what she could remember of Rose's actual words.

'Look, it sounds like a bit of a misunderstanding,' she

added, trying to be diplomatic. It wouldn't help matters to tell Marcus that his mother was an interfering snob and a tactless bitch.

He brooded silently on her words and she stared at her watch, almost dancing in frustration. She was now well and truly late for the meeting and Matt did not appreciate tardiness. After a few moments, Marcus spoke, sounding doubtful. 'Okay, I'll talk to her this evening when I get home. I'd better go – I've got to get to a meeting. Speak to you soon.'

Yes, I've got to get to a meeting, too; not that anyone seems to care, Faye muttered to herself, muting the volume on her phone and slipping it back into her bag. She knocked hastily on Matt's door and burst into his office, her apologies at the ready.

Whatever she had planned to say died on her lips as she took in the scene in front of her. Instead of the project team she was expecting to see, there were only two people in the room; Matt and a slim brunette whom she immediately recognised as Mandy Parker. The tension in the air was palpable and when they both whirled round to face her, Matt's face was a deep red while Mandy looked tearful.

'Oh, I'm so sorry...' Faye stammered in apology. 'I didn't mean to interrupt. I thought we had a team meeting?'

Matt took a deep breath and ran his hands through his luxurious mane of brown hair. Without looking at Mandy, he said in a cold voice quite unlike his usual jovial tones, 'You're not interrupting anything. Mandy was just leaving.'

Faye looked at Mandy, who was now staring at Matt, her

blue eyes swimming with unshed tears. Dressed in a fitted black skirt with tiny buttons down the front, her slender toned stomach peeked through the cropped matching jacket. Matt towered over her and even in her spiky black and cream heels, she barely reached his shoulder. With a quick glance at Faye, she forced a smile and pushed a lock of her long, dark hair behind her ear.

'Fine, Matt. If that's how you want it, I'll leave.'

He made no response and she turned to Faye, a distinct wobble audible in her voice. 'Hello, Faye, it's good to see you again.'

Without another word, she brushed past a startled Faye and walked out of the office. The tension in the room was excruciating and left alone with Matt, Faye didn't know where to look. For several moments neither said a word. Then Matt picked up a file and strode towards his desk, throwing himself into his swivel chair. Not sure whether to go or stay, Faye hovered uncertainly by the door.

'I told Britt to let everyone know that I'd postponed the team meeting to five o'clock'. Matt sounded terse and Faye stiffened, instantly irritated at his tone.

'Well, I didn't get the message. I've just come straight from an update meeting with Harriet Woollaston.'

Matt sighed. When he spoke, he sounded more like himself. 'Sorry. Didn't mean to snap at you.'

He tossed the unread file back onto the pile and his fingers drummed restlessly on his desk. Wondering why she seemed to have wandered into quite so many dramas today, Faye waited to see if Matt had anything further to say. He stared straight ahead for a few seconds, the only sound in the office coming from the restless tattoo of his fingers on the glass-topped desk. Suddenly he turned his gaze onto Faye, his dark blue eyes alight with curiosity.

'So did you ever talk to your boyfriend about whether he wants to take the next step?'

Faye gaped; this was certainly not what she had been expecting. Nor did it explain the scene she had just interrupted. Matt was still looking at her and she shrugged uncomfortably.

'No, I haven't. He's been really busy on a major financial deal over the past few months and there's never really been a good time to have the talk.'

For a few moments Matt said nothing and she decided that if he could ask personal questions, so could she.

'So, erm, are you and Mandy...?' Having started, she couldn't quite find the words she was looking for. He gazed at her quizzically; his hair had flopped over his forehead and there was a faint hint of stubble on his square jaw, and she was suddenly conscious of just how attractive he was.

'No, we're not,' he said brusquely. 'Maybe in the past, but it's been over for a good three years.'

'Oh,' Faye said blankly. The tension she had witnessed when she barged in didn't feel like ancient history but, as she reminded herself fiercely, she had enough problems of her own to contend with and her boss's love life – or lack thereof – was none of her business.

'Okay, then I'll go and fill Ruth in on my meeting with Harriet and I'll come back for the team meeting at five?'

Matt nodded and picked up another file and she left the room, closing the door quietly behind her. The vibrations from her phone broke into her thoughts as she walked across the corridor to Ruth's office. Praying it wasn't another crisis call from Caroline, she saw Amma's name flash up on the screen. Firmly rejecting the call, she tucked her phone back into her bag and knocked on Ruth's door.

10

Performing Arts

The five o'clock meeting with Matt and the team had gone well and with all the boxes ticked for their part in the opening of Justin's new gallery. Faye gathered her belongings and left the office, buttoning her jacket against the autumn chill. She was debating whether to ring and check on Caroline or to wait until she got home when she remembered the call from Amma which she had unceremoniously cut off. Bracing herself, she tapped out Amma's number and waited for the familiar long dialling tone.

'Faye? It's about time! I called you ages ago.' Amma's breathless, girlish voice came over the line clearly. Forgetting her earlier impatience, Faye smiled as she pictured her friend's earnest face. Amma's dramatic tendencies had intensified alarmingly since her engagement to Edwin, but she was still one of the sweetest and most lovable people Faye knew.

'Sorry, I was in a meeting. It is a working day for those of us not getting married, you know.'

Amma brushed aside any attempt at humour. 'Hmm...

Anyway, the reason I was calling was to ask about the seating at the reception and where you think I should put Clarissa – I'm guessing you don't want her near you and Rocky?'

'You didn't say you were inviting Clarissa to the wedding!' Faye protested. Rocky's ex-girlfriend was an unequivocal nightmare. A tall, leggy model with more front than Katie Price, Clarissa still behaved as if Rocky was her personal possession. After a few run-ins with her during her visits to Ghana, Faye had hoped to get through her forthcoming trip without the experience of another encounter.

'I hadn't planned to, but she's going out with one of Mama's good friends and he's bringing her as his plus-one.'

'She's got a boyfriend?' Faye was both curious and relieved.

Amma giggled. 'Haven't I told you? He must be around fifty – and the man is loaded! He owns a television station and he's just built a new hotel in the city. They've been going out for a few months now.'

Faye laughed. 'Well, I hope he can handle her – and keep her away from Rocky!'

'I wouldn't worry about that; apparently the guy is besotted. He bought her a top of the range Audi after they'd been going out for a month! And she's just launched a new talk show on his TV channel, so I think she's got enough on her plate without chasing after Rocky.'

'Let's hope so. Put her wherever you like, just so long as it's as far away from me as possible – you know she hates me!'

Amma chuckled. 'Clarissa doesn't like anyone getting away with something she wants, so just watch your back.'

Her tone changed and all trace of humour vanished. 'You won't believe what Mama did this morning! After all the effort we went through to finalise the menu, she's only gone and...'

Faye sighed and mentally switched off as Amma continued to rant about her latest spat with her mother. After a couple of minutes and with the entrance to the Underground station in sight, she broke in gently.

'I'm sure you'll be able to sort it out. How's Uncle Fred doing?'

Amma paused, took a second to take in the question and then changed gear. 'He's fine,' she said slowly, her voice taking on a tinge of anxiety. 'Well, he says he is, but I'm getting really worried about him. He's been working very long hours at the office and he's lost a lot of weight in the last few weeks. He says he's doing as he's told and eating healthily to look good in his suit for the wedding, but you know how much my dad loves his food. I don't remember ever seeing him look so slim. Mama was pleading with him yesterday to see the doctor, but he keeps insisting that there's nothing wrong with him.'

Faye hastened to reassure her. There was enough drama to go round with Amma's mother without introducing a new one with her father.

'I'm sure he's fine. He's probably been overdoing it – it's amazing how hard he still works at his age! Don't worry; he'll get plenty of opportunity to fatten up again with all the events you've got lined up around the wedding.'

'I hope you're right.' Amma still sounded doubtful but then, chameleon-like, she changed the topic again. 'How are things with you and Rocky? Has all the fuss over the merger deal died down or is he still being treated like some kind of finance superhero? There's been loads of reporting on the news about him here; you know, local boy made good and all that hype. Talk about over the top – it wouldn't surprise me if the President gave him a medal!'

Faye giggled at Amma's irreverent tone, amused at how normal and down-to-earth she could be when she forgot her bridal woes. Although Amma loved her brother and was far prouder of him than she would ever admit, she was singularly unimpressed by his frenetic work schedule and his consequent lack of availability to hear about her wedding dramas. She was also an unashamed romantic and had made no secret of wanting Faye to officially become her sister-in-law.

'Oh yes, he's definitely still the new wunderkind in the City. I haven't seen him in over a week – he just got back from Dubai last night. I'm on my way home now, but I might pop over to his place later.'

Amma tone turned serious. 'Faye, I do hope things are okay between you two? I assumed you'd be coming together but Rocky says he arrives in Accra the day after you. Please don't let all this fuss and attention get in the way; it's high time you guys sorted out your own wedding date!'

Faye shifted from one foot to the other and adjusted her shoulder bag, its weight suddenly feeling heavier. It seemed like everyone was keen to get them married off, except the man who mattered.

'Amma, you know your brother better than me. I haven't heard a peep out of him about marriage. In fact—' she paused abruptly, on the verge of spilling out the truth.

'In fact, what?' Amma was like a dog with a bone when she wanted to be and Faye cursed herself silently for the slip.

'No, it's nothing,' she said hastily. 'He hasn't ever mentioned marriage and I certainly don't want to be the one to bring it up. He seems to be quite happy with us just dating – although we don't exactly do much of that anymore.'

What she also failed to tell Amma was that if she had been under any illusion that the closure of the LaserTech deal would lead to more time with her boyfriend, it hadn't taken Faye long to realise that Rocky's success had created an even greater wedge between them. His business trips increased in frequency as more potential clients called on his time, and what little time they did spend together was almost invariably disrupted by phone calls. Although Yvette hadn't actively interrupted any more of their dates, she was often on the phone to Rocky and far more frequently, it felt to Faye, than any other member of his team.

Amma didn't sound entirely convinced by the explanation but let the subject drop. 'Well, he'll be in Ghana for at least a week which will give you both a chance to get things back on track.'

Feeling a sudden churn of excitement at the thought of a week in Ghana and time with Rocky, Faye cheered up. 'It will be so good to see you – gosh, only two more weeks to go! I can't wait to see how Ghana's looking.'

'Thankfully, the heavy rains have stopped, so fingers crossed we have a sunny day on the 28th. Oh! Sorry, Faye, I have to go, the caterer's here.'

With a good-natured roll of her eyes, Faye replaced the phone in her bag and skipped down the escalator into the Underground, suddenly exhilarated at the thought of seeing Rocky later that evening.

Pushing open the front door to her house, she stopped short as she heard the sound of a man's deep, rich guffaw coming from the kitchen. Her father was abroad at yet another medical conference and she walked into the kitchen, curious to see the source of the laughter.

Seated at the kitchen table with a tall glass of Guinness in one hand and a fork in the other, was none other than the star of *Getting Back with Bridget*. The empty plate in front of him bore the remains of a slice of Lottie's famous peach upside-down cake, the rest of which was on a floral glass platter set in the middle of the table.

'Mr Molloy!' Faye stared in stunned surprise, looking from him to her housekeeper in bewilderment.

'Sam,' he said.

'Sam,' she echoed dutifully. She grinned in response to his smile and tilted her head to one side in enquiry. 'Don't tell me you've locked yourself out again?'

His eyes twinkled and his smile grew even wider. He took a sip of his beer and gestured towards Lottie who was blushing hotly.

'No, darlin', not this time, thank the Lord. I was passing by and thought I'd stop in to say hello. Sure, it was so rude of me not to come by before this and thank you both for rescuing me. And my timing was excellent, seeing as I got here just in time to sample Lottie's delicious cake!'

Faye watched in amusement as he scraped the last crumbs off the plate. It had been several weeks since the incident with the keys and she had almost forgotten that they lived only a few doors away from the famous actor.

She had definitely forgotten quite what a potent combination his beguiling Irish brogue and hypnotic blue eyes made. Another quick glance at Lottie and it was patently obvious to Faye that the older woman was completely smitten by their celebrity guest.

Responding to his expansive gesture to join him at the table, Faye pulled out a chair and sat across from him. Not quite sure how to engage in conversation with a household name when he wasn't sitting on his doorstep groaning, she watched him take another long swallow of his beer. The tiny moustache of foam on his lip when he lowered his glass made him instantly more approachable and she watched in amusement as he wiped it off with the back of his hand. Dressed in a crumpled navy shirt with the sleeves rolled up to his elbows and equally crumpled chinos, Sam looked in need of more than a Guinness and she gestured to the cake on the table.

'Can I cut you another piece?'

Sprawled in the chair with his long legs crossed at the ankles, Sam shook his head and patted his lean stomach. 'No, darlin', but thank you. I've got to watch the old figure – the camera puts on twenty bloody pounds in my case, not ten.'

Faye looked appraisingly at his wiry frame. 'I don't

think you need to worry about your weight just yet,' she observed dryly.

He chuckled in appreciation. 'It's good of you to say so but let me tell you, my agent will kill me if I put on weight – I've just been signed up for a film part'. He winked at her, his cobalt-blue eyes mischievous. 'I'll be playing an ageing sex symbol who still thinks he can pull the birds.'

'Oh!' Faye looked at him with renewed interest. 'Does that mean you're not doing *Getting Back with Bridget* anymore?'

'Sure, I will be. We'll finish with this series at Christmas. The filming for the movie starts after that and will take about twelve weeks, so I'll be done with it by the time we start filming the next series of *Bridget*.'

Faye glanced at Lottie who had been listening intently and a teasing note entering her voice. 'Well, I'm sure your fans will be glad to hear that, won't they, Lottie?'

As Sam turned his gaze on her, Lottie flushed again and bent to open the oven, muttering something about her bread burning.

Oh dear, she's got it bad, Faye thought, torn between amusement and concern at the idea of Lottie falling for the handsome actor who could clearly charm the birds from the trees.

Making a mental note to call Lucinda to ask for help with this new development, she pushed her chair back from the table with a loud screech and stood up.

'Sam, it's been lovely to see you again but I need to get ready for an appointment. I hope we get to see you again?'

Sam winked at her, a wide grin splitting his craggy,

handsome face. 'You can count on it! I'm getting a real taste for Lottie's cooking, so I'll be back whenever she lets me through the door!'

With a glance at the flustered woman leaning against the oven door, Faye laughed and left them to it.

11

Guilty Parties

A week later, as she prepared for the Parker Gallery opening party, Faye was desperate for a dose of Sam Molloy's good humour. Instead of looking forward to an evening with her team to celebrate a job well done, she was dreading the idea of socialising with Justin Parker.

Giving her eyelashes a last flick of mascara, she stood in front of her full-length mirror and nodded slowly with satisfaction. The dress, straight from the sales rack at Whistles, fitted like a glove. The shimmering midnight blue fabric clung to her slim body, coming to a stop a few inches above her knees. From the front, the sleeveless dress reached up to her neck and looked demure enough. But when she twirled around, the deep cowl draping at the back plunged down to her pert African bottom, revealing a completely bare back. She chose a pair of large silver hooped earrings and pushed a cluster of thin silver bangles up her arm. Slipping on her favourite silver sandals, she sprayed a mist of Miss Dior over herself and faced the mirror again.

'Okay, then,' she murmured, tilting her face upwards for a final check on her make-up. 'Let's get this over with. And then it's good riddance, Justin Parker!'

Finding a parking spot on a Thursday night in Kensington wasn't as easy as Faye had hoped. She circled twice around the block where the gallery was housed before she spotted a car pulling out and quickly bagged the space. She gathered up her black pashmina and silver clutch bag from the passenger seat, checked her lipstick quickly in the car mirror and then stepped out, taking a deep breath to calm her jangling nerves. Trying to remember that this time she was here for a party and not to deal with Justin's never-ending complaints, she locked the car and walked quickly in the direction of the newly refurbished gallery.

As she grew closer, she couldn't help but smile at the dramas that had led up to today's opening, not least the unexpected collapse of the gallery wall. That was also the day she had first met Mandy Parker. Since the scene she had interrupted in Matt's office, there had been no sign of Mandy either at the office or at the gallery and although Faye had replayed the incident in her mind several times in a bid to work out what might have happened, none of her theories felt convincing. Matt had made no further reference to what she had witnessed and Faye was quite happy to keep her interactions with her boss at a completely professional level, not least because she had no desire to invite any further dissection of her own relationship. But unless Mandy was as psychotic as her brother, there had to be a good reason for that episode.

She paused for a moment outside the solid black door of the newest Parker Gallery to admire the window display. Against a plain white backdrop and bleached wood flooring, clever lighting highlighted three oil paintings propped up on easels. The pieces were clearly by the same artist and the vibrant colours of the abstract artwork provided a dramatic contrast to the stark backdrop. Extravagant swathes of blue velvet – Britt's handiwork – draped across the top and on either side of the huge show window, provided an elegant frame for the paintings.

Faye pushed open the heavy door and was immediately assailed by a wall of heat. Although she was only half an hour late, the party was already in full swing. Wherever she looked, groups of people were clustered around the exhibits holding animated discussions about the abstract paintings and sculptures.

Taking a chilled glass of champagne from the waiter standing by the door with a smile of thanks, Faye moved off in search of her colleagues. The gallery occupied a sizeable space and was made up of three large interconnecting rooms, each displaying a collection of paintings and sculptures. A narrow corridor right at the back of the gallery led to a small office and the washrooms.

Gripping her glass, Faye carefully weaved her way through the crowd, a mixed bunch of casually dressed young art student lookalikes and older, well-dressed and clearly well-heeled guests. Making her way into the second showroom, she immediately spotted Britt, looking elegant in a black lace knee-length dress, and hurried over to join her. She was chatting to a tall man with his back to Faye and intent on not spilling either of their drinks, Faye hugged Britt cautiously before turning to look at him. She did a rapid double-take when she realised it was Matt. Instead of his customary chinos and sports jackets, he wore a fitted black suit with narrow trousers that emphasised his long legs and sinewy physique. With a dark pink shirt open at the collar and his hair was slicked back tidily, he had clearly made an effort, including shaving off his perpetual stubble.

'Scrub up well, don't I?' His dark blue eyes twinkled at her shocked expression. He took a step back, looked her up and down and whistled appreciatively, leaving her flushed with embarrassment at the open scrutiny. She took a quick gulp of her champagne and looked past Matt to see Gemma and Antonia, two other members of the Cayhill team, flag down a passing waiter to refill their glasses. She waved at them and watched in amusement as they each grabbed an extra glass from the waiter's tray before sending him on his way.

Matt beamed and raised his glass to the two women. 'Well, guys, we did it! I know it wasn't the easiest job we've worked on but I have to say that this place looks fantastic.'

Britt sipped her champagne and laughed. Her deep, throaty chuckle was the product of the twenty cigarettes she got through a day – a habit that not even Ruth's nagging had managed to break. In her late forties, Britt was the oldest member of Cayhill's creative design team and had worked with Matt and Ruth since the early days of the company. Her broad face had a rich sprinkling of freckles and her deep-set brown eyes twinkled with mischief.

'We've all worked hard on this one, Matt,' she said. 'But I think Faye deserves a medal for putting up with—' She broke off abruptly as a tall, well-dressed figure moved towards them.

Faye stiffened and her skin prickled in alarm. She turned to see Justin approaching, as impeccably dressed as ever in a dove grey suit that looked custom-made. She could just imagine Justin ordering his suits from Savile Row and giving some poor tailor a major headache with his precise demands for perfection. His shirt was pure white and he wore a royal blue tie with a square of matching fabric flamboyantly thrust into the breast pocket of his jacket. His black shoes gleamed, their shine reflecting the brightly lit exhibition room.

There was one significant difference in their client's usual demeanour. Justin Parker was actually smiling! Faye wouldn't have believed his facial muscles capable of the act if she hadn't seen it for herself. With a wolfish grin that displayed large white teeth, Justin thrust a hand out towards Matt. Undeterred by Matt's unenthusiastic response, Justin pumped his arm up and down exuberantly before turning to Faye and an equally shocked Britt.

'Good evening, good evening! I'm so glad you could join us today to celebrate the opening.'

Coming even closer, he slipped his arms around the two women. Faye flinched as his hand came into contact with her bare skin, her discomfort increasing when he spread his fingers out across her back and pulled her closer, so close that she could smell the distinct scent of whisky on his breath. She instinctively tried to move away but he tightened his hold, pinning her against him. She looked helplessly at Matt but from his vantage point he had no way of seeing what Justin was doing to her. It was only when Britt broke away from his encircling arm to place her glass on a passing waiter's tray and pick up a fresh drink that Faye felt able to pull away. Her face burned with indignation at being manhandled so summarily and she turned to Justin, her expression stormy.

Innocent blue eyes returned her stare and she fumed silently as he turned away, the sheen on his fair hair gleaming under the spotlights.

'You and your team have done an excellent job, Matt. It certainly wasn't smooth – but at least we were able to get it done on time.' He smiled with satisfaction, letting his eyes roam around the crowded room.

Although he was still addressing Matt, he turned his gaze on Faye. 'All being well, once this gallery takes off, we can start discussing the next two that we want to open. Did I mention that we are looking to expand westwards – and possibly even open a gallery in Cardiff?'

Faye avoided meeting his eyes and tried to repress a shudder. Parker Galleries was an important client but she was damned if she was doing any further work on their account.

Matt didn't appear overly excited to her either and after making a few more self-congratulatory comments, Justin moved off to speak to some of the other guests.

Britt was the first to break the silence. 'Is it really bad of me to hope that he doesn't come to us for the next gallery design?' Without waiting for a reply, she signalled to a passing waiter and picked up a full glass, exchanging it for the empty one in Faye's hand.

'Here, I think you need this after that little scene.' She looked at Faye sympathetically. 'I noticed he was getting a bit touch-feely; are you okay?'

Matt frowned and looked hard at Faye. 'Why? What was he doing?'

Anxious to avoid a scene and to forget about Justin, Faye took a long gulp of champagne and shook her head dismissively. 'It's nothing; he was just being a bit handsy.' She looked past Matt and burst into giggles. 'Oh my God, what is Gemma doing?'

After another hour in the hot, crowded gallery, Faye was ready to leave. Conscious that she had to drive home, she had stuck to orange juice after the second glass of champagne. After chatting at length with her colleagues – or at least those who were still sober – she had made an effort to socialise and take in the paintings and other exhibits on display. She glanced at her watch and looked around hoping to say goodbye to Matt but the tall, familiar figure with flowing brown locks was nowhere to be seen. Antonia and Gemma had finally hit their limit of the free flowing champagne and sat slumped against each other on the white leather cubes in the centre of the main room. Unable to see Britt among the crowd, Faye decided to quickly pop to the bathroom before leaving.

She left her empty glass on a side table and hurried past the office at the back of the gallery. There was no-one queuing to use the three small cubicles and she dashed into one and locked the door behind her, grateful to escape the heat and the crush of people in the exhibition rooms. She washed her hands and tidied her hair and had just stepped out into the corridor when the office door opened and Justin walked out. His tall frame blocked the narrow passageway, making it impossible for her to pass without pushing him out of the way.

'Well, well, look who it is! Are you enjoying the evening, Faye?' Without waiting for a response, he continued smoothly. 'And, did I mention how very fetching you look tonight?' His blue eyes looked a lot less innocent now and Faye shifted uneasily from one foot to the other. Refusing to feel intimidated, especially now that she no longer worked for him, she raised her chin defiantly.

'Thank you,' she said, not caring if she sounded curt. 'It's been a pleasant evening but if you'll excuse me, I have to leave now.' She looked pointedly at the space over his shoulder but he made no effort to move aside, instead taking a step closer.

'What, so early? The party's going on for at least another hour or two. You should stay – it will give us a chance to get to know each other a lot better, don't you think?'

The walls of the corridor seemed to shrink around him as Justin came up against her and the smell of whisky coming off him was even stronger than it had been earlier. She felt the faint stirrings of alarm as she looked into the hard blue eyes boring into her and she tried not to give in to the dart of panic that shot through her. There was no-one else in the cubicles behind her and the corridor was so narrow, it was impossible to see past the man. She eyed him warily, instinct telling her not to push past when she had no obvious back-up.

'My boyfriend is expecting me.' Faye looked at her watch as if to prove that she really did have an appointment. 'I'm going to say goodbye to Matt and the others, and then I'll be off.'

Justin adjusted the cuffs of his shirt, revealing gold cufflinks that glinted in the semi-darkness. When he looked at her, his expression was thoughtful and his casual tone belied the import of his words.

'Ah yes, Matt. You know we've given Cayhill's a lot of business over the years?'

Unsure whether he was asking a question or making a statement, Faye nodded slowly, waiting to see what was coming next.

'I've got plans for a major expansion of Parker Galleries; not just here in the UK, but abroad as well. If Cayhill's gets the contract, it will be a huge coup for their business.' He paused, his eyes still on her face.

Fay had no idea where all this was leading and was far more interested in finding a way to get past him than in his plans for his business.

Justin hadn't finished. Clearing his throat, he smoothed back his hair and without warning clamped his hand around her bare upper arm and pulled her none too gently against him. Faye gasped and tried to pull away, almost toppling over in the process. Taking advantage of her wobble, his other arm snaked around the back of her waist and he pulled her up sharply against his chest. She was pressed so tightly against him that she could feel the hard edge of his jacket lapel through the thin jersey of her dress. His fingers felt clammy against the bare skin of her back and she wriggled helplessly within his surprisingly strong grip.

'Don't pretend you don't want this,' he whispered fiercely. 'You know there's been chemistry between us from the start.'

'Chemistry!' Faye practically spat the word out in her fury and disgust. 'You have got to be kidding! You've been a complete arse to me ever since I started working on your account. Let go of me... Now!'

She struggled frantically to break his hold, but his grip tightened even further, the acrid stench of whisky on his breath making her feel physically sick.

'What do you think Matt will say if I pull our account from Cayhill's because you don't want to play ball?' He muttered against her ear.

In a burst of anger, she wrenched herself away and stepped back from him, practically panting in fury. She pushed her dishevelled hair off her face and her almond-shaped eyes spat fire as she glared at him in disbelief.

'Are you crazy? Do you think Matt will even want to do business with you when I tell him that you attacked me?'

His eyes narrowed and he weaved unsteadily, holding onto the wall for support. She looked around, feeling increasingly more desperate. To get past him, she would have to tackle him head-on, and she had no desire for any further physical contact.

'You want to watch your words,' he snarled, his tongue snaking out to lick his dry lips. His eyes darted over her face and came to rest on her full lips. 'Why on earth would anyone believe that I would attack you? In any case, stop being so bloody coy – I thought your lot were always up for it!'

The sound of the slap reverberated around them and for a moment the background noise from the party receded into the distance. Her chest heaved painfully and she stared in horror at her arm, still outstretched, and then at the deep red mark on Justin Parker's cheek. It was hard to tell which of them was the more shocked, but Justin was the first to react.

He grunted with anger and then lunged towards her and grabbed her arm again. Before he could do any more, a sharp voice from behind him cut through Faye's anguished squeal.

'Justin! What the hell do you think you're doing?'

He gave Faye a searing glare and dropped her arm before whirling around to face his incredulous sister. Mandy seized her brother by the lapel of his suit and almost shaking him with rage, dragged him away from Faye.

He turned and Mandy gasped in shock as the red mark standing out vividly against Justin's pale complexion told its own story.

'Oh my God! Justin, what have you done?'

'What have I done?' He spat the words out and lifted his hand to his cheek. 'Why don't you ask that... that vixen who had the nerve to assault me?'

Trembling with shock, Faye's eyes were huge in her face as she stared at him. Justin was livid with rage and his face was now suffused with colour, making the redness from the slap less evident.

'You're drunk, Justin, but nothing excuses what you were trying to do. Just go, now!' Despite the differences in their size, he allowed Mandy to push him further away and with a final glare at Faye, he stalked off.

'Are you all right?' Mandy asked softly. She reached out to touch Faye's shoulder and bit her lip as the other girl flinched. 'I'm so sorry – Justin's a complete idiot and had no business doing what he did.'

Faye tried to speak but the words dried up before they left her mouth. She was still staring numbly at Mandy when Matt strode up, his height and broad shoulders almost filling the small hallway.

'Faye, we're taking off now. Are you-?' He broke off as he took in her shaken expression and Mandy's hand stroking her shoulder in concern. 'What's the matter? What's happened?'

Mandy looked up at him and for a moment they stared at each other in silence. Her slim figure was enhanced by a long, emerald-green dress and she had pinned her hair back to show off ornate silver and emerald drop earrings. She shook her head and glanced at Faye before turning her gaze back to Matt, her blue eyes anxious.

'I'm not sure. I think Justin tried it on with her. He's been at the whisky all evening and he probably came on too strong – he never knows how to take no for an answer!'

Horrified, Matt stared at Faye in concern. 'Are you okay?' His voice was sharp with worry and she snapped out of the daze threatening to overwhelm her.

'Thanks for pulling him off me, Mandy. I thought he was going to slap me back!'

Matt's eyes goggled in astonishment. 'You slapped him?'

'Yes, I did – and I'd do it again!'

'He deserved more than a slap, Matt,' Mandy added with asperity. 'Well done for standing up for yourself, Faye. I know he's my brother but his behaviour was inexcusable!'

Matt's eyes moved from Faye to Mandy and then back to Faye again, patently at a loss for words. Deciding that this was as good a time as any to make her escape, Faye cleared her throat loudly.

'It's been a long day and an eventful evening, and I'm leaving now.'

She brushed aside Matt's offer to find her a cab and shook her head firmly. 'Honestly, it's no problem. My car is parked around the corner and it won't take me long to get home at this time of night. You stay – I'll see you at work tomorrow.'

She gave Mandy a quick hug. 'That's twice you've come to my rescue – I owe you one!'

There was no sign of Justin as she pushed through the mass of people still crowding the over-heated gallery and made her way out of the front door. She hurried back to her car and once inside, locked it securely; resting her head on the steering wheel while she tried to make sense of the chaotic turn the evening had taken.

She shuddered as she remembered the look on Justin's face and the contempt with which he had spoken to her. *'Your lot!' Wow! Well, it looks like I was right about the colour thing.* Curiously, it also appeared that Matt's original theory wasn't too far off the mark. She shivered as she recalled his idea of the 'chemistry' between them. 'More like bloody biology than chemistry', she muttered aloud, rubbing her arm where his fingers had grabbed her.

'Faye!'

She jumped at the knock on the window and looked up sharply to see Matt standing by the car. Taking a deep breath to calm the rush of adrenalin flooding through her, she rolled down the window.

'Matt! You scared the life out of me. What are you doing here?'

'I wanted to make sure you were okay after what happened in there... look, could you please open the door? I'm getting a crick in my neck standing here.'

Touched by his concern, she smiled and released the car lock. He walked round and she turned to face him as he slid into the seat beside her, his long legs shifting awkwardly in the confined space.

'Matt, I said I'm fine; you really don't have to worry about me.' She sounded braver than she felt but the wobbly smile that accompanied her words was less convincing.

He sighed and held out his arms. 'Come here.'

She hesitated, then leaned in towards him and allowed him to wrap them around her. After a few moments she relaxed against him while he stroked her hair gently, comforting her as if she were his young nephew. The gear stick poking into her hip was becoming painful and she shifted away, ready to make a flippant remark about the unexpected end to the party.

The words died on her lips as her eyes met Matt's. In the darkness relieved only by the dim street light a few feet away, they looked like deep pools of liquid indigo and had she wanted to, she was close enough to count the lashes framing them. His face was only inches away and she could feel the warmth of his breath as he stared back at her quizzically, his eyes asking a silent question. Any comparisons to Charlie vanished as she felt her chest tighten and her breathing become constricted. The atmosphere suddenly felt oppressive and she moved back into her seat and cleared her throat, breaking the tense silence.

'Where's Mandy?'

He shrugged. 'I told her I was coming to check on you; I'm guessing she went back to the party.'

The silence in the car stretched and Faye could think of nothing to say. Then, with a sigh and a muttered 'Drive safely,' Matt leaned forward and kissed her gently on the cheek. Moments later, he had opened the car door and was striding back in the direction of the gallery.

Faye dropped her head onto the steering wheel with an audible groan. What just happened? *Absolutely nothing*, she told herself sternly. *It's not as if he kissed me or anything.* She remembered the expression in his eyes as she leaned up against him and a wave of intense guilt washed over her. *It doesn't matter that we didn't actually kiss; none of this should have happened.*

Suddenly, she felt an overwhelming need to be with Rocky and to forget everything that had happened that evening. More than anything, she wanted to feel his arms around her and to hear his heartbeat against hers; to eradicate the memory of being crushed against Justin's Savile Row suit and the temptation that Matt presented.

She glanced at her watch and wondered if it was too late to stop at Rocky's flat. She briefly considered phoning him but then calculated that if she went there directly, she could still get to him before ten o'clock. Spurred into action, she gunned the engine into life, oblivious to anything except the need to be with him. The increasing coolness evident in their relationship over the past few weeks and the widening gulf that had opened up between them suddenly meant nothing; after everything that had happened this evening, she wanted – no, needed – to be with the man she loved.

She drove through the quiet streets, her thoughts so agitated that she barely heard the soft strains of the music playing on the radio. All the doubts she had been harbouring about her relationship with Rocky and had never had the courage to voice now felt petty and she berated herself for allowing his work to become a wedge between them. *Amma was right,* she thought, steering the car through the winding back roads of Victoria, *I need to stop waiting for things to be perfect. His job isn't going to go away and I have to find a way to make this work.*

For the first time in months, she was clear about what she wanted: Rocky. There was no question that she wished to be married and to have a family, but the only person she could envisage doing that with was the same person she had been so successfully alienating over the past few weeks. She bit her lip anxiously, conscious of how her own actions had caused things to deteriorate even further. In her efforts to force him to choose her over his business, she had pulled away from him, cancelling dates at the last minute and spending much more time with Caroline and Lucinda. She felt ashamed thinking of how she rarely visited the flat they had found and decorated with such joy, somehow hoping that by not going to him, he would ignore his hectic schedule and make the effort to come to her.

Determined now to put things right and to set a new course forward for the two of them, she parked her car down the road from his apartment block and stepped out, wobbling slightly in her high-heeled sandals. The chilly evening breeze went straight through the thin fabric of her dress, and she wrapped her pashmina tightly around her. When she reached the large double doors to the mansion block, she punched in the security code and hastened up the stairs.

The corridor light was still on when she pushed open the front door to Rocky's flat. The security chain lay slackly by the side of the door lock, telling her that he had not yet retired for the night. Rocky was paranoid about security and couldn't sleep unless the door was securely locked, bolted and chained.

The light was on in the living room and she could hear voices from the TV as she hurried into the room with a sigh of relief and anticipation. It was immediately apparent that the voices she had heard were not from the black and silent television, but from the two people seated at the dining table, laughing as they looked over a pile of papers. A couple of slices of congealed pizza lay in an open cardboard takeaway box on the table and two half-filled glasses of white wine stood next to a bottle that was almost empty.

Yvette looked up first, her eyes widening in surprise at the sight of Faye standing silently in the doorway; and a second later, Rocky turned around. For a moment he said nothing, his smoky brown eyes taking in the stunned expression she couldn't mask. He was still in his work clothes with his tie loosened around his neck and the top two buttons of his white shirt unfastened. His sleeves were rolled back and one hand was poised in mid-scribble over a sheet of paper on the table.

All her good intentions vanished as fast as they had come and Faye stood stock still, unable to speak. Gone was her desire to apologise and explain to him how she felt and to put things right between them. Her aching need to hold him and to be held by him slithered away in the face of Yvette's confident smile and the realisation that she could see no hint on her boyfriend's face that having a work colleague in his home at this time of night was not acceptable. *So now*, she thought grimly, *'work' had really come home and there was nowhere safe or sacred as far as Rocky's job was concerned.*

Just as he opened his mouth to speak, Faye lifted a hand to stop him. 'No, I'm sorry to interrupt; I didn't realise you had company.'

The irony of her choice of word was not lost on her. She glanced at Yvette but the other woman's face gave nothing away. She shrugged as if bored and took a sip of her wine, her eyes back on the papers in front of her.

Rocky's expression was a mixture of concern and impatience and he tossed the pen he was holding onto the table.

'Faye—'

She cut in before he could say another word. 'You know what? It's fine. I should have realised that you would be doing what's most important to you.' She laughed mirthlessly. 'Which, quite clearly, isn't me. My mistake.'

Rocky got up from his chair but before he had the chance to take a step, she turned and ran from the room, not stopping until she was outside his flat. Her sandals clicked loudly on the tiles in the vestibule and she raced down the stairs sobbing, not caring if she broke her neck in her spiky heels. All she knew was that she had to get away from him and that nothing was going to stop her.

Heading Home

Faye paid the taxi and waved away the offer of a receipt, stepping back smartly from the curb as the impatient driver sped off. A warm breeze gently lifted the hem of her dress, exposing her bare legs and trainers. She smoothed down her grey maxi dress and settled her bag firmly on her shoulder. Pushing down hard on the handle of the trolley, she made her way to the airport terminal.

It was a beautiful October day and the light, hazy clouds of early morning had drifted away, leaving the skies a bright, sunny blue. The automatic double doors swished open and she pushed the trolley into the air-conditioned building, looking round for the gates for her flight.

She allowed herself a mental pat on the back for checking in online; an aisle seat always made the six-hour flight to Ghana more tolerable. The airport terminal was busy and she steered past long queues to find an automated check-in machine. After printing off her boarding pass, she joined a short line of people waiting to deposit their bags; many of whom had at least three or four suitcases each.

She had never quite understood why people travelling to Ghana always took such prodigious amounts of luggage.

Faye watched in amusement as the couple at the front of the queue struggled to steady the suitcases and boxes stacked on their trolley and topped by a large parcel tightly strapped with masking tape. The woman, dressed in a pair of skin-tight red jeans with perilously high scarlet stilettos, squealed nervously as her partner pushed the trolley forward and the parcel nearly toppled onto the clerk behind the counter. Reaching out to steady it, her heavy shoulder bag swung forward almost knocking her out. Distracted by the couple, it took Faye a moment to realise that she was being called forward to the adjoining baggage drop counter. She slung her suitcases onto the conveyor belt, relieved to see that Amma's shopping list hadn't pushed her over the free limit.

She manoeuvred the empty trolley into a nearby stack and scanning her boarding pass at the barrier, took her place in the queue to go through security. She smiled sympathetically at a harassed woman trying to control three unruly children; a smile which turned into an agonised wince when the youngest, a solidly built little boy jumping up and down in excitement, landed heavily on her foot. Her soft black Converse offered no protection and as the blood slowly flowed back into her traumatised toe, she groaned silently. *I really can't get away from children, no matter where I go!*

Not a good idea. Thinking about children meant thinking about Rocky and she was determined not to go down that particular road. After twenty minutes spent wandering around the perfume counters in the duty-free shop, liberally spraying a variety of fragrant samples onto her wrists and arms, she left the store with a large bottle of Daisy Dream. Stopping at the newsagents to buy some water and magazines, she made her way to the shuttle that would take her to the departure gate and nipped smartly into a tiny space on the crowded train just as the doors slid together.

Waiting in the departure lounge for her flight to be called, Faye watched the other passengers for Ghana take their seats, smiling as she spotted the woman in the tight red trousers sitting with her companion, a large blue and red striped bag secured between her legs. In an attempt to zone out the conversation between two men behind her on the merits of mosquito nets in the tropics, Faye skimmed through the latest issue of Cosmopolitan. But after a few minutes, she tossed the magazine aside, feeling far too excited about her trip to concentrate on tips for skincare in winter. It was over two years since her last visit to Ghana and she couldn't wait to get out of London and spend ten days doing nothing except have fun and witness one of her best friends get married.

The fact that the friend in question just happened to be Rocky's sister and that the trip would involve spending a week in the same house as her boyfriend, was an added complication. It wasn't the first time that she and Rocky had stayed at his parents' – albeit in separate bedrooms – but it was the first time when they were barely on speaking terms.

It was also the perfect time to get away from Cayhill's. While she appreciated his concern, Matt's constant enquiries about how she was feeling were driving her mad. It didn't help that he had assumed that her tear-swollen eyes the morning after the party were the result of Justin's attack and not from sobbing half the night after the scene in Rocky's flat. With the Parker project now completed, once her holiday was over she planned to focus her attention on Harriet's crèche. Dealing with Ruth's acerbic personality was infinitely more appealing than Matt's cosseting.

Thinking of Justin reminded Faye of the other Parker. After the party, Mandy had turned up at the office unannounced. Pleading for a few minutes of Faye's time, she had apologised profusely for her brother's behaviour. Having repeatedly assured Mandy that she had no plans to take any action against Justin and assuming that the matter had been settled, Faye had been surprised to see her walking into the lobby a few days later. It was past six o'clock and most of the staff had left for the day.

Judging from the guilty smile and the colour that flooded Mandy's face when she saw her, it was obvious that Faye was not the object of her visit.

'Oh, hi! I didn't expect to run into you.'

'Mandy! What on earth are you doing here at this time? I'm pretty sure everyone's gone home. Is it about the gallery – did you need something?'

Mandy blushed even deeper and her words ran into each other nervously as she answered. 'No, no! I just thought I'd stop by to see if Matt was still here. I thought, well, that maybe he'd leave his desk long enough to take me out for a drink—'

She ground to a halt and her eyes – disconcertingly like those of her obnoxious brother – fell. Faye felt a stab of pity; Matt probably was still in his office but given the scene with Mandy she had witnessed and Justin's recent behaviour, she doubted if he would welcome his visitor with open arms.

But with no desire to get involved in whatever was – or wasn't – going on, she had simply wished Mandy luck and headed home. Much as she liked the girl, she was in no mood to for any further involvement with the Parker family or with her boss's love life, particularly when she had enough problems with her own.

The call to board through the crackling loudspeakers brought forth a flurry of activity in the departure lounge. Pushing unwelcome thoughts of Rocky aside, Faye wheeled her case along the elevated walkway that led into the plane, slowing down to wait as two ladies struggling with heavy carry-on bags blocked the narrow corridor. Once on the plane, she stowed her suitcase in the overhead compartment and took her seat, idly watching the stream of people coming down the narrow gangway. She could feel the vibrations from the plane's idling engine, and the whirring of the air conditioners cooling the interior of the jet and she shivered in excited anticipation of her long-awaited holiday.

The woman in red trousers, closely followed by her exhausted partner, staggered past dragging her striped carry-on bag behind her, and moments later a heavy-set man in a blue checked shirt approached. He slowed down when he reached Faye and she watched in dread as he glanced at the seat next to her and checked his boarding pass. Sweating profusely, his massive stomach poked out from between the buttons of his shirt and weighed down heavily on a well-worn leather belt. He rummaged in his pocket, pulling out a large red handkerchief to wipe his face and to her relief, took a step back to sit down heavily in the seat in front.

'Please, excuse me.' The apologetic request came from an attractive young woman in a long black dress and a black headscarf standing in the gangway. Faye stood up to let her through, her duty-free perfume mix wafting around them as she settled back into her seat.

The cabin staff were now urging passengers into their seats and helping to stow away luggage. Across the aisle, a harassed flight attendant struggled to shove a large cosmetics case into one of the overhead spaces while its owner, a curvy black girl in a blonde wig and tight black leggings that strained against a sizeable bottom, stood watching him with narrowed eyes as if convinced he wasn't trying hard enough. Faye bit back a smile; the girl was a dead ringer for Amma's best friend, Baaba, who, despite having the widest pair of hips Faye had ever seen on a woman, insisted on wearing the tightest clothes possible. With a last, desperate heave, the attendant shut the overhead compartment and apparently satisfied that he wasn't going to disappear with her case, the girl smoothed down her blonde locks and took her seat.

'Crazy, isn't it?' The woman seated next to Faye shook her head in amusement. Up close, she looked older than Faye had first thought, and she could see tiny lines around her eyes and cinnamon brown lips.

'You do have to wonder,' Faye agreed with a smile.

'Do you live in Ghana or are you just paying a visit?' Her neighbour's accent had a strong North American twang and her chocolate-brown eyes matched the colour of her smooth skin.

'My friend is getting married and I'm going over for the wedding,' Faye said. 'What about you? Are you on holiday?'

'Not exactly. My father passed away a couple of weeks ago and I'm on my way home to bury him.'

'Oh, I'm so sorry!' Before she could say any more, the airline safety video started to play and they both fell silent. Shortly afterwards, Faye felt the shudder of the plane as it moved off with a jerk and she leaned back as the lights in the cabin dimmed and the jet tore down the runway before lifting smoothly into the sky.

Releasing her grip on the arm rest, she expelled the breath she had been holding in and turned to see her companion smiling at her.

'Are you scared of flying?'

'A little,' Faye admitted sheepishly. 'I'm okay once we're airborne; it's the taking off and landings that make me nervous.' She paused for a moment and then, unable to help herself, ploughed on. 'Was your father very ill or was it sudden?'

'It was all very sudden, but I'm grateful that he was spared a long illness. I live in New York and don't get much vacation time, so I can only stay for the main activities before I have to head back to the States.'

From her earlier visits to Ghana, Faye was only too aware that funerals could be lengthy and very costly. 'I'm really sorry for your loss and I hope everything goes well.'

'Thanks; I appreciate that. I'm Brenda, by the way.' She smiled at Faye, revealing beautifully white, even teeth.

After a few minutes, Faye plugged in her earphones and was soon lost in a movie she had hoped to watch with Rocky. *It's just as well we didn't go*, she thought moodily. *We'd probably have ended up taking Yvette and her bloody notebook along.*

Refusing to allow depressing thoughts of Rocky ruin her day, she selected another movie as soon as the credits rolled up on the first. Despite the movies and chatting to Brenda, after several hours into the flight Faye was feeling more than ready to get back onto solid ground. She hated flying and missed having Rocky's strong, calming presence beside her. Somehow, she didn't think Brenda would appreciate her gripping her arm if they were to experience turbulence.

When the Captain eventually announced that they would be landing shortly, Faye whipped off her earphones with relief and tidied her dishevelled hair. The plane was descending steadily and they circled around the bright lights twinkling out of the darkness of the city below. A sudden dip of the aircraft caused her stomach to plummet and she gripped her armrest nervously. Brenda's hand moved over and rested calmly on her straining knuckles, her soft palm dry and reassuring.

'Don't worry; we'll be on the ground soon.'

Faye looked across at her, at once embarrassed and grateful. 'I'm so sorry; you must think I'm such a wimp!'

Brenda laughed. 'Not at all. But I've always believed

that when it's your time to go, it's your time, and there's absolutely nothing you can do about it. I know it's not my time to die yet, so I'm not worried. Besides, there's not much we can do – it's all in the hands of the pilot.'

Faye's smile was a little shaky but she took a couple of deep breaths and forced herself to relax as the plane circled lower. *It could have been worse*, she conceded, remembering how she had almost ended up in Caroline's lap during a turbulent flight to Spain. She sighed as she thought of her best friend, her fears about their descent paling into insignificance.

Since the row, Caroline had stubbornly refused to speak to her mother-in-law or allow her to visit the house, and Marcus, torn between the two women in his life, was at his wits' end. Rose had taken to ringing him at work every morning, alternatively berating him for allowing Caroline to deprive her of her only grandchild and weeping bitterly at being misunderstood. After each call, Marcus would, in turn, ring Faye and beg her to help him deal with his wife. Caroline, for her part, was so outraged that Marcus hadn't immediately taken her side that she would refuse to speak to him if he so much as mentioned his mother's name. Much to Marcus's annoyance, Anastasia had been conscripted to help with Coco, underlining Caroline's determination to cut Rose out. Faye's pleas to Caroline to relent had gone unheeded and she genuinely had no idea how to help with the crisis that had beset her friend's marriage.

With a gentle bump, the plane landed on the tarmac and the relieved passengers broke into a spontaneous round of applause. The aircraft taxied down the runway and eventually came to a stop. Ignoring the appeals from the pilot and the cabin staff to remain seated, the passengers were immediately up on their feet, tugging their baggage from the overhead lockers.

'Now I know I'm in Ghana!' Brenda remarked with resigned amusement as they watched the pandemonium. They winced in unison as the heavy cosmetics case belonging to the girl in the blond wig tumbled out of the overhead compartment. Luckily, it landed harmlessly on the recently vacated seat below, although that didn't stop its owner from sucking her teeth loudly and glaring at the man who had opened the locker.

'It's been lovely flying with you – and thank you for keeping me calm!' Faye smiled at Brenda, who sat serenely adjusting her head scarf amid the hubbub of activity. 'Good luck with the funeral.'

'Thank you, and enjoy your friend's wedding.' Brenda's eyes twinkled. 'Weddings can be a great place for finding romance.'

On the verge of protesting that she already had a boyfriend, Faye held her tongue, wondering if she really still did. She hoisted down her small suitcase and gathered up her jacket and magazines. Waiting for the line of people in front of her to move towards the exit, she peered through the plane window into the darkness and couldn't help grinning. She was home – for Ghana felt like home to her in many ways – and it was time to look forward to her trip.

She waved goodbye to Brenda and shuffled past the vacated seats and discarded blankets to the exit, where she stopped for a moment to absorb the sudden blast of tropical heat and searing humidity. She stepped carefully down the metal steps and climbed into the waiting bus, holding tight to a strap as the vehicle jerked forward for the few metres to the airport terminal.

The air-conditioned building was a welcome relief and Faye pushed her hair back, allowing the chilled blasts of air to cool her heated face as she trailed behind the other passengers down a wide corridor. The harsh strip lighting highlighted colourful posters carrying stern warnings against drug trafficking and busy officials in white shirts hastened up and down barking commands into mobile phones and doing their best to look important.

Faye spotted the woman in the tight red jeans just ahead of her. She had discarded her heavy cardigan and her fitted white sleeveless top clung to her shapely curves, although the overall effect was somewhat marred by the effort required to carry her heavy striped bag.

Faye pulled out her passport and joined the queue to go through immigration and when it was her turn, she moved forward and placed her passport and landing card on the counter. The man behind the reinforced plastic screen was not much older than her and he gave her a piercing stare before scrutinising her documents. At his command, she dutifully stared into the small round camera facing her while he took her picture. He stared at her again before handing back her papers with a nod and a brief smile.

Faye walked towards the baggage area, pausing to bag a trolley from the stack near the entrance. She moved towards the conveyor belt that would bring in the luggage and it wasn't long before she spotted her case. Heading for the exit, she tried not to stare as she passed the woman in red remonstrating with a customs officer going through her striped bag. Mopping his brow, her partner stood to one side, looking far too exhausted to argue with anyone.

13

Soul Food

'Faye! I'm over here!'

Faye smiled with relief at the sight of Amma waving vigorously from behind the barrier. Emerging from the brightly lit terminal into the steamy darkness of a tropical evening, she had been overwhelmed by the crowds straining against the barriers clamouring for the attention of the arriving passengers. A number of people carried signs for hotels and jostled for space with taxi drivers in search of business.

Amma was almost hopping with excitement as she watched Faye push her way through the crowd. Her long braids swung from side to side and she launched herself at Faye with a scream of excitement, hugging her fiercely.

'I can't believe you're actually here!' Finally releasing her hold, Amma stepped back to examine Faye critically. After a moment, she gave a satisfied nod and a broad smile lit up her pretty, round face.

'I'm so glad you haven't put on weight; the dress should fit perfectly.'

Faye rolled her eyes. 'Amma! At least get me out of here before you start talking weddings!'

Amma hugged her again and seized her trolley. 'Come on then, the car's over there. Let's get you home – this place is crazy!'

She waved away a hopeful porter and led the way towards the car park. With the cases securely in the boot, she handed the empty trolley to a young boy hovering nearby and pressed a coin into his hand before ushering Faye into the car. Amma drove slowly out the car park, tooting impatiently to disperse a group of porters obstructing the exit, and within minutes they were on the highway. Faye leaned back in her seat, enjoying the cool air blasting through the open vents, and surveyed the passing landscape of skyscrapers, shops and the occasional kiosk.

'You're looking very well, Faye.' Amma's dark eyes danced mischievously and her white teeth sparkled against the dark copper brown of her complexion. 'It's just as well Rocky will be around or you'd have real trouble fighting off the men.'

Faye laughed, ignoring the stab of anxiety at the mention of Rocky's name. 'Thanks for the compliment, but the only romance I'm interested in during this trip is yours. I can't wait to see you and Edwin tie the knot.'

She tugged her seatbelt aside and turned to Amma. 'It's so good to see you. You're looking pretty fabulous yourself; I love that dress!'

Amma glanced down at the halter-necked dress in a vibrant African print. 'Thanks, it's one of Baaba's designs. She's doing really well for herself now – did I tell you she has her own outlet in the Accra shopping mall? Mama's had to hire someone else to run her shop, which has been good for everyone, to be honest. Mama says Josephine is a far better saleswoman than Baaba ever was – you know how she was always getting into arguments with the customers.'

Amma rattled on as she drove expertly along the smooth highway, barely pausing to take a breath and yet still managing to honk impatiently at the buses and taxis that pulled out into the road or threatened to overtake without warning. Faye watched her affectionately and tried to keep up with the flood of observations. *It's good to know some things don't change*, she thought. With the exception of Caroline, Amma was the closest thing she had to a sister and she was eager to see the rest of the family that she had grown so close to in recent years.

Amma paused, clearly waiting for an answer and Faye blinked, taken off guard. 'What did you say?'

'I said what time's Rocky's flight getting in tomorrow?'

Faye shrugged. 'I'm not sure. Probably the same time as mine did; he's flying with the same airline. He made his own arrangements, or rather, his very helpful colleague made them for him.'

Amma slowed down and indicated to turn off the highway onto a wide road lined with big houses tucked behind tall gates. She stopped to let a few pedestrians cross and glanced over at Faye with a frown.

'What's going on with you two? It's almost impossible to get hold of my brother these days, no matter how late in the day I call him. You guys were getting on so well the last time you were here; what's happening?'

'I wish I knew,' Faye said wistfully. 'It's a long story, but let's just say things aren't great between us right now. We'll talk about it later; right now, I want to hear all about the wedding plans.'

Amma needed no further encouragement and she launched into a litany of complaints about the caterer, only pausing when she turned into a short driveway and drove up to a pair of black iron gates. She tooted the horn twice and moments later a skinny figure in a dark T-shirt emerged. With his arms folded across his chest, he stared hard at the car for a few seconds and then slowly swung the gates wide open. Faye rolled down her window and grinned at Togo, the Asante family's gardener-cum-security guard. He stood back and saluted her as they drove in, a broad smile splitting his narrow dark features. His baggy khaki shorts swung loosely around his thin legs as he shut the gates behind them and removed the suitcases from the boot.

Faye stepped out of the car and sniffed the air appreciatively. The profusion of flowering frangipani and pink hibiscus in front of the big white-walled house gave off a perfume that spiced up the evening air, while the shrill sibilant sounds of crickets at play supplied the familiar soundtrack of an African evening.

'Good evening, madam. Welcome.' Togo hoisted her heavy suitcase onto one shoulder, unfazed by the weight, and smiled warmly at her.

'Hi, Togo! It's good to see you again. How is your family – are your children well?'

'Everybody is fine, madam. We are happy to see you

are back with us.' Amma watched as he strode off around the back of the house, dragging the smaller wheeled case behind him, and she shook her head in wonder. 'I don't know how you do it. That man is so cantankerous and doesn't give any of us the time of day. And how do you know about his family, anyway?'

'Erm... Maybe because I ask?' Faye retorted. 'Some of us actually think of our staff as human beings!'

Amma rolled her eyes in exasperation. 'Oh, don't start with your 'we are all equal' speeches! Talking of staff, Martha can't wait to see you – she's been going on about it all day and cooking up a storm in the kitchen.'

They had almost reached the double doors when they were flung wide open. Faye dropped her handbag and walked straight into the warm embrace of the woman standing on the doorstep, holding on tight as she breathed in the familiar scent of Mrs Asante's favourite Chanel perfume.

'My dearest child, it's so wonderful to have you back with us! Let me look at you.'

The older woman dropped her arms and stepped back, allowing Faye to take a closer look at Amma's mother. Her high cheekbones, so like Rocky's, were accentuated by the head scarf wrapped tightly around short natural hair shot with streaks of grey. The same caramel-coloured eyes that wrought havoc when Rocky looked at her, now held such a loving expression that Faye felt her eyes well up.

'It's so good to see you again, Auntie Amelia,' she said, her voice husky with emotion. 'I've missed you all so much!'

Although there was no blood relationship between

their two families, as was the custom in Africa, older people were automatically given the title of 'Auntie' or 'Uncle'. Auntie Amelia smiled and put an arm around her, ushering her into the house.

'Come inside, girls. We don't want to let in mosquitoes!'

Faye walked into the large hallway and looked around with a sigh of pleasure. The beautiful space with high, white-painted walls felt as familiar as walking into her own home and she moved across the cool terrazzo floor, past the polished wooden banisters leading upstairs, and into the elegant family room, with Auntie Amelia and Amma close behind her.

Faye had barely sat down on the brown leather sofa when she jumped up again to embrace a plump, dark-skinned woman dressed in a plain blue dress with a tiny white lace collar.

'Martha!'

Martha smiled and gently extricated herself from the enthusiastic embrace. 'Good evening, Miss Faye. Welcome home.' Her voice was soft and her brown eyes sparkled with pleasure.

'I've prepared your favourite jollof rice and kelewele, so I hope you are hungry.'

Faye groaned with pleasure. 'Martha, you are the best! I'm starving – the food on the plane was pitiful.'

Auntie Amelia chuckled and turned to her housekeeper. 'Mr Asante will be back shortly, so please lay the table and warm up the food. Amma, why don't you take Faye up to her room so she can freshen up before dinner? I'll give Martha a hand in the kitchen.'

Faye needed no further prompting and she took the lead, with Amma a few paces behind holding up her long dress to avoid tripping. Halfway up the winding staircase, Faye stopped at the display of ebony framed family photos hanging on the wall. Her favourite was of a teenaged Rocky dressed in blue denims and a wide collared shirt, with his back against the trunk of a sturdy tree. With a short afro, high cheekbones and languourous eyes, he looked like a 1990's pop star posing for a fan calendar.

Amma caught up with her and followed her gaze. 'He hasn't changed much, has he?' she remarked. 'Apart from that awful hair and the fact that he's a lot more muscular across his arms and chest now, there's not a lot of difference.'

Faye nodded in agreement, her heart tugging as she looked at the young, uncomplicated Rocky smiling back at her. '...and the fact that he wasn't a finance whiz kid with no time for anyone.'

The words slipped out before she could stop them and she carried on quickly up the stairs, hoping Amma wouldn't probe further. The guest room was across the landing and she pushed open the solid mahogany door to find her suitcases stacked neatly by the wall. She looked around the spacious room with its familiar tie-dye curtains and matching bedspread. The huge bed in the middle of the room was covered by a thin white mosquito net which hung from four tall wooden posts fixed at each corner. The air conditioning unit fixed against the far wall hummed quietly and the room felt cool and inviting.

She walked over to the dressing table and raked her

hands through her hair, grimacing at her reflection in the mirror. Her smooth brown skin was shiny and her lipstick had long since faded.

Amma was still standing in the doorway and Faye turned to her with a wry smile. 'Give me a few minutes to wash my face and change and I'll see you downstairs.'

Amma nodded and closed the door behind her, leaving Faye to unlock her suitcase and pull out the clothes she had packed with more haste than care. After using the en suite bathroom to freshen up and repair the damage from the day's travelling, the thought of Martha's cooking waiting for her downstairs spurred her on and she quickly changed into a pair of black trousers and a loose silk top. Slipping her feet into a pair of leather-soled flip-flops, she ripped open the packaging of the perfume she'd bought at the airport and sprayed some onto her wrists before heading back downstairs.

The sound of a male voice coming from the family room had her speeding to the bottom of the stairs and she raced into the room, almost knocking over the older man standing inside the doorway.

'Uncle Fred! I'm back!' Faye threw her arms around the man who hugged her back just as hard before releasing her.

Faye looked at Amma's father and tried to hide her shock. Instead of the familiar portly man with a round laughing face, Uncle Fred seemed to have shrunk before her eyes. His cheeks had lost their customary roundness and sagged against the fine bones of his face. His chestnut brown skin, normally glowing with health, looked dull and his belt was pulled tight to hold up trousers that would otherwise have hung off his waist. About the only thing that hadn't changed were the twinkling brown eyes that looked her up and down in turn.

'Our very own supermodel! Welcome home, Faye, you have been greatly missed. And I'm sure Amma hasn't stopped talking since you arrived?' He looked at Amma who had been observing Faye's shocked expression with pensive eyes and she quickly turned her attention back to her father and pouted.

'Dad, I've hardly had a minute to talk to her since she got here – ask her!'

Faye laughed, trying to hide her concern at the dramatic change in Rocky's father. Something was clearly wrong and she felt a pang of remorse for brushing aside Amma's concerns. Not wishing to dampen the jolly atmosphere, she gave the older man a gentle squeeze before putting her arm through Amma's.

'She's been very good, but I do want to hear all about the plans for this week. I'm really looking forward to everything.'

Auntie Amelia appeared and ushered them through to dinner. Taking a seat at the dining table, Faye eagerly scanned the heaped platters of food on the table while Amma poured water into both their glasses and then passed the jug across the table to her mother. Martha brought in some serving spoons, wished them a good evening and headed off to her quarters.

Amma waited for a few minutes and then left the table, returning shortly afterwards with a bottle of chilled white wine and four glasses. 'I didn't want to ask Martha to bring in the wine – I could do without a lecture on what her church says about the evils of alcohol!'

While her mother passed around the heavy serving dishes, Amma filled the glasses and set one by each of their places. Taking her seat, she helped herself to the rich tomato flavoured rice and crispy fried chicken. She hesitated and then added a spoonful of the heavily spiced plantain, inhaling the aromas from the food with pleasure.

'Mmm... It smells amazing! I'm not supposed to be eating fried food this close to the wedding, but this looks so good.'

Faye looked down at the heap of food she had piled onto her own plate. 'I know. I can't wait to get started.'

Uncle Fred laughed and raised his wine glass. 'Let's not keep you waiting, then. Here's to you, my dear. Welcome home. Now, all we need is my son and we will be complete!'

Faye took a quick gulp of her wine and hastily shovelled some food into her mouth to forestall any awkward questions about Rocky. The soft rice melted into her mouth and she took a bite of the deliciously herbed fried chicken, almost swooning at the mix of flavours. She stabbed her fork into the kelewele on her plate and closed her eyes as she savoured the contrast of the spicy blend of pepper and ginger against the sweetness of the crispy fried plantain.

Auntie Amelia was watching her in amusement. 'You really have missed Martha's cooking!'

Faye nodded enthusiastically, her mouth too full of food to speak; which was probably just as well in light of Auntie Amelia's next sentence.

'Faye, I still don't understand why you and Rocky didn't travel together. I know he's very busy but it seems ridiculous that your flights are only one day apart.'

All eyes were upon her and Faye chewed slowly, hoping to buy some time while she thought up a diplomatic response. The last thing she needed was an inquisition from Rocky's parents about the state of their relationship, particularly when she had no ready answers. Ever since she and Rocky had become a couple, she had been left under no illusion that his family were keen to see them formalise their relationship. From the moment she had graduated from art college, Amma's not so subtle hints had been echoed by those of her parents' who were increasingly impatient to see their bachelor son finally change his status. Faye sighed inwardly; she knew that with Amma's wedding looming, the question of when Rocky would also get married would be high on everyone's agenda. The Ghanaians she knew were not known for holding back from asking personal questions and given the current tensions between herself and Rocky, she dreaded the endless speculation that they were bound to face over the coming week.

'To be honest, we had a bit of a misunderstanding. Rocky thought I'd already bought my ticket and Yvette, his colleague, went ahead and sorted out a flight for him. By the time I got my ticket, his flight was fully booked – which is why I came today instead.

Saying it out loud didn't make any more sense to her than it had before and judging from the puzzled expressions on the faces around her, she wasn't the only one.

Amma spoke first. 'But why didn't this Yvette person

check with you before making the booking? Surely she knows you're a couple?'

Faye shrugged and took another bite of her food. It wasn't the best time to share her theory that Rocky's sexy French colleague was actively trying to sabotage their relationship.

'I've no idea. It was all in the lead up to that mega deal they pulled off and, apparently, she was trying to be helpful because Rocky had a lot on his plate.'

Auntie Amelia and Uncle Fred exchanged glances. Breaking the silence, Rocky's mother raised her wine glass again. 'Well, he'll be here tomorrow, so we can all spend a wonderful week getting Amma and Edwin married off.'

'Hear, hear!' Uncle Fred touched his glass lightly against his wife's and took a sip before setting it down. Faye watched him from under her lashes, disturbed at the small portion of food which he was appeared to be pushing around his plate rather than eating. This hollow-cheeked person was definitely not the same man who loved to eat generous quantities of his traditional Ghanaian food.

'What, no pigfoot tonight, Uncle Fred?' she teased.

He twinkled back at her. 'We're making an exception this time because Martha knows how much you love jollof. But, make no mistake; pigfoot will be back on the menu tomorrow.'

Auntie Amelia smiled but, like Faye, her eyes were on her husband's plate. 'Fred, is that all you are eating? That is not enough to feed a bird, let alone a grown man! Here, let me serve you with a bit more—'

Her husband hastily put out his hand to stop her. 'No,

thank you, my dear; I'm really not very hungry. I had a late lunch with Kwabena and the new architect we have taken on – he seems like a bright young man.'

Amma pursed her lips. 'Dad, it's not just tonight. You're hardly eating anything these days. Why won't you see the doctor?'

Without waiting for an answer, she turned to Faye.

'Faye, don't you see how much weight he's lost? Maybe you can persuade him to get a check up!'

Uncle Fred looked at Faye, his mouth turned downwards in an expression of mock sorrow. 'My dear, you see how these two women trouble me all the time? Please tell them that I'm perfectly fine.'

Faye stabbed at another piece of kelewele, torn between telling the truth about his changed appearance and not wanting to upset her favourite African uncle.

'You're so much thinner than you were the last time I was here,' she admitted. 'Why don't get a check-up, and then I'm sure they'll leave you alone.' She looked enquiringly at the two women who both picked up their forks and carried on eating in silence.

Uncle Fred winked at her. 'If it will make you happy – and keep these ladies off my back – I'll make an appointment with my doctor on Monday. Now, let's talk about more important things. Amma, your wedding is exactly one week away, so what is the agenda for this coming week?'

Amma brightened up and burst into her usual high-speed, breathless patter. 'Well, after we've picked up Rocky from the airport tomorrow, we're going to my hen night at the Lido Lounge. Baaba's arranged everything, so

I hope it goes okay; she's not the most organised person.'

Her mother rolled her eyes but said nothing and Amma continued with scarcely a pause. 'I'll take Faye to the dressmaker's on Sunday for the fitting for her bridesmaid's dress.' She turned to Faye with a smile. 'I've also got her to make a boubou for you for the day after the wedding. We'll be hosting lunch here for our families and closest friends and everyone will wear traditional clothing.'

Faye nodded, her mouth occupied by the chicken drumstick she had picked up and almost stripped clean of meat. Holding up the remains of the chicken leg, she paused for a moment to swallow.

'Thanks, that sounds lovely. I've always meant to have one made but never got round to it.'

'I chose a very nice peach coloured fabric,' Amma said. 'She's making the skirt bit in a wrap-around style and the top will be square cut with loose sleeves – I'm sure you'll like it.'

'Wow, you have been busy. What about the rest of the week?' Faye reluctantly abandoned the remains of her chicken and took a sip of her wine.

'Well, Stuart's offered to take us all out to dinner on Monday. So that will be Edwin and me, and you and Rocky. Oh, and Baaba, of course.'

Faye grinned at the mention of Amma's best friend. 'It's amazing that those two are still an item. They've been together for, what, nearly four years now?'

Amma pulled a face and put down her wine glass. 'Tell me about it! Baaba's desperate to get married and poor Stuart doesn't hear the end of it. She's not exactly diplomatic about the subject and keeps saying she doesn't believe in sitting around waiting to be asked.'

Faye spluttered with laughter. The words diplomacy and Baaba did not belong in the same sentence. Amma's friend was renowned for being blunt to the point of rudeness and saying whatever happened to be on her mind. Rocky's one-time boss Stuart, on the other hand, was a genial laid-back Brit who had spent most of his thirty-nine years enjoying the company of a variety of women and successfully dodging any serious entanglements. It was still a mystery how Baaba had managed to keep him on a leash for so long.

With a shake of her head which Faye assumed was probably in sympathy for Stuart, Auntie Amelia stood up and began to stack the empty plates. Urging her back into her seat, Faye and Amma quickly cleared the table and carried the used dishes through to the large kitchen off the hallway.

Amma started washing while Faye scraped the remains from the dishes into the large dustbin. The younger girl lowered her voice and looked cautiously at the door.

'I saw your expression when you first saw Dad. So now you know why I've been so worried – It's really scary how thin he's grown!'

Faye paused in mid-scrape, making no attempt to hide her anxiety. 'He has lost a lot of weight from when I last saw him. Something's not right.'

Amma looked downcast and Faye tried to inject a positive note into her voice. 'Look, he's promised to see the doctor so let's wait and see what they say. I'm sure he'll be fine; he's probably been overdoing it at work. Isn't it time he retired?'

Amma snorted. 'Mama's been trying to persuade him to retire, or at least cut down his working week to two or three days, but he won't hear of it. He set up the architectural practice with Uncle Kwabena thirty years ago and he can't bear the thought of no longer being in charge.'

'So at least we know where Rocky gets it from,' Faye said absently, passing the last few dishes to Amma. Her friend dropped the wooden spoon she was washing back into the sink with a loud thwack.

'Okay, so what's going on with you two? There's something wrong and I don't believe it's just because Rocky is a workaholic. He's always been that way, so there's obviously more to it than that.'

Faye removed the clean dishes from the drainer in an effort to buy time. Although Amma was a close friend, she was also Rocky's sister and it was at times like this that she was torn between her innate need to be honest and the desire not to put her friend in an awkward position. Honesty won the day as she slowly explained the growing distance between them, her increasing resentment at the intrusion of Rocky's work – and colleagues – into their lives, and her frustration at his apparent lack of interest in settling down with her.

Amma listened in silence, quietly washing the rest of the plates and glasses, and then dried her hands.

'Okay, I understand how you must feel; after all, I've been nagging you two to tie the knot for ages, although my brother always acts deaf when I say anything. But why don't you talk to Rocky about all this and tell him how you really feel? You never know, he might be worried that you're the one going off him!'

Faye sighed. 'It sounds simple when you put it like that but, honestly, trying to get your brother's attention in the past few weeks – no, months – has been impossible. He always used to be the first person I would talk to about anything, but we spend so much time apart these days that by the time I see him, I've either forgotten what I wanted to tell him or I can't be bothered any more. There's no point planning anything with him since he always ends up being called to the office and cancelling at the last minute. We never seem to be on the same page at the same time and I've stopped including him in any social events because it's so embarrassing to keep making excuses when he doesn't show up. I really have tried! Look, we'll arrange to have a quiet night in and I'll be all geared up to talk about how I feel and then within minutes, he's on the phone or texting someone or other about some meeting, or just crashing out because he's shattered!'

She twisted the tea towel she had been using to dry the plates into a convoluted knot. 'There's no point talking to him about marriage; the man's already married to his work!'

Amma had perched on the edge of the wooden kitchen table and she watched Faye thoughtfully through narrowed eyes.

'I really hoped that my brother would have realised by now that there are things in life more important than work.'

'I know, but according to my brother, we're all being too critical. William reckons we just don't understand how much harder it is for a black man to succeed in the corporate world in Europe.'

'Maybe,' Amma conceded, 'but Rocky has been obsessed about being financially successful for years; in fact, ever since he got back from the States. It's not as if he's short of money; he doesn't even have time to spend half of what he earns. I think that whole experience with Celine really scarred him.'

Faye frowned at the reference to Rocky's old girlfriend. 'I know she turned out to be a gold-digging bitch that dropped him for someone wealthier, but that was years ago! He's doing so well now; why on earth would he still worry about that?'

'I don't think being damaged is something that just goes away,' Amma said soberly. 'It's always there; it just shows up in different ways.'

Faye looked at her in surprise. 'Wow, that's very profound.' She pondered for a moment. 'But if he's never going to be satisfied with what he's achieved and doesn't trust me to love him for himself and not his money, where does that leave me? How long am I supposed to wait for him to see that financial success isn't everything?'

'Faye, Rocky can be annoying but he's not stupid. I'm sure he knows that you can't continue like this indefinitely and I don't think he would want that for himself anyway.'

'But, Amma, we both know he's never going to quit his job; it's become his whole identity. Maybe he's still hung up on Celine, I don't know! Be honest, when have you ever heard your brother talk about getting married or having kids?' Faye demanded.

'But that doesn't mean things can't change. I mean, look how long I've had to wait for Edwin to finish his Master's in America and then come back home and find a decent job!'

Faye sighed and shook out the tea towel before hanging it on the hook above the sink. 'Maybe you're right. Anyway, let's get you married off and we can worry about me and your brother afterwards.'

'On another note, Mama was reading an article about your Harriet Woollaston the other day and she's really impressed that you actually work for her.'

'I find it hard to believe, sometimes. But she's really nice and very down to earth. It's amazing to watch her at work but the more I see of her, the more I realise that even the super rich don't have it all.'

With that, they went through to the living room to join Amma's parents who were glued to the TV watching the evening news. After a few minutes, Faye gave up feigning interest in the latest Middle Eastern crisis and yawned widely. The day's travelling, the delicious dinner and the wine had all combined to make her suddenly feel weak with fatigue.

'I'd better go to bed before I fall asleep in this chair.'

She shooed Auntie Amelia back onto the sofa as she made to get up. 'No, don't bother getting up; I know where everything is. I just want to have a quick shower and crawl into bed.'

She gave Amma and the older couple a quick hug, wincing as she squeezed Uncle Fred's thin frame, and headed upstairs. After a refreshing shower, she slipped on a T-shirt she had liberated from Rocky's wardrobe several months earlier, lifted the corner of the mosquito net and snuggled under the soft covers.

'It's so good to be home,' was her last thought before she fell into a deep sleep.

14

Hen Night

Faye craned her neck to get a better view over the crowd of people standing between her and the barriers. Only twenty-four hours earlier, she had been standing in almost the same spot hugging Amma. Now, as they waited for Rocky to emerge from the airport terminal, she concentrated on trying not to get crushed between the enthusiastic welcoming committees jostling for prime position. She winced as a plump woman cannoned into her side in her eagerness to reach a young man dressed in a T-shirt, saggy denims and a pair of white trainers that looked as if they had seen better days. Faye watched the woman push through the cordon and seize him around the waist in a tight grip that brought to mind Coco at her best.

From where she had been standing on the other side of the walkway, Amma circled back to stand beside Faye.

'I still can't see him,' she said, turning to scrutinise another group of people walking out of the terminal. 'He's so tall, he's not exactly hard to miss—' She broke off and waved frantically, jumping up and down to be seen above the row of people in front of her.

'Rocky!' she bellowed.

A grey-haired man standing directly in front of her flinched visibly at the unexpected assault on his eardrums and cast an aggrieved look back at her, pointedly rubbing his right ear. Amma paid no attention as she forced her way past him and was soon hugging her brother in a tight embrace.

'Hey, kiddo, it's good to see you.' Rocky returned the hug and dropped a light kiss on the top of her braids. He leaned back to take a look at her.

'Well, well! So my little sister is finally going to tie the knot, huh?'

He released her and turned to Faye who had been watching them with an indulgent smile. Their eyes locked and she detected a hint of wariness in his eyes as if he wasn't quite sure how she was going to react. In her flip-flops, she reached only as high as his shoulder and before she could say a word, he stooped and kissed her softly on her lips.

'Welcome home, stranger,' she said lightly, unable to prevent the wide grin that found its way onto her face.

Amma slipped her arm through Rocky's and prattled away as she steered him and his trolley towards the car park. 'I like your haircut – I haven't seen it this low before. But that's fine; it will still look good in the wedding photos. The tailor has finished the waistcoats for the other groomsmen but wants to see you to check he's got the sizing right... oh, we're parked over there!'

Faye trailed behind them and waited while they loaded Rocky's bags into the boot before sliding in behind the driver's seat. Wiping his hands on his jeans, Rocky climbed into the front passenger seat and grimaced as he pulled the seat belt across his chest.

'Amma, are you sure you don't want me to drive?' The implication that he didn't trust her behind the wheel was clear. She glanced at him dismissively, refusing to rise to the bait.

'Just chill out! I've been driving for years – and if anyone's used to dealing with crazy Ghanaian drivers, it's me. I bet you've gone soft after living in London.'

Moments later, an impatient driver cut in ahead of her as they approached the exit barrier to leave the car park, forcing her to brake sharply.

'See what I mean? Relax... So, how was your flight?'

Rocky turned in his seat so he could see both his sister and Faye and shrugged. 'Okay, I suppose. I managed to do some work and at least I didn't to have to deal with any phone calls. But it would have been a lot more fun if I had some company.' He looked at Faye with an innocent smile. 'We really should have come together, don't you think?'

She glared at him, ready to launch into a heated attack, when he winked at her with an impish expression on his face.

'You are such a—!' She shook her head, laughing in exasperation, and he gently smoothed back the lock of the silky hair that fell across her face.

Amma smiled, clearly relieved to see them behaving as normal. She sped down a poorly-lit dual carriageway while launching into a long explanation about the events planned for the wedding week. Rocky listened patiently, wincing as cars cut into the lane in front of them without indicating.

'I've almost forgotten how mad the driving is here,' he muttered, when a large minivan ahead packed with passengers abruptly pulled in to the side of the road.

'Amma, you were saying that the two of you have a girls' night out this evening? That's fine with me; I'd like to spend some time with the folks and catch up properly. When I last spoke to Ma a couple of days ago, she sounded really worried about Dad. What's going on with him?

'You haven't seen him in, what, six months? Well, prepare to be shocked when you do – he's lost so much weight! At first I thought it was because of the wedding, but he's hardly eating anything these days and his clothes are hanging off him.'

Rocky's grin vanished and his forehead creased into lines of worry. 'Do they know what's wrong? What's the doctor saying?'

Amma honked in irritation at a slow moving pedestrian crossing the road she was turning into. 'He's been refusing to go and see Dr Kankam up until now, but last night he promised Faye that he'll make an appointment to see him on Monday. Dad's really looking forward to seeing you – he's already complaining that he's outnumbered by all the women in the house.'

Rocky chuckled and turned to Faye who had been listening quietly in the back. 'So, what have you been up to since you got here?'

'Not a lot; I slept in this morning and I've just been hanging out with Amma and eating loads of kelewele.'

'Well, doing nothing is obviously working; you're already a lot less cranky.'

She gasped in outrage and swatted his head, missing as he ducked away laughing. He grasped her arm gently but firmly and lowered his head to kiss the palm of her hand, sending a host of tingling butterflies fluttering around inside her. He kept a hold of her hand and looked into her eyes, his voice softening.

'Ghana suits you; you look gorgeous. Missed me?'

'I don't know; I'm still making up my mind about that,' she said tartly. The image of Yvette sitting in his flat still rankled.

'I thought absence was supposed to make the heart grow fonder?' he replied. His eyes twinkled mischievously and despite herself her lips twitched.

'Really? I've always found that "out of sight, out of mind" works better for me.'

He burst out laughing and leaned in to kiss the tip of her nose. 'Well, how about we make sure we don't let that happen, then?'

'And how exactly are we going to do that?' she said, smiling openly.

'I'm sure I can think of a few things...' he murmured meaningfully

'Hey, you two – I'm still here!' Amma protested.

Faye laughed; thrilled to see the return of the teasing, affectionate Rocky she had fallen in love with. With any luck, the workaholic boy-wonder of recent months would be put out to pasture over the coming week. Appalled that Rocky had originally intended to stay for only three days, it had taken Faye an hour of cajoling to persuade him to spend at least a week, arguing that he owed his sister more than a couple of days for the most important event in her life. She studied his chiselled profile as he turned back to chat to Amma and her spirits lifted at the thought of a week of nothing more complicated than having fun. Maybe this was their chance to reconnect with each other, and for her to finally share her concerns. A few days without the stresses of working life would give her a chance to explain her changing priorities and to understand what he wanted from their relationship.

Minutes later, Amma pulled up at the gates of the house and sounded the horn. The quiet street was in darkness, the only light coming from the twin beams of the car's headlights and a couple of dim security lights fixed to the gate posts.

The gate creaked open slowly and a head peeked round looking for the source of the noise. Togo stared at the car intently; the look of suspicion on his face suggesting to anyone who didn't know better that he had never seen the vehicle before in his life.

Amma groaned and slapped the steering wheel. 'Togo! How many times do we have to go through this charade? He's so annoying! And who's he kidding; he was probably fast asleep until I honked.' She leaned out of her window and barked an instruction at him in their local language and within seconds, his head was back inside and the gates thrown open.

Rocky returned Togo's salute as Amma drove through the gates and he jumped out of the car as soon as it stopped. He walked over and slapped palms with the security man, exchanging greetings in Togo's dialect. The older man beamed at Rocky, and then swung the gate shut and shuffled over to the car to retrieve the cases. His baggy khaki shorts dwarfed his thin dark legs and his hips were so narrow, Faye wondered how he managed to bend over without breaking, never mind actually lift anything.

In an almost exact replay of the previous evening, Auntie Amelia appeared on the doorstep, clapping her hands in excitement as her son strode towards her. She hugged him to her fiercely for a long moment and then reached up to kiss him on both cheeks. With their faces close together under the light of the porch, the resemblance between mother and son was striking.

'Come in, everyone,' she said, scarcely taking her eyes off Rocky as she spoke. 'Son, come in. I'm so happy to have you back home.'

Amma and Faye trooped in behind him and followed them through to the living room where some drinks and snacks had been arranged on a side table.

'You must be tired after the flight, Rocky. What would you like?' she nodded towards the refreshments. 'I've just taken the drinks out of the fridge'

'I'll have a beer, please.' He shrugged off the lightweight jacket he had been wearing and tugged his short-sleeved white Polo shirt out of his jeans. Stretching, he grunted and flexed his back.

'I hate long-haul flights; all that sitting around kills your back!'

'With all the travelling you do, I should have thought you would be used to it by now. I hope you remember to get up and walk around; it's very important if you want to avoid getting blood clots,' his mother fussed.

He smiled and reached for the glass of beer she held out to him, kissing her affectionately on the cheek. 'Don't worry, Ma. If flying was going to kill me, I'd be long gone by now.'

She shook her head and settled herself on the sofa next to him, watching him take a long, slow sip of his drink. Amma and Faye helped themselves to drinks and sat down.

'Where's Dad?' Rocky asked.

Auntie Amelia sighed and slumped back against the cushions, anxiety descending like a mask over her beautiful face.

'He should be back soon. He's gone to pick up some plans from his office for a site meeting tomorrow. He's finally agreed to see Dr. Kankam first thing in the morning and he won't have time to get the papers before his meeting.'

Rocky put his glass down carefully on the side table and leaned towards his mother, his voice gentle with reproach. 'Ma, what's going on? I had no idea that he was unwell – why didn't you say anything? You know I would have come home straightaway.'

Auntie Amelia shrugged helplessly, her beautiful brown eyes shadowed with worry. 'I should have told you, son, but you've been so busy I didn't want to worry you.

You have enough to cope with at work without us adding to your worries.'

Amma snorted impatiently. 'Mama, I told you to let me tell him and you insisted that things would sort themselves out. Rocky doesn't need to be protected – we're all busy – and he might have been able to talk some sense into Dad!'

'Amma!' Faye jumped in, looking anxiously at Auntie Amelia's crestfallen expression. 'Your mother's got enough to deal with already. Look,' she glanced at her watch. 'Baaba told us to be at the club at ten o'clock so we'd better start getting ready. Let's focus on your hen night and leave Rocky to talk with your mum.'

She dragged Amma off her chair and urged her out of the room and up the stairs, only releasing her hold when they reached Amma's door. 'I'll see you downstairs in an hour; that should give you plenty of time to get dolled up.'

Amma nodded, a sly smile creeping onto her face. 'You and Rocky seem to be getting on well; you had me quite worried yesterday.'

Faye grinned cheerfully. 'I know; I'm actually looking forward to spending time with him.'

Shortly after ten, Faye walked carefully back down the wide terrazzo staircase, praying that she wouldn't trip. Her high-heeled sandals were little more than strips of velvet ribbon that looped through tiny metal tabs which started from her toes and criss-crossed over her feet to tie at the ankle. While they looked beautiful, walking in them was a different matter. And if her shoes felt precarious, they were in good company with the low cut top she wore over a fitted black three-quarter length skirt. The silky midnight blue fabric was cut in a loose wrap-over style and the front plunged down in a revealing v-shape that just about covered her breasts. A long silver chain hanging down almost to her navel and large silver hoops in her ears completed the look. Her hair was brushed into a silky bob and her make-up was understated with a ruby gloss on her full lips.

Arriving downstairs in one piece, she ran straight into the Asantes. Rocky's eyes widened as he took in the daring cut of her blouse and Uncle Fred chuckled appreciatively. 'Our supermodel is certainly back!'

Faye smiled at Uncle Fred's nickname for her and she looked at Rocky, her eyes challenging him to comment. Her boyfriend could be surprisingly conservative on occasion but after his initial intake of breath, she could see only admiration and an unmistakable gleam of desire in his eyes.

'You look lovely, Faye. But how will you keep the sides of that top together?' Auntie Amelia looked dubiously at the flimsy fabric that barely covered the swell of Faye's breasts.

Faye laughed. 'It's a lot more secure than it looks. And, if you think this is bad, wait until you see Amma. I've just left her room and—'

'—and what?' Amma demanded, marching down the stairs, her high heels clacking against the marbled flooring. The full skirt of her mid-calf length black dress was a frothy combination of satin and sheer transparent panels that revealed most of her shapely legs, elongated by her spiky black heels. The top half of the dress was made almost entirely from sheer black netting with a heart shaped satin panel covering her full bust and leaving little else to the imagination. She had tied her long braids up into a high pony tail and accentuated her smoky dark eyes with a sparkling navy eye shadow.

Her father gawped and Rocky raised an eyebrow, but said nothing. Her mother, on the other hand, gasped audibly.

'Amma! My goodness... Are you sure that dress isn't too...revealing? Ladies, you both look beautiful but... Oh dear, I think I'm getting old!'

Amma kissed her mother on the cheek. 'You'll never be old, Mama! It's my hen night, so I'm allowed to be daring – I'll be a married woman soon and won't be able to get anyone's attention!'

Glancing at her watch, Faye gave Amma a nudge. 'We'd better move it before Baaba starts getting worked up. The party can't begin without you, so let's go!'

Amid a chorus of goodbyes, she and Amma hurried out to the car, forcing a slumbering Togo to open the gate to let them out. The Lido Lounge was only a short distance from the Asantes' house, and within a few minutes Amma had pulled outside.

Faye glanced at the sleek top-of-the-range models in the car park, marvelling at the disparity between the young people on the streets hawking newspapers and plastic knick-knacks and the high-earning professionals that frequented clubs like the Lido. Following Amma inside, it dawned on her that there were probably people who lived in run-down parts of inner London with the same thoughts about her privileged life in Hampstead.

As soon as she walked in, Faye was struck by the club's unusual décor. Light shades in the shape of giant balls hung in clusters from the high ceilings, and chrome spotlights cast a warm glow onto coffee-coloured walls. The clever lighting and mellow jazz combined to create an intimate atmosphere. A number of tables had been set up around the dance floor and at the far end of the room she could see a few private booths. The club was busy and waiters bustled between tables taking orders and depositing trays of food and drink. Judging from the mix of people around the crowded tables and at the bar, the club was popular with expats as well as Africans.

Amma had been scouring the room and her eyes lit up in excitement as she spotted Baaba waving her over. 'Look, there they are! Oh, good, they've got a booth!'

Her black dress swished around her legs as she sashayed confidently across the empty dance floor to give her best friend an exuberant hug. Baaba wore a scarlet dress in a soft jersey fabric with a neckline that dipped to reveal a generous cleavage. The bright fabric strained tightly across the widest hips and biggest bottom Faye had ever seen on a woman not in the entertainment industry. Instead of the short twists she had worn two years ago, Baaba's hair was now styled in long waves that fell from a centre parting down her back. She disentangled herself from Amma's grip and smoothed down her hair and dress before turning to Faye. Pursing her full lips, she stared hard at Faye, her heavily kohl-outlined eyes taking in every detail from her stylish hair cut to her plunging wrap-over top and strappy black shoes.

Her inspection complete, a smile lit up Baaba's small, pointed face, and she threw her arms open.

'Welcome back, Faye. It's been a long time!'

Taken aback by the warm welcome – Baaba was not known for being affectionate – Faye cautiously returned the hug, amazed that such a tiny waist could support the curvy hips below.

Baaba released her and smoothed her hair back into place before gesturing towards the four other women at the table. 'You know Frieda and her sister, Mansa.' Faye nodded and smiled at the two women closest to her, leaning over to hug Frieda, Amma's good friend and a teacher at the international school. Mansa was darker in complexion than her sister, but had the same wide-eyed smile. In contrast to Frieda's plain black dress, Mansa's strapless white top clung to her slim frame and full breasts, leaving little to the imagination.

Amma turned to introduce Faye to the other two women in the booth. 'Faye, this is Trudie. We work in the same department and we've become good friends.' She gestured towards a fair-skinned woman with light brown braids twisted into an elaborate top-knot. In the muted lighting, her eyes were a curious blend of green and hazel and they crinkled at the corners as she smiled warmly at Faye.

The other woman, whom Amma introduced as Sena, was as dark as Trudie was fair. Her natural hair was cut low at the sides in a style that flattered her high cheekbones and she wore a bright gold sleeveless top that glowed against the ebony hue of her skin. She held out her hand, her smile revealing perfect white teeth.

'Hi! It's good to meet you at last. Amma never stops talking about you.' Her accent had a transatlantic twang that instantly reminded Faye of Brenda.

With the introductions over and Faye and Amma seated, Baaba poured out two glasses from the bottle of wine in the ice bucket beside her and passed them over.

'We've started without you,' she said, taking a sip from her own glass. 'Why are you so late?'

Amma raised her glass in a silent toast to her friends and took a long sip of her wine. 'Hmm... Delicious! Yes, I know; sorry. We went to pick Rocky up from the airport.'

Trudie leaned forward, her eyes alight with interest. 'Oh, is that your brother? I've heard so much about him! How long is he going to be in Ghana?'

Amma grinned and glanced at Faye. 'Well, he's here for the wedding, obviously. Then I suppose he'll stay for a few more days before he – and his girlfriend, Faye—', she added meaningfully, 'head back to London.'

'Oh!' Trudie flushed in embarrassment and took a sip of her wine. Then she shrugged and looked cheerfully at Faye, her green-ish eyes sparkling. 'Well, you can't blame a girl for asking – I've heard the man is unbelievably good-looking!'

Faye giggled; she could see why Amma liked Trudie. The conversation jumped between topics, invariably coming back to the upcoming wedding. Baaba was to be maid of honour and Faye a bridesmaid, Amma explained. Her cousin Betty's eight year-old twins, Sheba and Sidonie, would be her flower girls. Edwin had chosen to have three groomsmen; his best friend, Kofi, his brother, George, and a reluctant but resigned Rocky.

'Amma, what are you and Edwin doing for your honeymoon? Are you travelling somewhere exciting?' Sena put down her wine glass and looked across at her friend.

'To tell the truth, we've spent so much on the wedding, we can't afford to go anywhere expensive,' Amma confessed. 'Rocky offered, but he's doing so much already that we decided to spend a week in Aburi instead. Edwin's friend manages a guest house there and he's given us a good rate. The plan is to go up after lunch on Sunday; it won't take long to drive and the weather is lovely and cool up in the hills.'

Mansa sighed. 'That sounds really romantic! You are so lucky, Amma. And Edwin has his own house, so you won't have to live with your in-laws.'

Amma spluttered with laughter. 'Mansa, we might not be living in the same house, but don't forget Edwin's parents will be literally right door! I am lucky, though. It's really good of them to let us live in their guest house because on our salaries we'd never have been able to afford anywhere central.'

'Plus you get babysitters within easy reach,' Sena added.

Amma rolled her eyes in alarm. 'There's no rush for that, thank you very much! I'm not ready for kids – and besides, Edwin and I want some time to ourselves before we start a family.'

'Good luck with that,' Mansa chipped in. 'Just wait until your mum starts harassing you about wanting grandchildren. Ask Frieda how annoying our mother's become since she got married.' She grinned at Frieda, who scowled in annoyance. 'Don't look at me like that, you know it's true!' She turned back to Amma. 'She's so fed up with Mummy going on about it that she hardly ever visits now.'

Three bottles of wine and two sizeable platters of canapés later, the waiter approaching their table looked more than a little apprehensive. Amma was laughing hysterically as Sena recounted the details of the date she had been on the previous week; Trudie and Faye were arguing loudly over which Hollywood film star had the best body, and Mansa was rapping along to the club mix, her arms raised and swaying from side to side.

Baaba noticed the waiter's hesitation and her stern look did nothing to reassure him.

'Please, madam, sh-should I bring some more drink?'

He glanced at Mansa and his eyes widened. Instantly forgetting his question, he stared at her, mesmerised. With her eyes closed and her arms high in the air, Mansa's top was revealing even more than was intended.

Baaba cleared her throat loudly and the waiter reluctantly tore his gaze from the unwitting performance.

'Yes, please bring us another bottle of wine.'

She stared pointedly at him until he took the hint and left. Tutting impatiently, she leaned across and yanked up Mansa's drooping top, causing the girl's eyes to fly open.

'Hey! What?' She glared at Baaba, who shrugged carelessly.

'If you want to give the waiters a floor show, carry on. I was just trying to be helpful.'

Mansa grimaced and took a sip of her wine. 'Have you

looked around the room? The waiters are probably the only ones who would be interested in me. Where have all the decent men in this town gone?'

Frieda looked askance at her sister. 'Mansa, it's not like you don't get offers. You are just so picky; it's your own fault that you're still single!'

Trudie leaned over to pat Mansa's hand sympathetically. 'I feel your pain, Mansa. I haven't had a boyfriend for almost two years and there's still no sign of Mr. Right.'

'Don't you know there's no such thing as Mr. Right?' Sena drawled, her dark eyes glowing in amusement, '... there's only Mr Right Now!'

Trudie and Mansa shrieked with laughter while Baaba topped up her glass and took a large gulp. 'Well, I've found Mr. Right – it's just driving me crazy that he won't put a ring on it.'

She tossed her hair back and stared moodily into her wine glass, swirling the contents around with a ferocious glower. 'I've done everything I can to get him to propose; if I don't hear those words soon, I'm going to have to move on and stop wasting my time.'

'Baaba! Don't do anything rash,' Amma protested. 'Why don't you leave the subject alone and give Stuart a chance to actually ask you, instead of going on about it all the time?'

'That's easy for you to say.' Baaba threw back the wine and immediately refilled the empty glass, her glossy lips pouting in frustration. 'You're getting married in a few days while I'm still sitting on the sidelines. No, I should probably try and find someone else.'

'Don't be silly – you know he's mad about you!' Amma giggled. 'He must be if he manages to put up with all your craziness!'

Faye tried to hide her smile but Baaba's sharp eyes were onto her. 'Yes, and I don't know why you're laughing, Faye. How long have you and Rocky been dating? Four, five years? You should be asking yourself the same question!'

Faye winced and Amma rolled her eyes in irritation. Sena looked at Faye and raised her eyebrows, the smooth dark skin on her forehead puckering in surprise. 'Wow, you guys have really been together that long?' Her accent sounded more pronounced than before and Faye shifted uncomfortably against the cushioned banquette.

'Well, yes, I suppose so,' she muttered, quashing the urge to wring Baaba's neck for putting her on the spot. As if she didn't already have enough doubts of her own without inviting contributions from virtual strangers.

Baaba hadn't finished. 'So, what's the problem? Don't you want to get married? Is Rocky going to be a bachelor for the rest of his life? '

She was starting to slur her words and Amma yanked the wine glass out of her hand.

'Okay, I think you've had enough of that. Come on, let's go and dance. Mansa, there are plenty of guys here, so cheer up!'

She stood up and dragged Baaba along with her and within seconds they were all on the dance floor, whooping and bobbing up and down to the music. It was well past two o'clock by the time they finally dragged themselves out of the club and headed home.

15

Dress Rehearsal

The strident crowing of the neighbourhood rooster was the alarm call that penetrated Faye's deep sleep. Cursing silently, she rolled over and burrowed her head beneath her pillow, desperate for a few more hours of sleep. Just as the cock stopped his cacophony, the sound of loud, angry voices wafted in through the half-open panes of her bedroom window, penetrating the downy pillow. Although she didn't understand the language, there was no mistaking Martha's voice or Togo's plaintive tones.

Knowing it would be impossible to go back to sleep, she sat up and immediately regretted it as the room gently swirled around her. She groaned softly, feeling the after-effects of the wine from the night before kicking in. Her mouth felt dry and her head throbbed in a rhythm reminiscent of the music at the club. Her legs ached after the hours of dancing in her strappy high heels and she lay back against the pillows trying to muster the strength to get out of bed. After a few minutes, she made her way to the bathroom and stood under the shower, clutching the tiled wall for support. It took her another half an hour to wriggle into a pair of shorts and a T-shirt and drag a brush through her hair.

Desperate for a cup of coffee, she walked downstairs, her leg muscles protesting at each step. She wandered into the kitchen and stopped dead at the sight of Rocky standing by the window staring out into the garden. His expression was bleak, although it changed the instant he saw her.

'Hi, you're up early. Good morning.' He smiled at her and held out his arms and she walked into his embrace, leaning gratefully against his chest and breathing in the fresh lemon scent of his aftershave. She could feel the strong beat of his heart and for just a moment, her hangover moved into a state of suspension. The moment over, she stepped away from him and headed straight for the coffee pot on the table, willing her hands not to tremble as she poured the hot black liquid into one of the empty mugs on the table. She slumped down into a chair and clasped the mug between her hands, letting the heat from the drink seep into her nerveless fingers.

'What the hell were you girls up to last night?' Rocky leaned back against the kitchen counter and watched her painfully slow movements with amusement.

'Shhh... Not so loud.' She frowned at him over the rim of her mug.

'Are you sure you're okay?' he asked. 'Look, I've decided to go with Dad to the doctor's tomorrow morning – I want to make sure he keeps the appointment.' His smile faded and clenched jaw emphasised the sharp angles of his face.

'I can't understand why he's let things get this bad. I should have been here sooner.'

'You had no way of knowing that he wasn't well,' Faye reminded him.

He shook his head impatiently and strode over to the window, folding his arms against his chest. 'If I came home more often, I would have. I've been so caught up with work that I had absolutely no idea that my own father is sick.'

With his back still turned to her, he sighed in frustration. 'I feel like I'm caught between a rock and a hard place right now and I can't seem to get it right with any of you. You're pissed at me, and my mother won't even tell me what's going on because she thinks I'm too busy to care.'

'Rocky, your dad will be fine,' Faye said gently, her hangover temporarily forgotten. She knew how much he adored his father and her heart went out to him. 'The important thing is that he's finally agreed to see a doctor. At least now we'll know what we are dealing with.'

He turned and looked at her quizzically. 'You said "we. We'll know what we are dealing with." Do you still feel that way – that you and I are a "we"? Because I've wondered for a while now if that's still the case and I really wish I knew what you wanted.'

Stunned into silence, she stared at him in disbelief. She really wished that her head felt clearer. Was this honestly when he wanted to have this conversation? she wondered miserably. Now, after all the weeks and months of interrupted moments and intermittent silences? Now, when she had the mother of all hangovers; this was when he wanted to raise the thorny subject of their relationship?

'Rocky, are you serious?' Her voice mirrored her incredulity. He stared at her impassively and she sighed and put her coffee cup safely on the table. With something else to worry about, she noted that her hands had stopped shaking.

'You know what? I – we – can't do this right now. This isn't the time to talk about us and it's definitely not the place.'

He nodded silently. After a moment, he pulled open a drawer and rummaged around, pulling out a small blue packet. Popping a couple of tablets out of a blister pack, he deposited them on the table in front of her.

'Here; take these and go back to bed. We'll talk later,' he said, and left the room without waiting for a response.

She swallowed the tablets and sipped her coffee, grateful that he cared enough to look out for her, yet suddenly dreading the showdown she thought she had wanted. She was still mulling over whether to return to bed when Martha burst into the kitchen singing one of her church hymns at full volume. Faye's head throbbed in response and she retreated to the veranda off the living room.

Faye stretched her aching limbs out on the blue and white cushions of the wicker sofa and grabbed a cushion from the adjoining chair to prop up her head. Although it was still early in the day, it felt warm on the porch. She jammed her sunglasses onto her face and closed her eyes, the gentle breeze and the soft swishing of the garden hose Togo was using to water the flower beds lulling her to sleep.

'Faye!' Startled, she jerked awake to find Amma peering down at her. 'I've been looking for you everywhere! Come on, we've got to get to the dressmaker's for your final fitting.'

Considering the exertions of the previous night, Amma looked remarkably fresh. But then, Faye thought sourly, the bride-to-be had been the designated driver and had only consumed a couple of glasses of wine the entire evening.

'Why are you so perky?' she groaned. 'It was your hen night and I feel like I've been ten rounds with Floyd Mayweather!'

'I've got far too much to do to allow myself the luxury of a hangover,' Amma said virtuously, no trace of sympathy in evidence. 'I'm getting married in six days and you,' she nudged Faye with her knee, 'are going to get dressed now so we can go and sort out your bridesmaid's dress.'

'You are a hard woman; I hope Edwin knows what he's letting himself in for!' Faye rolled off the cushions and slipped her feet into her flip-flops. She stood up cautiously and was relieved to find that the room spinning had stopped and that everything stayed in its proper place.

'Give me a few minutes to change.'

She stopped in the kitchen for a long drink of water and then went upstairs. After changing into a white shift dress, she walked out to the car with Amma. The heat of the sun was blistering and Faye stood aside while Amma started the engine and rolled down the car windows to let out some of the stifling hot air. After a few moments, she slipped into the front and smoothed down her dress to protect her bare legs from the heated leather.

Amma reversed and swept out of the gate, held open by a morose looking Togo. After a few minutes, she switched on the air conditioner and the windows slid closed.

'Oh, that's so much better,' Faye murmured with relief as the oppressive heat give way to the chilled air. Feeling more energised, she opened her eyes and sat up to gaze out of the window, slipping on her sunglasses against the intense brightness of the sun and the cloudless blue sky. The traffic was light and they were soon off the highway and driving along a quiet, leafy road fronted by large houses behind high gates and past brightly painted wooden kiosks set back from the road. From these tiny shops, their owners sat staring out at the passing traffic in the hope of selling the stacks of tinned goods and packs of mobile phone cards on display.

'Where are we?' Faye asked. She was still unfamiliar with much of Accra, and had to keep checking on her bearings.

'North Ridge,' Amma said. 'Efua lives down that road. With any luck we should be able to get this done quite quickly so we don't have to stay out long in this heat. She's made all the clothes for the bridal party; we had the final fitting for the twins' dresses last week. They looked adorable!'

'What's Baaba's dress like?'

'Let's just say it's not as revealing as the style she wanted,' Amma sniffed. 'I had to remind her that she's wearing it to a wedding and not a nightclub! It's made from the same fabric as yours but it's been tricky getting the fit right – poor Efua has had to adjust it quite a few times.'

She turned into the driveway of a house set a fair distance back from the road and tooted the car horn. Moments later, the light blue gates swung open and Amma drove through, waving at the young man standing to the side.

'Good morning, madam.' He gave a respectful salute and ran back to close the gates.

Amma parked in the driveway and they walked up the loose gravel path to the house, a white-washed villa with a wide front porch. The veranda was lined with a colourful array of pots and plants that gave off a sweet aroma and Faye looked with longing at a cushioned hammock swaying invitingly at the far end of the shaded porch.

She reluctantly followed Amma inside and into a bright living room with silver-framed family photographs and assorted knick-knacks crammed onto every available surface. Moments later, a small woman dressed in a long skirt with a matching kaba, the fitted top made from traditional Ghanaian fabric, walked in.

'Amma, good morning, good morning! How are you feeling? Only a few more days to go, eh?' She beamed at the two women and Amma hugged her before turning to introduce Faye.

'Efua, this is my friend and bridesmaid, Faye.'

Efua shook her hand warmly and then inspected Faye from head to toe, nodding in satisfaction.

'Yes, I think the dress will be fine.' She disentangled one of the hangers from a pile of clothes on the table and handed it over. 'Faye, why don't you try this on? You can change in the study and come back to use this mirror.'

Faye took the dress and walked through the door Efua had pointed out and into a small room lined with books. She slipped out of her dress and hung it over a chair before carefully stepping into the new one. The fabric was an unusual shade of dark orange and the soft, silky material hugged her body.

She went back to join Amma and the dressmaker and laughed as Amma gasped with pleasure and clapped her hands excitedly. Standing in front of the full-length mirror by the dining table, Faye stared in wonder. The draped cowl neck fell softly over a fitted bodice and the skirt, cut on the bias, emphasised her slender hips and the curve of her bottom. The distinctive colour glowed against the duskiness of her skin, lending her an air of sophisticated elegance.

'Oh my God, you look amazing!' Amma was practically squealing in excitement. 'I knew that style would be great with your figure. You'd better not upstage me on Saturday.'

Faye grinned. 'I don't think you need to worry about that. But wow...' She turned back to admire her reflection which even in the rather dusty mirror, she had to admit looked stunning. Her eyes met Efua's in the mirror and she smiled gratefully.

'Thank you so much, Efua; it's perfect!'

The dressmaker nodded and turned her attention back to the dress. She tugged lightly on the bodice and smoothed down the fabric at the back.

'Amma, I don't think we need to adjust anything. The shoes you showed me have quite a high heel, so we can leave the length of the dress as it is.'

Amma pursed her lips and studied the hem of the dress which was pooling around Faye's bare feet.

'I think the length is fine.' She looked up at Faye.

'Remind me to give you the shoes when we get home so you can get used to walking in them. You don't want to get blisters on the day.'

Faye groaned silently; her legs still ached from the heels she had worn the night before but she knew there would be no sympathy from Amma on that score. After a last glance in the mirror, she held the dress up carefully and went back to the study to change.

She walked back into the room as Amma was arranging for the clothes to be delivered on Thursday.

'Faye, your boubou will be finished by then. Oh, Efua, before I forget, Baaba will come to you tomorrow for her final fitting.'

The dressmaker grimaced but made no comment and they said their goodbyes and headed back to the car.

16

Stormy Weather

The next morning brought a dramatic change in weather. From her bedroom window, Faye was surprised to see dark clouds overhead in place of the usual sunny skies.

She showered quickly and went down for breakfast, dismissing the brief temptation to knock on Rocky's door as she walked past. There was far too much going on already without adding any further drama. After the scene in the kitchen, it was clear to her that Rocky had his doubts about their future, and she now found herself dreading the serious discussion that she knew lay ahead.

The overcast skies had infected the mood in the house and even the bright kitchen felt gloomy. Martha, who could always be counted on to blast out cheery hymns every morning, hummed quietly to herself while she cleaned around the kitchen sink.

'Good morning, Miss Faye. I hope you slept well?' Without any prompting she filled a large mug with steaming coffee from a flask on the table. 'Mr Rocky made it not long ago, so it is still hot.'

Faye took the mug gratefully. 'Thanks, Martha. You're an angel.' She pushed back a chair and sat down at the table watching the housekeeper resume her work.

'How are your children – has Genevieve finished school yet?' Faye took a cautious sip of the hot coffee and carefully set it down on the wooden table.

'Oh, they are very well indeed! Pa Joe has been teaching at his school for almost two years now, and he and his wife are expecting their first child,' Martha said proudly.

'That's wonderful, Martha; you're going to be a grandmother!'

The housekeeper's smile widened. 'Yes, Miss Faye, God is good. I just wish my husband was still alive to see our first grandchild – it's hard to believe that he has been gone for almost twenty years.'

Faye's eyes softened in sympathy. A tragic road accident had left Martha a young widow with four young children. After her hostile in-laws threw her out of her marital home and destroyed her livelihood, the Asante family had stepped in to provide her with a home and a job.

'I can't complain, Miss Faye,' she added. 'I was very fortunate to find this job and my mother has taken good care of the children. Araba, my oldest girl, has a good job in a nice hotel. Matilda is also working now and helps my mother to look after Genevieve – although at seventeen, she says she doesn't need anyone taking care of her!'

Faye chuckled. 'Well, you don't look old enough to have four grown-up children, never mind a grandchild.'

The door swung open and Rocky strode in carrying an empty mug. As soon as he spotted Faye, he walked over to drop a kiss on her head, oblivious to her glance of embarrassment at Martha who was studiously scrubbing at a spot on the counter and pretending she hadn't seen a thing.

'It's pretty gloomy out there – what are your plans for today? I'm surprised Amma's not in here already with a clipboard and that ridiculous to-do list of hers.'

'Just give it a few minutes,' Faye remarked. 'I've no idea what she's got planned. All I know is that we're all having dinner with Stuart tonight.'

Rocky nodded. His former boss was now a close friend and his offer to host dinner for Amma and Edwin at a local restaurant was a typically generous gesture. 'I know; I'm meeting up with him after I've seen Amma's tailor about the wretched waistcoat for the wedding.'

Faye bit her lip, trying not to laugh at his disgruntled expression. She knew how unappealing he found the idea of being Edwin's groomsman and that the only reason he had relented was to keep his sister happy – and put a stop to her persistent phone calls.

As if on cue, Amma strolled into the kitchen. She brightened up as soon as she saw them and immediately whipped out her notebook, causing Faye to snort with laughter.

'What's so funny?' she demanded. With barely a pause for breath, she then reeled off a series of instructions from her list, only grinding to a halt when Rocky stood up, his chair scraping loudly against the flagstone floor.

'Amma, you lost me at "tailor's." I'll go and see him after lunch; I promise. Stuart's booked a table at the Jewel of the Orient for eight o'clock, so please make sure you're ready on time.'

Unmoved, he returned her glare with a smile. Faye, meanwhile, was looking at Rocky in surprise. 'Where are you going?'

'I'm going with Dad to see Dr. Kankam, remember? After that, I may stop by the bank and take the opportunity to check on a few things for my clients while I'm in town. I need to put in a quick call to the team at some point, so it will be easier to do it from there.'

'So you're not going to be around today?' She tried to keep her tone even despite the disappointment churning inside her. She could feel the resentment she thought she had put away in anticipation of their time away from London start to rise up again.

'Once I've finished with Dad, I won't be that long. I'm sure I'll be back in time for lunch.'

'Yes, but you're still going to work! I thought we were supposed to be on holiday?' Even to her own ears, her voice sounded whiny, and she mentally kicked herself for being so pathetic.

'Faye, I can't just drop everything – business still goes on. Look, it's no big deal; I just need to check on a few things and I'll see you back here afterwards.'

He walked past his open-mouthed sister still clutching onto her notepad, and she stared after his retreating back in disbelief.

Faye shrugged. 'See what I mean? Even on holiday, he finds some excuse to work.'

Deciding for once that a prudent silence was the best

option, Amma poured the remains of the coffee into her cup and sat down at the table, ticking off a couple of items on her list.

'Forget about Rocky, we've got a lot to get done today,' she said briskly. 'You'll come with me to the caterers – I need to do a final check on the drinks. I simply can't trust Edwin to get the order right. Then I need your opinion on the flowers; well, actually, it's all decided, but it would be good for you to see the bouquets I've ordered...' Faye listened in fascinated horror as Amma went through the full list. Rocky's decision to escape suddenly sounded like a very smart move.

The skies remained overcast all morning and the dark clouds showed no signs of dispersing when she and Amma finally arrived home early in the afternoon. Sporadic rumbles of thunder throughout the morning had contributed to the heaviness in the air and after spending hours tailing after Amma as she descended on caterers, videographers, florists and even the people providing ice for the drinks at the wedding, Faye was ready to collapse.

She stepped out of the car and shivered as a sudden gust of wind cut through the still humidity. 'I don't like the look of this weather. How far away is the restaurant we're going to this evening? I really don't fancy getting caught in a rainstorm.'

Amma glanced up at the dark clouds and shrugged. 'Hopefully the rain will hold off until much later. The Jewel of the Orient is in Osu, so it's quite close by. I'm really looking forward to it; they opened quite recently and I've heard good reports about the food.'

She squealed as a strong gust of wind swept across the compound, whipping up swirls of dust and almost flattening the flowers in their beds.

'Come on, let's go inside!'

Auntie Amelia was in the sitting room when they walked into the house, her faced pinched with worry as she read a message on her phone.

'It's from Rocky. He says Dr Kankam has ordered several tests for Dad, so they will probably be at the hospital for another hour or so.'

She rubbed her forehead anxiously. 'I was hoping they would be home by now but I suppose it's a good thing that Dr Kankam is so thorough. I just hope he can get to the bottom of all this.'

But they were none the wiser by the time Rocky and his father returned. It would be a few days before the test results were available and until then, Uncle Fred insisted, life was to carry on as normal.

'No long faces in this house, please. We have a wedding to plan!'

The winds were still high when they set out later that evening, and this time Rocky insisted on driving. Amma slid into the back seat, trying to avoid creasing her purple linen dress while Faye sat up front flexing her legs to ease her aching calf muscles. An hour's practice run earlier that afternoon in the bridesmaid's shoes Amma had bought had been enough for one day and she had slipped her tired feet into flat black ballerina pumps for the evening.

A rumble of thunder cut through the music playing on the radio and Faye shivered with trepidation. She had seen the power of a tropical storm in Ghana at first hand and had no wish to get caught up in one while out on the road.

Rocky glanced across at her and squeezed her hand briefly in reassurance. 'We'll be there in a few minutes,' he said quietly. She nodded and tried to shake off the feeling of unease that had been hovering over her since morning. After a short drive, Rocky manoeuvred the car into an impossibly small space in the cramped car park alongside the restaurant and came round to open her door, before helping Amma out.

Amma smoothed down her dress and led the way to the entrance of a building painted in an eye-catching combination of red and gold. Rocky held open the door for Faye to go through and she looked around with interest at the striking décor. A huge tank filled with multicoloured tropical fish and exotic coral lined the wall of the brightly-lit reception area and peeking through, she could see the restaurant was buzzing. The Chinese maitre d' escorted them straight to a table, partially concealed by a screen from the main restaurant, where Baaba sat sipping a bright green cocktail through a translucent pink straw. Edwin and Stuart were also at the table and stood up as soon as they walked in.

Stuart hugged Amma and kissed her soundly on both cheeks before turning to Faye. At over six feet, he was only slightly shorter than Rocky, and his rangy physique made him appear younger than his years. She kissed him and flicked the light brown curls of his unruly fringe with a giggle.

'Aren't you bankers supposed to be all buttoned up

with short back and sides?' she teased. Stuart defied every stereotype of a banker and it was a mystery to many quite how he had managed to progress so far and so fast in his career. In stark contrast to Rocky's driving ambition, Stuart was the very definition of laid-back, only putting up a fight when he had faced the threat of a transfer out of Ghana.

He brushed his hair back and grinned, revealing a slightly crooked front tooth which, along with the sprinkling of freckles along his nose, always reminded Faye of a grown-up Dennis the Menace.

'It's all coming off tomorrow, love. The boss–', he broke off and glanced at Baaba ruefully, '—insists I've got to get it trimmed before the wedding. Here, let me take a good look at you; you're even more beautiful than the last time you were here.'

Pretending not to notice Baaba rolling her eyes at her boyfriend's effusive compliments, Faye scrutinised his beige linen trousers and matching long, loose fitting shirt and nodded in approval. 'I like the outfit, my friend; it's very African – suits you.'

'Where's my hug?' Edwin demanded. In the soft lighting of the restaurant, his dark chocolate skin was almost luminous, and in dark trousers and a short-sleeved African print shirt, his lanky build was in sharp contrast to Amma's short, curvy figure. He nudged Stuart aside and seized a laughing Faye in a warm embrace.

'I need all the hugs from beautiful women I can get before I'm officially off the market this weekend.'

This time it was Amma who rolled her eyes impatiently, propelling her fiancé into the seat next to her.

'I'm starving; can we all sit down and order?'

Rocky pulled out a chair for Faye and sat down next to her just as an attractive Chinese woman in a red silk gown appeared clutching a sheaf of menus. Her silky dark hair was caught up on top of her head in a loose bun, from which she pulled out a pencil to take their drinks order. Returning a few minutes later, she set the drinks down on the pristine white table cloth and pulled a small notepad from her pocket.

Stuart had been studying the extensive menu. 'I think we should go for the Oriental banquet. It's got five courses and a good selection of dishes.'

The waitress retrieved her pencil from her bun and scribbled the order. Just as she turned to leave, Stuart called her back.

'Just one last thing, love. Please bring us some hot chilli sauce, will you?'

Baaba shot him a look of complete incredulity. 'So you really can't eat anything now without adding chilli sauce?'

She looked at Amma. 'Can you believe I actually had to beg him not to put some in his yoghurt the other day?'

Amma burst out laughing. 'Okay, Stuart, now you've definitely become an honorary Ghanaian.'

'I think I am, love,' he said cheerfully. 'I couldn't imagine living anywhere else now.'

'Yeah, well maybe you need to think about what else you can't imagine living without,' Baaba muttered, stirring the dregs of her cocktail with the pink straw and earning a nudge and a warning glare from Amma.

Rocky tapped his fork against the side of his glass and

the gentle ping had everyone looking in his direction. His copper brown eyes were alight with humour.

'Okay, I just want to say a couple of things. First of all; Stuart, on behalf of my sister and Edwin, thank you for hosting dinner this evening. We all appreciate it very much.'

His friend nodded in acknowledgement and Rocky continued, 'Amma and Edwin, in five days you'll be officially man and wife and we wish you both a very long and happy marriage.'

He raised the foaming glass of beer in front of him and the others followed suit. After taking a quick sip of his drink, he winked at Edwin. 'Don't say you weren't warned... those handcuffs don't come with a key.'

Amma, Baaba and Faye – all with their drinks still suspended in mid-air – turned in unison to glare at him, while the men roared with laughter. Amma elbowed her fiancé sharply and he looked at her sheepishly, his lips still twitching.

'What?' he protested defensively, rubbing gently on his injured rib. 'He's only joking.'

That's what you think. Faye sniffed audibly, fighting the impulse to do more than dig an elbow into the man beside her. Instead she took a sip of the deliciously chilled white wine, savouring the tartness of the grape on her tongue.

Stuart prudently changed the subject. 'So, Amma, all ready for the big day? Got your meringue all sorted out to shimmy down the aisle?'

Amma giggled and shook back her long braids. 'Well, it's not quite a meringue; but yes, the dress is finished and it's beautiful!'

Baaba sighed deeply. The sharp intake of breath swelled her already ample bosom and Faye stared in fascination at the black fabric straining against the pressure, wondering what would constitute breaking point.

'Amma, you will make a lovely bride. God knows I've been to enough of other people's weddings to know...' She arched a pencilled eyebrow and glanced meaningfully at her boyfriend, paying no attention to Amma's less than subtle finger across the throat gesture.

The arrival of the waitress provided a welcome distraction and the aroma from the freshly cooked food instantly defused any tension. The dishes sat on a revolving platform which whizzed back and forth as they ploughed through the delicious array of golden fried crab claws, spicy chicken kebabs smothered in a tangy satay sauce, deliciously sticky spare ribs, long crisply battered prawns, and the nutty shredded seaweed that Faye loved to hold on her tongue until it melted away. Even Baaba brightened up as she munched on a spare rib, delicately wiping her fingers on her napkin between bites.

When the second course – a tangy hot and sour soup with dumplings – had been demolished, Edwin regaled them with a tortuously long story about his first apartment in America. He sounded wistful and Amma shot him a troubled look. Although he had been back in Ghana for a year, Edwin's passion for America still made her nervous.

'I'm glad you enjoyed America, but you're home now and doing so well in your job,' she said brightly.

Edwin reached for her hand and kissed it gently and

his amused grin made it clear that he knew exactly what was on her mind.

'You don't have to worry; I'm not ever going anywhere without you.'

The waitress arrived with a loaded trolley and set out huge portions of fragrantly spiced dishes and for the next few minutes the only sound to be heard was the scrape of cutlery against plates.

Amma was the first to break the silence, licking fingers still sticky from the garlic sauce smothering the sautéed lobster she had just consumed.

'This was a great choice, Stuart; the food is delicious!'

Nodding, Stuart spooned some more chilli sauce onto the seasoned lamb on his plate and wiped his forehead with a cotton handkerchief.

'Here, Baaba, try some of this chilli sauce on the meat – it's incredible!'

She stared in alarm at his flushed features and the rivulets of sweat trickling down his neck. The damp curls of his fringe were pasted flat onto his forehead and he took a long gulp of the ice-cold lager in front of him.

'Don't you think you've had enough of that stuff?'

Faye smiled inwardly at Baaba's wifely tone and turned her attention back to her food just in time to see Rocky surreptitiously trying to steal a prawn from her plate. With a squeal of protest, she jabbed at the seafood with her fork, succeeding only in breaking it into two. Rocky swiftly tossed the other piece into his mouth with a cheeky smile that had her giggling helplessly.

Amma was watching in amusement when her attention

was caught by a couple walking past their table. Her eyes widened and she quickly ducked her head, but it was too late.

'Rocky!' the loud squeal cut through the quiet hum of conversation, causing everyone to jump. Faye groaned silently; although Amma had warned her that Rocky's ex-girlfriend would be at the wedding, she had hoped to avoid any other encounters with her.

'I thought it was you! I'd know that handsome head anywhere.' A tall woman in a tiny black dress that showed off very shapely legs stood by the dividing screen, a radiant smile lighting up her beautiful face. 'When did you come to Accra? You should have called me!'

Rocky pushed his chair back with a smile, standing up to give the new arrival a perfunctory hug. Stuart and Edwin nodded politely in Clarissa's direction and then turned away.

Clarissa's attention was focused exclusively on Rocky and without even a glance of acknowledgement at the others, she tossed back the long mane of hair tumbling down her back and seized Rocky's arm. Pinning him securely to her side, she called out, 'Henry – come back! Guess who's here?'

An older man dressed a long pale blue shirt over loose trousers turned and approached their table. He was short and quite stocky with neatly trimmed dark hair. He smiled and raised a hand in greeting to everyone before shaking Rocky's hand warmly.

'Congratulations on the LaserTech deal, Rocky. That must have taken some doing.'

His dark eyes narrowed speculatively. 'I don't want to interrupt your party but do you have a minute? We've been looking at some financing options for our new hotel and I'd value your opinion.'

Rocky hesitated and looked around the table. Faye made no comment and kept her eyes fixed on her plate, and after a moment Rocky nodded and the two men walked across the restaurant towards the door, deep in conversation.

Looking down at Faye, a flash of spite crossed Clarissa's flawlessly made-up face and her glossy lips curved into a malicious smile.

'Back again so soon, Faye? At this rate, you'll be moving over to live with us.'

Faye continued eating and evidently unhappy at being ignored, Clarissa waved her pink-tipped, perfectly manicured hand in the direction of Faye's now almost empty plate.

'I'm not surprised to find you at a Chinese restaurant; you never looked comfortable eating our local food – even if you did manage to find your way around our men.'

Faye almost choked on the wine she was sipping; it was abundantly clear that Clarissa had still not forgiven her for taking the man she had considered as hers.

But Clarissa's attention and saccharine sweet smile was now being directed at Rocky's sister.

'Amma, I'm really looking forward to the wedding this weekend; I'm sure you'll look beautiful! Baaba, you're the bridesmaid, are you?'

'Maid of Honour, actually.' Baaba practically snarled. There was a long history of animosity between the two women and there was a collective intake of breath at the table.

As if Baaba hadn't spoken, Clarissa injected a note of false concern into her voice. 'Weren't you a bridesmaid at Frieda Ansah's wedding last year as well? Do be careful, you know what they say about always being a bridesmaid and never a bride?' She tittered in amusement and Amma looked nervously at her best friend, waiting for the usual explosion that accompanied encounters between the two women.

But, for once, Baaba had no comeback and just stared into her wine glass, an expression of pure misery on her face. Stuart had been listening to the exchange with a raised eyebrow and he looked thoughtfully at Baaba, an unusually serious expression on his flushed features. He raised his head and caught Faye watching him. She couldn't resist smiling back as he gave her a cheeky grin, followed by a conspiratorial wink. She shook her head, curious as to what was going through his mind.

Patently disappointed at Baaba's stony silence, Clarissa turned back to Amma and reverted to her normal tones, almost babbling in her excitement. 'Amma, did you see my talk show on TV last week? It's going so well and we've some really big celebrities lined up. Henry thinks we might even be able to get Marcel Desailly as a guest when he's next in Ghana!'

She glanced across to where Rocky and Henry appeared to have finished their conversation, and her eyes lit up.

'Oh my God, I've just had a great idea!'

With a brief wave of farewell to the bemused group at the table, she rushed over to where the two men were shaking hands and grabbed Rocky's arm excitedly. They were too far away to hear her words, but they could see Rocky immediately shake his head. Clarissa clearly wasn't taking no for an answer and continued to protest and tug his sleeve until he laughed and nodded, gently prising her fingers off his arm. Exchanging a final handshake with Henry, Rocky walked back to the table.

'What was all that about?' Amma asked curiously. Her brother picked up his fork, took a mouthful of the food cooling on his plate and chewed it quickly before he answered.

'Just Clarissa being Clarissa. She wants me to be a guest on her TV chat show and talk about "the world of high finance."' He drew quotation marks in the air in gentle mockery. 'I told her I wasn't interested, but she wouldn't let it go. It was easier to agree than to have her keep talking at me.'

Faye raised an eyebrow. 'And when exactly is this supposed to happen?' Her hopes of spending time with her elusive boyfriend were rapidly dimming, and now his former girlfriend appeared to have commandeered more of the limited time available.

'Apparently, they record the show on Thursday and it's broadcast on Sunday evening.'

'Yes, it's on Channel 33, Henry's TV station. If you're going to be on it, we'll try and watch, but I can't promise. It will be the first night of our honeymoon and we'll be all tucked up in our hotel in Aburi,' Amma said dreamily, squeezing Edwin's arm.

'Oh my God, you two are so nauseating!' Baaba had found her voice again although the loving smile she directed at Amma robbed her words of any malice.

Faye finished her food quietly, feeling hollow inside. Her earlier buoyancy had been squashed by Clarissa's appearance and Rocky's continuing willingness to make time for what seemed like everyone except her. The sense of unease that she had felt earlier in the day returned full force and she quickly swallowed the remainder of her wine and held out her glass for a top-up from Edwin. Oblivious to the puzzled looks Rocky was giving her, she steadily drank her way through a further two glasses and was more than a little unsteady on her feet when it was time to leave the restaurant.

After farewell hugs and kisses had been exchanged with Stuart and Baaba in the foyer, Faye followed Rocky outside, feeling the sharp, rough gravel scraping the thin soles of her shoes. She gasped as a sudden, powerful gust of wind slammed against her and swept through the branches of the trees in the car park. Looking up into the dark sky, she shuddered at the sight of the ominously large clouds swirling against the bright moonlight. The air felt heavy and oppressive and she could almost taste the moisture in the air. The storm that had been threatening all day looked set to break and with a shiver, she tugged her wrap around her bare shoulders and hurried towards the car.

Edwin draped a protective arm around Amma and kissed her quickly before opening the back door. There was a loud rumble of thunder and he cast an anxious glance upwards. 'You need to hurry! Call me when you get home.' He waited for Rocky to start the car and then raced towards his own.

The gentle strains of jazz from the radio did nothing to calm Faye's jangling nerves as flashes of lightning lit up the sky. The claps of thunder were now louder and more frequent and she heaved an audible sigh of relief when they pulled up into the driveway of the Asantes' house. Even Togo dispensed with his usual pantomime and swung open the gates within seconds of the car horn sounding.

Just as she scrambled out of the car, she felt the sting of raindrops on her skin. Scampering after Amma, she had just reached the safety of the front porch when an ear-bursting clap of thunder sounded and the heavens opened, sending heavy sheets of rain beating onto the ground.

Safely inside the house, Amma and Faye looked at each other, chests heaving as they tried to catch their breath. The main lights had been turned off and the house was in semi-darkness with the only illumination in the hallway coming from the single overhead light. Seconds later, Rocky raced in, his shirt soaked and sticking to his muscular torso. Drops of water clung to his long lashes and he blinked hard and looked at the girls, a grin of relief softening the hard planes of his face.

'That was close!' He shook the rain drops from his hair and unbuttoned his shirt gingerly, pulling the wet fabric away from his skin. Amma took one look at him and turned towards the stairs.

'I'm going to ring Edwin to check he's got home safely, and then I'm going to bed. There's a lot to get done tomorrow, so Faye,' she turned and looked pointedly at her friend, giving a slight nod in the direction of the half-dressed man standing next to her, 'don't stay up too late.'

Faye felt herself blushing and watched as Amma climbed up the stairs and out of sight. She turned to Rocky, trying to keep her breathing steady even as her eyes raked over him. His wet shirt was wide open, revealing his bare chest and her eyes travelled down his muscled abdomen to the black belt at his waist. Looking up into his eyes, she felt an overwhelming rush of desire flood through her.

'Well?' he said slowly, his eyes boring into her. 'Do you want to stay up late?' His invitation was unmistakable and her first instinct was to throw herself into his arms. After all, this was what she had been hoping for, wasn't it? Time alone with the man she loved. Then, from nowhere, a little voice in her head sounded a warning. *What are you doing? You haven't had the talk yet; you still don't know if this is going anywhere.*

Rocky reached for her, pulling her up against the warmth of his bare skin. His kiss, at first gentle and exploratory, quickly deepened as he wrapped his arms tightly around her. She allowed herself to sink into his embrace, feeling the passion in the strong body pressed against her. *Uninvited*, the voice returned. *He wants you now, but what about tomorrow? What about after that?*

Faye gasped as his hand slipped up under the thin fabric of her blouse and caressed her bare skin. The overhead light flickered but the only sound came from his heavy breathing and the torrential rain drumming onto the roof and whipping against the windows. She grabbed at his wet shirt still hanging open and peeled it off, uncaring that they were standing in the hallway, and Rocky groaned, pulling her even tighter against him. Her head swimming both from the wine she had consumed so freely and from the onslaught of passion against her senses, she closed her eyes, her mind whirling in indecision. As if sensing her hesitation, he pressed his cheek against hers, and whispered, 'Let's go upstairs.'

He reached for her hand and started towards the stairs. All at once, she pulled back, the voice pounding furiously in her head even as her body wanted nothing more than to follow him up to his room.

Rocky dropped her hand and looked down into her eyes, his own dark with frustration. His normally cool demeanour was gone and his breathing was as laboured as if he had been running. She stared up at him speechlessly; her eyes dark pools of agony in her face, and gave an infinitesimal shake of her head, wishing she knew how to put into words what she needed from him.

'Damn it, Faye!' He groaned loudly and ran his hand over his hair, causing her to flinch at the sudden movement. Immediately, as if a shutter had come down, his eyes went blank and his face lost all expression. He dropped his hands to his sides and took a step away from her, shaking his head in disbelief.

'Damn it, Faye,' he repeated, this time quietly. 'What's going on with you? One minute, everything's fine, the next minute you're pushing me away. You won't talk to me and now, what... now you think I'd actually hurt you?'

'No, of course not,' she whispered miserably. 'How could you even think that?'

'What the hell else am I meant to think? For God's sake, Faye, what do you want?'

Not stopping for an answer, he bent to pick up his discarded shirt, and then turned and walked away, taking the stairs two at a time.

17

Singletons and Secrets

For the next couple of days, there was little sign of Rocky outside of meal times and Faye felt a physical ache each time she remembered his expression before he walked away. On Wednesday morning, commandeered by Amma to accompany her around Accra as she finalised the outstanding arrangements for the wedding and reception, Faye was given little opportunity to dwell on the unhappy end to the dinner on Monday.

Amma's continued barrage of instructions provided a welcome distraction and consequently, she meekly tied flame coloured ribbons onto countless little mesh bags filled with sugared almonds for the place settings at the reception and filled scores of gift bags with keepsakes for the guests without protest.

After lunch, they paid a visit to the hotel where Amma painstakingly went through each item on her list for the reception. A final trip to the florists to satisfy herself that the flowers and boutonnieres would be delivered early on Saturday was followed by a brief stop at the church to agree on when the florists decorating the church could get to work. Giving in to his pleas to get involved and muttering dark threats if he messed up his assignments, Amma had reluctantly put Edwin in charge of organising the ice coolers for the lunch to be held at the Asantes' house on Sunday and for coordinating delivery times with the hire company bringing the tables, chairs and canopies to be set up on the lawn.

Amma and Faye were back at home nursing their tired feet when the impatient toot of a car horn sounded at the gates. A few minutes later, Baaba burst into the living room and threw herself on Amma, who squealed in shock as she fell back against the cushions.

'What the-!' Amma struggled up, pushing her braids back from her face and glaring at her friend, convinced that she had finally lost her mind.

'Baaba! What's wrong with you?'

Baaba simply danced gleefully around the room; her generous curves on display in a tight fitting dress. Eventually coming to a stop in front of the sofa where both girls were now sitting bolt upright, she held out her hand without a word to display a very large round diamond set in a gold band.

Amma gasped in shock and then leapt up off the sofa, her tired feet forgotten in her excitement.

'Oh my God, oh my God, he asked you! He finally asked you!'

She flung her arms around Baaba's neck and they jumped up and down screaming like hysterical teenagers. Completely stunned by the unexpected news, Faye sat frozen for a moment and then stood up, ready to hug Baaba when she came down to earth. Seconds later, she was seized in a suffocating hug by the other girl and whirled around.

'Yes! He finally asked me! Can you believe it?' She released Faye as abruptly as she had grabbed her, and flung herself onto the sofa, panting furiously. Amma sat down next to her, drawing her legs up underneath her and bouncing excitedly on the leather cushions.

'When did it happen? How did he ask you? Tell us everything!' she commanded, reaching out to grab Baaba's hand and scrutinise the ring.

Baaba's small pointed face was radiant with happiness and her usual cynical expression was nowhere in sight. In her rush to reach Amma, she hadn't bothered to apply the heavy make-up she tended to favour and she looked younger than Faye had ever seen her. If she had ever harboured any doubts about Baaba's feelings towards Stuart, the joy radiating from the other girl instantly quashed them.

'We went out to dinner last night at Chez Lucille and I didn't suspect a thing. We had almost finished our meal when he just stood up and took the ring out of his pocket. Before I could say a word, he was kneeling on the carpet – right there in front of everybody!'

Amma's round eyes widened and her mouth formed a silent 'o'. 'You're kidding! What, you mean right there in the middle of that posh French restaurant?'

'Yes!' Baaba crowed. 'It was incredible. Everyone started clapping and the manager brought us a bottle of champagne!'

Faye had perched on the arm of the sofa next to Amma and couldn't help the grin that spread across her face. Baaba's joy was infectious and she was genuinely happy for her.

'That's so romantic! How long do you think Stuart had been planning it?'

Baaba sobered for a moment. 'He said he always meant to ask me to marry him, but Clarissa's crack at the Chinese restaurant made him realise that he needed to get on with it.' She had the grace to look shame-faced as she continued. 'He bought the ring ages ago but he said that every time he was on the verge of saying something, I'd make a comment about it and he didn't want to make it look as if proposing to me was something I had forced him to do.'

Amma clapped her hands with excitement. 'This is such great news – now we can plan another wedding! I know – there's a bottle of wine in the fridge. Let's celebrate with a drink.'

After a couple of glasses of wine and slightly the worse for wear, Baaba set off for home, leaving Faye and Amma to finish the remains of the bottle. There was still no sign of Rocky at dinner and after they had finished eating, pleading a headache, Faye went up to her room for an early night.

She eventually drifted into a restless sleep from which she woke just after midnight, feeling parched after the wine she had consumed earlier. Trying hard to get back to sleep, she tossed and turned for what felt like hours until, desperate for a drink of water, she slipped her feet into her rubber flip-flops and headed downstairs.

She padded through the dimly lit hallway to the kitchen and pushed open the door quietly, giving an involuntary gasp of fright at the outline of a figure silhouetted against the moonlit window. She fumbled for the switch and her hand flew to her mouth in shock as light flooded the room. Uncle Fred was hunched over the sink with a glass of water in one hand. His silk dressing gown hung open over loose blue cotton pyjamas, causing her to gasp once more as she took in the full extent of his weight loss. His face looked grey and drawn with pain and she rushed forward instinctively.

'No, no, I'm okay.' He straightened up and gestured for her to stop where she was. 'I just came down to take the painkillers the doctor prescribed. I'll be fine in a few minutes.'

'Let me get someone... Auntie Amelia, Rocky...' She tailed off uncertainly. Surely painkillers weren't enough to deal with whatever was wrong. 'Uncle Fred, please... you don't look at all well.'

He grimaced and took a few sips from the glass in his hand before setting it down in the sink.

'Faye, please promise me you won't say anything. Your aunt is already worried sick and until we get all the tests back from the hospital, there's no point in adding to her stress.'

She looked at him doubtfully and he added quickly, 'Look, Amma's wedding is in three days. I'm already seeing the doctor, so it won't make any difference to anyone if you keep this to yourself, hmm?'

Faye remained standing in the doorway, her expressive

features mirroring her turmoil and uncertainty about what to do for the best. While Uncle Fred's words made perfect sense, her instincts were to race upstairs and wake Rocky or his mother. But with Amma's wedding only days away, she reasoned silently, would adding to the stress on Auntie Amelia and her family serve any purpose, particularly as Uncle Fred was already under the care of a doctor?

She went to the fridge and poured herself a glass of chilled water. She gulped it down quickly and refilled the glass, sipping more slowly this time, still uneasy that she was effectively agreeing to say nothing about what she had seen. As if sensing her anxiety, Uncle Fred tied his robe firmly and walked towards the door, his pyjama trousers flapping loosely about his spindly legs. He stopped to give her a reassuring pat on the shoulder.

'Faye, everything will be fine, don't worry. Now, go back to bed and forget you saw me here.'

By the next day, the encounter with Uncle Fred had taken on a dream-like quality, particularly when he wished her a cheery good morning without making any reference to the incident in the kitchen. She continued to wrestle with her conscience about whether to share what she had witnessed, but with Rocky still keeping his distance and Amma increasingly prone to dramatic outbursts, she reluctantly decided not to upset everyone, particularly in light of the growing tensions at home as the big day approached.

With only two days to go before the wedding, the frazzled nerves in the Asante house were increasing exponentially. Having double and treble-checked every possible detail for the big day, Amma had taken to micromanaging everyone else's schedule and exasperating her mother beyond belief. Just before lunch, Efua had delivered the clothes for the bridal party; including an exquisite boubou that Faye was to wear for the post-wedding lunch. Later that afternoon, Rocky left the house, overriding Amma's protests with a reminder that he had promised to film the interview for Clarissa's TV show.

Taking the opportunity to remove Amma from her stressed mother's orbit before any blood was shed; Faye suggested that they go out for drinks. Amma, who was secretly relieved to get out of the house now that she had literally nothing left to organise, readily agreed and promptly texted Baaba and her other girlfriends to join them.

'I've told them to meet us at Maxwell's,' she said, referring to the popular wine bar that Faye had visited on her last trip to Ghana. 'It's in the mall so I can pick up a couple of things I'll need for when we're in Aburi.'

After an hour of inching along in slow moving traffic in the late afternoon sun, the air conditioned shopping mall was a relief. They strolled through the busy shopping precinct towards the pharmacy and Faye slowed to admire the striking fashions on display in the shop windows. Instead of the muted, dark and autumnal colours in the shops in London, the clothes on the mannequins in the windows were almost uniformly made from bright colourful fabrics.

The sales assistant behind the counter was also far more stylish than the part-time students that usually manned the checkouts at her local Boots, and while Amma paid for her purchases, Faye cast a covetous eye over the young woman's African print wraparound dress tied with a broad blue sash.

It was still early and Maxwell's was almost empty when they walked in. Baaba was sitting at a booth near the door and she waved them over impatiently, making sure to use her left hand so she could flash her ring in the process.

'I closed the shop early today,' she said airily, giving them each a perfunctory hug. Her make-up was back to full strength and her slickly glossed lips curved into a satisfied smile as she stretched out her left hand and gently stroked the sparkling jewel.

Amma smiled indulgently. 'I bet you haven't taken it off since he proposed, have you?'

Baaba smirked. 'Are you kidding? Look at the size of that rock – can you imagine if I lost it?'

They had just placed their orders with a rather bored looking waiter when Frieda and Mansa walked in. Mansa's dark blue skinny jeans looked as if she had been poured into them, and her bright pink cropped top clung to her small high breasts, emphasising her flat stomach. Frieda, on the other hand, was dressed like the schoolteacher that she was in a simple blue dress with white piping at the hem and around the pockets. She held a large and slightly battered briefcase which she dropped onto the leather banquette where she sank with an exhausted sigh.

'Is it only Thursday? That school will kill me!'

Amma looked at her with sympathy. 'Are the children

driving you mad? One year of teaching during my National Service was enough for me. I don't know how you do it.'

'It's not the students I mind, it's their wretched parents.' She beckoned impatiently to the waiter. 'Just because they pay school fees, they seem to think we have nothing else to do except to be at their beck and call at any time of day.' She ordered a drink and turned to her sister. 'Mansa, what are you having? Choose carefully – you're driving us back, remember?'

Her sister pulled a face and ordered a Coke, adjusting the thin straps of her halter top. 'Where's Sena? Is she coming?'

Baaba nodded. 'She should be here soon. I called Trudie as well, but she's working late today.'

Right on cue, Amma's phone pinged and she picked it up, giggling as she read the message. 'It's from Trudie. She says she has a report that she needs to finish today because she's taking the day off work tomorrow. She's booked an appointment at the Body Factory to have her hair and nails done. Listen to this... "Everyone knows weddings are the best place to find a man."'

Faye laughed. 'That's exactly what the woman on my flight said to me when I was coming over.'

'Not that you're looking,' Mansa said enviously. She took a long sip of the chilled glass of fizzy liquid the waiter had deposited in front of her. 'You're so lucky you have Rocky, he's such a catch!'

Amma cleared her throat loudly. 'Enough about my brother; let's talk about my wedding instead. No, stop groaning, you guys – it's only two days away!'

In the midst of her protests, Sena sauntered in. The white silk blouse tucked into the short black lace skirt she was wearing accentuated the dark chocolate of her skin. As soon as she saw Baaba, her face lit up and she sped towards her, almost screaming in excitement.

'Oh my God, I can't believe you're engaged! Show me the ring!'

Baaba stood up and waved her hand with an exaggerated flourish right under the noses of the women seated around the table. Amma giggled while Frieda and Mansa gaped in astonishment.

Sena threw herself onto the empty chair next to Faye and gestured to the waiter who perked up as soon as he laid eyes on her. With considerably more energy than he had shown before, he moved over swiftly to take her order, giving her a wide smile that showed off strong white teeth.

Mansa glared at him through narrowed eyes, clearly irritated by this burst of charm which was in marked contrast to the indifferent service he had given her.

After a couple of hours, Frieda beckoned for the bill, pleading a pile of homework that needed to be marked before the next day.

'We'll see you all on Saturday,' she said, briskly counting out some notes and laying it on the silver plate the waiter had deposited on the table. 'Amma, I can't wait to see your dress! I've warned Ken that he's driving because I plan to have a good time at the reception – the Beacon Heights Hotel is such a lovely venue.'

Tugging her reluctant sister to her feet, Frieda blew a

flurry of kisses around the table and the two women went off. Shortly afterwards, the others finished their drinks and Faye and Amma headed back to Labone.

The evening traffic was heavy and minivans and taxis fought for supremacy on the roads, weaving in and out of the choked lanes. In the absence of pavements, pedestrians trudged wearily along the dusty verges, occasionally shouting out in alarm as drivers attempting to dodge potholes drove dangerously close.

They came to a stop at a set of lights and Faye impulsively wound down her window and dropped some coins into the outstretched palm of a disabled elderly man who had approached her side of the car. His smiled and gave a nod of gratitude before moving on to the car behind.

Not to be outdone, a gaggle of hawkers descended upon them, causing Amma to tut with irritation. She ignored the ingratiating smiles of the young salesmen and women selling batteries, magazines and garishly coloured plastic gadgets, driving off as soon as the lights changed.

The evening passed without incident and although Rocky was civil enough, despite Faye's repeated efforts to talk to him privately, since the night of the thunderstorm he seemed intent on ensuring that they were never alone.

Friday saw Faye caught up in the last minute arrangements for the big day. In the morning she left with Amma to meet Baaba and the young bridesmaids at the hairdressers where a relaxed pampering session involving facials, manicures, pedicures and hairstyling had been arranged.

Having come this far, Faye was determined to help Amma enjoy the experience and she forced herself to put aside her increasingly gloomy fears about a future with Rocky.

18

'To Have and to Hold...'

Faye bit down hard on her lip in an effort to hold back the tears that threatened to tumble down her cheeks and ruin the make-up that had taken almost an hour to apply. She blinked hard to clear her vision and stared at Amma's reflection in the full-length mirror.

'Oh my God, you look so beautiful!' Her voice trembled with emotion as she took in the figure standing next to her. Amma's wedding gown was a long satin ivory sheath overlaid with delicately beaded lace. The cut was simple; a fitted bodice with cap sleeves and a skirt that fell straight to her feet with a short train at the back. What made the dress so striking were the tiny shiny glass beads that had been painstakingly sewn by hand into the ivory lace, creating a beautiful shimmer of brilliance that cascaded down to the ground almost covering the strappy high heeled ivory sandals on her feet. Her long braids had been styled into a bun high on the crown of her head, below which a long ivory veil edged with glass beads had been attached.

Jeanette, the beautician from Amma's hair salon who had been drafted in for the preparations, carefully brushed a fine layer of powder onto the bride's nose. Chewing ferociously on a piece of gum that had been a fixture in her mouth since she arrived early that morning, she stepped back to admire the overall effect through narrowed eyes.

'Amma, you look fabulous! Edwin will be very proud when he sees you. Auntie, don't you think so?'

Auntie Amelia smiled at Jeanette and nodded. Her eyes were also in imminent danger of spilling tears as she looked at her only daughter. 'We are all proud. Faye's right. Amma, my darling, you look so beautiful.'

'Mama, don't cry,' Amma said with an affectionate smile. In marked contrast to Baaba and Faye, who were fanning their faces in a frantic attempt to stop their threatened tears, she looked incredibly calm and serene. 'Can you please check on whether Dad's ready yet? And have the twins had something to eat? The last thing I need is Sidonie bawling her eyes out at the church because she's hungry. I've never known a child who eats so much!'

She twisted her head to check the back of the dress in the mirror and smiled with satisfaction. 'Efua and her girls have done an amazing job with the dress, haven't they? It took them ages to sew in the crystals, but it's really worth it.'

Baaba nodded, still trying to keep her emotions in check, and smoothed down the dress she had just changed into. To Faye's surprise, Efua had succeeded in making a dress that both flattered Baaba's figure and discreetly skimmed over her hips and substantial bottom. The fabric was the same burnt orange silk as Faye's dress, but the built in support held Baaba's full bust in check, while the clever draping of the skirt merely hinted at the curves of her backside. Her hair was curled into loose ringlets and along with the matching high-heeled sandals Amma had bought them, she looked stunning. Even more stunning was the sizeable diamond on the third finger of her left hand.

The morning of Amma's wedding had dawned with a clear blue sky and a light, cooling breeze. For once the raucous crowing of the neighbour's rooster didn't generate the usual gnashing of teeth; instead Faye had leaped out of bed, excited at the prospect of the day ahead. Jeanette had promised to be there by nine o'clock and Martha had warned everyone that she would clear up early in the kitchen to allow herself enough time to get ready for the wedding.

After a leisurely shower, her hair carefully tucked up into a waterproof cap, Faye smoothed a rich, fragrant cream all over her body. It had cost her an extortionate amount in Debenhams and even the sweet aroma it gave off smelt expensive. The trip to the salon the day before had left her hair shiny and silky smooth and she brushed it out with care. She examined her nails critically; their perfect oval shape had been painted a pale pink and the manicurist had scrubbed her feet without mercy, leaving the skin soft and smooth before painting her toenails.

Faye wriggled into a short cotton playsuit and went in search of the bride. She rapped on Amma's bedroom door and pushed it open. Still in the T-shirt she had worn to sleep, Amma was craning her neck between the glass louvre panes to see out of the window.

She turned to Faye with a relieved smile. 'Good morning! I was just checking and there's no sign of rain, thank goodness!'

'I think God got your memo.' Faye smiled as she came into the room and sat down at the end of the bed. 'Haven't you showered yet? I thought you'd be ready by now so we could have breakfast together before Jeanette gets here.'

Amma looked at the Mickey Mouse clock on her bedside table and squealed in panic. 'Is that the time? How long have I been standing there?' She grabbed her dressing gown and sprinted into her bathroom, slamming the door behind her.

Faye uncurled her long legs and called through the closed door on her way out, 'I'm going downstairs; see you in a few minutes!'

Jeanette arrived shortly after breakfast, closely followed by Baaba, and the rest of the morning was a blur of make-up, hair and clothes. Eager to escape the house filled with women, Rocky left for Edwin's to join the other two groomsmen. Just before midday Amma's cousin, Betty, arrived with her twin daughters, Sidonie and Sheba. The girls looked like perfect mirror images of each other in ivory dresses with puffed sleeves and sashes made from the burnt orange fabric Efua had used to make Faye and Baaba's outfits.

After dutifully kissing everyone, the flower girls were shepherded into the living room with sharp instructions from their mother to sit down in front of the television and not touch anything. Sidonie, having been pacified with a packet of sweets, was content to sit cross-legged on the leather couch, her dimples flashing with each chew of her jelly tots. Sheba, on the other hand, sat bolt upright, terrified of creasing her satin gown or putting a run in her white tights.

With Amma dressed, it was time to leave. Auntie Amelia cast an anxious glance at the elegant gold watch on her wrist. From the top of the elaborately twisted gold and ivory chiffon headscarf, highlighting her high cheekbones and beautiful copper-brown eyes, to the tips of her low-heeled gold sandals, she looked every inch the mother of the bride. Her gold boubou was accessorised with an elegant gold and pearl necklace and matching earrings.

'Ladies, the cars are here and we need to make our way to the church now.' She waved off Amma's protests. 'Yes, I know some guests will arrive late – this is Ghana isn't it? But that doesn't mean we should also be late. I told Father Joseph that we would be on time today, so don't make a liar out of me!'

Amma was in too good a mood to argue with her mother. She held up the hem of her dress and allowed Faye and Baaba to help her navigate her way down the stairs and out to where two limousines decorated with white ribbons were parked. Uncle Fred looked frail despite his well-cut dark suit. He hugged and kissed his daughter on both cheeks before helping her into the back of the car. Auntie Amelia carefully arranged Amma's veil before taking a seat next to her.

Popping the last sweet into Sidonie's willing mouth, Betty ushered her girls into the second car and strapped them in. Faye and Baaba followed and once they were all seated, the cars set off onto the highway, the bridal car in front flashing its headlights and the driver sounding an occasional toot of his horn.

The sun was high in a brilliant blue sky and bystanders, alerted by the lights and the persistent honking, stopped to smile and wave at the beautiful bride. The limousines cruised past a group of women with baskets of fruit on their heads walking alongside the road. In spite of the joyous occasion, Faye couldn't help feeling guilty that she was in a luxurious air-conditioned vehicle while other women had to trudge through the dust and heat to make enough money to feed their families.

The lights on the car ahead continued to flash as the driver turned off the dual carriageway. Two young boys shepherding a flock of goats beat the excitable animals back with sticks and watched in awe as the limousines came to a stop at the junction. Sidonie, already bored with sitting still, surreptitiously stuck her tongue out when one of boys approached the car to take a closer peek.

The Saturday traffic was far lighter than the normal weekday commotion on Accra's roads and in less than twenty minutes they were driving into a large car park. The bridal car came to a halt with a final toot of its horn and as they drew up to park alongside the bridal limousine, Faye peered through the lightly tinted glass, fighting to contain her excitement.

The church was a towering building with a tall spire topped by a cross. Its white-washed walls dazzled in the bright sunlight and folded back wooden shutters revealed high narrow windows and colourful panes of stained glass.

At the front of the church, shallow steps led up to a set of double doors manned by ushers in dark suits handing out copies of the order of service to the guests still streaming in to find seats before the service started. The latecomers were dressed in a mix of colourful traditional outfits, formal suits and dresses. From where she sat, Faye counted a fair few elaborately trimmed hats and feather fascinators that would have gone down well at Royal Ascot.

Her people-gazing was interrupted by a wide-eyed Sidonie pulling on her arm insistently.

'Aunty Faye, Aunty Faye, why aren't we going into the church?' The eight year-old unhooked her seatbelt and scrambled up impatiently to look out of the back window. In her haste, she knocked against Sheba and earned an angry glare from her twin.

Faye smiled at the child's exuberance, secretly wishing she could do the same. 'Sit down, Sidonie. You're going to crumple your dress.'

Taking a quick peek out of the window, Baaba smoothed down her hair and took advantage of the pause in proceedings to whisk out a compact from the tiny clutch purse on her lap and dab some powder onto her nose. She took another look out of the window and quickly put the compact away.

'They're bringing the bouquets over and... oh, look! Amma's getting out the car. Let's go!'

As soon as she stepped out of the limousine, Faye seized each twin by the hand, forcing them to walk sedately. The loose pebbles on the ground crunched under her high-heeled sandals and she could feel the warmth of the sun on her bare shoulders and penetrating through the thin fabric of her dress. Amma was standing by her car and she waited patiently for Baaba to help Aunty Amelia drape the veil over her face and straighten the train of her gown.

The florist handed Amma her bouquet, a lush arrangement of ivory and flame blooms accented with dark green leaves, and then passed Baaba and Faye matching bouquets of white African lilies and trumpet shaped orange hibiscus. The twins were given small posies made up of tight globes of ivory flowers secured with vibrant dark orange ribbons.

Almost all the guests had made their way inside the church and a few stragglers stood well back waiting for the bride to go in. Walking slowly up the steps to enter the church, Faye couldn't help the shiver of excitement that ran through her. It was actually happening; after all the years of waiting and the months of preparation, Amma was finally getting married!

Father Joseph, a stocky man with a head of wiry, dark hair liberally salted with grey, waited at the top of the stairs to greet them. He exchanged handshakes with Uncle Fred and Auntie Amelia before turning to kiss Amma gently on each cheek, careful not to dislodge her sheer veil. He waited for the bridesmaids to take their places in line and then turned and strode into the church.

Blowing a kiss at her daughter, Auntie Amelia gave her husband a gentle squeeze and followed the minister, gratefully taking the arm of one of the ushers standing by to escort her.

A few moments later the sound of the organ swelled

and Faye gently propelled the twins forward. Holding hands and clutching their posies, the two girls started their walk down the aisle. Sidonie looked around, unable to contain her excitement or the wide grin almost splitting her face in two. Sheba, on the other hand, had her eyes firmly fixed on the ground in front of her, frowning as she concentrated on walking at the pace they had practiced earlier that day.

After a few seconds Faye followed, holding her bouquet between hands suddenly damp with nerves and silently praying that her feet wouldn't buckle in the stiletto heeled shoes. The church was packed with guests on both sides of the aisle and she swallowed nervously, feeling the pressure of almost two hundred pairs of curious eyes boring into her as she made her way down. Keeping one eye on the flower girls, she smiled at Martha as she walked. The housekeeper was clutching her bible tightly and looked resplendent in a blue and white lace outfit with a wide-brimmed hat trimmed with blue flowers and ribbons.

Faye was almost at the end of the aisle when she looked up and her heart flipped a double somersault in her chest the instant her eyes rested on Rocky. Towering over the bridegroom, it was hard to miss him. He wore a dark grey suit and a white shirt that set off his burnt orange tie perfectly and he stood alongside Edwin and a couple of other men, one of whom Faye recognised as Edwin's brother, George. The three men wore identical suits and floral patterned waistcoats and Faye shifted her glance to a nervous looking Edwin dabbing at his forehead with a handkerchief.

Her eyes met Rocky's and for a split second she imagined that she was the bride and he was the groom waiting there for her. His face offered her no clue as to what he was thinking although she noted the small smile he gave her with relief. After days of near silence, she was ready to take any sign that they could break through the coldness that seemed to have engulfed them.

The music stopped for a moment and then the organ burst into life again, this time even louder than before. Faye gently nudged the twins into the front pew to make room for Baaba who was right behind her, and then turned to watch Amma walk down the aisle. She couldn't resist casting a quick glance back at Edwin who suddenly looked more self-assured as he watched his bride approach.

Streams of light came in through the high narrow windows and bathed Amma and her father in a gentle light as they walked slowly to the triumphant chords of music. Her hand rested lightly on his arm and the smile of pride on his face brought a lump to Faye's throat. For a moment she thought of her own father and imagined how he would feel escorting her towards her future husband. She blinked back the threatened tears and instead concentrated on keeping a tight hold on Sidonie. The ten-year-old was almost dancing with excitement and even Sheba had lost her customary reserve and was craning her neck around the adults to catch a glimpse of the bride.

The music stopped when Amma and her father reached the end of the aisle where Father Joseph stood waiting. Uncle Fred gently lifted up the veil and kissed his daughter. Shaking hands with Edwin, he took Amma's hand and placed it firmly into the younger man's and moved to stand in the front pew. Baaba straightened the train of Amma's dress and relieved her of the bouquet while Rocky and the other groomsmen took their seats next to Edwin's parents across the aisle.

'Dearly beloved...' The minister started the service with the familiar words and the guests rustled their programmes in unison. As Faye sang along to the first hymn, she glanced over at the young couple. Not even pretending to sing, Edwin was instead grinning at Amma who was smiling radiantly back at him. For a moment Faye's voice faltered and she blinked rapidly and looked across the aisle at Rocky, head bent over his programme, singing cheerfully and predictably off-key. Her tears forgotten, she smiled remembering how he used to hold her tight and croon against her ear in retaliation for her pleas for him to stop singing in the shower. Those carefree times felt like a lifetime ago.

Her eyes followed the subject of her thoughts as he strode up to the pulpit to deliver the first reading. A collective sigh went up from the women in the church when Rocky reached forward to adjust the microphone upwards. He cleared his throat and looked around for a moment before reading out the short piece confidently. He paused on his way back to his seat to kiss his sister gently on the cheek, earning another loud 'Aaah!' from his fans.

A second hymn followed the reading and then Father Joseph beckoned to Amma and Edwin to join him at the foot of the altar. The silence in the church was palpable as the guests leaned forward in anticipation. Edwin reached for Amma's hand and she gave him a quick smile of reassurance.

The minister glanced down at the book in his hands and then looked intently at the man facing him.

'Edwin, this is when you are asked to make the most important promise of your life. Are you ready?'

The grin on Edwin's face had become a permanent fixture and he looked straight into Amma's eyes before responding with a loud 'Yes.'

'Then, say after me. I, Edwin Kobina Forson...' He paused while Edwin said the words in turn. '...take you, Elizabeth Amma Sapomaa to be my lawful wedded wife. To have and to hold from this day forward; for better, for worse, for richer, for poorer, in sickness and health, to love and to cherish, until death do us part.'

Edwin repeated the words, his eyes never leaving Amma as he spoke. When it was her turn to say her vows, Amma spoke softly and there was another sigh from the guests which erupted into applause immediately after Father Joseph announced that the couple were now man and wife. Clapping her hands in excitement, Faye looked up to find Rocky's eyes on her, his expression unreadable. She felt the heat rise in her cheeks and bent to brush an imaginary piece of fluff off Sidonie's dress to hide her sudden confusion.

After Amma and Edwin, followed by their parents and Baaba holding up Amma's train, had left to sign the register, Faye tried to distract the over-excited twins. It was only when Betty slipped her daughters a small pack of biscuits that they finally sat still, munching quietly, until the newly-weds came back to take their seats.

Bounding up into his pulpit, Father Joseph launched into a long-winded homily on marriage. After fifteen minutes, the little bridesmaids were visibly wilting and even Faye was struggling to suppress a yawn. Sensing that his restive audience had suffered enough, the minister ended the service with a short prayer. The organist thundered out his own version of the wedding march to accompany Amma and Edwin as they walked hand-in-hand down the aisle waving at their guests. Faye and Baaba each gripped on to a twin and followed after the couple, with Uncle Fred, Auntie Amelia and Edwin's parents falling in behind them.

After the coolness of the church, the sunshine was a welcome relief. The guests poured out of the front and side doors and soon the steps and the forecourt of the church were packed with people. Traditional African clothing blended seamlessly with suits and dresses, and families and friends exchanged hugs and greetings in snatches of English fluently interwoven with local languages.

To one side of the steps, Amma and Edwin had created an informal receiving line with their parents, greeting guests as they came out. The official wedding photographer had been primed by Amma to start taking pictures as soon as they emerged from the church, but was failing miserably to break into the long line of people waiting to speak to the family. Looking more harassed by the minute, he clung onto the expensive looking camera dangling around his neck, practically leaping up and down to get Amma's attention.

'You look beautiful!' Faye jumped as the voice spoke close to her ear. She turned around, almost falling into Rocky's arms. He reached out to steady her and she leaned against him for a moment before straightening up.

'You don't look so bad yourself,' she said with a teasing smile. 'Did you enjoy the singing?'

He grinned unashamedly and for a moment the commotion around them receded into the distance and it felt like the world had shrink down to just the two of them.

The moment was lost as Sidonie jumped up excitedly onto him, closely followed by Sheba who had decided to relax and enjoy herself now that the formalities were over.

'Uncle Rocky, Uncle Rocky! Carry me!' They chanted in unison as Rocky smiled indulgently at them. To Faye's astonishment, he bent down and lifted Sidonie high into the air and she squealed with excitement. With a loud groan, he dropped her gently onto the ground and hoisted Sheba up, hastily moving the little girl away from Faye as she kicked her heels in excitement.

Putting her back down as carefully as if she were made of glass, he gave an exaggerated sigh and pretended to wipe his brow. 'You girls have grown so much that you're way too heavy for me to carry any more.'

They giggled in unison and hugged his legs like excited puppies while Faye gaped, unable to believe her eyes. With the exception of Coco whose path rarely crossed with his, thanks to his work schedule, Faye had never seen Rocky around children and had anyone asked, she would have sworn that he would have avoided them like the plague. Uncomfortably aware that perhaps she didn't know her boyfriend quite as well as she thought, she almost missed his next words.

'I'm going to round up the family for the photos or we'll be stuck here for hours.' He gestured in the direction of the photographer frantically trying to push his way through the throng of people surrounding the newlyweds. 'That poor guy is going to have a stroke if he carries on like that.'

Faye nodded and held on firmly to the twins, following close behind Rocky as he made his way towards Amma and Edwin. He gently manoeuvred them away from the crowd surrounding them and cleared a space along the top of the steps for his parents and Edwin's family to join the couple. The photographer was almost babbling in gratitude and quickly adjusted the settings on his camera before clicking away. After assorted combinations of family members and friends had been photographed, the bridal party climbed back into the limousines for the drive to the reception.

Faye kicked off her sandals as soon as she was in the car and wriggled her toes, relieved to be free of the pretty and extremely uncomfortable strappy shoes. Baaba pulled out her compact and checked her face critically, dabbing at her nose gently with the sponge.

'If those shoes hurt now, I don't know how you're going to handle the rest of the day,' she drawled, raising an eyebrow at Faye who had pulled her legs up under her in an attempt to massage her sore feet. 'The reception is going on until midnight and there's no way you are getting away without dancing.'

'I know,' Faye grimaced, rubbing her toes. 'I should

have spent more time breaking them in. Oh well, if it gets too bad I'll just have to go barefoot.'

Baaba's response was cut short as Sidonie attempted to climb onto the seat and had to be restrained and strapped back in. Thankful that the reception was only a short drive away, Faye leaned back, reliving the novel experience of seeing Rocky at play with his nieces.

A few minutes later they pulled into the grounds of a beautiful hotel, its well manicured front lawns a rich verdant green. The limo came to a smooth stop in front of the main entrance and Faye reluctantly strapped on her sandals and stepped out onto the paved walkway. Seizing the twins, she and Baaba followed close behind Amma and Edwin across the plush lobby into a huge banqueting hall.

Topped by high ceilings with moulded cornices, the room was dominated by a huge, glittering chandelier streaking light across the beautifully decorated space. The dining tables were covered in white linen cloths and set with gleaming silver cutlery and sparkling crystal glasses. In each place setting was one of the beribboned pouches of sugared almonds that Faye had painstakingly finished. At the far end of the room, a stage overlooking a dance floor had been set with a long table draped in a white tablecloth for the bridal party. As soon as he spotted them walking across the hall, the DJ slipped on a pair of headphones and turned the volume up on an upbeat version of *Here Comes the Bride*.

As ushers quietly escorted new arrivals to their tables, Amma and Edwin took their seats at the high table along with their parents. Baaba helped Amma unpin her veil and then sat down, gesturing to Faye to take the seat next to her. To the relief of both of them, Betty had reclaimed her children and was settling them at a table just below the stage.

Edwin's brother, George, took the last seat at the high table and Rocky and Kofi joined Betty and the twins. Moments later, Frieda and her husband, Ken, along with Mansa, Sena and Trudie arrived and made a beeline for the remaining seats at the table. Faye watched in amusement as Trudie bagged the seat next to Kofi and smiled flirtatiously while pushing her chair closer to his.

Faye watched enviously, wishing she were down there with them rather than stuck up on stage where she would have to eat and drink in full view of everyone in the room. Baaba, on the other hand, was having the time of her life. Having made an ostentatious show of fussing around Amma all day, as far as she was concerned she was now officially off-duty and had already made significant inroads into the bottle of wine Stuart had snuck up to her before going to join Rocky's now very crowded table and which she was hiding behind the stunning flower arrangement on the table.

'Don't you want a drink?' Her heavily kohl-lined eyes were almost cat-like as she turned to Faye, who shook her head.

'I'd better not; I haven't eaten much today and it will go straight to my head. I'm having enough trouble staying upright in these heels as it is.'

Baaba shrugged. 'Okay, but I warn you, there are going to be a lot of very boring speeches. So heels or no heels, I'd get something into that glass.'

Forty-five minutes later, Faye had to concede that Baaba had a point and she eyed the bottle longingly. Speeches at the weddings she had attended in England were generally confined to the bridegroom, the best man and the father of the bride. Today, however, it seemed as if every family member and close friend was intent on having their say. The fruit juice she was drinking hadn't come close to drowning out the tedious, long drawn-out addresses, starting with Amma's elderly uncle – whose speech alone had gone on for almost a quarter of an hour – right through to Edwin's godfather. It was Uncle Fred's short, funny and sentimental speech that had finally roused her from her torpor. And now it was Edwin's turn.

The guests fell silent as the nervous bridegroom rose to his feet, microphone in hand. The only sound came from the chink of bottles and glasses as the waiters moved around the room refilling drinks. All eyes were on him and he cleared his throat and carefully unfolded a small sheet of paper.

'Ladies and gentlemen...' He paused and cleared his throat again and took a quick glace around the room. Not reassured by the stares focused on him, he coughed and hastily returned to his notes.

'Erm... Ladies and gentlemen. My wife and I—' Before he could say another word, the guests erupted into a cacophony of whooping, clapping and whistling and Amma blushed and hid her face between her hands. At first startled by the interruption, Edwin grinned at his bride in delight and then banged on the table to get the attention of the room.

'Ladies and gentlemen,' he shouted into the microphone. The guests gradually settled into an expectant silence. Now sounding much more self-assured, Edwin barely glanced at his notes as he thanked everyone who had helped with planning the wedding and complimented the bridesmaids.

'I know you are all hungry and dinner is about to be served, so let me finish by thanking my wonderful in-laws.'

His voice took on a serious note as he looked across at Auntie Amelia and Uncle Fred. 'Amma and I have been a couple for quite a few years now and you have both been so supportive and loving. Thank you for welcoming me into your family. Rocky, thanks for everything you've done to let Amma have the wedding of her dreams.'

He paused, a grin back on his face. 'I know how protective you are of your sister, so I also want to thank you for not beating me up when I first asked her out.'

There was widespread laughter and Rocky smiled in acknowledgement. When the room fell silent again, Edwin continued. 'Finally, to my beautiful wife...' He turned to face Amma, his eyes fixed on hers. 'I know this has taken us longer than we planned, but I'm so glad that you agreed to marry me. I love you and I promise you that I will be the best husband I can be and make you glad that you said yes.' Cutting into the collective 'Aaah' that filled the room, he raised his glass to her and said softly, 'To my wife!'

The tear that spilt out onto her cheek at the sincerity in Edwin's voice took Faye by surprise and she dashed it away quickly. She didn't dare look at Rocky and instead turned to Baaba who was still whooping in response to Edwin's speech.

'To hell with the high heels,' she whispered fiercely. 'Pass the wine!'

Baaba had already consumed more than half the bottle and she tittered as she tipped a generous amount into Faye's empty glass. 'Now you're talking! Relax and have some fun. Look at Trudie,' she nudged Faye and laughed throatily. 'She's practically sitting on Kofi's lap. She's certainly getting her money's worth from her pamper session. That girl really knows how to go after what she wants!'

Thankful that it wasn't Rocky on Trudie's target list, Faye swallowed a huge gulp of wine and decided for once to take Baaba's advice and let loose. After dinner was over, the guests began to circulate and Faye made a beeline for Rocky's table. He was deep in conversation with Stuart who, judging from his ruddy complexion, had consumed about as much alcohol as his fiancée.

'Faye!' Stuart stood up and gave her the traditional three kisses on the cheek and stepped back, openly admiring what he saw. 'You look fabulous, doesn't she, Rocky?'

She could smell the beer on his breath and had it been anyone else, she would have given them a wide berth. But Stuart's cheeky smile was irresistible and she hugged him affectionately. Rocky stood up and held out his chair.

'Here, sit down. I'll get you a drink – wine all right?'

She nodded and he moved off towards the bar. Her eyes were still on him when Stuart spoke, his speech more than a little slurred.

'Is everything all right between you two? Feel free to slap me down if I'm speaking out of turn, but I'm not seeing the same happy couple that came to Ghana a couple of years ago.'

Faye felt the heat rush up her face. She picked up an unused dessert fork and idly traced a pattern on the white tablecloth.

'I wish I knew what's going on. Let's just say that we're going through a bit of a rough patch, although, if I'm honest, I'm not sure if we'll get through it.' She blinked back the tears prickling the back of her eyes and he hastily changed the subject.

Weaving from the effects of the bottle of wine she had almost single-handedly consumed, Baaba had taken the empty seat next to Sena while Trudie and Kofi stood deep in conversation a few feet away. She looked up as Rocky returned to the table and placed a large glass of wine in front of Faye, and her deep voice carried across clearly in the sudden hush that fell upon the table.

'So, Rocky, now that Amma's married off, when are you and Faye going to set a date?'

Utterly mortified, Faye groaned aloud. Frieda raised an eyebrow and Stuart glared at Baaba, who shrugged unrepentantly. If Rocky had any intention of answering the question, there was no chance to find out as a very purposeful Clarissa marched up to their table.

'Rocky! There you are, sweetie. Thanks so much for doing the interview; I can't wait to watch it tomorrow night!' Clarissa's long mane of hair was caught up in a half ponytail and secured with an emerald green hair comb, while her make-up was giving Baaba's a run for its money. She had applied a deep green sparkly eye shadow to the lids of her heavily lashed eyes and her thickly glossed lips, curved into their familiar pout, were painted a deep ruby. She wore a short, silky green dress that emphasised the length of her slim legs and maddening though the woman was, Faye couldn't deny that Rocky's ex-girlfriend was a beauty.

Clarissa was also intent on her usual mission of aggravating Baaba and Faye took a gulp of her wine and waited for the inevitable fireworks. But before the usual thrust and parry could commence, Clarissa gasped and her jaw dropped in shock.

Baaba smiled sweetly and waved her left hand a second time to make sure that the other girl was in doubt about what she had seen. Clarissa's eyes widened even further, giving her beautiful face a suddenly comical look as she croaked out the words that seemed to stick in her throat.

'What…? When…?'

Dumbfounded, she looked at Stuart who simply grinned and took another swig of his beer, clearly enjoying the floor show. Dispensing with any subtlety, Baaba smirked openly at Clarissa's stunned expression.

'Yes, you are seeing right. Stuart and I just got engaged – aren't you going to congratulate me?'

Muttering something which could have been good wishes but probably was not, Clarissa turned on her heel abruptly and stalked off, her back stiff with anger. Faye sighed and tossed back the remaining contents of her glass before reaching for a half open bottle of red wine in the centre of the table. If it was going to be one of those nights, she decided, her brain would need all the numbing that it could get.

The DJ stopped the music to announce that the bride and groom were about to cut the cake. Still grinning triumphantly, Baaba tottered unsteadily over to Amma and made a half-hearted attempt to hold up her train as Edwin escorted his bride to stand behind a table bearing an elaborately decorated four-tier wedding cake. Both Auntie Amelia and Edwin's mother moved forward to stand behind the couple.

'Come on,' Stuart tugged gently on Faye's arm. 'Let's get a closer look at this.'

'Why are their mothers standing there?' Faye asked curiously, hastily picking up her wine glass before following his lead.

'It's a lovely custom they have here where someone – usually an older lady – "helps" the couple to cut their cake.' He smiled ruefully. 'Bloody hell, you can tell I'm right at home in this country now, can't you?'

The guests gathered round and a huge cheer went up as the newly- weds, together with their mothers, clasped hands around the beribboned handle of a cake knife and plunged its sharp blade into the soft white icing of the largest cake.

The upbeat music switched to a slow ballad, and hand-in-hand Amma and Edwin walked over to the dance floor, moving together easily in their first dance. For a few minutes the guests stood around watching them and then Uncle Fred and Auntie Amelia took to the floor, closely followed by Edwin's parents. Before long, the dance area was packed and Kofi pulled a squealing Trudie onto the floor, taking advantage of the crowd to hold her close to him.

Rocky gently extricated the wine glass from Faye's fingers and set it down on a nearby table. He slipped his arm around her waist and pulled her up against him before she could protest.

'Dance with me.'

Not sure if it was a request or a command, and now far too tipsy to care, she followed him and fell into his arms as they swayed in the tiny space he had created on the dance floor. Her sore feet were forgotten as she relished the feel of Rocky's strong arms around her, and she nestled into his chest wishing she could stay there forever. She stumbled slightly in her heels and his arms tightened around her, causing the familiar heat to rise up through her body, the feeling growing more intense as his hands gently played against her back. Cocooned by the thick crowd surrounding them and wishing they were back at his house, she clung onto him, feeling the heavy thud of his heartbeat against her cheek, and was soon left in no doubt about what holding her was doing to him.

Having done his duty by the bride and groom, the DJ switched up the tempo and Faye reluctantly unpeeled herself from Rocky. He ran a hand over his hair and even in her condition she could see that he looked shaken. She sighed in happy anticipation of how the evening would end and gave him a beguiling smile before moving away to dance with Amma and the girls beckoning furiously to her to join them.

Amma and Edwin were spending the night in the hotel and after the last guests reluctantly stumbled out of the ballroom just after midnight, Rocky helped a very tipsy Faye to the car, leaning in to click her seatbelt into place. He waved goodbye to a bleary-eyed Stuart who was attempting to climb into the back of his car with the help of his long-suffering driver, Amidu. The minute the driver shut the door, Baaba, who was already inside, slumped heavily against her fiancé's shoulder.

Rocky gunned the car into life and Faye closed her eyes and leaned back against the soft leather seats, enjoying the cool breeze wafting through the windows. The soulful music from the radio combined with the alcohol she had downed to raise her state of arousal even further. Rocky drove in silence and put his food down hard on the accelerator once they reached the main highway, and it felt like only minutes before they were turning into the driveway of his house.

Faye slipped off her sandals as soon as she walked in, wincing as the blood ran back into her constricted feet. The house was quiet and the hallway was in almost complete darkness. Rocky locked the door and took her by the hand. Clutching her shoes in the other, she leaned heavily against him as he guided her up the stairs. This time, she vowed dreamily, she would not be swayed by the voices that warned her to watch her heart. This time, I'm not going to think about what happens tomorrow; I'm just going to let go.

Rather than stopping at his room, Rocky continued to the door of her bedroom and opened it before turning to her. Slightly dizzy from the wine and the intensity of her aroused emotions, she pressed herself up against him and raised her lips eagerly for his kiss.

She felt the warmth of his lips touch hers briefly, and then move to her forehead.

'Goodnight, Faye. Sleep well.' Without waiting to see her go in, he turned and walked down the corridor into his room.

19

'...In Sickness
and in Health...'

The sound of angry voices and repeated banging roused Faye from her drink-induced stupor. Shielding her eyes from the sunshine streaming across her bed, she crawled out slowly from under the white mosquito netting that shrouded her bed like a ghostly veil.

Stumbling to the window, she pulled back the light muslin curtains to peer out into the spacious garden behind the Asantes' house. The source of the commotion was quickly established: a group of men were hard at work setting up canopies to cover tables and chairs and erecting a large marquee. Part of the process involved hammering long metal rods deep into the ground to anchor the tent, and the shouting that had awoken her came primarily from Togo, obviously incensed at the damage being done to his immaculately mown lawn. Although she didn't understand the language, his fiery tone and the very expressive gestures he was directing at the men didn't need an interpreter.

Besides enraging Togo, the hammering was also exacerbating the throbbing in her head and she stumbled into her bathroom to take a long, hot shower. When she eventually emerged from the steam filled room, she slipped on a cotton dress and wandered downstairs. Rocky's door was firmly closed as she walked past and she shuddered with embarrassment; being turned down by him was a novel experience and one that she was not particularly keen to remember.

Martha, back in her customary uniform of white-collared navy dress, was at the sink rinsing a tall stack of dishes when Faye walked into the kitchen. She looked up with a smile and raised an arm to wipe away the beads of sweat on her forehead.

'Good morning, Miss Faye. Did you sleep well?'

Faye nodded, and instantly regretted the movement as a stabbing pain shot through her temples. Forcing a smile, she poured a cup of coffee from the flask on the table. Martha was the last person she could confess to about a hangover; convinced as she was that alcohol was the work of the devil.

'I wasn't expecting to see you today. Isn't Sunday your day off?'

'We have a very big lunch to organise today, Miss Faye. I can't just leave my kitchen to the caterers to cause confusion.'

She looked pointedly at the cup in Faye's hand, making it clear that it wasn't her idea of a decent breakfast. 'There are bread rolls and fresh fruit on the dining table.'

Instantly queasy at the thought of food, Faye shook her head and took a sip of the hot, dark liquid. Martha picked up a dishcloth to wipe the plates and her dark brown eyes twinkled with mischief.

'Now that Amma is married, I am sure it will be your turn soon.'

Faye studied the coffee in her cup, marvelling yet again at how shamelessly Ghanaians expressed what was on their mind, no matter how personal.

'Martha, I have no plans at all to get married; I have a really busy job in London and if everything goes well, I might have a shot at a promotion one day.'

Martha said nothing for a few minutes and concentrated on wiping the dishes she had stacked in the drainer. She hung the damp cloth on the hook by the sink and then turned to look at Faye, her generous curves straining against the soft nylon of her dress.

'Miss Faye, you are a woman and you will want to marry. Your job cannot give you children, so you must not let your work become a problem. By God's grace, you and Amma will soon give Mrs Asante very beautiful grandchildren.'

With that parting shot, she hurried out of the back door and could be heard shortly afterwards loudly berating Togo who had to be physically restrained from punching one of the workers.

With no sign of Auntie Amelia or her husband in the living room, Faye wandered out onto the veranda. She stretched her tired limbs out on the wicker chaise longue and watched the preparations for the post-wedding lunch. The heat, combined with the tiredness from the late night, conspired to send her to sleep, and she awoke with a start at the sound of the gate creaking open.

The arrival of the caterers signalled a frantic rush of activity in the house and Faye crept up to her room to change into the traditional two-piece outfit that she would be expected to wear for lunch.

She jumped at the loud knock on her door and yanked down the top she had been easing over head.

'Come in!'

Practically flinging the door open, Amma bounded in and rushed over to hug Faye. She looked happy and relaxed and was wearing a beautiful boubou made from a white lacy fabric shot through with gold thread, and a matching headscarf. Her braids had been set free from the high bun she had worn the day before and they bounced rhythmically as she almost hopped in excitement.

'I still can't believe I'm actually married!' she crowed. After a few more twirls, she sank onto the edge of the bed, gasping breathlessly. 'Edwin keeps calling me Mrs Forson – it sounds so weird! I know I've wanted this for a long time but now it's actually happened, I can't quite believe it.'

Faye watched with amusement as Amma prattled on happily.

'You look stunning, by the way,' she said, when she was finally able to cut in. 'And I'm really glad you're here; I need some help with the headscarf bit. Here–' She brandished the peach coloured piece of fabric and Amma grabbed it with a giggle.

'You'd better get used to tying these things.' She laid the fabric out on the bed and folded it into a long strip and then deftly wrapped it around Faye's head, slipping the tied ends into the folds of the cloth.

'With Baaba getting married next year, not to mention

when you have your own engagement ceremony, you are going to wearing boubous a lot.'

Refusing to rise to the bait, Faye contented herself with looking in the mirror, silently admiring how the headdress accentuated the delicate oval of her face and the slanted oriental cast of her eyes. The royal blue top flowed closely along the lines of her slim body and the tightly wrapped long skirt with delicately embroidered designs emphasised the curve of her hips. Her outfit was complemented by stylish sling-back shoes, their comfortable kitten heels guaranteed to spare her feet the torture of the wedding sandals.

'You look lovely!' Amma exclaimed. 'Rocky is going to have to fight the men off today.'

Keen to distract Amma from the topic of her discussion, Faye quickly sprayed a few blasts of Daisy Dream and propelled her out of her room, slipping her arm through hers as they walked downstairs.

The tables and chairs had been arranged on the lawn under white canopies and the spacious marquee provided shelter from the blazing sun for long trestle tables covered in white linen. His arms folded aggressively, Togo stood watching the caterers set out large stainless steel chafing dishes on the tables, his eyes narrowed in suspicion at the intruders traipsing in and out of the kitchen.

Edwin was on the veranda talking to Rocky when Faye walked out and he broke off to issue a piercing wolf-whistle. Wearing a long shirt and loose trousers in the same white and gold fabric as Amma's boubou, there was no sign of yesterday's nerves. Kissing Faye warmly on both cheeks, he slipped an arm around his new wife. 'You both look amazing.'

Rocky's eyes widened as they took in Faye's transformation from modern Western girl to traditional African woman. He kissed her gently on the cheek, his murmur for her ears alone.

'You look delicious. How's your head this morning?'

She pouted, at once delighted at the admiration she could see in his eyes and incensed at his rejection the previous night.

'Perfectly fine, thank you,' she lied.

Rocky looked sceptical but Baaba's appearance seconds later in a tight fitting skirt and top made from traditional kente cloth, and with Stuart in tow, put paid to the conversation.

By two o'clock, all the guests were seated around the tables and relaxing with drinks and canapés. The DJ was back in action and the sounds of Ghanaian high-life music filled the air. After the formality of the wedding reception, lunch was a far more relaxed affair and Faye sat with Amma, Baaba and an obviously love-struck Trudie who could scarcely keep her eyes off an equally besotted Kofi. Across the table Rocky, Stuart, Edwin and George were deep in an argument over football teams.

Her hangover had receded and Faye seized one of the tiny meat pies making their way round, enjoying the taste of the light pastry that melted on her tongue. Stuart made short work of three sticks of spicy beef kebabs, immediately downing a bottle of ice cold beer before moving on to the fried yam balls stuffed with seasoned tuna.

When it was time for the main course, Faye walked towards the buffet in the marquee, her tight skirt and heels slowing her progress. Breathing in the tantalising aromas, her stomach growled in anticipation. The food, an eye-catching array of Ghanaian dishes, was set out in huge steel serving dishes manned by waiters.

She picked up a plate and held it out for some fluffy white rice and rich lamb stew and helped herself to a small serving of Ghanaian salad, although drenched as it was in juicy red tomatoes, creamy vegetable salad, boiled eggs and baked beans, with only slivers of green lettuce to be seen, it bore little resemblance to leafy salads she was used to. Faye's plate was almost full and she shook her head regretfully to the offer of kenkey, the fermented corn dough balls which were a staple of Ghanaian cuisine, instead opting for a slice of spit-roasted pork. She paused in indecision when she spotted the last dish on the trestle table. The spinach stew swimming in rich red palm oil looked appetising enough, but the unmistakable pieces of pigfoot in the dish held her back. She still associated the bony pink meat with memories that were not altogether pleasant and it was never going to be her first choice of food. With a final glance, she turned away and walked back to her seat.

The conversation at the table was sporadic as everyone focused on the food. True to form, Stuart had loaded his plate with lashings of hot pepper sauce and his flushed face grew progressively moister as he ate. Taking pity on his friend, Rocky silently handed over a clean white handkerchief which Stuart took with a grateful smile.

Kofi was sitting next to Trudie and the couple laughingly sampled food from each other's plates as they ate. Baaba had finished her meal and while manoeuvring a toothpick around her mouth, watching them through narrowed eyes. She cleared her throat and Stuart looked up and followed her gaze. He quickly put a warning hand on her arm which she glanced at indifferently before turning her attention back to the couple.

'You two seem to be getting on very well.' Baaba held her toothpick aloft and returned the ominous glare Trudie sent her way with an innocent smile.

'What? I'm just saying. You know, someone recently told me that a wedding is the best place to meet your future spouse... Trudie, what do you think?'

Whatever Trudie thought, her outraged expression suggested that it was as well that she didn't get the chance to say. The music stopped suddenly and the loud pinging of fork against glass brought an immediate hush. The guests turned expectantly towards Uncle Fred who was standing in front of the DJ's table holding a microphone. He raised his arm to speak and his loose shirt fell back to expose his forearm. It looked stick thin and Faye bit her lip anxiously.

Despite the dramatic change in his appearance, Uncle Fred sounded cheerful enough as he welcomed everyone and thanked them for coming to celebrate Amma's wedding. Before taking his seat, he looked over to Amma and Edwin's table with a mischievous smile, and continued.

'I'm a very proud father today because I have just gained another son. But let me just add that I'm very much looking forward to the day when I get another daughter!'

He sat down to loud whoops and catcalls and Faye blushed furiously, conscious of the eyes looking over curiously at Rocky who sipped his beer coolly and turned back to George to pick up on their interrupted conversation.

Faye pulled a face and Amma gave her a tiny smile of sympathy, leaning in to whisper. 'Take no notice. You know what Rocky's like; he has to do things his own way. He's never responded to being pressured.'

She glanced pointedly at Baaba, who was stroking her engagement ring as if seeing it for the first time, and smiled in affectionate exasperation. 'Not everyone's like Stuart!'

Faye stared bleakly into her glass for a moment and then forced herself to smile. This was Amma's day and she wasn't going to let her feelings about Amma's brother cloud the happiness in the air.

It was late in the afternoon when the guests finally started to disperse. Trudie and Kofi were the first to leave from their table, closely followed by George. Finishing his fourth bottle of beer with a satisfied sigh, Stuart took Baaba by the hand to pull her up from her seat. Her generous hips were wedged firmly into the chair and it initially resisted her attempts to rise; forcing her to wriggle her bottom vigorously and push down hard on the arm of the chair before it finally released her.

Stuart bent to kiss Amma and shook Edwin's hand with both of his.

'It's been a wonderful weekend and we wish you both a long and happy marriage. We'd better leave so Amidu can get himself home before it gets late.'

Baaba pouted, but with little choice in the matter, she kissed Amma and Edwin before turning to do the same to Faye.

'When did you say you were leaving?'

'I'm flying back to London on Tuesday. I'd love to have stayed longer, but there's a big project at work that I'm involved in and I was lucky to get the time off.'

Stuart gave her a warm, slightly inebriated hug and she laughed, giving his damp back a brief pat before extricating herself. He shook hands with Rocky and draped an arm around Baaba.

'Make sure you come back soon, won't you? We'll let you know when we've sorted out our wedding date so you can put it in your diary.'

He turned to leave and a second later, turned back, his blue eyes twinkling. 'Hey, Rock, you do know they say weddings come in threes, don't you?'

A few hours later, the caterers had left and the back garden was deserted. The hire company was scheduled to return in the morning to dismantle the marquee and remove the garden furniture and an exhausted Martha had retired to her quarters, leaving Togo to secure the gate.

Edwin and Amma had set off on their honeymoon and Faye joined her hosts in the living room. She curled into an armchair and tucked the wrap-around skirt around her, listening to the light-hearted banter between Rocky and his parents. She looked thoughtfully at Rocky; his loose shirt strained against the muscular arm casually resting across the back of the sofa. Watching him chuckle at his mother's acerbic description of the elderly relative who had only reluctantly been persuaded to go home, Faye couldn't help the quickening of her pulse. Just at that moment he turned and caught her gaze and a curious smile played across his lips.

Without breaking eye contact, his voice was suddenly husky. 'Ma, you look tired. Why don't I make you a cup of that peppermint tea you like so much? Faye – will you give me a hand?'

Auntie Amelia looked so astonished that Faye almost burst into giggles. Rocky offering to make tea was a very rare occurrence; his usual mode of operation was to cite his traditional African man excuse to get out of doing most things that involved the kitchen.

'Thank you, but don't be long. Clarissa's show starts in a few minutes and I want us to watch your interview.'

He grimaced but made no comment. Faye followed him into the kitchen and set out cups and saucers on a tray while he filled the kettle and then leaned back against the kitchen counter to watch her at work.

'So how's your head now?' he said, his tone dry. 'After all that wine last night, I'm pretty sure you felt like hell this morning.'

She laughed, pausing for a moment from dropping teabags into the old-fashioned teapot to look at him. 'I did feel pretty rough, if I'm honest. I have drunk more wine in the last few days than I have in weeks! It's just as well we're heading back to London soon because I don't think my liver would survive another week here.'

The kettle whistled and clicked off, but Rocky made no move to pick it up.

'And then what happens?' His attractive features were unreadable and her smile faltered as she looked at him.

'What do you mean?' She felt the tiny tremor in her voice and she cleared her throat, trying to sound more assured as she repeated herself. 'What do you mean, "and then what happens?"'

He shrugged. 'Faye, it's pretty obvious that things aren't right between us. You've been pushing me away for weeks – in fact, you only seem to want me after you've knocked back a bottle of wine.'

She stared at him, suddenly speechless. Where the hell had that come from?

'Rocky, I—' The rest of her sentence was cut off by Auntie Amelia's excited cry.

'Faye! Rocky! Come quickly! The programme is starting!'

He clicked the kettle on again and poured the boiling water into the teapot while she stood by, still lost for words. He said nothing further and she held open the door for him to carry the laden tray through, and then followed him back to the living room.

On the large television screen, the camera had panned to a close-up of Clarissa. Faye settled back into the armchair and watched the former model introduce the first segment of her show. Although no fan of Rocky's ex, Faye was forced to admit that, putting her over-exuberant hand gestures and a voice that sounded rather nasal aside, Clarissa looked stunning in a fitted red suit with a short pleated skirt that made the most of her elegantly crossed legs.

'Today on *Clarissa's Hour*, my very special guest is

someone whose name has been in the headlines not only in Ghana, but across the world. I am really honoured to introduce our most attractive and exciting export and the darling of the global financial world, our own Rocky Asante!'

Uncle Fred chuckled and Auntie Amelia clapped in excitement, almost knocking over the cup of tea on the table beside her. 'Oh, look, Rocky – there you are! You look so handsome.'

Faye stared at the screen as the camera zoomed in. Rocky did indeed look very handsome; his close cropped hair accentuating his clean-cut features and the strong line of his jaw. With one leg crossed lazily over his knee, he looked confident and relaxed. She glanced over at the live version sitting on the sofa by his mother, rubbing the back of his neck uncomfortably and clearly wishing he could be anywhere else.

On the screen, Clarissa leaned in towards him, the camera closing in on the cleavage exposed by her jacket. 'Rocky, welcome to the show. First of all, congratulations on your success with the...' she paused and consulted her notes for a moment, '...the LaserTech deal. You've made Ghana proud. Now, my first question is...'

Faye tuned out and just watched Clarissa's shapely lips moving, noting how she barely giving her guest time to respond to a question before jumping in with another one. *I don't think Oprah's got anything to worry about just yet*, Faye thought, as once again Clarissa cut into Rocky's response. He didn't appear fazed and answered her questions about investment banking and the intricacies of the Alexander Electronics deal smoothly and fluently.

Faye listened raptly; impressed by his skill in making the complex deals he had been involved in sound so simple and straightforward, and even making sense of the incomprehensible acronyms. She felt a pang of guilt, suddenly wishing that she had made more effort to understand the work that he was obviously so passionate about.

'Rocky, you should have your own TV show – you're so natural!' his mother exclaimed. She creased her forehead in irritation. 'I think Clarissa could do with some training in how to interview people; she doesn't seem to listen to anything you're saying.'

As the interview came to a close, there was one question that Clarissa had no problem giving Rocky time to answer.

'So, Rocky...' she paused dramatically and the camera panned across and zoomed in on his face, one eyebrow raised expectantly. 'We know that there isn't a Mrs Rocky, sooo... my final question is this; tell us how such a handsome man as yourself has managed to stay single?'

Faye's eyes widened and Rocky leaned back in his chair and roared with laughter. He shook his head slowly before replying, 'Well, I certainly didn't see that one coming!'

Clarissa tilted her head and waited pointedly for him to elaborate. Showing no inclination to oblige, Rocky simply smiled in response, and then added graciously, 'Thank you for the compliment and for the opportunity to be part of your show.'

With a smile and a helpless shrug that said 'Well, folks, I tried,' Clarissa leaned back and introduced the next segment of the show before the picture faded into a commercial break.

Uncle Fred was the first to speak. 'Well, that was very interesting, son – well done! I've learned a lot about the financial markets. Your mother's right; you should do more public speaking.'

Auntie Amelia's eyes were on Faye, and the pensive look that had settled on the younger woman's expressive features was not lost on her.

'It's been a long day, my dears; I think it's time we went up to bed.' Without further ado, she walked over to Faye and bent to give her a gentle kiss on her cheek, whispering softly, 'Don't look so sad, my dear. That wretched girl ambushed him with that question.'

Faye forced a smile and stood up to kiss Uncle Fred good night before moving across to sit on the vacated sofa. Why was it, she wondered, that everyone except Rocky was keen to reassure her that she had a place in his life? She replayed his response to Clarissa's question and again felt the stab of hurt disappointment at the way he had skilfully dodged admitting that he was in a relationship.

Rocky shifted over and she stiffened as he reached for her hand. He frowned and turned to face her. 'What's wrong – have I upset you?'

She glared at him, suddenly furious that he had no inkling how his words might have been received.

'What's wrong? Are you serious? You've just humiliated me in front of hundreds and thousands of people and you're asking me what's wrong?'

Taken aback, he stared at her for a moment, visibly

dumbfounded. 'How did I humiliate you?'

'So, as far as you're concerned, you are single, are you?' She demanded. She watched as comprehension slowly dawned upon him. Then unexpectedly, he grinned, enraging her even further.

'Is that what's bothering you? Come on, what did you expect me to say? Faye, you of all people know that I don't discuss my personal business. Think about it – how long did it take you to get anything out of me about my past relationships? Besides which, I didn't even answer her question, so how could I have humiliated you?'

'It's because you didn't answer the question that you've given everyone the impression that you are single,' she bit out through gritted teeth. For someone so smart, why was he suddenly being so dense, she fumed.

He shrugged carelessly and shook his head. 'Look, I wasn't prepared to discuss my personal status on national television and I think you're reading far too much into how that comes across.' Suddenly, his voice lost its humour. 'And if I'm not single, perhaps you can tell me why my girlfriend is blowing hot and cold all the time? In fact, can you tell me whether I have a girlfriend or if I actually am single? Because, frankly, that's exactly how you've been making me feel for a while now.'

She scrambled off the sofa furiously. 'Don't turn this back on me, Rocky! I wasn't the one who denied you existed – especially in front of your ex-girlfriend who would be only too happy to see us split up and me out of the picture!'

The muscle at the side of his jaw twitched and his eyes

hardened. 'This isn't about Clarissa, Faye – it's about you and me. Maybe you're the one who doesn't get it. Don't you think it's time we stopped playing games and that you tell me where we stand? Because the truth is... I don't know how long I can keep doing this.'

Her eyes flooded with hot tears and she stared at him wordlessly. So there it was finally, she thought miserably. So much for the reasonable talk she had hoped that they would have and which would give them each the chance to share what was on their minds. Here was confirmation, if ever she needed it, that he didn't love her and that their relationship was going nowhere. She bit her lip as a tear slid down one cheek, closely followed by another.

His expression changed and he stood up with a groan of frustration. But his move towards her came to an abrupt halt as his mother's scream shattered the tense silence in the room.

With a muffled exclamation, he turned and raced up the stairs followed by Faye, moving as fast as her tight wrap-around skirt would allow. She dashed her hands impatiently across her eyes to wipe away the tears blurring her vision and her heart thudded in horror as Auntie Amelia's cries grew louder.

She reached the top of the stairs in time to see Auntie Amelia running into Rocky's outstretched arms. Sobbing hysterically, his mother screamed again.

'It's your father! He's collapsed on the floor and he's not moving!

20

'... 'Til Death Do Us Part'

The house was deathly quiet and not even the sound of Martha's singing could be heard. The cacophony of car horns from the Monday morning traffic filtered in through the open windows of the kitchen where Faye sat, trying to make sense of the horrific events of the night before.

Rocky's quick thinking and a rapid call to his father's doctor had brought an ambulance to the house in what felt like hours, but was in fact less than twenty minutes. During that time, he had gently draped a blanket over his father's still form. Careful not to move him, he propped his head on a pillow and after checking his pulse and verifying that his airways were clear, he sat on the bed with his arm around his distraught mother, murmuring quiet words of comfort.

Unable to think of anything else she could do, Faye's instinctive British response had been to put the kettle on and bring Auntie Amelia a strong cup of tea. She had then sat cross-legged on the carpet by the unconscious man, stroking his hand gently and praying that he would survive. Their argument forgotten, she watched agonised as Rocky glanced down repeatedly at where his father lay, visibly fighting to keep his own emotions under control and support his mother.

Togo had been primed and was waiting at the gates to swing into action at the first sign of the emergency vehicle. He led the medical team up the stairs as soon as the ambulance arrived, and moments later they had gently transferred Uncle Fred onto a stretcher and manoeuvred their way down the staircase and into the waiting van. Faye followed closely behind Rocky and Auntie Amelia and watched the paramedics place an oxygen mask over Uncle Fred's face, her eyes blurring as fresh tears flowed down her cheeks.

'I'll drive with my mother to the hospital.' Rocky's voice jolted her out of her reverie and she stared at him for a moment in bewilderment. He was clutching his car keys, his knuckles white with the force of his grip.

'Of course. I'll come, too.' She turned to go back into the house, intending to grab her bag.

'You don't need to come,' he said abruptly. 'I'll call and let you know what's happening as soon as I can.'

'Rocky.' She turned back and shook her head impatiently. She gestured towards his mother who stood deathly still watching the ambulance driver slam the back doors, her face taut with fear. 'You need me and your mother needs both of us. We don't have time to argue. Not now; let's just go!'

He stared at her for a moment and then nodded and gently steered his mother to the vehicle parked under the carport. He screeched out of the gates mere inches behind the white ambulance, following it out onto the main highway and through the quiet, dark streets. From where she sat in the back seat, Faye gnawed on her lip anxiously and gazed out of the window, barely registering the almost deserted roads and the wooden shacks battened down for the night.

With little traffic to slow them down, it had been only minutes before they turned into a spacious compound encompassing several white buildings, on the largest of which was a neon sign with the words 'Accra Metropolitan Hospital.'

Rocky parked in front of the hospital and they rushed towards the building in time to see the ambulance crew lowering the stretcher to the ground and wheeling Uncle Fred in through the main doors. Faye placed a protective arm around Auntie Amelia while Rocky hurried inside to catch up with his father.

Auntie Amelia clutched Faye's hand as it rested on her shoulder and the two women walked into the building. Most of the chairs in the waiting area were empty and Faye helped the older woman to a seat before going across to the reception desk where Rocky was quietly speaking to a woman wearing a white uniform. Just as Faye reached the desk, a man dashed in through the main doors and hastened towards them. He looked young despite a generous sprinkling of grey hair, and his steel rimmed glasses gave him an air of authority.

'Dr Kankam!' Auntie Amelia left her seat and rushed towards the new arrival. 'I'm so glad you are here. Thank you for getting the ambulance to the house so quickly!'

The doctor shook hands with Rocky and nodded briefly at Faye before placing a reassuring hand on Mrs Asante's shoulder.

'You did well to call me,' he said, glancing briefly at Rocky before turning his eyes back to his mother. 'Let me go and examine him and I'll come and update you as soon as I know what the situation is. We got the test results a couple of days ago and I pleaded with him to come in so we could start the treatment immediately. Unfortunately, he insisted that he would only do so after your daughter's wedding.'

Auntie Amelia looked stunned. 'But he didn't say a word about it! I would have forced him to come sooner if he had told us – he acted as if he was fine and he didn't seem to be in any pain.'

Faye stared uncomfortably at the ground, feeling wretched as she remembered her encounter with Uncle Fred a few nights before Amma's wedding. Desperately wishing she could turn back the clock and that she had not promised to keep his obvious agony a secret, she prayed even harder that he would pull through.

With a nod, the doctor sped towards the room where the medics had taken Uncle Fred, and Rocky put an arm round his mother and gently led her back to her seat.

'Do you think we should call Amma?' Faye looked fearfully at Rocky, who shook his head decisively.

'No, there's nothing she can do at this point and it would just ruin her honeymoon. Let's see what the doctor says first, and then we can figure out what needs to happen.'

Thankful that he was at least including her in the 'we,' she lapsed into silence and sat holding his mother's hand while older woman murmured quietly to herself, her lips moving over and over in a near silent prayer. For the next two hours, they remained in the waiting area, Rocky occasionally getting up to pace restlessly up and down the terrazzo floor before resuming his vigil beside his mother.

Despite the lateness of the hour, it was relatively busy with hospital staff bustling around clutching files and porters wheeling empty trolleys into the lift and ferrying equipment into different rooms. With little else to do, Faye watched the staff going about their business, impressed by their professionalism. After another hour of waiting and with no further word from the doctor, Auntie Amelia was quietly weeping and Rocky's pacing had become increasingly more agitated.

Holding tightly onto Auntie Amelia's shaking hand, Faye's eyes wandered across to where a little girl of about five who had just been brought in by her parents lay listlessly across her mother's lap while her father frantically sought help at the reception desk. Faye watched the woman cradling her daughter and gently stroking her little puff-ball pigtails and her heart contracted in sympathy. Having children didn't just involve happy times, she reflected, wondering how she would cope if her own child was seriously ill. Her thoughts flew back to the picture of Uncle Fred lying immobile on the floor of his room and a rush of fear pierced through her, tightening her grip on the older woman's hand.

Just as the suspense of waiting was becoming almost

unbearable, Dr Kankam strode into the reception area, his white coat flapping open as he hurried towards them. The doctor looked solemn and Rocky's face was almost ashen with dread as he jumped to his feet. Auntie Amelia pressed a hand against her chest, unable to move. Her reddened eyes stared piteously at the doctor, who removed his glasses and slowly knelt down in front of her.

'I'm sorry it took so long for me to come back to you but it was a close thing and we were forced to operate immediately. Luckily, because we already had the test results, we could target the problem immediately.'

'How is he?' Auntie Amelia whispered; her voice choked with fear.

The doctor smiled and his dark eyes crinkled, their expression mirroring the relief in his voice. 'We still need to monitor him but from what we were able to do in surgery, he should be fine. Your husband is a strong man and put up a good fight. He will need to take it easy for some time but all being well, he should make a full recovery.'

'Doctor, what was the problem?' Rocky ran a shaky hand over his hair and although his voice was calm enough, it held an unmistakable tremor. Faye glanced at him sharply, but his eyes were fixed on the man in front of him.

'The tests we carried out showed that he had a severe gastrointestinal infection. It had inflamed a significant part of his digestive tract and made it uncomfortable for him to eat, which accounts for his loss of appetite. He has lost a lot of weight over the past few weeks which also weakened his resistance. I really wish he had come to see me much sooner so we could have dealt with it before the infection reached this stage. As it is, he must have been in a great deal of pain.'

Auntie Amelia shuddered and Dr Kankam patted her shoulder gently. 'Please don't distress yourself. Unfortunately, men can be particularly difficult about seeking medical help and you couldn't have known what was going on unless he told you.'

Mentally berating herself for the umpteenth time for allowing Uncle Fred to persuade her into silence, Faye tried to focus on what the doctor was saying.

'He is comfortable now and sleeping, so I would advise you to go home and get some rest. We have him on very powerful antibiotics and we'll do some more tests first thing in the morning to monitor the affected area for any further sign of infection.'

With that, the doctor settled his glasses back onto his nose and left them. Auntie Amelia sagged with relief against her son and he put a gentle arm around her as they walked back to the car. Faye climbed into the back while he settled his mother in the front seat and drove them carefully back home.

Waking up a few hours later from a fitful sleep, Faye had wandered downstairs to learn from a sober looking Martha that both Rocky and his mother had already left for the hospital. Now, seated at the kitchen table while Martha was outside personally supervising the men dismantling the marquee in a bid to keep Togo from venting his frustration on them, Faye tried to assuage her feelings of guilt about her complicity in Uncle Fred's behaviour.

Compounding her worry about his health was the

realisation that she was scheduled to leave Ghana the following day. She remembered the fear in Rocky's eyes as his father lay prone on the bedroom floor and her heart ached at the idea of leaving him alone to deal with the uncertainty that still lay ahead. Despite Dr Kankam's reassuring words, her father had always cautioned that doctors were not infallible and didn't always get it right. And no matter how badly their relationship had deteriorated, she simply couldn't imagine abandoning Rocky now when he most needed her. She briefly considered calling Matt to tell him she was staying on and then decided to wait until she had a better idea of how long she might be needed before stirring things up at the office.

She grimaced inwardly at the thought of Ruth's reaction to her extending her trip; the Woollaston project was in full swing and all hands were needed on deck to get the infamous baby haven ready in time for Harriet's scheduled delivery date – the deadline she had given Cayhill's. She chewed on the end of a strand of her hair, her thoughts returning once again to the night in the kitchen.

Why the hell did I listen to Uncle Fred and not tell anyone about what I'd seen? She sighed deeply, frustrated at her acquiescence to his instructions, even as the voice of reason told her that spilling the beans would have made no difference if Uncle Fred wasn't willing to go along with the treatment until he had seen his daughter get married.

Martha marched back into the kitchen, her dark round face shiny from the humidity outside. Her grumpy expression lightened as she took in Faye's wan appearance and she took a seat opposite her, clasping her hands together on the wooden table top.

'Miss Faye, don't worry. Mr Asante will be fine. I called my pastor this morning and we are all praying for him. He is a good man and God will spare him. I am sure of it.'

Faye dredged up a reluctant smile. If Martha and her fellow prayer-warriors were on the case, it would take a very strong adversary to thwart their plans. 'I hope so, Martha. I just feel so sorry for Auntie Amelia – and I don't know what to tell Amma, if she calls.'

'Ah, you must say nothing,' Martha said firmly, standing up and tying an apron around her plump waist. 'Amma has to enjoy her time with her new husband in peace. She cannot do anything if she comes home, so she is better where she is.'

Faye sighed again. Not disclosing the truth, it seemed, was fine in some circumstances, but not in others. Everyone was agreed that not telling Amma the truth was a good thing but she doubted that not revealing the truth about their father's pain would have merited the same response.

The sound of the phone ringing in the hallway had Faye and Martha staring at each other in alarm. Faye spoke first. 'Martha, you get it! If it's Amma, I won't be able to hold it together.'

Martha sped out into the hall and returned a minute later, her eyes filled with trepidation. 'Miss Faye, Mr Rocky is on the phone. He wants to speak to you.'

Faye raced out into the hall, her heart thumping wildly in her chest. She seized the old-fashioned telephone sitting on the hall table. 'Rocky?'

When he said her name, her first thought was that he sounded normal, and she sighed with relief and perched her bottom on the marble-topped table.

'My mother wanted to get here early this morning and I didn't want to disturb you. We've seen Dad and he looks weak, but he was able to say a few words. The doctor says he's hopeful that they can start him on fluids in the next day or so when the swelling goes down at the site where they operated. In the meantime they've got him on a drip but at least he's not in any pain, thank God.'

Faye was nodding vigorously as she listened. 'How's your mother?' she asked, when he fell silent.

'She looks exhausted, but she wants to sit with him for a while. I'll give them some time alone and then bring her home so she can get some rest. I'd better go now.'

With that, he hung up and she replaced the handset and walked slowly back to the kitchen to tell Martha the news. With a loud 'Hallelujah!' the housekeeper broke into song and Faye hastily removed herself and went to sit out on the veranda. The air was warm and still and she watched with a wan smile as Togo marched up and down the lawn stamping grass down into the holes left by the metal rods used to secure the marquee and canopies.

After the dramatic events of the previous evening, it was strange to think that Amma's wedding lunch had taken place only twenty-four hours earlier. At that moment, she would have given anything to turn the clock back to when, only a few feet away, they had all been laughing and enjoying the occasion. She tried to take comfort from Rocky's update and decided to close her eyes and relax on the lounger for a few minutes. It would be better to hold off calling the office until after she had discussed it with him, she reasoned. Within minutes, the tension from the previous night's drama slowly seeped away and she drifted off to sleep.

She jerked upright as the creaking of the main gates broke into a muddled dream about ambulances and speeding taxis. Slipping on her sandals, she ran through the living room and into the hall just as Rocky and his mother came in through the front door. Auntie Amelia was in a loose black dress and casual low-heeled sandals. Her face looked drawn with exhaustion and a dark scarf covered her short, grey streaked hair. She stopped as Faye came towards her and a smile lit up her tired but still beautiful features.

'Good morning, my dear. How are you today? I told Rocky not to wake you this morning; you needed to get some rest after everything that happened last night.'

Faye returned the warm embrace and then stepped back and scrutinised the older woman's face, noting the dark shadows beneath her eyes. 'I'm fine, thanks, but I think you're the one who needs to rest, not me. How's Uncle Fred doing?'

Before his mother could answer, Rocky cut in. 'He'll be fine. He's pretty weak, which isn't surprising, but the doctor sounded very optimistic.'

Faye glanced at him and her heart constricted in sympathy. Rocky's normally cool demeanour was nowhere in evidence. His eyes were red-rimmed from lack of sleep and the faint stubble on his unshaven face underlined the dramatic transformation from his usually impeccable appearance.

'Martha's in the kitchen; should I ask her to bring you a cup of tea and some breakfast?' Faye looked from mother to son, desperate to help in some way.

'I think I'll just go upstairs and lie down,' Auntie Amelia said. 'Please ask Martha to bring some tea to my room.' She turned to Rocky and patted his arm gently. 'Son, you need to get some sleep.'

With that, she walked slowly up the stairs, leaving Faye and Rocky in the hallway. He heaved a deep sigh and rubbed his chin, the faint rasp of the stiff bristles audible.

'Your mother's right, you look exhausted.' She moved towards him instinctively and slipped her arms around his waist. After a moment's hesitation, he relaxed and wrapped his arms around her, letting his chin rest gently on her head. For a moment they stood in silence, her head resting against his chest, feeling the reverberations from the strong beat of his heart.

With another sigh, he dropped a light kiss on her head and stepped away. 'I need some coffee and then I have to take a nap. We'll go back to the hospital this afternoon and check on him. I know Ma's not going to rest easy until we get Dad home again.'

Faye followed him to the kitchen and relayed Auntie Amelia's message to Martha, sitting quietly while the housekeeper assembled a tray of tea and biscuits and Rocky brewed a fresh pot of coffee. She opened the door to let Martha through with the laden tray and turned back to see Rocky stirring three spoons of sugar into his mug.

She smiled, resisting the urge to chide him about his sweet tooth. He glanced up and caught her gaze and a faint smile crossed his face for the first time that morning.

'What, no lecture today?' He took a sip of the steaming liquid and sighed with pleasure. She shook her head and tucked a strand of hair behind her ear.

'I think you've more than earned the sugar so, no; no lecture today.' She took a deep breath before continuing. 'I'm going to call Matt and tell him I'm staying on here for a few more days.'

He looked up from his coffee, an eyebrow raised in surprise, and she frowned. 'Why are you looking so shocked? Did you think I was just going to leave you here tomorrow with all that's going on?'

He hesitated and then took another sip before replying. 'Don't take this the wrong way but, yes, I am surprised. With the way things have been lately, I really wasn't expecting you to change your plans because of me.'

He put down his mug and leaned back against the kitchen counter, folding his arms across his broad chest. The sleeves of his pale blue shirt were rolled back and in casual denims and dark brown loafers, even the fatigue imprinted on his face couldn't detract from his vitality.

'You're right in the middle of that Woollaston design project, aren't you?' His copper brown eyes probed her face and she stared back at him defiantly.

'I'm sure they'll manage without me for a few more days. I'd much rather be here with you. Besides, with Amma away, I can help Auntie Amelia if she needs anything.'

He nodded thoughtfully. 'I offered to call one or two

of the relatives to come over, but Ma's adamant that she doesn't want anyone told – even Auntie Akosua – until we're sure he's turned the corner.'

Faye nodded at his reference to Auntie Amelia's close friend who came from the same hometown as her own late mother and had been her best childhood friend. Having spent some time chatting with Auntie Akosua at the lunch the day before, and knowing how close the two families were, Faye knew that she would be horrified to hear about Uncle Fred's illness.

'I can understand that,' she said. 'Everything's happened so quickly, your poor mother needs time to process it all herself before having to deal with other people.'

'You're sure you want to stay on?' He took a large gulp of his coffee, his eyes never leaving hers. 'I wouldn't blame you if you had to leave, you know?'

'Rocky, whatever's going on with us, I still care about you – and I love your father, you know that.'

He swallowed the rest of the drink and set the mug down beside the sink. 'I'm going up to catch up on some sleep. We can visit Dad later; I'm sure he'll want to see you.'

Faye smiled and watched him leave the kitchen, relieved that he had accepted her offer without argument. She glanced at her watch and poured a mug of coffee from the pot, then raced upstairs to fetch her iPad to contact the office.

Lunch was a quiet affair with only Auntie Amelia and Faye at the dining table. The older woman ate sparingly and for once Faye was unable to summon up much of an appetite for the fried rice, spicy chicken and vegetable stew that Martha served up.

Rocky resurfaced later in the day, freshly shaved and with renewed vigour in his step. In a crisp white shirt and dark trousers, he seemed much more his old self although his smile didn't quite mask the anxiety still lurking in his eyes.

The sky was a clear, cloudless blue when they set off for the hospital and despite the air conditioning, the intense sunlight filtered through the car window. The traffic was heavy and Faye could sense Rocky's irritation as he inched forward trying not to run into the street hawkers dodging in and out of the slow moving vehicles. Reflecting on the sudden shift in fortunes for Uncle Fred, her thoughts flew to her own father and she pictured him in his study in London, his head bent over his notes and his favourite tortoise-shell glasses balanced across his broad nose. Just imagining how she would feel if anything were to happen to him made her shudder and she watched in sympathy as Rocky thumped impatiently on the steering wheel, barely able to conceal his frustration at the delay.

The sound of tapping on the car window startled her and she turned to see an old man clutching a walking stick in one hand, his other hand outstretched. She realised with a start that he was blind and that the young boy standing next to him and holding onto his arm was his guide. Scrabbling in her handbag, she snatched up a few loose coins and wound down the window to drop the change into the beggar's outstretched palm.

Auntie Amelia turned with a smile of approval. 'That's very kind of you, Faye. So many people find it irritating to be accosted for money but, sadly, a lot of our people are in need and we still have far too much poverty in this country.'

A gap opened up in front of them and Rocky pressed down on the accelerator and cut smoothly across the choked lanes of traffic, turning down a side road which passed through a quiet residential area. With less congestion to contend with, they were at the hospital within twenty minutes.

Faye's last visit had been in the middle of the night and the institution appeared quite different in daylight. The car park was almost full and visitors milled around the entrance to the main building. Neatly trimmed shrubs and flowers lined the paved pathway leading to the main hospital block, and Faye hurried to keep up as Rocky and his mother made their way down a side path and into a large white-washed building that housed the wards.

Entering through glass doors into a cool vestibule, they approached the large reception desk manned by a pretty woman pointing out directions to an elderly couple. Rocky waited impatiently and when the receptionist finally turned her attention to him, Faye saw the woman's eyes instantly widen in appreciation.

'How can I help you, sir?' She curved her lips into an inviting smile and patted her elaborately styled braids.

The second he tetchily rapped out his father's name, her flirtatious manner quickly transformed into a mask of professionalism and she checked the list in front of her before quietly pointing towards a side door marked 'Acute Unit.' Rocky put an arm around his mother, guiding her through the doorway, with Faye following closely behind. They walked down a short corridor and into a large room where curtains screened off four beds at each corner. A nurse, clipboard in hand, emerged from behind one of the partitions and smiled in greeting. In answer to their enquiry, she pointed to where Uncle Fred lay before moving on to the next bed.

Auntie Amelia moved towards the closed curtains at the far end of the room and slipped inside. Faye's heart was thudding so hard at the thought of Uncle Fred in here that she barely registered Rocky taking her hand and leading her into the enclosed space. Her first impression from her position behind Auntie Amelia was how small Uncle Fred appeared from the little that she could see. She scanned the array of machines positioned around the bed and shuddered at the menacing coil of plastic tubing leading from the humming machines into his thin arm.

Auntie Amelia straightened up and stepped away from the bed and Faye gasped, trying to conceal her shock as she saw him properly for the first time. Uncle Fred's upper body was propped up on two or three white pillows and a transparent plastic mask covered his mouth and nose. The sheet that lay over his body clearly showed the outline of his small frame, a far cry from the once rudely healthy and well-rounded man.

But if his body was unrecognisable, the twinkle in his warm brown eyes was as mischievous as ever and he winked broadly as she leant over to kiss his cheek. She couldn't help smiling back at him and with the hand unencumbered by tubes, he lifted the mask off his face.

'Don't look so worried, my dear. I'm a tough old man...

I'll be fine.' His voice was halting but clear and she felt a rush of relief.

'Dad, put the mask back on!' Rocky looked reprovingly at his father, who obeyed meekly but not without giving Faye a mock piteous look belied by another crafty wink.

For the next twenty minutes, the three visitors sat around the bed chatting while Uncle Fred watched and listened, giving the occasional nod to something that was said and on one occasion defying Rocky by removing his mask long enough to insist that Amma should not be told about his operation.

After a while, they left Auntie Amelia alone with her husband and wandered out into the corridor. Before leaving his bedside, Faye bent down to kiss Uncle Fred goodbye and he grasped her arm tightly. His expression was suddenly urgent and she shook her head gently, not sure what he was trying to say. His eyes flashed towards Rocky and back to her and then, with a grimace, he slumped back against the pillows, clearly exhausted. Giving his hand a gentle squeeze, she whispered goodbye, and slipped out through the gap in the curtain.

Neither she nor Rocky spoke for a few minutes as they waited for his mother outside the Acute Unit and Faye looked around the hospital, impressed by the high ceilings, stylish furniture and the electronic boards and other hi-tech equipment in the reception area. The walls were painted a stark white and the floors were spotlessly clean. A couple of orderlies walked past, one pushing a wheelchair occupied by a patient wearing a dark green hospital gown. A private hospital of this calibre would not be cheap, Faye speculated. She wondered how this facility compared with the public hospitals that most people were forced to use.

'What's on your mind?' Rocky sounded amused. He had been quietly observing the changes in her expression as the different thoughts flitted across her mind.

She shrugged. 'I was just wondering how many ordinary people could afford to come to a place like this. You were able to get an ambulance to the house and have Uncle Fred operated on even quicker than would probably have happened in London. I can't imagine that's the case for everyone.'

Rocky sighed. 'Look, money talks here just as much as anywhere else, particularly as the National Health Service here only covers the most basic items. It certainly helped that I know Dr Kankam personally and there's no question that this place isn't exactly cheap, but I'm just relieved that having money means that my father's life was saved. There's not much point to any of it if you can't help the people you care about.'

A few minutes later, Auntie Amelia emerged from the double doors leading to the Acute Unit and they walked slowly back to the car. The sun had started its descent and although it was still humid, with the air conditioner on full blast, the journey back home was far more comfortable.

Martha hurried out of the kitchen as soon as she heard the front door shut. She looked at them anxiously, almost wringing the damp cloth she was clutching between her hands in her agitation. Her dark blue dress strained against her solid curves and her generous bosom rose and fell rapidly.

Auntie Amelia smiled in reassurance. 'Martha, it's okay. Mr Asante is feeling much better. He sends his regards and I'm sure he will soon be strong enough for us to take him some soup. When he comes home, you will have to cook all his favourite dishes to build him up again.'

Martha clutched her chest with relief and took a deep breath, a smile finding its way back onto her face. 'Thank the Lord, Madam! My pastor called me this afternoon and I said that you were at the hospital. Everyone at my church is praying for him. When he comes home, we shall celebrate with some fine kontomire and pigfoot!'

Faye repressed a shudder, praying in turn that she wasn't going to be subjected to that particular meal. Almost skipping with joy, Martha returned to the kitchen and could be heard in full voice from behind the closed door shortly afterwards. Faye shook her head with a smile and turned to Auntie Amelia who was about to head upstairs.

'I've sent an email to my boss to say that I'll be staying on for a few more days,' she said. 'I don't want to leave when there's so much going on here.'

Auntie Amelia exclaimed in dismay. 'But Faye, why? No, my dear, you mustn't do that! You saw your uncle – yes, he's weak, but he's going to be fine. You have a very important job now and you've already taken time off to be with us for Amma's wedding.'

Taken aback by the vehemence of her reply, Faye hesitated. Auntie Amelia came forward and gently touched her cheek. 'I know how fond you are of Uncle Fred, my dear. If I really felt that it was necessary for you to stay, I would tell you.'

She turned to Rocky who had remained silent during the exchange. 'Son, tell her she doesn't need to change her plans.'

He looked from one to the other, clearly in a quandary. 'Ma, you could do with having someone at home with you while Dad's in the hospital. If Amma was around...' he tailed off as his mother frowned at him.

'You heard your father; Amma must absolutely not be told. Rocky, Faye... I have people I can – and will – call if I need anything. My dear child, you are so lucky to be working on such a big and important project and I don't want you to jeopardise anything by hanging around here. I love you for offering but I must insist that you go back to work as originally planned.'

Now I know where Rocky gets his stubbornness from, Faye thought ruefully. Unwilling to argue any further and suddenly feeling emotionally drained by the events of the past twenty-four hours, she nodded in a bid to placate the older woman.

'Okay, let me speak to Matt – my boss. If he thinks it's important that I get back to the office right away, I promise I'll stick to my original plan. If a few extra days won't make any difference, then please let me stay on for a bit to help out?'

Auntie Amelia patted her on the cheek gently. 'I'm going to rest for a little while before dinner.' With that, she walked up the stairs and was soon out of sight.

With Rocky close behind, Faye walked into the living

room and sank onto the brown leather couch with a deep sigh. Feeling weary, she lay back against the cushions, pulling her long legs up under her. Rocky sat down next to her and rested his arm across the back of the sofa, the warmth of his body radiating across the small space dividing them. She turned her head to look at him; he was staring straight ahead and she silently took in the handsome profile and the hard planes of his jaw. Sitting this close to him, she could also see fine lines at the outer corners of his eyes, something she hadn't noticed before.

As if aware of her scrutiny, he turned his head and their eyes locked, neither of them speaking. With a fluid movement, he moved his arm from the back of the chair to encircle her shoulders and draw her close against his chest. When he spoke, he sounded almost matter-of-fact although she could detect a faint tremor in his voice.

'I didn't tell Ma, but Dr Kankam said that it really was touch and go during the surgery. At one point they had to resuscitate him when his heart stopped.'

Faye gasped and sat up, pushing away from the comfort of his hold.

'Oh no, how awful! Thank God we got him to the hospital in time.' Suddenly it was all too much for her. Exhaustion, anxiety and the stress of the past day all combined to cause her eyes to well up with tears.

With a soft exclamation, Rocky leaned forward and gently brushed away the teardrops that spilled over onto her cheek. 'Hey, don't cry. He's over the worst now.'

She nodded and he sat back and shook his head with a puzzled sigh.

'What I still don't understand is how he managed to function with the kind of excruciating pain the doctor said he must have been experiencing. How the hell could he have gone through this with none of us noticing?' He slammed a clenched fist against the sofa in frustration.

Torn apart by the pain in his eyes, Faye couldn't contain her guilt any longer and before she could consider her words, blurted out, 'I did notice.'

His looked at her sharply, clearly baffled by her response. 'What? What do you mean?'

'I knew he was in agony... I saw him in the kitchen a few nights before the wedding. I was getting a drink of water and I saw him taking painkillers, and I knew he didn't look good.' The tears were spilling in earnest now and he stared at her dumbfounded, as if she was a complete stranger that had wandered brazenly into his house.

'But... but why didn't you tell me – or my mother?'

She was too upset to notice the grim set of his jaw. 'He told me not to... he made me promise not to say anything; he didn't want to ruin the wedding!'

'And you agreed to that, knowing how much pain he was in?' He looked – and sounded – incredulous.

'Rocky, that's not fair,' she protested. 'He said he had medication for the pain and that the doctors were taking care of him. Besides, what could you have done?'

'At least I'd have known we needed to get help straightaway instead of leaving it,' he shot back. 'The delay was almost fatal!'

Faye was now openly sobbing, his anguished expression more than she could bear. 'I'm so sorry! I felt awful about not telling you. I know how much you love your dad and that this is killing you.'

With a groan, he dropped his head into his hands. She reached out tentatively to stroke his back and bit her lip as he flinched away from her touch.

'Rocky, I'm sorry; don't be angry with me. Look, I'm not going to leave tomorrow. Let me stay – please! You need me.'

'No, I don't.' He raised his head and looked straight at her, his expression bleak. 'I don't need your pity – or your guilt, if that's why you think you need to be here. I've had to do without you for months now, and I'm used to it. So no, I don't need you now.'

He stood up with a weary sigh. 'You heard my mother. Don't change your flight – go back to London.'

Without another word, he left the room.

21

Revelations

'So, then what happened?'

Caroline pushed her empty bowl aside and leaned forward eagerly as Faye recited the events of the previous week.

'What do you think happened – I'm back here, aren't I?' Faye said bitterly. 'I tried again to tell his mother that I wanted to stay on, but she insisted that I should get back to work.'

Auntie Amelia had indeed insisted, during another subdued meal rendered even quieter when Rocky failed to make an appearance for dinner. Adamant that Faye should return to London, Auntie Amelia suggested instead that they make a quick trip to the hospital the following day to say her goodbyes to Uncle Fred.

Long after the older woman had climbed wearily up to her bedroom, Faye waited alone in the living room. Torn between her gut-wrenching guilt at not revealing Uncle Fred's obvious pain sooner, and hurt at Rocky's brutal response to her confession, she knew she wouldn't be able to sleep easy without clearing the air. Wishing she had Amma or Caroline around for reassurance, she sat on the sofa through what felt like hours of raucous talk shows and an improbable village drama. When the clock struck midnight, there was still no sign of Rocky and she finally gave up and dragged herself up to bed.

The next morning, the coffee dregs in the mug on the kitchen table were the only clue that Rocky had been around. After making a fresh cup for herself, Faye had reluctantly returned to her room to pack, leaving out the T-shirt and cotton trousers she planned to wear for the flight later that day. After a final check, she went down to find Auntie Amelia in the living room reading the papers.

'Good morning, Faye. I hope you slept well? Rocky's gone to buy a few things for his father, but he should be home soon. We'll visit Uncle Fred after lunch and Rocky can take you to the airport later.'

All the way to the hospital, Rocky had been uncharacteristically quiet, giving brusque responses to his mother's questions instead of their usual easy banter. His interaction with Faye had been confined to a polite 'Hi' when he returned home just after lunch and nothing thereafter. Gritting her teeth in irritation at his obstinate refusal to meet her eyes, and still smarting from his harsh words of the night before, she had sat silently in the back seat staring out at the afternoon traffic during the drive to the hospital. Her gloom was temporarily lifted by the sweet smile Uncle Fred gave her when she walked into his cubicle and the gentle kiss he planted on her cheek.

Although he was still in the Acute Unit, the oxygen mask had been replaced by tiny tubes which puffed out little bursts of oxygen just below his nostrils and for the first time since his collapse, Faye allowed herself the hope that he would recover.

They had no sooner arrived home than Rocky announced that he was heading off to the bank to join an urgent conference call with his team in London. His mother looked taken aback, and then shocked when he said to Faye.

'I'm not sure how long it will take so I had a word with Stuart earlier and he's offered to drive you to the airport.'

Dismayed at his obvious desire to avoid her when she had hoped to talk some sense into him on the drive to catch her flight, Faye bristled in exasperation at his stubbornness. A quick glance at Auntie Amelia forced her to bite back the angry retort on her lips; the woman had enough to worry about without adding her son to the mix.

'Fine,' she said evenly. 'I've finished packing so I'll hang around until he gets here.'

Rocky hesitated for a moment and then nodded. He kissed his mother's cheek gently, giving no indication that he had noticed her troubled expression.

'I'll see you later, Ma. Get some rest and we can go back this evening to check on Dad.'

Before Auntie Amelia could formulate a response, Rocky bent to give Faye what felt to her like a very reluctant peck on her cheek.

'If I don't get back before you set off, have a good trip and I'll call you tomorrow.'

'And did he?' Caroline's voice broke into Faye's thoughts and she jerked herself back into the present.

'No – well, okay, he sent me a text the next day to check that I'd got back safely. I've called the house a few times since then and spoken to his mother, but he never seems to be at home when I ring and I've given up calling his mobile. I hate the way he retreats into himself when he's unhappy about something!'

Caroline gave her a sympathetic smile and gestured towards the plate in front of her. 'Go on – finish your food. I've never yet known you to let a man get between you and pasta.'

Faye gave a wan smile and forked another mouthful of penne into her mouth.

'These meatballs are divine,' she breathed, her Rocky-shaped troubles momentarily forgotten. 'The sauce is seriously tasty – who made it? Don't tell me it was you!'

'Oy! Do you mind? I can cook, you know!' Caroline tossed her head and her red-gold curls bounced indignantly. Ignoring Faye's obvious scepticism, she went on. 'Actually, Anastasia made it – she's a brilliant cook as well as a great nanny. Haven't you noticed that you've managed to get through a meal without Coco climbing all over you and decorating you with food?'

Faye looked around. 'I thought something was missing! Where is the little dev-, I mean, angel?'

'I told Anastasia to take her down the road to the park. It's a bit chilly but I thought it would be good for her to get some fresh air. They should be back soon and you can finally meet my personal Mary Poppins.'

Faye nodded absently and focused on finishing the pasta in her bowl, her thoughts returning to her last day in Ghana.

With Amidu at the wheel, Stuart had arrived late in the afternoon to take her to the airport. On the way she replied quickly to a long text from Amma, another of her regular updates with lengthy descriptions of the guest house in Aburi and the lazy days she was spending exploring its beautiful grounds with her new husband.

Switching off her phone, she turned to Stuart who was sitting quietly beside her checking his own e-mails.

'Well, Amma is certainly enjoying her honeymoon! I guess they were right not to ruin it for her by telling her about Uncle Fred.'

Stuart put down his phone and nodded thoughtfully, his expression unusually serious. 'Yeah, it's best she gets to enjoy the break. She's been planning this wedding for ages and deserves to have a few days off to relax.'

'Thanks for taking me to the airport, by the way,' Faye said with a wry smile. 'I know how busy you are and I know Rocky strong-armed you into it since he can't bring himself to even look at me!'

Shortly after leaving the house, she had filled Stuart in on the incident with Uncle Fred and Rocky's total withdrawal after her confession.

He patted her hand in sympathy. 'Don't beat yourself up about what happened. You didn't do anything wrong and you shouldn't let Rocky get away with taking his own guilt out on you.'

'So why do I feel like I'm to blame, then? He was furious with me and he's scarcely said a word to me since last night.'

Stuart sighed. 'Faye, you've known Rocky long enough to know he's a bit of a complicated one. I don't know what's going on in that head of his half the time! What I do know is that he puts a lot of pressure on himself to be Mr. Fixit and he hates letting anyone down. When he worked for me, he was ten times more driven than I ever was.'

He grinned mischievously. 'Not that it takes a lot to put my ambition in the shade, mind you.'

Despite her heavy heart, Faye couldn't help smiling. Stuart was probably the most unlikely banker she had ever come across, but his unfailing good nature, sharp instincts and generosity of spirit had made him popular at the bank and with his clients.

'You know what, Faye? I haven't seen Rock this emotional since I've known him, which tells me that he's really cut up about his father's illness. When something like this happens, it can come as a real shock – it happened to me when my father had a heart attack a few years ago. This is something he can't fix and he more than likely feels really guilty for not spending more time with his old man – but that's still no excuse for him blaming you.'

Touched by his kindness, Faye remained silent for the remainder of the drive, gazing out at the Accra skyline. Dusk was falling and the strident sound of car horns sounded by impatient drivers filtered through the windows of the luxury car. *I'm going to miss being in Ghana*, she thought wistfully as they drove down the palm tree-lined thoroughfare that led to the airport. Despite the emotional turmoil of the past couple of days, she was sad to leave the tropical warmth to return to the autumn chill awaiting her in London.

She scraped at the last remnants of rich tomato sauce and Caroline whisked away the empty bowl and rinsed it out before dumping it into the dishwasher.

'Does Amma still not know about her father?' she asked curiously.

'Her mother called her a few days after I left to break the news. As they suspected, Amma wanted to cut their trip short and go straight home, but they wouldn't let her. According to Auntie Amelia, she had to threaten that it would make her dad worse if he thought he had ruined her honeymoon. In the end, it was the only reason she agreed to stay on.'

Faye took a sip of water and wiped her mouth with a paper napkin. 'Judging from her texts, she seems to be coping with the news okay. Luckily, Edwin knows how to keep her calm; he's brilliant at taking care of her.'

'And what about you?' Caroline said quietly. 'Who's taking care of you?'

Faye shrugged. 'I just wish I knew how Rocky was doing. It's been really tough not being able to reach him to clear things up. However bad things are between us, he worships his father and none of this can be easy for him.'

Caroline slammed the dishwasher shut, looking less than sympathetic. 'Well, he must surely be coming back soon now that his father is on the mend? I can't imagine

Rocky staying away from work any longer than he needs to.'

She took in Faye's brooding expression and her voice softened. 'He's probably missing you, too. My guess is that he's feeling guilty about not spotting what was going on with his father under his own nose. You just gave him a good excuse to deflect the blame. He's not stupid – he'll get over it when he's had time to calm down.'

'That's what Stuart said – that he's feeling guilty. But it doesn't make it any easier—'

The sound of the doorbell cut her off and Caroline glanced at her watch, puzzled. 'I'm not expecting anyone...' She hastened to open the front door and moments later Faye heard the familiar baritone voice as it approached the kitchen.

Dermot Duffy, Caroline's younger brother, swept into the room with the usual high drama that accompanied every appearance. With a mop of bright red hair that framed a narrow pale face and wearing black skinny jeans that accentuated his long lean legs, Dermot was an unconventional and very successful teenage heartthrob. As the lead singer of the band Guns in Clover, he was a regular feature on gossip websites and in teen magazines, obligingly falling out of nightclubs with a different girl whenever possible, and giving the paparazzi a field day and his Irish Catholic parents heartburn in the process.

Faye hung on for dear life as Dermot flung his arms wide open to envelop her in a tight hug that lifted her right off her feet. Regaining her balance, she frowned at him in mock disapproval.

'I hope you haven't dragged any impressionable girls

over here or allowed any dodgy photographers to follow you?'

Dermot laughed and threw his jacket over the back of a chair. 'No chance. I just wanted to see my darling sister, and look – I get my gorgeous Nubian princess as a bonus.'

Caroline rolled her eyes, trying to look unimpressed, although secretly pleased to see him. 'Well, it's about time you stopped by for a visit. I know you're a famous pop star and—'

'—and producer,' he interjected proudly. 'I've just finished putting down some tracks with Sadie Monck.'

Faye raised her eyebrows in astonishment. 'Really? That's amazing! I love her voice – it's so deep and smoky!'

Caroline cleared her throat. 'Yes, well, as I was saying, it's been ages since we've seen you. Coco's practically forgotten who you are!'

'Never fear, I'm here now,' he said grandly. 'Where is the little dem—' He coughed hastily as Caroline glared at him. '—I mean, darling?'

The sound of the front door slamming followed by the tapping of light footsteps provided the answer. Seconds later the kitchen door was thrown back with such force that it bounced gently back from the wall. Coco stood in the doorway in dungarees almost identical to her mother's. Her chubby hands were planted on her hips and her tousled strawberry blond curls stood up in a golden halo around her head. Her eyes darted from Faye to Dermot and she bit her fist, squealing with joy, unable to decide who to toddle over to first.

Her uncle solved the problem by swooping down to lift

her up high in the air before lowering her to blow a loud raspberry against her ruddy cheeks. She gurgled with pleasure and wrapped her arms around his neck.

'What the...?' Dermot choked and turned puce, while Coco's smile grew even wider as the pressure of her hug intensified.

'For God's sake, take your godchild before she kills me!' he croaked.

Openly laughing at Dermot's discomfort, Faye disentangled Coco's arms from around his neck and hugged her cautiously, keeping a firm grip on the little hands that immediately tried to reach up to embrace her. Dermot flicked the switch on the kettle and rummaged in a cupboard for a mug and teabag, his face slowly returning to its normal hue.

Moments later, a thin, dark-haired girl walked into the kitchen and Faye glanced curiously over the baby's head at Caroline's new nanny.

'Anastasia, this is my best friend, Faye.' Caroline waved a vague hand in Faye's direction and then pointed at Dermot. 'And that's my brother, Dermot.'

Anastasia's smile when she looked at Faye didn't quite reach her eyes and Faye watched the girl glance at Dermot and then, predictably, swivel back in shock when she realised who he was. Dermot smiled at her cheerily before returning to the task of making his favourite builder's tea. Although no stranger to champagne, his real addiction was to PG Tips, a detail that Faye frequently threatened to leak to his adoring fan club.

With her hands thrust into the pockets of a rather

grubby red padded jacket, Anastasia stared disbelievingly at Dermot's back for a second and then reluctantly turned to respond to Caroline's question. As the nanny walked past her, Faye sniffed at the faint but unmistakable aroma of tobacco and the sour odour of wine. She bounced Coco on her hip and watched Anastasia closely. The girl's heavily plucked eyebrows curved in thin arches above her pale blue eyes. Her narrow face and ultra thin lips, twisted into a saccharine sweet smile reminiscent of Clarissa, did little to inspire Faye's confidence. Her scrutiny was brought to a sudden halt by her god-daughter's attempts to burrow down the front of her top.

Looking up to say a hurried goodbye to the departing nanny, Faye deposited Coco gently onto the plastic floor mat in her nook and left her to play with Elsa. She looked across at Caroline who was busy emptying out the picnic basket the girl had left on the kitchen table.

'Where did you say you found her again?'

'Who? Anastasia?' Caroline glanced up before returning to her task. 'She used to work at Coco's nursery. Why?'

Faye tried not to let the unease she felt creep into her voice. 'I don't know exactly. There's just something about her that's a bit...well... hard?'

Caroline bristled, immediately on the defensive. 'Well, she's been fine so far. And at least she doesn't accuse me of being a crap mother. Besides, Coco seems to have taken to her – although that child would hug a snake if she was allowed to, so maybe that's not the best recommendation.'

Faye smiled and tried to shrug off her concerns. If Anastasia was doing her job properly and Caroline was happy with her, it seemed churlish to criticise her without any real evidence.

'So there's still no prospect of a reconciliation with Rose, then?' she asked hopefully.

'Not a chance in hell!' Caroline dumped the empty picnic basket under the table and wiped her hands on her baggy denim dungarees. 'And I've told Marcus to stop moaning about having a nanny around at weekends, because the only way Anastasia goes is if he decides to spend more time at home and does more to help with Coco.'

Caroline's scowl was fierce and Faye prudently changed the subject. 'How are things going with the new show?'

Her friend's face lit up with excitement. 'It's looking really good! We've lined up almost all the people we want to interview as role models. Eliza Henry has been fantastic – I thought she'd be a bit of a dragon, but she's so easy to work with and she's pulled strings to get us some big names for the show.' She paused and looked at Faye thoughtfully. 'I've been meaning to ask you, what do you think about me inviting Rocky to be one of the role models?'

Taken aback by the question, Faye looked nonplussed and Caroline continued before she could respond. 'We want a cross-section of people and professions for the series and as much as we hate the fact that he's a workaholic, Rocky has made a bit of a name for himself. He's a high profile black man and we want the show to be diverse. I think he'd be great, don't you?'

Faye bit her lip dubiously. There was no doubt that

Rocky had been an impressive guest on Clarissa's show but knowing his distaste for being in the limelight and his near paranoia about his privacy, whether he would agree to Caroline's request was another matter altogether.

'Well, there's no harm in asking him. But I'm not exactly flavour of the month at the moment, so you're better off doing it yourself – just send him an email.'

Returning from seeing off the nanny, Dermot wandered back into the kitchen and dumped his empty mug by the sink. He perched on a barstool and after a few minutes, the subject turned to his band's upcoming European tour.

'Are you sure you don't want to come with me, my lovely one? We can visit all the romantic spots as we tour.' He smiled at Faye, stretching his lips out into an exaggeratedly lascivious leer and wiggling his eyebrows like a comic villain. She punched him lightly on the shoulder.

'I have no interest in fighting off those raging little fans of yours. The last thing I need is a bunch of trolls stalking me on the internet because they've seen me out with you and think I'm your sugar mama!'

Dermot smirked. 'Don't put yourself down; you'd make a great sugar mama. I mean look at those legs... and don't get me started on the bum.'

'Eeew, Dermot, stop that! It's practically incest!' Caroline protested. 'And you'd better make sure you don't let Rocky hear you talking to her that way. I don't think there'd be much left of you to go on tour.'

Faye smiled sadly. 'Quite honestly, I don't think he'd be bothered. I'd probably need to wrap myself up in a copy of the Financial Times to get his attention.'

Dermot dropped his pantomime villain expression and looked at her with quizzical eyes. 'Is there trouble in paradise?'

His sister sighed. 'Let's just say that the great love story is in a bit of a stall right now.'

'More like freefall, you mean,' Faye said gloomily.

'You know what, Amma's right. You really need to sit him down and make him listen to you,' Caroline instructed. 'Hasn't all this gone on long enough? Look, just drop it into the conversation when he's feeling all lovey-dovey. The next time he says "I love you," just say "In that case, why don't we take the next step?"'

'He doesn't.' The words escaped before she could help herself.

'What do you mean "he doesn't"?' Caroline frowned, the freckles on her nose scrunching up into a single brown patch.

Mortified at her slip, Faye looked at the floor. 'He doesn't say "I love you." He's never said "I love you."'

There, I've said it! The one thing she had never shared with her friend was now out in the open and glancing up at her, there was no mistaking the impact of the admission.

Caroline's jaw had dropped and she made a visible effort to regain her composure.

'Faye, what do you mean? Are you saying that in all the time you two have been together, Rocky's never said the "L" word?'

Faye nodded, misery etched on her expressive features. Her eyes returned to the white floor tile under her foot and she traced the edge of it with the toe of her

347

shoe, desperately wishing she had kept her mouth shut.

Caroline said nothing and after a moment, Faye looked up resignedly. Knowing her friend as she did, she knew there was no way she would drop the subject without further details.

'Okay, he says things to me like "you're so amazing" and "you are so incredible" and "I've missed you so much," if he's been away. But no, he's never used the "L" word. So now do you understand why I'm never totally sure of him?'

'But why have you never said anything about it?'

'Because it's horribly embarrassing to admit that your boyfriend, the guy you are crazy about, has never actually said he's in love with you. Don't you get it?'

'Oh, come on, Faye! You know he loves you. Haven't you seen how the man looks at you?' Caroline exclaimed in exasperation.

Faye shrugged. 'I suppose so – or, at least, I used to think so. But if that's true, would it kill him to say "I love you," even once?'

'Well, I'd much rather have someone show me they love me even if they can't say it, than have some idiot spouting it every ten seconds and then cheating on you as soon as your back's turned.'

'Well, if there's one thing I do know about Rocky, it's that cheating isn't his style; especially after what he went through with that bitch of an ex-girlfriend. Not that it stops women from trying their luck. Take that French cow, Yvette, that he works with – I don't trust her an inch!'

She hesitated. 'I honestly don't know if this is one of his long list of "I'm an African man and we don't do this" taboos or if it's simply not what he feels.'

Clearly at a loss as to how to answer, Caroline just stared at her and scratched abstractedly at her makeshift bun.

Dermot broke the awkward silence, his expression an exquisite blend of complete wonder and incomprehension.

'What exactly is the big deal here? Some guys just don't use those words! Faye, seriously, you can't have any doubt how Rocky feels about you. And if it matters that much to you, why don't you just ask him?' His face brightened as another idea dawned. 'Or, say it to him yourself and see if he reciprocates.'

Faye and Caroline spun around in unison to glare at him with identical expressions of horror. His sister found her voice first, and it was pitched so high she was almost squealing. 'Are you crazy? Tell a man "I love you" first? Why would you do that?

'To find out if he does, maybe?' Dermot suggested helpfully.

Faye chipped in impatiently. 'If you say it first...' she started, and then stopped to look at him with a pained expression that clearly said 'Have we taught you nothing?' She took a deep breath and tried again. 'If you do, you'll never know if he really means it or if he just feels that he has to say it back.'

Dermot stared impassively at them. He shook his head slowly in a way that signalled that women would forever remain a mystery to him, and picked up his niece.

'Coco and I are going to the living room to watch the rugby. You two can carry on without us – I can see my advice is totally wasted on you.'

Caroline watched her brother walk out of the room before turning to Faye, all trace of humour gone from her face. 'Seriously, Faye, what are you going to tell Rocky? What do you want to do?'

Faye sighed and raked her hands through her hair, leaving the ends sticking out awkwardly. 'Caro, you know what, I've gone back and forth on this in my head and it always comes back to the same thing. What I want is... is... I want to matter. Before I met Rocky, there was Michael. I finished with him because I knew I didn't mean that much to him – as a cultural project, yes, but not as a girlfriend. You remember what I was like when I was with him; I let him make all the decisions and just put up with it. I can't keep making the same mistakes! I know Rocky cares about me but to be honest, it just feels like he's used to having me around and that he takes me for granted. It's not just the fact that he never says he loves me. I just don't feel like I really matter to him.'

She ticked off the list on her fingers as she carried on heatedly. 'His work is always more important than spending time with me – I can't count the number of times he hasn't showed up to something when he promised he would. He's never said a word about our future together; he was horrified when I told him Lucinda was having twins and made some comment about being glad it wasn't him; and then, when he's asked point blank, he doesn't even admit that he's in a relationship!'

Caroline didn't interrupt and Faye's voice rose in agitation. 'I mean, look at what's just happened! His father's seriously ill and he practically bundled me onto the plane instead of wanting me to be there to support him. The way he spoke to me, you'd think that I caused his father's collapse!'

At this, Caroline interjected hastily. 'Faye, I think you're reading this all wrong! Yes, he flew off the handle, but he was just really worried about his dad. Of course, it's not your fault. You couldn't have changed anything – even if you had told him about seeing his father in agony that night, what difference could it possibly have made?'

'I know. But I really wish now that I had woken him – in fact, all of them – that night. At least then he wouldn't have an excuse to be so angry with me.'

'What are you going to say when he comes back to London? You can't continue like this, surely?'

Faye shook her head slowly. 'No, I don't think it's fair on either of us. I love him... I really do, but it's not enough.'

Her friend smiled faintly and tucked a stray red curl back into her bun. 'Before you start getting all Tina Turner-ish about this, can I just say that love has got everything to do with it? Whether he says the words or not, I know Rocky loves you, but perhaps you need to think about the mixed messages you're sending him. To be fair, you haven't exactly been forthcoming about how you feel and what you want from him, so how can you decide for him what he wants without giving him the chance to tell you that himself?'

Caroline shook her head. 'Okay, now I've confused myself. But you know what I mean!'

Faye smiled half-heartedly, but Caroline hadn't finished. 'What was it you told me that Amma said about

351

him? That sometimes being damaged shows up in other ways? Don't you think that's true about you as well?'

'How do you mean?' Faye frowned in confusion.

Caroline sat down and looked directly at her friend for a long moment, and then said calmly, 'Sometimes when you think you've learned a lesson, maybe you really haven't. You let things drift with Michael for so long because you thought having him was better than being on your own. I've heard you say how you feel about Rocky, but nothing about what you are going to do about it. I know it's not exactly the same but you've let Rocky get away with murder sometimes and it's like you're still waiting for something to happen to you rather than taking a stand for what you want. Isn't that also what you did with Michael?'

Faye opened her mouth to protest and then shut it again, weighing Caroline's words carefully.

'I hate it when you're right and in some ways I have put up with a lot of crap because I don't want to lose Rocky. But to be honest, Caro, I don't want to go down that road again of being with someone for the sake of it and then losing who I am in the process. I don't want to be that girl anymore.'

'So, what are you going to do about it?' Caroline repeated.

22

Change of Heart

The question was still reverberating around Faye's head as she sat in her cubbyhole of an office at Cayhill's a few days later. It was one thing to make brave declarations of emotional independence and quite another to figure out how to execute them.

She tapped a pencil against the blank sketch pad in front of her, for the first time seeing the patterns of her own behaviour as clearly as if she was standing outside herself looking in. Although Rocky's innate kindness and generosity was light years away from Michael's self-centred and patronising attitude, she couldn't deny that his forceful personality, good looks and easy charm had blinded her to her own needs in a bid to keep him happy... or just to keep him.

She picked up her phone and re-read Amma's text, not sure how to feel about Rocky being back in London. A week without contact while he was in Ghana had saved her from making any decisions. But knowing that he was back – and no doubt back at work, she thought sourly –

she couldn't put things off much longer. If she was ever going to be brave enough to change the pattern, it had to be now.

Change certainly seemed to be in the air – and not just for her. Despite herself, Faye smiled at the memory of the scene she had walked into the day before.

With the cold November days bringing a sharp nip to the air, she had stopped at home on her way from work to pick up a scarf before carrying on to see her brother and Lucinda. Hearing male voices in the kitchen, she had walked straight into a most curious tableau.

'Ah, Faye! Good evening, my dear.' Her father was sitting at the kitchen table holding a loosely bound sheaf of papers. He removed his tortoiseshell glasses and gestured to the man sitting across from him.

'You know our neighbour, don't you?'

Faye kissed her father and looked with amusement at the actor who was becoming a regular fixture in their kitchen. She gave him a nod of greeting which he returned with a bright smile.

Her father cleared his throat. 'Yes, well, Mr Malone—'

'Sam,' came the helpful interjection.

'Yes, er... Sam. Sam is auditioning for a role as a doctor and wants my advice on some of the technical points of his character's development.'

In spite of his carefully modulated tone, she could tell instantly that her father was bursting with excitement. Only those close to him knew that Dr. Bonsu was an avid film buff, and the idea of contributing his medical expertise to a movie was bound to be irresistible. Struck by a sudden suspicion, she looked sharply at the actor.

'Is that the part you mentioned some time ago, Sam – the one about the ageing Romeo? Is he a doctor, then?'

'If needs be,' Sam replied laconically, his cornflower-blue eyes wide with innocence. He glanced at Lottie who, to Faye's astonishment, promptly flushed a fiery red.

'Oh,' Faye said. 'Ohh…!' she repeated, as comprehension dawned. Of course! Anyone who wanted to be with Lottie would first have to get past her very protective boss. *I wonder who came up with this sneaky idea,* she thought in reluctant admiration. Looking at her star-struck father, it was patently obvious to her that Sam would now have the run of the house.

Doing her best to hide her amusement, she turned back towards the door. 'Okay, well I'll leave you to your male bonding, Dad; I'm heading off to see Lucinda so we can have a good honest catch-up.'

She looked pointedly at Lottie, who had the grace to look abashed. With a hurried goodbye, her father eagerly returned to the script in front of him. 'Right, Sam. Now, in this scene where you enter the operating theatre, you need to remember that…'

The peremptory knock on her office door startled her out of her reverie and she sat up hastily as Ruth glared at her from the doorway.

'I do hope I'm not interrupting anything important,' she said, her voice dripping with sarcasm. 'If you need another holiday to recover from the last one…'

'Oh no, sorry,' Faye muttered, wishing the ground would open up and swallow her. Curious about what the great Ruth Wendell, who rarely ventured into the lowly junior designers' section, was doing there, she hurriedly turned over the blank sketch pad and looked attentive.

'Right. I've just had a call from Harriet. She can't come over here for the final project meeting because she's "about to burst."' Ruth rolled her eyes and raised her hands to draw air quotes. 'But she wants to go over a couple of last minute things with someone from the team and has asked you to go and see her.'

Faye was bewildered. 'Why me? She's been dealing mostly with Harvey for the past few weeks; he's more up to speed on where things are at the moment than I am.'

Ruth's snort suggested that she thought exactly the same thing. 'Yes, well ours is not to reason why. When our biggest client says she wants to see you, all we ask is "When?"'

'When?'

'Are you deliberately trying my patience?' Ruth growled. 'Now!' She turned on her heel and marched off, her short body quivering with irritation.

Faye grimaced and reached for her bag and a notebook. She rang Harvey's extension hoping to get an update on any issues with the almost completed baby haven, but it went straight to voicemail. She left a hurried message asking him to call her back, snatched up her mobile and jacket and made her way out of the office towards the tube station. She briefly considered hailing a cab and then dismissed the idea, reluctant to test Ruth's uncanny knack for spotting what she considered unnecessary expenses.

A little under an hour later, Faye walked into Harriet's suite of offices just in time to see Jessica slipping on her jacket and looking uncharacteristically harassed.

'Oh, Faye, go on in. She's having a quiet lie-down for a few minutes, but she is expecting you.'

At Faye's enquiring look, the PA grimaced. 'I've got to rush home to let the plumbers in – my neighbour's just rung to say there's a leak coming from my flat down into hers. Please tell Harriet I'll be back as soon as I can!'

With that, she grabbed the bag dangling from the back of her chair and dashed out.

Faye clutched her notebook to her chest and marched up to the solid oak door of Harriet's office. She knocked tentatively and hearing nothing, knocked again more firmly. Instead of the usual brisk 'Come in,' the sound of a muffled groan was the only response. Alarmed, she pushed open the door and stood horrified as she saw Harriet bent over on all fours on the soft pile rug by the sofa. Whatever was taking place, it was clearly not the quiet lie-down that Jessica had described.

'Oh my God! Are you okay?' She rushed forward in a panic and stopped as Harriet looked up at her, breathing heavily. The impeccably made-up face of the cosmetics queen was ashen and streaked with perspiration, and she glared at Faye through mascara smudged eyes, her words coming out in short bursts.

'Do I look okay?' She tried to heave herself back onto the sofa and groaned again. Panting heavily, Harriet gasped, 'Call… Jessica. She knows… what… to do!'

Faye stared at the woman on the floor in dismay. 'She's just left,' she stammered. 'She said something about a flood in her flat.'

Harriet's face turned even paler and she whimpered softly. 'Damn it! I thought... the pain would die down if I gave it a few minutes. Oh my God... this hurts so much!'

'Is the baby coming already?' Faye asked urgently. 'I'll call an ambulance. Try to relax.'

Harriet nodded and inhaled deeply, visibly trying to keep calm. Faye ran to the desk and dialled the emergency services, quickly spelling out the nature of the problem and the office address. She slammed the phone and rushed back to where Harriet had managed to prop herself up against the sofa, one hand rubbing her large bump protectively.

'Can I call one of your staff?' Faye asked. Although anxious about leaving Harriet alone, she was also conscious that there were people outside the executive suite who should know what was going on.

Harriet shook her head decisively. 'No! I don't want anyone to see me like this. Call down to the ground floor reception desk and tell them to let me know when the ambulance gets here. You'll have to help me downstairs – we can take the lift at the back for privacy.'

Faye nodded, not about to argue with a woman in her condition. Hanging up the phone after passing on Harriet's instructions to a curious receptionist, she asked, 'Is there anyone else I can call? What about your husband?'

Harriet groaned again and Faye snatched a clean tissue from her handbag and wiped the woman's damp brow.

After a moment, Harriet took a deep breath and exhaled noisily. 'No, don't bother. What's the point? He's made it perfectly clear that he doesn't care!'

Faye crouched down next to Harriet who continued taking long deep breaths and short pants with each contraction. Struck by the fact that she was sitting on the floor waiting for an ambulance for the second time in a matter of weeks, Faye tried to soothe the agitated woman, jumping to her feet the instant the phone rang.

'The ambulance is here; let me help you up.' She hoisted Harriet gently to her feet and stared at her doubtfully.

'Are you sure I shouldn't get someone from your office?'

Harriet closed her eyes and took another deep breath. 'No, absolutely not! I'm having a baby, not a heart attack, and there's nothing any of these people can do about that. I'll call Jessica when we get to the hospital. Pass me my mobile and my bag and we can take the service lift down to the lobby.'

Faye followed the instructions and then slung her own bag around her shoulders before walking slowly with Harriet out into the corridor. The area outside the executive suite was deserted and both women breathed a sigh of relief when the lift at the end of the corridor finally reached their floor. Faye punched the button and a few moments later, they were on the ground floor.

The doors slid open and a man and a woman in dark green scrubs waiting in the lobby rushed towards Harriet, who was now clutching her swollen belly and groaning in agony. The receptionists watched wide-eyed as the paramedics whisked her outside to the waiting ambulance and Faye climbed in, sitting quietly on the jump seat in the back while the female medic quickly examined Harriet and barked out instructions to her colleague. With sirens blaring, the ambulance shot off and Faye hastily strapped on her seat belt. As they sped through the streets, cutting through the mid-afternoon traffic, Harriet's groans intensified.

Faye leaned forward to pick up the mobile Harriet had dropped and looked uncertainly at the woman lying on the stretcher, now in far too much agony to make use of the canister of nitrous oxide and oxygen that the paramedic had administered to relieve her pain.

Without waiting to reconsider, Faye scrolled through the contacts list on the phone and punched the call button when she reached the name 'Jamie.' On the second ring, she heard a deep voice.

'Harriet?'

Faye glanced across at the owner of the phone and satisfied that she wouldn't hear her, whispered into the handset. 'Mr Woollaston, my name is Faye. I'm working on a project for your wife. Unfortunately, she seems to have gone into early labour. We're in an ambulance on our way to the Kensington Memorial Hospital. Can you get there as soon as possible?'

She had scarcely finished her sentence when she heard an abrupt 'I'm on my way' and the line went dead.

A few minutes later, the ambulance pulled up into a wide courtyard and the paramedics sprang into action. As soon as the doors opened, they gently lowered the trolley with Harriet onto the ground and sped through double glass doors into the emergency ward, leaving Faye to scramble after them, clutching bags, jackets, and Harriet's phone.

Faye was one of only a handful of people sitting in the Accident and Emergency waiting room when a solidly built man strode in. Faye stood up, immediately recognising him from the pictures she had Googled of him with Harriet. He hastened towards her, rubbing his full beard nervously. He had a thick head of chestnut brown hair with more salt than pepper and he stared at her intently.

'Faye?'

She nodded and held out a hand. He shook it with a firm grip and then looked past her. 'Where is she? Is Harriet all right?'

'They've taken her into the emergency labour ward – it's over that way.' She pointed down a corridor leading away from the reception desk.

'I'll go and find her. I'm really grateful to you for calling me.'

'Wait!'

He turned back, startled by the urgency in her voice.

'She doesn't know I called you – she didn't want me to because she said you wouldn't care.'

His thick eyebrows lowered into a deep frown and she hesitated. Then remembering the pain on Harriet's face when she had first confessed about her separation from her husband, she pressed on.

'Look, she thinks you hate her. She's going through a lot right now so if you're just going to upset her, then I don't think it's a good idea for you to go in there.'

She tried to sound firm although she was quaking inside and she held her breath with trepidation. Telling anyone's husband, never mind the great and powerful Harriet Woollaston's, that they should keep their distance from their pregnant wife was not something she was accustomed to doing, and she had no way of knowing how he was going to react.

James Woollaston gave an appreciative chuckle and looked at Faye properly for the first time. Taking in her anxious but defiant expression, he smiled and scratched his bearded chin ruefully.

'Thanks for the warning, Faye, but don't worry, I'm not going to upset her. I love the silly cow, but she's as stubborn as hell; always has been. The only reason we fell out is because she thinks she knows it all. She's even having a bloody crèche built at her office because she thinks she can just schedule appointments to see the baby between meetings!'

Faye flushed with guilty embarrassment and decided that it wasn't the best time to tell him that she was one of the designers of the 'bloody crèche.'

'I, for one, can't wait for her to have this baby and finally realise that she can't control everything in her life.' He chuckled and hurried off down the corridor.

Faye wandered slowly out of the hospital, feeling mentally drained by the drama of the last hour. She looked back wistfully at the imposing building. Somewhere up there, Harriet was bringing a new life into the world with her husband by her side. Once again, she felt the pang of desire for a child of her own with the man that she loved, a prospect that seemed to be growing more distant by the day.

It was too early to finish work and she reluctantly headed back to the office, bracing herself for Ruth's acerbic reaction to the cancelled meeting.

'Well, she can hardly blame me if the woman went into labour instead of giving me her feedback on the project,' she muttered under her breath as she marched past the security desk and headed for the lift, knowing full well that it was exactly what her boss was likely to do.

A quick chat with Chelsea confirmed that Ruth had left for an external meeting and thankful for the reprieve, Faye headed back to her office. Walking down the corridor, it dawned on her that she could simply tell Matt about Harriet and leave it to him to break the news to Ruth.

She turned round and walked back the way she had come. Deep in thought, she knocked on his office door and walked straight in, stopping short as both Matt and Mandy turned to glare at her.

This is becoming a very bad habit, was Faye's first thought as she took in Mandy's flushed cheeks and Matt's stormy eyes. They had obviously been arguing again and she hesitated for a moment before deciding to feign ignorance.

'...Erm, sorry to interrupt, but I thought you should know that Harriet's gone into labour. It happened while I was there, so I had to go with her in an ambulance to the hospital...' She tailed off as Matt's scowl morphed into an expression of complete horror.

'You're kidding! Is she okay? Are you okay? God, how awful for you!'

Faye backed away towards the door. Matt in over-protective mode was something she could do without. He had only just started treating her normally after the Justin fiasco and she didn't need him thinking she was some hothouse flower that needed protecting when she would far rather have him consider her as promotion material.

Out of the corner of her eye, she noticed Mandy surreptitiously wiping away a tear and sighing inwardly, she turned to leave. She later decided that she had either taken temporary leave of her senses or else was so fed-up with warring couples – even if one of them happened to include her boss – that she had to speak her mind.

As it was, the words tumbling out of her mouth seemed to take on a life of their own and she felt powerless to stop them.

'Okay, so this is none of my business but as I seem to have ended up playing cupid today, let me just say this.'

Sounding like an exhausted school principal, she launched into an extended rebuke. 'Mandy, you are obviously crazy about Matt and I think you would be perfect for him. Matt, you are obviously just as crazy about her and you need to stop denying it and sort this out. Whatever happened three years ago is clearly not history because looking at you both, whatever's going on is very definitely in the present. I've just spent the last two hours with a very scary and very stubborn multi-millionaire and all I know is that life is just too short for all this drama. If you didn't care about each other, you wouldn't be arguing all the time. So whatever your problem is, just sort it!'

With the two of them safely stunned into silence, Faye turned on her heel and left. She felt far too fired up to return to her office and didn't fancy sticking around in case Matt came seeking retribution.

She glanced at her watch and finally made the decision. It was time to deal with the other warring couple uppermost in her mind. The afternoon's events had given her the impetus to do what needed to be done and if she was honest, what she should have done a long time ago. With her mind made up, Faye was determined to take the bull firmly by the horns, and right away.

23

Confessions

Hurrying out of Canary Wharf tube station an hour later, she fought her way through the hordes of workers streaming in the other direction. Rocky's office was only a short walk away and in a few moments she was crossing the large foyer leading to the reception desk, her heels clicking lightly against the polished marble tiles.

The receptionist, a smartly dressed blonde in a dark grey suit, had a telephone headset clamped around her head and she touched the microphone to end her call, greeting Faye with a smile.

'Hi... erm, could you please give Rocky Asante a call for me?' Faye asked.

The receptionist took her name and tapped on the switchboard with perfectly manicured nails. After several rings, she shook her head and tried another number. After a short conversation with someone, she looked at Faye apologetically.

'I'm sorry, Madam, but apparently he's already left for the day.'

'Oh!' Faye said blankly. She hadn't even considered the possibility that Rocky wouldn't be at work. Now wishing she had called before heading over so impulsively, she turned and walked back slowly towards the revolving doors that led out to the street. She was reaching into her bag to retrieve her mobile when she heard her name.

'Faye?'

She stopped in her tracks and turned in surprise to find Yvette looking at her curiously.

'I was sure it was you! What are you doing here?'

Dressed in a fitted black suit that showed off her petite, curvaceous figure, Yvette's jet-black hair was smoothed back into an elegant chignon. Faye couldn't help glancing down at her own poppy print shift dress which suddenly seemed very frivolous compared with the other woman's serious suit.

'I was hoping to see Rocky,' she said shortly. *Why else would I have wandered into this massive, soulless building*, she thought, her irritation with the other woman rising.

'He left the office a few hours ago; I'm assuming he went home.' Yvette looked at her appraisingly and dropped the bulky briefcase she had been holding onto the marble floor. 'You look upset – is there something wrong?'

Torn between annoyance that her agitation was that obvious and incredulity that Yvette would imagine that she would confide in her if she did have a problem, Faye stared at her in silence. Then, not quite sure where the words were coming from, she heard herself answering.

'No. Well... yes.' She paused and took a deep breath. 'Look, I just need to speak to Rocky. I should have called first to check that he was still here...'

She tailed off as Yvette gestured towards the black chrome and leather seats in the waiting area.

'Why don't we sit down for a minute?' Her French accent sounded suddenly more pronounced and before Faye could respond, Yvette picked up her briefcase and walked over to the nearest seat. With little choice but to follow, Faye took the armchair next to the sofa where Yvette had perched; cringing at having to make conversation with the woman she was convinced had her sights set on her boyfriend.

Yvette leaned in towards her and with her face in such close proximity, Faye could see the lines radiating from her dark eyes, their elongated shape emphasised by thick eye liner. Seen up close, she was older than Faye had initially assumed and now seemed more likely to be in her late thirties or even older.

The silence stretched out but Faye was determined not to be the first to speak. *I didn't ask for this little tête-à-tête*, she thought moodily. *If she's got something to say, she can damn well spit it out without my help.*

Yvette cocked her head to one side. 'You are probably wondering why I think that you being upset is any of my business, no?'

It was patently clear that it was exactly what Faye was thinking and Yvette smiled, her ruby lips parting to reveal evenly spaced white teeth.

Even her teeth are perfect, Faye noted abstractedly.

'I don't blame you; although I have worked with Rocky for some time, it's not like you and I have become friends now, is it?'

Faye shrugged, wondering where this was leading. She looked around at the procession of tired workers pushing through the electronic turnstile by the reception desk to head home and tried to calculate how long it would take her to get back onto the tube and over to Rocky's flat. She was intent on finally having the long awaited showdown and the last thing she needed was his disturbingly attractive colleague distracting her from her mission.

Undeterred by Faye's impatient fidgeting, Yvette didn't speak for a moment and her eyes narrowed thoughtfully as she took in the emotions flitting across Faye's revealing features.

'I know you don't like me very much, Faye. No—' She raised her hand as Faye snapped to attention and attempted a feeble protest. 'No, really, I can understand it. After all, I spend a good deal of time with your man and I am involved in the work he does and for which he has so much passion, is that not so?'

It was indeed so, and Faye stayed silent, waiting to see what was coming. When she continued, Yvette's voice was unexpectedly gentle.

'While it is correct that your relationship is not my business, I have grown very fond of Rocky and I feel I must say something.'

Her heart beating loudly in her chest, Faye stared at the woman sitting opposite her, a feeling of dread settling on her like a heavy blanket. Then in a sudden rush of fury and oblivious to the curious stares from some of the people walking past, she leaned forward with her eyes locked on Yvette's, almost spitting out her words.

'What exactly do you mean by that?'

Undaunted, Yvette smiled. 'Not what you are thinking, if I am to judge by your expression. My English, perhaps, is still not so good.'

She sighed. 'Faye, I do not have bad intentions here. Rocky has been very kind to me, and also to my family. I don't know whether he told you that he helped my husband to find another job after he was made redundant? Jean-Bernard had grown very depressed and Rocky used his personal contacts to help him. To tell you the truth, it saved our marriage.'

'Oh...' Like a birthday balloon punctured by a curious child, Faye's rage subsided and she sat back in her chair, stupefied. Yvette was married?

She felt even more deflated when she glanced surreptitiously at Yvette's left hand and noted the slim silver band on her third finger. Groaning silently at her own stupidity, she smiled weakly at the other woman, who laughed softly. But there was no malice, only amusement, as she watched Faye struggle to find words.

'I see Rocky didn't tell you about that. Why does that not surprise me? He is very... modest, no?'

That wasn't quite the word Faye would have used when she thought of the energy she had expended on hating Yvette because Rocky hadn't seen fit to tell her the full story about his colleague.

'You could say that, I suppose. Or very un-communicative.'

Yvette's shrug was typically Gallic. 'Sometimes it is better when people do not say everything that they do, is it not? I asked you to speak with me because I think it is the case that you and Rocky are experiencing some... difficulties, shall we say?'

Faye stared at her through narrowed eyes, her relief short-lived as the other woman ventured once again onto dangerous terrain.

'I cannot tell you what to do, but I think you should realise that Rocky has been quite unhappy since his return to work. I know that his father has not been well, but I think there is more to it than that.'

Faye didn't hide her scepticism. 'If Rocky is unhappy, I can assure you that it's not because of me. It's more likely to be about some deal he's working on that isn't going according to plan!'

A flash of irritation crossed Yvette's face. 'Faye, I do not know you well, but I can assure you that Rocky is totally devoted to you.'

'Really?' Faye couldn't help the note of bitterness that crept into her voice. 'And what exactly gives you that assurance, Yvette? It surely can't be all the time that he spends with me or the messages that he asks you to deliver when he can't be bothered to pick up the phone and call me himself?'

'Faye, what I know is that there is a certain level of dedication required to be successful in particular jobs, and Rocky's is one of them. It is very hard to explain this to people who do not work in our industry but he carries a lot of responsibility and it can be very tough – and sometimes, I would add, very lonely – at that level. You should realise that if you are not prepared to concede a little and to give

371

him what he needs, someone else will!'

'Are you suggesting that Rocky would cheat on me? Because if that's what you believe, you don't know him as well as you think you do,' Faye retorted defiantly.

'Cheating isn't always about sex, you know.' Yvette eyed her shrewdly. 'It can also be about intimacy. Ask yourself how much he talks with you and shares with you? What do you know of his work and the pressures he is under? Have you given him the attention you say you need for yourself?'

Faye shifted uncomfortably under Yvette's scrutiny, but said nothing.

Yvette shrugged. 'I can understand the frustration you feel – Jean-Bernard also becomes annoyed at the long hours I have to keep in my job, not to mention the constant travel. But Faye, this is what Rocky's job demands. In our business we don't get the luxury of regular hours every day and that is part of the reason why we are paid so much. But as long as he is in this job, this is his life – if you don't accept it, I don't see how your relationship can survive.'

Faye stared down at her hands, her eyes blurring as the truth hit home. Yvette was right; it was always going to be Rocky's job versus her and whatever dreams she had for a life with him. Even if Yvette was no longer a rival, she thought, her boyfriend's job was never going to take a back seat.

Faye blinked rapidly and then looked up, forcing a smile as she saw the concern on Yvette's face. She stood up and stuck out her hand.

'It was good to chat to you but I'd better get going.'

372

The tube ride to Rocky's flat took less than an hour and caught up in the crush of commuters heading home on a Friday evening, she was forced to stand for most of the journey. Lost in thought, she punched in the door code when she reached his apartment block and walked slowly up the stairs, her nervousness increasing with each step. She scrabbled in her bag for the key she had used so rarely in recent months, slightly surprised that it was still there.

As soon as she pushed open the door, she heard the strains of Rocky's favourite jazz band coming from the living room and she walked down the corridor, stopping in the doorway. Rocky looked up in surprise from where he lay on the sofa, his head propped up on a throw cushion. Caught off-guard, he looked tired and drained of his usual energy and vitality.

'I didn't hear you come in.' He spoke softly, his voice barely audible above the music.

She walked into the room, slipped off her coat and tossed it over the back of an armchair. Shifting his legs to make room for her at the end of the sofa, he picked up the remote control lying next to him and turned down the volume of the music.

Smiling faintly, she faced him squarely. Although it was less than two weeks since she had left Ghana, it felt like an age since she had seen him, and even longer since they had been alone without someone or something interrupting.

'How's your father?' she asked.

He grinned and for a brief moment she caught a glimpse of the old Rocky.

'Extremely vocal, so he's definitely getting better. He came home a few days ago but the doctors are taking regular blood tests to check that the infection doesn't recur. Dr Kankam is keeping a close eye on him and even my mother is finally starting to relax.'

Faye listened silently, thankful to hear that Uncle Fred was safely on the mend. She drew her legs up under her and said casually, 'I've just been to your office; I thought you would be at work.'

'I left early for a meeting.'

'Oh.'

'Well, actually it was more of an interview.'

'What kind of interview?' Her mind flew to the television programme Caroline had mentioned, and which her friend had jubilantly reported that he had agreed to do.

'It was with an investment company I've been talking to; they're interested in me joining them. Marcus knows the partners well and I think it would be a good move, particularly as my London contract is about to expire.'

Faye looked as stunned as she felt and it took a minute before she could gather her thoughts into a coherent sentence. 'So you went for a job interview and didn't see any reason to talk to me about it beforehand?'

'Faye, you're the reason I'm talking to them in the first place.' Rocky sat up and crossed one leg underneath him, his copper-brown eyes fixed on her indignant face. 'We obviously can't go on like this. I know you resent my work but there are limited options for moving out of investment banking at my level. Even if I switched to another bank, it wouldn't make any difference to my lifestyle. So unless I move to another type of firm, nothing's going to change. That's why I'm talking to these guys about a partnership. It's a niche business with fewer and more select clients and with the network I've built up and my client base, particularly after the LaserTech transaction, I can bring a lot to a private investment consultancy. The deals won't be as big but as a partner, I'll have much more independence and a bigger percentage of the rewards. I'll still have a busy job – I won't lie – but there's a lot less travel involved and I – we – will be able to have more time together.'

'But... but why haven't you said anything about all this? I had no idea you were even thinking about leaving the bank!'

'I didn't want to get your hopes up in case things didn't pan out. The board has been pressuring me to sign an extension to my contract, which I didn't want to do until I'd exhausted all my other options, so Marcus' advice to talk to Jensen Capital made a lot of sense.'

His expression was fast changing into one of suppressed impatience as it became apparent that her reaction to his news was not what he had anticipated.

Faye stretched her legs out in front of her and tried to gather her thoughts. On one hand, the fact that Rocky was actually willing to move jobs in order to have more time for her was good, no great, news. On the other hand, she couldn't fight the nagging sense of disappointment that he hadn't confided his thoughts and plans sooner. Once again he had turned to someone else for counsel rather than her and much as she tried to appreciate him wanting to protect her from disappointment if a job offer didn't materialise, she also couldn't help feeling resentful at being treated like a sheltered child instead of an equal and trusted partner.

'Rocky, I'm not saying changing jobs is a bad idea. I just wish you had shared what you were considering with me and actually included me in your decision making, instead of telling me what you've decided after the fact. How do you think that makes me feel?'

'I can't win with you, can I?' He sighed and shook his head slowly. 'You want me to share stuff with you, but how do you expect me to do that when you don't want to hear about my work and push me away all the time? When was the last time you even came over here? How do you expect me to confide in you when I don't know if you're going to be around from one moment to the next?'

She gasped at the unfairness of his accusation. 'Do you know what it's been like for me? You're on a plane to New York or Frankfurt or Johannesburg half the time! When you are here, all you've cared about is your job—'

'Life hasn't exactly been a bed of roses for me, you know,' he cut in bitterly. 'I've felt all alone out here but I didn't take that out on you. I know you don't give a damn about my job, but I thought you at least cared about me.'

She flinched as the accusation about his job hit home, but she steamed ahead regardless.

'I do care about you – but I'm not the one who doesn't have the time to invest in this relationship, the one who cancels our plans and drops me at a moment's notice! I'm not the one who literally brings work home and thinks there's nothing wrong with having a late night meeting in my house with a sexy colleague. I mean, really, where was the next merger going to take place? In your bedroom?'

'Don't be ridiculous,' he snapped impatiently. 'You know me better than that!'

'But that's the thing, Rocky; do I? You give more of yourself and your time to everyone else than to me. Marcus is the one you turned to about this job situation and William knows far more about what's going on with you than I do! Even Caro's got you roped into her TV series. So where do I fit in?'

'Come on, Faye,' he protested hotly. 'Don't you think you're exaggerating? I admit it hasn't been perfect, but I've always tried to be there for you.'

'Really? Is that what you tell yourself, that you've always been there for me? So where exactly were you when that pig Justin Parker tried to force himself on me?' she lashed out.

His eyes darkened in anger. 'What are you talking about? When did that happen – I'll kill the bastard!'

She laughed mirthlessly. 'Well, it's a bit late now. And when I came to see you to tell you about it and to say sorry for having been so distant towards you, what did I find? You and your work colleague—' she stressed the words, 'all cosied up and without a care in the world.'

She watched the comprehension dawning in his eyes and he fell silent. After a moment, he spoke quietly. 'That's not fair. I had no idea and no way of knowing what had happened to you. I tried to stop you leaving and explain to you that we were on a deadline to get a proposal to a new client by the next day, but you didn't stay to listen.'

'The same way that you thought it was reasonable for me to stay and listen to you talking to another woman who had crashed our date?'

'Faye, that LaserTech merger was the biggest transaction I've ever been involved in and I was the lead for the team. Everything – my reputation, my future at the bank – was riding on that deal. Everyone had warned me that it was impossible and to leave it alone, but I knew I could get Marshall Alexander to sign onto the merger. And if it meant—'

She finished his sentence for him. '—if it meant never spending any time with me and always putting me – us – second, then it was a choice you were ready to make. Just like all the times you've made the choice to cancel dinners, forgotten to show up for appointments or rushed us through a meal because you want to get back to the office. Even getting you to spend time with me when we were on holiday was a problem. I'm a person, too, Rocky! I have my own needs and desires, not that you would know that. Because for you, it's a case of never mind my feelings and what I want or need; work always comes first, isn't that right?'

'Faye, what exactly is it that you want me to say?' His tone was mild and reasonable and totally enraged her.

'What is it that I want you to say?' She looked at him, her eyes wide with a fury born of pent-up frustration. Aware that she probably looked as crazy as he was driving her, she practically hissed at him.

'Let's play charades, then, Rocky! Three words. One syllable each. Any guesses?'

He looked at her and there it was; the look. The blank expression that told her that he had disengaged and retreated into his inner castle and that she was wasting her time. As quickly as it had flared, her anger abated, leaving only a tired little piece of barely glowing coal at its core as the energy in her died. There, you've done it. You've managed to push him away and now it's over.

'You can't do it, can you?' She stared at him challengingly. There was nothing else to lose now, she decided, so why hold back. 'Why is that, Rocky? Why can't you say those words to me?'

His expression didn't waver and he could have been carved from the very substance that was his name. Only a twitch of the muscle by his jaw proved that he was human and was able to hear her. The music playing in the background stopped but neither of them noticed.

'Is it because of Celine?'

Did he flinch, or did she imagine it? Still he said nothing and then, like a dam bursting its banks, she lost all restraint. 'You wanted us to talk? So, let's talk! It is Celine, isn't it? You've never been able to say those words to me because you said them to her and she broke your heart.'

Tears were streaming down her face and she dashed them away impatiently. She needed to say everything she had held back for months; no, if she was honest, for years.

'Faye, you need to stop. You don't know what you're saying,' he ground out, his eyes like flint.

'Really, why? Because I'm right, aren't I? You've never really gotten over her. Amma was right; you're still broken but I just couldn't see it. Instead of dealing with what she did by cheating on you, instead of feeling it, you've just hidden it all inside. She's still there between us, isn't she? You've never really let her go or let yourself deal with your feelings about her. Let's see, you don't smoke, you hardly drink, so did you hope that work would be your drug of choice to self-medicate? Is that why you can't bear to be away from your office for any length of time?'

'Faye, stop!' He was staring at her as if he had never seen her before.

She shook her head wildly, more sure than ever that she was right. 'No, Rocky, I won't stop! Because I'm right, and you're supposed to admit I'm right, not avoid the truth.'

He groaned and dropped his head between his hands, shaking his head from side to side.

She looked at him sadly. 'Let's face it, Rocky; you don't really see me as my own person, do you? I've just become some accessory for when you have the time or the inclination. You don't love me. Despite all the time we've been together – four whole years – you've never once said 'I love you' to me. What does that tell you?'

She stood and snatched up her coat, fresh tears flowing down her cheeks as she headed for the door.

'That it's not enough.' The words were muffled and spoken so quietly she could barely make them out.

She stopped and turned around. 'What?'

He raised his head and looked straight at her. 'It's not enough,' he repeated.

She looked at him blankly and he sighed deeply, rubbing a hand helplessly over his cropped hair.

'Faye, I don't say "I love you," I never thought I needed to say I love you, because it's not enough. Because it doesn't even begin to define how I feel about you; how much I need you and how my world makes no sense without you in it.'

His eyes raked over her shocked face. 'Faye, if it makes you happy, I will say "I love you" a million times a day. But if I haven't, it's not because I don't; it's because it's not enough and it will never be enough.'

He stood up and walked over to where she stood. He gently removed her coat from her nerveless fingers and pulled her into his arms. He buried his face in her hair, inhaling the scent of her perfume, and for a long moment neither of them spoke.

Faye pulled away first. He reached down and gently wiped away a tear clinging to her eyelashes.

'Please don't cry,' he whispered. 'I had no idea that you thought all those things. I don't love Celine; don't ever think that. Since the day I met you, it's been you, and only you.'

She tried to step away but he kept a tight grip on her. 'No, sweetheart, now you listen. You were right about one thing; I did think I was losing you. But instead of trying to talk to you about it, I did the only thing I could think of to keep you – work like a dog so I could prove that I was worthy of you.'

She frowned, but didn't interrupt as he continued. 'I don't have any feelings for Celine, I promise you. But it's been harder than I thought to forget the lesson she taught me. I was desperate to be a success; to show you that I could take care of you and to stop you leaving me, and instead I ended up pushing you away.'

She opened her mouth but couldn't find any words. He gave a short laugh. 'You know, sitting by my father's hospital bed made me realise that all the success in the world means nothing if you don't have someone who loves you by your side. When Dad came out of hospital, we talked on the phone for a long time. He was relieved that I'd finally seen sense and warned me to get my act together and fix things with you or not bother coming home again.'

She smiled properly for the first time that evening. *Trust Uncle Fred to tell it like it is*, she thought.

He sighed deeply and pulled her closer to his chest. She rested her cheek against him, feeling the familiar thud of his heartbeat against her ear. Her head swam with the revelations that had poured out of him. But mixed in with the comfort that he didn't have feelings for his ex-girlfriend was the fact that he had still made no reference to a longer-term future.

Knowing that he wasn't in love with Celine and hearing him finally say the words she had almost given up on was a huge relief – but was it enough? Was that really all that she had been waiting for?

She stepped back and looked at him, really studying him. She looked past his ridiculously handsome face, warm brown eyes and perfectly sculpted body. She looked at the beautiful man standing in front of her, the man who had finally declared his love for her, and at that moment, the words she had spoken to Caroline only a few days earlier sounded loudly in her head. Perfect as he was, Faye realised, for the first time, that she had a choice as to whether he was perfect for her. And having come this far, she knew she had to take the time to find out.

She reached up and kissed Rocky on the cheek and then bent to retrieve her coat.

'Where are you going?' He looked at her and his puzzled expression was reason enough for her to press on. If he still didn't get it, she thought, it was time to leave.

'You've told me everything that you want, Rocky, and I'm so glad you were honest with me.'

'So why are you going?'

She steeled herself against the hurt in his eyes and walked to the door. Turning round, she looked at him, a tremulous smile hovering around the edge of her full lips.

'I'm truly glad you opened up to me. I know you love me now and I know you want me. It took a while, but I also know that I don't have to be that girl, the one that just accepts what's on offer. You asked me once what I wanted and, to be honest, I couldn't have answered you then. How could I know what I want when I've always said yes to everything and never been brave enough to put my own needs first? I don't want to be that person any more. Because while everybody else seems to think they know what's best for me, I've never really asked myself that one very important question.'

He stared at her in stunned silence and she smiled sadly. 'Rocky, I have to go because I need time to figure out what I want before I know if I can give you what you're looking for.'

With that, she turned and walked out of the flat, closing the door gently but firmly behind her.

24

Moving On

Faye looked at the caller ID on her mobile, torn between rejecting the call or answering it and having to deal yet again with a plea to which she was powerless to respond. Gritting her teeth, she punched the green button and took a deep breath.

'Hi, Marcus.'

She listened patiently while her best friend's husband went through the daily litany of recounting his mother's latest phone call and tirade about her separation from her only granddaughter, finishing up with his usual entreaty. 'Faye, this can't go on. Please, talk to Caro again – you're the only one she listens to. It's not fair on Coco, either, to be deprived of her grandmother.'

Faye had been doodling absently on her sketch pad as she listened patiently to Marcus's plaintive tones. When he finally came to a stop, she suppressed a sigh and went through her own practiced routine.

'Marcus, I know this must be difficult for you, but your wife is as tough as they come. Rose really pushed her luck speaking to her the way she did – you know how sensitive Caro is about being seen as some kind of trophy wife or—'

'Yes, I know,' he broke in impatiently. 'My mother's not the most diplomatic person, I'll admit, but she has a good heart. I just wish Caro would see that instead of letting her wind her up her all the time. I can't always be around and—'

'—maybe, that's part of the problem,' Faye murmured, deviating from the script; interruptions could work both ways. There was a moment's silence and then Marcus spoke again.

'What do you mean?' He sounded wary and Faye sighed impatiently.

'Marcus, you know exactly what I mean! Okay, so Caro's taken things a bit far with banning Rose from the house but honestly, ask yourself why she's being so difficult about this. Maybe instead of just seeing this as her being stubborn, you should recognise that it's a cry for your attention.'

'Faye, both Caro and I are busy people...'

'Exactly, and that's my point,' Faye said with asperity. 'You both agreed to have a baby and to spend time together at weekends being full-time parents. The trouble is that you are never around and she feels like she's doing all the work by herself. Your mother criticising her parenting skills was the last straw and unless you recognise that you've got a part to play in all this, I can't persuade Caro to back down.'

She felt a pang of sympathy for Marcus, torn as he was between two equally strong-willed women. But it was high time he acknowledged his own contribution to the conflict that was threatening to tear his family apart. As much as Caroline pretended otherwise, Faye knew how upset she was about the rift with her mother-in-law, but she also knew that her friend was desperate to replicate the close family set-up she herself had known and always envisioned for her children; a vision that Marcus's increasingly frequent absences was close to sabotaging.

He sounded subdued when he eventually spoke. 'You're right, of course. I'll speak to Caro when I get home tonight; it's high time we sorted this out. My mother's in London for a few days so maybe I can get them to sit down together and put an end to this feud.'

Faye stayed silent and he continued. 'I'm sorry I've been putting all this on you, but I really love Caro and I can't bear to see her so miserable.' He gave a short laugh. 'And maybe it's the wake-up call my mother needed to stop her being quite so opinionated.'

Faye chuckled to herself; this was the first time Marcus had actually voiced any criticism of his mother, giving her hope that he noticed more than either she or Caroline had given him credit for.

'Anyway, that's enough about my troubles; how are you doing?' His voice softened and she knew instantly that he was referring to Rocky. She immediately suspected Caroline of revealing state secrets and then remembered that Marcus was independently in touch with her boyfriend – if indeed that was how she could still refer to him.

When she didn't immediately answer, Marcus pressed ahead. 'I know things aren't great between the two of you at the moment, but don't give up on him. You know he's taken the position with Jensen's, don't you?'

Faye didn't, not having spoken to him for two weeks, but she had to admit that she wasn't surprised. If, as Yvette had suggested, he had been that unhappy at the bank, it was probably time for him to make a change and attempt to find a more balanced life.

Before she could say so, there was a peremptory knock on her office door and Jojo stuck her head around, a look of apprehension on her pale face. Her silver piercings were in full array on both earlobes and the baggy black top she wore drooped over the top of skin-tight black jeans.

Raising an eyebrow at the panic on her colleague's face, Faye spoke hastily. 'Marcus, I need to go now. Let's speak later.' Without waiting for an answer, she punched the disconnect button and looked up at Jojo who had slipped into the room and was standing with her back against the closed door.

'What's going on?'

'Ruth's called a meeting in the boardroom at two thirty for the whole team, no exceptions. It's about the Woollaston project and she didn't sound happy. You weren't answering your phone so I thought I'd better let you know.'

Faye smiled gratefully; Marcus had been in full flow when her office phone had rung and she hadn't had the heart to cut him off.

'Thanks, Jojo, I appreciate that. I could do without Ruth tearing a strip off me for missing a three-line whip. Do you have any idea what's happening with the project?'

Jojo shook her head, her jet black hair tumbling over her shoulders. 'Not a clue. Harvey doesn't seem to know much either.' She lowered her voice to a whisper. 'The guys are taking bets that the project has been cancelled – apparently Harriet didn't finalise the paperwork before she went on maternity and no-one else knows what's going on.'

She looked at her watch and bit her lip anxiously. 'I'd better get back to my desk – I've got a couple of calls to make before the meeting starts!'

She disappeared, shutting the door behind her with a firm thud, and Faye sat for a moment reflecting on the latest from the rumour mill. Her eyes fell on the huge bouquet of flowers in the corner of her tiny office and she sniffed the fragrance appreciatively. The luxurious arrangement of pink roses and purple and white freesias studded with green fern and baby's breath looked almost as fresh as when it had arrived in a cut glass crystal vase three days earlier, causing a stir among Cayhill's staff. At first convinced that Faye had a secret lover, they were even more shocked to learn that the bouquet had been sent by a grateful Harriet Woollaston.

Even Ruth had been stunned into temporary silence by the note on the accompanying card which Faye had reluctantly handed over. 'With love from a very grateful Woollaston family.' It has been signed 'Harriet, James and baby Oliver.'

It had been a fortnight since her mercy dash to the hospital with Harriet and with no further word from the tycoon, work on the almost completed baby haven had come to an abrupt halt. Faye could only pray that the Woollastons' gratitude extended beyond a card and flowers; she couldn't begin to imagine Ruth's reaction if Cayhill's was to lose the cosmetics queen's account.

Her mobile buzzed again, vibrating against the wooden veneer of her desk. Faye looked at the screen in surprise and answered the call immediately. She knew Caroline was on a shoot and would never normally make a phone call.

'Faye, where are you?' Caroline sounded frantic.

'I'm at work. Why, what's wrong?'

'Oh my God, you were right about her! Look, can you get to my house right away and get that girl out of there?'

'Which girl?' For one brief moment, Faye wondered if Caroline had finally succumbed to the stress of recent events.

'Anastasia, of course!' The panic in Caroline's voice flooded down the phone line.

'Caro, calm down! What's going on? What's Anastasia done?'

She heard the sharp inhalation of breath as her friend struggled to keep her agitation under control. 'Sorry, I know I sound like a lunatic, but I need to make sure Coco's okay. I rang the nursery to tell them that she's not very well today and that Anastasia was watching her at home. It turns out the nursery sacked her months ago for neglecting some of the kids in her care. It seems she behaved appallingly to the children and she was only caught because of the security cameras. Apparently they only told the parents involved and kept it all hush-hush to save their reputation. But as soon as I said she was alone with Coco, Elaine spilled the beans and told me to get rid of her right away!'

Her voice started to rise again. 'Faye, I'm stuck out in bloody Hertfordshire supervising this shoot and even if I could leave right now, it would take me at least an hour to get home. I need to make sure my baby's safe! Please can you help me out?'

Faye looked at her watch, groaning inwardly. The Woollaston team meeting was in fifteen minutes and Ruth would personally slaughter her if she failed to attend. On the other hand, this was Caroline asking, and the person in possible jeopardy was her own adored god-daughter. Suddenly, the solution was obvious.

'Leave it with me, honey,' she said soothingly. 'Don't worry; I'll sort everything out. Just get back to work – I'll call you later on if there's anything to report.'

'Faye, you're the best friend ever!' The relief in Caroline's voice prompted a brief pang of guilt, but not enough to change her mind. She ended the call and scrolled through her list of contacts until she found the number she was looking for. She tapped on the phone before she could change her mind, and her call was answered almost immediately.

Faye took a deep breath. 'Mrs O'Neill? It's Faye here, Caroline's friend. We need your help.'

Ten minutes later, she scurried into the boardroom, her notebook in hand, praying that she had made the right decision. Although one tiny part of her acknowledged that she had been right to be suspicious of Anastasia, her overriding concern was that Rose would get there in time to ensure Coco came to no harm. How she would square the decision she had taken with Caroline was something she would have to face up to later. Having given Rose strict instructions not to let Anastasia out of her sight until reinforcements arrived, her plan was to escape from the office immediately after the team meeting and take over from Rose before Caroline returned home.

Although she was the first to arrive for the meeting, within a couple of minutes the other members of the project team trooped in. Looking solemn, Jojo had tied her hair back as a concession to the occasion, while Harvey, in black jeans ripped above the knee, wore a Black Sabbath T-shirt with a black hoodie and his usual deadpan expression. Nathan looked pale and fidgeted nervously with his glasses. Although never known to appear excited about anything, today he looked as if he was preparing for his own funeral. The other designers looked equally uneasy and Faye chewed on her lip anxiously, wondering what was coming.

They didn't have to wait long as Ruth strode into the boardroom, closely followed by Matt, both of them looking very serious. The team members looked at each other in alarm; it was highly unusual for one senior partner to attend the other one's team meetings. Something was clearly amiss.

Unaware that she had been holding her breath while the two directors sat at the head of the table, Faye eased the tight hold on her notebook and exhaled slowly in a bid to calm the nervous thudding in her chest. Ever since Cayhill's had resigned the Parker account, a move for which she still felt guilty despite the fact that Justin was the one who had behaved badly, she knew how important it was for the firm to have a client like Harriet Woollaston on its books. Even if the actual project wasn't exactly worth a fortune, the prestige of having such a high profile client would help draw other big name brands to their design consultancy. If Harriet had decided to pull the plug on the nursery project – and James Woollaston was clearly no supporter of the idea – it would leave Cayhill's in a precarious position.

Ruth cleared her throat and the room fell so silent that Faye was convinced everyone could hear the thump of her heartbeat. The senior partner's dark eyes scanned the anxious faces around the table, her impassive expression giving nothing away. She looked at Matt briefly before speaking.

'Right, well, let's get started. Thank you all for coming – I know it's short notice and that you're all busy.' She paused, and Jojo glanced at Faye as if to say, 'Did she actually think we had a choice?'

'As you all know, Harriet had her baby earlier than expected and, unfortunately, before she was able to feed back her comments and give the final sign-off on the crèche—'

'—baby haven,' Matt broke in absently.

Ruth fixed him with an impatient glance and repeated in an acerbic tone, '...baby haven. Well, Matt and I have just come back from a meeting with Harriet at her home and we both thought that we ought to let you know what's happening as soon as possible.'

His face ashen, Nathan gulped audibly and turned his glasses over and over between his damp hands. As the lead designers, he and Harvey had spent countless hours on the project and he was clearly dreading what was to come.

Ruth sighed. 'There's no easy way to say this, so I'll just spit it out. Harriet's decided that she no longer wants the crèche.' There was a collective gasp around the table and she held up her hand immediately to call for silence. 'Okay, let me rephrase that. Harriet doesn't want the crèche any longer for herself; she's going to take maternity leave for a bit like a normal person, and then leave her baby at home when she comes back to work. However, she does want us to complete the job so any staff members that want it for their kids can make use of it.'

Another collective sigh, this time of relief, went up and the team members grinned at each other. Nathan popped his glasses back on and scratched the bald patch at the back of his head, a wide smile making him look ten years younger.

Harvey was the first to voice the unspoken question. 'But if we're still going ahead with the crèche, why's Matt here?'

Ruth looked at Matt. 'Do you want to tell them or shall I?'

He grinned at her, his brown hair flopping into his navy blue eyes. 'Go right ahead; I think you've earned it.'

Faye and Jojo exchanged puzzled glances while the other team members looked expectantly at Ruth.

'Harriet says she's been really impressed by the talent and professionalism of our team and, of course,' Ruth paused to glance at Faye, 'we all know that Faye here practically delivered her baby.'

Faye squirmed as everyone's head spun in her direction but Ruth's flippant tone made it clear that she was joking. 'Anyway, the great news is that Woollaston Cosmetics is planning to open concessions in at least fifty major department stores around the country over the next three years and she's asked us to design the branding and architecture and to manage the installation in every single one of them!'

She looked around at the stunned faces staring back at her and broke into a grin. 'Yeah, magic, isn't it? We're going to have to get some more hands on deck and get started on this right away. Harriet's taking a couple of months off but we'll need to have something to show her when she's back in the office. So, well done, you lot – you've really brought home the bacon!'

Matt looked at the incredulous expressions around the table and burst into laughter. He started clapping and the rest of them joined in, dazed at the enormity of the job they had just landed.

Ruth stood up and signalled that the meeting was at an end and the team members scrambled to their feet and headed towards the door, laughing and chattering in excitement.

Ruth called out above the hubbub, 'Faye, could you stay for a moment?'

Faye turned back at the command, and sat down again. She watched with apprehension as Ruth closed the glass door and returned to her seat next to Matt. Ruth looked at her business partner and gestured. 'Okay, this time it's your turn.'

Matt ran his hands through his luxurious curls and turned his gaze fully onto Faye, and she bit her lip nervously. Mindful of the less than respectful haranguing she had delivered the day she stumbled into his office, she couldn't help the sudden feeling of trepidation. Matt had made no subsequent reference to her outburst and she had felt no desire to prompt him to do so, instead making sure to keep her head down and deal with the numerous design tasks assigned to her as speedily as possible. With no Rocky in her life and with Caroline busy filming her show, the extra work had proved a welcome distraction.

But Matt's lazy smile didn't suggest a man ready to take umbrage at being told what to do with his love life, and she was suddenly struck by the fact that he looked happier than she had ever seen him. She sat upright and waited with bated breath for hear what was on his mind.

'Faye, Ruth and I both felt that it was important to acknowledge the contribution that you've made to Cayhill's,' he said. 'You've done an amazing job since you joined us and your contribution to the Parker account was invaluable – even though I know you had to deal with some unwarranted unpleasantness from Justin in the process.'

She grimaced but didn't interrupt. 'Harriet singled you out for praise – and not just because you almost delivered her baby!' He grinned at Ruth, who had scowled at the mention of Justin's name, and she relaxed and returned his smile.

'Anyway, both Ruth and I agree that we want to recognise this with a promotion for you. It's not huge, but it does come with a bump in salary. So, with immediate effect, instead of Junior Designer, your new title is Design Consultant. Congratulations, you're now a fully fledged interior designer!'

Faye stared in disbelief at the two people in front of her and the grin that appeared on her face was so wide she thought her cheeks would crack.

'Oh my God! Seriously?' She jumped up from the table, far too agitated to sit still. Clutching her notebook to her chest, she gave a squeal of excitement and literally jumped into the air.

'Omigod, omigod, omigod...! I can't believe it!'

Ruth turned to Matt, a wry smile on her face. 'I think we can safely assume that she's happy.'

Faye just about managed to restrain herself from racing around the polished oak table to hug them, and instead she backed away towards the door, grinning and babbling incoherently.

'Omigod! Thank you so much! I can't believe it...'

She ran out of the room and skipped across the deserted reception area with a loud whoop, causing Chelsea's mouth to drop open in stunned surprise.

25

To the Rescue

Faye raced back to her office and seized her phone to call Rocky, then sobered up rapidly as she remembered her self-imposed period of reflection. She was about to tap Caroline's number when it hit her that she had almost forgotten about the mission she had entrusted to Rose.

Cursing under her breath, she grabbed her coat, snatched her bag from under her desk and raced out of the building to catch a taxi to Fulham. Thanking her lucky stars for a cabbie that seemed to know every back street in West London, Faye tipped him generously when he screeched to a halt outside Caroline's house and then ran up the path to press frantically on the doorbell.

Within seconds, the front door was flung open and Rose O'Neill stood inside the doorway, breathing hard. Framed against the brightly lit hallway, she stood tall; her legs slightly apart, with her hands planted firmly on her hips. For a moment, she looked ready to breathe out flames.

'I did exactly as you said, Faye,' she declared triumphantly. 'I've got her in the sitting room – although the slippery madam has tried a couple of times to escape. In the end, I threatened to call the police if she so much as made a move near the door again!'

Faye hurried in, rather more alarmed at the fire dragon that Rose appeared to have morphed into than pale, shaken Anastasia corralled in the living room under threat of imminent arrest. Whatever fears she had harboured during her mad taxi ride were dashed as she saw the subdued nanny huddled in the corner of the sofa, visibly terrified of Coco's grandmother.

'Where's Coco?' Faye demanded, her eyes darting around the empty room. Anastasia cast a wary glance at Rose and then stammered nervously.

'She's taking a nap upstairs in her room. I gave her some medicine like her mum said, and she's been asleep for ages.'

'Well, you'd better hope that she is fine when she wakes up, you deceitful creature!' Rose advanced menacingly towards the girl who cowed back against the cushions.

'...Erm, Mrs O'Neill, I think we can let her go now,' Faye intervened hastily, keen to avoid any bloodshed. After her prolonged separation from her beloved grandchild, Rose was looking a little too ready to unleash her suppressed grandmaternal instincts on any potential threat to the baby.

'Humph!' Rose glared at the nanny but stepped back and allowed the girl to gingerly peel herself off the sofa and edge out of the room. Once she was past Rose, Anastasia sped out of the front door, stopping only to snatch her red padded jacket from the table in the hallway.

There was a moment's silence after the door banged behind the fleeing child minder and then Rose grinned, a sight that a startled Faye was not used to seeing.

'There! After today, I don't think that little minx will dare to try and work with children again.'

Dumbstruck, Faye nodded, not quite sure what to do next. Rose had no such inhibitions.

'Since Camilla's still asleep, I'll put the kettle on and make us both a nice cup of tea!'

Although she would have much preferred coffee, Faye prudently kept silent and followed Marcus's mother through to the kitchen, watching silently while the older woman poured water into the kettle and retrieved mugs and a teapot, humming cheerfully all the while.

'I am so glad you telephoned me, Faye. I knew Caroline would come to her senses. It's just such a pity that it's taken so long,' she said, pouring the freshly boiled water into the teapot and setting it on the kitchen table before settling herself comfortably on a chair. She gestured to the chair across from her and Faye dutifully sat down.

'Shall I play mother?' Rose asked cheerfully. Without waiting for a response, she filled both mugs with what appeared to be very weak tea. Faye reluctantly reached for the one that Rose had pushed in front of her. She shook her head at the offer of milk and gingerly sipped the tasteless brew, wondering how to get Rose out of the house before her friend returned. While she had every intention of eventually confessing the truth to Caroline, she needed time to plan her explanation for inviting the enemy onto home soil. Unfortunately, Rose was no Anastasia who could be summarily evicted and judging by the relaxed manner with which she was sipping her tea, she clearly had no intention of leaving anytime soon.

'Mrs O'Neill, thank you for getting here so quickly.' Faye put her mug down on the table and picked her words with care. 'As I said on the phone, I was called into an urgent meeting at work but Caroline sounded so frantic that there was no way that I could leave Anastasia alone with the baby.'

Rose nodded thoughtfully and took another sip of tea without comment. Faye cleared her throat and tried again.

'So the thing is, I didn't actually tell Caro that I was going to call you—' She broke off abruptly at the sound of the front door slamming.

'Faye? Where are you?' Caroline's anxious voice wafted through the open kitchen door.

Faye flushed guiltily and looked across at Rose who seemed completely unperturbed as she continued to sip her tea.

'Mrs O'Neill, please... let me do the talking...'

Seconds later Caroline rushed into the kitchen and stopped dead as she took in the unlikely sight of her estranged mother-in-law calmly taking tea with her best friend.

'What's going on here?' she demanded, her face turning as red as the dishevelled curls spilling over the collar of her navy coat. Her blue eyes wide with incredulity, she glared at Rose and then at Faye.

'Where's Coco?'

Rose pushed back her chair and stood up, her voice

soothing and surprisingly gentle. 'She's perfectly fine and is fast asleep upstairs. Now, Caroline, you really mustn't worry; we managed to get rid of that ghastly girl and Faye did absolutely the right thing in calling me.'

Faye groaned silently. *Which part of 'Let me do the talking' had not been clear?*

Caroline's eyes widened even further.

'Faye called you?' She croaked out the words in disbelief and turned her ire back onto her friend. Faye raised an apologetic hand but the sound of a loud wail coming from the floor above interrupted her attempts to calm the situation. Still remarkably calm in the face of Caroline's obvious fury, Rose clapped her hands together.

'Oh, Camilla's awake at last! Let me go and see to her while you and Faye have a nice little chat.' She turned back as she reached the door. 'Oh, and Caroline, there's still some tea in the pot. You must be parched after working all day.'

Caroline stood open-mouthed as Rose hurried up the stairs and then she exhaled heavily, clearly at a loss for words. She unbuttoned her coat and sat down on the chair her mother-in-law had just vacated and stared helplessly at Faye.

'What just happened? Is that woman for real? Faye, why the hell did you call her when you know how—'

'Whoa, hold on a minute, Caro!' Faye pushed her mug aside impatiently and leaned forward to look her friend dead in the eye. 'Look, when you called, I had to go to a team meeting and I couldn't just leave that girl alone with Coco. I understand that Rose is not exactly your favourite person right now, but I knew she was in London and that she'd be able to get here before either of us.'

Caroline hesitated and Faye plunged on. 'Honestly, talk about Rose to the rescue; you should have seen her when I got here! I actually felt sorry for Anastasia – the woman was practically about to wring her neck.'

Caroline smiled reluctantly. 'She can be rather a force of nature when she wants to be.' She sighed and stood up to struggle out of her coat. Opening the cupboard, she brought out a mug and sat down again, filling it with the remaining tea from the pot. She spooned in some sugar and poured in a generous measure of milk, then took a long sip before speaking.

'I suppose the important thing is that Coco is safe,' she began. 'Although it means I'm stuffed as far as having a nanny is concerned. I don't dare imagine what Marcus is going to say when he hears about all this.'

'It could have been worse,' Faye reminded her. 'Coco doesn't seem to have come to any harm from that girl and he'll be relieved that you and his mother can actually be in the same house together.'

'I'm still not sure about that,' she scoffed, taking another swallow of her tea.

Faye looked at her soberly. 'Caro, give her a chance. I know she's a bit full-on, but you do need some help with the baby and she really came through for us today.'

Caroline raised her hands in surrender. 'Okay, fine! If she can keep her opinions to herself – which I doubt, by the way – we can try again. But things are going to have to change around here. I'm fed up with Marcus thinking he can get away with being the phantom of this opera; I don't care how he does it, but he's going to have to spend more time at home and get stuck in with helping with Coco, and that's not negotiable!'

She tossed back the rest of her tea with a ferocious frown and Faye bit back a smile. Marcus might well rue the price he had to pay for peace but knowing how much he adored his wife, Faye suspected that he had already accepted the inevitable. Knowing how much he had suffered from the rift between the two women in his life, she had no doubt that he would agree to any terms that would get their lives back to normal.

'Enough about me, how are you doing?' Caroline asked softly, sounding exactly like Marcus had earlier that day.

Pretending not to know that her friend was referring to Rocky, Faye grinned happily. 'Guess what?'

Taken aback, Caroline shook her head. 'What?'

'I got a promotion today! Can you believe it? Matt and Ruth have promoted me, and I'm a designer now!'

Caroline still looked puzzled. 'That sounds great, but aren't you already a designer?'

'Yes, but now I'm a designer designer! I was only a junior before, so everything I do – did – had to be closely supervised and signed off. But I'll be able to take on my own clients now and do everything from taking the brief to first design. I'll get to manage a budget and pick people to work with on my projects. I'm so chuffed!'

Caroline grasped her hands and squeezed them tightly, her blue eyes shining with excitement. 'That's amazing, Faye, well done! You really deserve it, you've worked so hard.' She paused for a moment. 'Have you told Rocky?'

Faye pulled a face and sat back. 'No-o. He was actually the first person I was going to call – until I remembered that I'm not going to ring him until I'm really sure of what I want.'

Caroline pursed her lips. 'So how long are you planning to keep up the silent treatment?'

'Caro, I'm not doing this to hurt him,' Faye sighed. 'I know he loves me but that seems to be all that's on offer and it's not enough for me. I want the whole white meringue dress and drooling babies and career juggling thing! Maybe I'm being selfish by wanting him to want the same things as I do – I don't know. But none of that seems to be on his agenda, which is why maybe we should both just move on.'

'What about Matt, then?' Caroline suggested helpfully. However much she liked Rocky, her primary goal was to see her friend settled and getting the life she wanted. 'He seems really taken with you. And you know he loves kids – look how great he is with Charlie.'

'Yes, but then I'd be with Matt and still be thinking about Rocky. Anyway, besides the fact that he's also my boss, I don't have feelings for Matt – which is just as well since he's nuts about Mandy Parker. I just wish he'd stop being so bloody stubborn and admit it. I don't know what went on between the two of them before but you can cut the tension with a knife when they're both in the same room.'

With Matt off the list of possible options, Caroline returned to her favourite candidate. 'So let me understand this. You love Rocky but you don't think he's the settling-down kind because he's never raised the marriage issue. And even though he's told you that he loves you, because he doesn't understand what you want, you don't know if he's the right man for you? Have I got that right?'

Caroline looked sceptical and Faye shook her head impatiently. 'Look, it's like going for a job that you think you really really want and being so anxious that you're not good enough for it and that there's no chance that they'll offer it to you anyway, that you don't even think about what it involves. Then, when they do offer it to you, you start wondering if the job's really what you actually want to do.'

'So... What? Now, Rocky's a wrong career move?' Baffled, Caroline scratched her head. 'Sorry, but I don't get it.'

Faye smiled. 'Rocky would be a lovely career move for anyone. But the truth is I've let him have his own way for so long that it's all been really easy for him. He's incredibly sweet and caring when he wants to be, and I know he wants to make me happy but I've allowed the whole power balance of our relationship to shift completely over to his side. So, of course, he quite rightly thinks he holds all the cards and can take all the decisions, even when they affect both of us. He's a strong man; he's used to bossing everyone around and, let's face it, with every woman – including me – falling at his feet, he's never really had to struggle. Even his own mother didn't want to upset him by telling him his father was unwell!'

'So now you want him to struggle?'

Faye shrugged, at a loss for words. 'I don't know, but at least... I don't know... put up a fight, make an effort. If he really wants me, he has to show me, not just tell me!'

'Faye, he's left his job for you!' Caroline protested. 'Or, at least, that's what he told Marcus.'

'True. But, to be honest, I suspect that was as much for his sake as it was to make time for me. He still loves the whole world of finance and making deals but even Yvette had noticed that his heart wasn't in the bank any more. His father's illness really hit him hard and I know he felt guilty about his job taking over his life so much that he hardly saw anything of his parents. I also think seeing Uncle Fred so sick made him finally realise that he was heading down the path of destroying his own health if he kept up the crazy schedule that his job required.'

'So you're willing to throw away four years and a gorgeous guy who loves you if he doesn't what... fight for you?'

Faye thought for a long moment. 'I don't want to; I love Rocky and you know that. But if I have to move on, Caro, it won't be the end of the world. It will be really hard, I won't lie, but I'll survive; I know I will. I want Rocky, but I have no intention of just rolling over and accepting everything on his terms.'

'Hear, hear!' Rose walked into the kitchen with a sleepy Coco nestling in her arms just in time to catch the last part of her sentence. Faye spun around, startled by the interjection. She had completely forgotten that Marcus's mother was still in the house and was even more shocked at the next words that came from her mouth.

'You absolutely mustn't let any man think that they can just click their fingers and you'll come running!'

Caroline dropped her head into her hands with a

silent groan. Any faint hope that Rose would have learned to keep her opinions to herself flew straight out of the open window. Coco spotted her mother and struggled out of Rose's arms to march over and grab Caroline's leg, burbling her own version of hello. Faye, meanwhile, watched in fascination as Rose, uninvited, pulled up a chair to join them, all the while prattling away.

'Men will always try and steamroller you into doing what they want if you let them, dear. Now you take my husband, a very forceful man if ever there was one. When I first met Patrick he wasn't at all the kind of man that my parents wanted me to get involved with and he was certainly nothing like the other young men in our county. For a start he had made all his own money through stockbroking which, as far as Daddy was concerned, was no better than gambling. And then, of course, he was far too brash and self-confident, not to mention...' She dropped her voice into a conspiratorial whisper, '...Irish.'

Caroline whimpered and buried her face in Coco's neck, wondering how much more she could take. Faye bit back a smile as Rose, totally oblivious to any discomfort she might be causing, carried on with her story.

'Daddy made it perfectly clear that Patrick wasn't welcome but that didn't stop him from courting me. I'll never forget Daddy's face when Patrick asked to meet with him – he wanted his permission to propose to me and even though I warned Patrick that he was wasting his time, he was determined to get my father's approval.'

'So how on earth did he manage to persuade your father?' Despite herself, Faye was wildly curious to hear more. She was seeing a whole new side to Rose today and she ignored Caroline's eyes silent pleading to stop encouraging her.

'Well, it turns out that Patrick knew exactly what to do to change Daddy's mind. He invited him to take a drive and then took him to Crayleigh Manor which he had bought and just finished redecorating, and showed him where he intended to set up home with me. Of course Daddy was so bowled over by the size of the place, not to mention that it came with the use of the adjoining golf course, that he couldn't give his blessing fast enough!'

Caroline stared at her mother-in-law in astonishment. 'Marcus has never told me that story!'

'That's because I've never shared it with him, dear,' his mother said placidly. 'One must preserve a little mystery sometimes, even with one's own children.' She turned to Faye. 'The point is that it took a big gesture from Patrick to change Daddy's mind. So my advice is to stick to your guns; if your young man is really the right one for you, he needs to demonstrate that. And if – or when – it feels right, you'll know.'

With that, she stood up and rubbed her hands together briskly. 'Right, then, I'd better be off! I mustn't outstay my welcome.'

Caroline snorted and quickly tried to cover it up with a cough. She handed Coco over to Faye and they followed the older woman out into the hallway to see her out. Rose took her coat from the rack by the front door and slipped it on. She stroked Coco's cheek tenderly and planted a warm kiss on the child's face.

She turned to Caroline and her smile faltered a little. 'Caroline, thank you for letting me stay and I am so very sorry if I offended you before. I really do think you are the most marvellous mother to little Camilla and I shall see to it that Marcus appreciates all the work you do and that he does much more to support you!'

Rose leaned in to clutch her in a strong embrace and Caroline gingerly returned the hug, her face the picture of incredulity. It was the first time she had been on the receiving end of anything more than a perfunctory kiss on the cheek from her mother-in-law and Faye watched her gasp for air in the suffocating grip. She's definitely Coco's grandmother, she thought, wondering how to rescue her friend. Luckily Coco started wailing in annoyance that she was no longer the centre of attention, allowing Caroline to break free.

Rose looked at Faye and an impish smile transformed her severe features. Faye returned the smile, now seeing Rose O'Neill in a completely new light.

'Faye, thank you for phoning me today and I do wish you the best of luck with your young man. Now, remember what I said and don't sell yourself short; you are a very good-looking girl.'

'Erm... Thanks, Mrs O'Neill.'

Rose beamed. 'I must say, you coloured girls do have the most marvellous skin!'

Bundling her mother-in-law out of the house before she could say another word, Caroline closed the front door firmly behind Rose. She turned back to Faye and they stared at each other for a long moment before bursting into hysterics. Faye clung to the door knob almost weeping with laughter while Caroline was doubled over gasping for air, tears streaming helplessly down her cheeks. Coco, her protests forgotten, stared at them nonplussed.

When the two women finally calmed down, they went back into the kitchen with the disgruntled and hungry child and Caroline rummaged through the cupboards.

'Right, let's get some dinner sorted out. What do you feel like?'

They glanced at each other and chorused: 'Pasta!'

Caroline giggled and brought out a packet of spaghetti, setting a pot of water on the cooker to boil. She opened the huge fridge and poked her head around in search of ingredients for a sauce.

'There is one thing I really regret about Anastasia going,' Faye said wistfully.

Caroline looked up curiously. 'Really, what's that?'

'I shall miss her meatballs,' Faye sighed. 'They were really tasty.'

26

Transition

Faye was at her desk sketching out a design idea for the Woollaston project when she was startled by a loud knock. The door to her tiny office was wide open and she looked up to see Mandy Parker standing in the doorway. Dressed in a long pleated navy skirt and a simple white shirt, her blue eyes danced with merriment.

'Surprise!' she laughed,

'Hardly,' Faye remarked drily. 'You really should think about getting a job at Cayhill's, or at least getting your own security pass.'

Mandy blushed a fiery red. 'I know. I must come across like some kind of deranged stalker. Actually, I came to meet Matt – we're going out to dinner – but I wanted to stop by and say thank you.'

'Oh?' Faye raised an eyebrow in surprise and put down her pencil. 'Why, what have I done?'

'Well, you knocked some sense into both Matt and me, for a start,' Mandy replied. 'After your little speech that day, we stopped yelling and actually started talking to each other.'

Faye was burning with curiosity and although she didn't say the words, her expression spoke volumes. After a brief moment of hesitation, Mandy walked into the room and sat in the chair across from Faye.

'I think I owe you an explanation.' She brushed aside Faye's feeble protest that it wasn't necessary and took a deep breath. 'The truth is that Matt and I used to be engaged.'

'Oh!' Faye had definitely not expected that. 'Well, I suppose it goes some way to explaining the tension between you two.'

She gave up all pretence at indifference. 'So what went wrong?'

'I was offered a promotion at work a few months after we got engaged. Unfortunately, the job was in France. At the time, Matt and Ruth were working flat out to build Cayhill's and there was no chance of him coming out there with me. He hated the idea of a long-distance relationship and more or less gave me an ultimatum. I was absolutely furious that he expected me to drop my ambitions while he was working on his own, and we ended up having a huge bust-up. In the end, I left for France and we just stopped speaking.'

Faye looked at her sympathetically. 'That must have been hard. But I have to say that it really doesn't sound like the Matt I know; being so sexist, I mean.'

Mandy's smile faded. 'Well, what I didn't know at the time was that Justin had been planting ideas in Matt's head about the guy who was going to be my boss in France. It turns out that evil brother of mine was making out that

Frédéric had a thing for me, and the more I argued with Matt about taking the job, the more he believed that it was because I wanted to be with Frédéric.'

'How could he? I thought Matt was his friend!' Faye exclaimed furiously. She shook her head, trying to stay calm. 'I wish I could say that it doesn't sound like Justin but from my dealings with him, it's exactly the kind of behaviour I would expect from your brother.'

'Well, let's hope that slap you gave him has taught him a lesson!' Mandy smiled wickedly and jumped to her feet. 'Anyway, don't let me take up any more of your time; I just wanted to say thanks for stepping in when you did. Matt and I are trying to work things out – fingers crossed, we'll get it right this time.'

Feeling more than a little self-satisfied, Faye went back to her sketchpad and was so lost in concentration that it took her a moment to register the ping of a new e-mail in her inbox. She glanced at her monitor and did a double-take when she saw Harriet's name.

Clicking open the message, she burst out laughing at the picture of a tiny infant sporting a small, yellow baseball cap with a large 'W' woven into the peak. The message below read: 'Thought you might like this picture of young Oliver flying the Woollaston flag! Loving the time off, but looking forward to getting back to work soon. Congratulations on your promotion! Harriet'

Faye stared wistfully at the picture of the baby and felt a pang of sadness. Although work had been incredibly busy, she missed Rocky intensely. She knew from Marcus that he was on garden leave from the bank and wouldn't be starting his partnership with Jensen Investment Management until the New Year. She had lost count of the number of times she picked up her phone to call him and then dropped it again, knowing that nothing had changed. They hadn't exchanged a word since the day she had walked out of his flat and although part of her was grateful that he had respected her request to be left alone to think things through, a bigger part of her couldn't help feeling crushed that he had made no move to overcome her objections.

With a sigh she looked at her watch and decided it was time to go home. Oliver's picture had put paid to her concentration and she suddenly yearned to be at home with Lottie and a huge bowl of comforting pasta.

The dark November evening was even more depressing when she stepped out of the building and she buttoned her thick wool coat all the way to the collar, ducking her head to avoid the biting wind. Coming out of Hampstead station, she walked briskly way down the High Street and into the tree lined avenue that took her home. She glanced idly in the direction of Sam Malone's house as she walked past and stopped dead in her tracks.

In the dim porch light, she could see two figures embracing. A minute later, they moved apart and she watched Sam lean across to tenderly kiss the lips of the tall woman in front of him. He stepped back into the shadows and Faye gasped as the light revealed a very familiar face.

'Lottie!' Faye blurted out before she could help herself. Sam and Lottie spun round to see Faye standing open-mouthed at the end of the driveway. Feeling like a mother catching her errant teenager behind the bike shed, Faye folded her arms across her chest and waited as Lottie said goodbye to Sam and walked towards her.

'And how long has this been going on?' Faye demanded sternly. She looked up as Sam called her name and he sent a broad wink and a cheeky smile her way before stepping back into his house and closing the front door.

Lottie, meanwhile, slipped her arm through Faye's and propelled her down the road towards their house.

'Lottie, tell me! What's going on between you and Sam?' Faye protested, reluctantly allowing herself to be hustled along.

Lottie put up the collar of her coat and shivered. 'Let's get home first; it's freezing out here!'

Once inside the house, Faye peeled off her boots, stamping her feet to get the blood flowing back into her frozen toes, and hobbled into the kitchen. With her father away on another business trip, she and Lottie preferred to eat in the warm, spacious kitchen rather than the more formal dining room.

Lottie turned on the heat under a large pot and briskly set out two large soup bowls. 'Right, I made a lovely spicy minestrone soup earlier – I put loads of pasta in, so I know you'll like it.'

She cut up some thick slices of home made brown bread and set the plate down on the table with the butter dish. A few minutes later, Faye was tucking into a steaming bowl of soup and slurping happily on the broken spaghetti. Slathering a thick coating of butter on a hunk of bread, she took a big bite with a groan of contentment.

'This tastes so good, Lottie!'

Lottie smiled as she watched Faye greedily make her way through the food in front of her. 'You know there are times when you still behave exactly like that little six-year old girl I came to look after!'

Faye scraped the last bit of soup from the bowl and swallowed it, and then leaned back in contentment. 'That was delicious; thanks, Lottie.'

She walked over to the fridge and took out a couple of small bottles of water, offering one to Lottie as she resumed her seat. 'Well, I'm certainly not six years old any more. Can you believe I'm actually turning thirty next week?'

Lottie's expression softened. 'No, I really can't. You know I don't get sentimental, Faye, but I'm so proud of you and what you've made of yourself. You've turned into a wonderful, strong young woman and although I never knew your mother, my bet is that she would be enormously proud of you too.'

Faye blinked back the tears pricking the back of her eyes. 'Well, you've been like a mother to me since I was tiny, Lottie, so it means everything to hear you say that.'

Lottie took a sip of her water and cleared her throat. 'Well, that's enough of that. Now, tell me, what are your plans for your birthday?'

'Caroline's in charge of organising everything but I've told her I just want a quiet dinner with her and Marcus and a few of our friends. Because my birthday's on Friday, I'll be at work that day, anyway. Dermot's on tour with the band in Sweden at the moment but he's promised to fly down and have dinner with us and travel back to Stockholm on Saturday.'

Faye took a large gulp of water and continued. 'Dad gets back on Saturday morning so I thought we could have a family dinner at home that evening. Lucinda's so huge now she hates going out in case she goes into labour in public. What do you think?'

Lottie hesitated and then blurted out; 'What about Rocky – surely you'll invite him?'

Faye shook her head and a wave of despondency swept over her. 'I haven't spoken to him in almost three weeks.' She shrugged and injected a note of bravado into her voice. 'Well, chances are he's moved on...'

'Oh, Faye, give the man some credit!' Lottie exclaimed impatiently. 'You're the one who asked him to give you some space; shouldn't you be the one to call first?'

'The trouble is that nothing's changed,' Faye said sadly. 'Trust me, Lottie, I've been on the verge of calling him a million times to say let's just carry on as we were. But I can't – it just wouldn't be right.'

Lottie looked at her levelly, and a reluctant note of admiration crept into her voice. 'Well, Faye, I must say that you never cease to surprise me. But I'm really pleased that you're strong enough to stand up for what you want.'

'Yes, well, it still leaves me single at thirty... which is not exactly what I had hoped for,' she retorted glumly. Struck by a thought, she sat bolt upright and fixed Lottie with a penetrating stare. 'And, by the way, don't think you can duck my question for ever. What exactly is going on between you and Sam?'

Lottie's pale skin flooded with colour and her eyes dropped to the empty bowl in front of her.

'Well, really, Faye...' she murmured, suddenly at a loss for words.

Taking pity on Lottie's obvious discomfort, Faye relented. 'Okay, okay, it's none of my business...but you know Dad will lose his mind if you leave us?'

Lottie's flush deepened. 'Faye! There's no question of that happening – this isn't just a job to me, you know. It's my home!'

'Yes, but we all have to leave home at some point, don't we?' Faye said gently. 'Come on, Lottie, never mind about Dad! You've taken care of all of us for years; don't you think it's time you put yourself first for a change?'

Lottie smiled and looked straight into the depths of Faye's almond shaped brown eyes. 'My goodness, you really have grown up, haven't you? Well, it's really very early days but let's say that if – and I do mean if – I ever decide to move out, I won't be going far. My guess is that it would only be about four houses away!'

27

Questions and Answers

The next few days passed by in a blur. Faye interspersed her growing volume of design projects with fetching and carrying for Lucinda who was absolutely convinced that the twins would arrive the minute she set foot in Sainsbury's. William was involved in a major court case and his long days and occasional nights away from home were proving an even greater trial for his heavily pregnant wife.

On the morning of her birthday, Faye woke up early. It was still pitch black outside and cocooned under her duvet, she could hear the high-pitched scream of the wind howling outside. She thought ahead to the evening's celebration and felt a sharp stab of pain that she would be marking such a momentous milestone without Rocky, something which only weeks before she would have never believed possible.

Her birthday also brought to mind her hazy memories of her mother whose sudden death twenty-five years earlier had left her devastated husband alone with two young children. If she felt this bad not being with Rocky, she brooded, she could only imagine how much worse it would be if they had started a family together.

Her mobile buzzed and she reached out from under the covers to check the message, her heart racing at the thought that it might be from Rocky. Her excitement faded when she saw the text was from Amma but she tapped the phone and was forced to smile as she read. Albeit marriage meant living in close proximity to Edwin's parents, Amma was clearly relishing her new life.

However, there was one piece of unexpected news. 'Edwin's persuaded me to visit America; he's convinced that I'll love it and want to live there (I don't have the heart to tell him that's never going to happen!). We're saving up to go over on holiday next year, so maybe we'll come through London on our way and see you all. Have a lovely birthday!'

Glancing at her bedside clock, Faye slipped out of bed and headed for the shower. Since her promotion the work had been coming in thick and fast and birthday or no birthday, she had a pile of things needing her attention at the office. Trying to push aside the thoughts of Rocky that kept intruding, she dressed quickly in a pair of fine grey wool trousers and a cherry red top and picked up her portfolio and handbag.

There was no sign of Lottie when she stopped to grab a couple of apples from the kitchen before heading to the tube and she smiled, wondering if the woman was even in the house. For the past week, her housekeeper cum surrogate mother had been flitting between home and Sam's house and Faye was now accustomed to walking into the kitchen and seeing the handsome actor at the table, more often than not tucking into something Lottie had just made.

After escaping the stifling crush of the underground, Faye hurried into the office and immediately got down to work. In between fielding calls and text messages from friends and family members, including a very welcome phone call from Auntie Amelia and Uncle Fred, who sounded almost like his old self again, she was able to get through the pile of e-mails and requests from her newly assigned clients. Trying hard to swallow her rising hurt at Rocky's continued silence, she smiled cheerfully at everyone who stopped by to wish her a happy birthday, including a very chipper-looking Matt who deposited a vase full of flowers on her desk with a bashful 'Happy birthday from Mandy and me.'

Caroline's call later in the afternoon provided a welcome – and brief – distraction. 'Okay, I've only got a minute, so listen carefully and don't interrupt. The plan is we're all meeting at my house this evening at seven o'clock. Dermot's promised to get there on time for once, so don't be late!'

'I thought you booked the table for eight o'clock?' Faye cut in, ignoring the instruction.

'I did, but I want to watch the Role Models interview before we go. It will only take half an hour.'

Faye had already seen two episodes of the TV series which had become an instant hit. Eliza Henry was a skilful interviewer and the guests that Caroline had selected had so far been as entertaining and inspirational as she had hoped.

'Okay, fine,' Faye said absently, her eyes drifting back to the email she had been composing. 'I'll see you at seven.'

Keen to avoid a lecture on being late, it was actually ten minutes before seven when Faye rang the doorbell. She rubbed her cold hands together, marvelling at how quickly the warmth from her car had vanished in the chilly winter evening.

Caroline opened the door and bundled her in without ceremony.

'Thank God, you're on time! Quick, take off your coat and grab a glass of wine; the show starts in a few minutes and then we're meeting up with the others at the restaurant. I've planned an amazing menu with the chef!'

'You're more excited about my birthday than I am,' Faye laughed. She walked into the living room where a very relaxed Marcus lay on the sofa playing with Coco.

He stood up with the child and folded Faye in a tight hug with his free arm. Taking her hand, he twirled her around.

'Happy birthday, beautiful. You don't look a day over twenty-one!'

Laughing, Faye reached up to kiss his cheek and give a burbling Coco a squeeze, taking a hasty step back before her goddaughter could raise her arms.

'Coco, this dress is pure silk and cost me a fortune. I absolutely refuse to let you drool all over it!'

The doorbell rang and Caroline rushed out to open it. Moments later Dermot strolled in; a grey beanie covering his hair and a long scarf wound around his neck partially concealing his face.

'Sorry, I'm not late, am I?' he asked, looking round curiously before kissing Faye and hi-fiving Marcus. He peeled off the scarf and tossed his hat onto the sofa. 'I had to shake off a couple of paps that caught me getting into a cab.'

Caroline shook her head impatiently and thrust a large glass of red wine into Faye's hand. 'Here, you go! Now, everyone sit down – the programme's about to start!'

Dermot flung himself into the nearest armchair and Faye perched on the arm, taking a cautious sip of the wine.

'Jeez, Caro, how much did you pour in here? I still need to walk tonight, you know!'

'Shhh!' Caroline ordered, picking up the remote to switch channels. Even Coco subsided into silence as they watched the opening sequence with Eliza Henry swivelling round in her chair to speak straight into the camera.

'Good evening and welcome to another in our series of Role Models. My guest this evening is someone who has taken the rather staid world of finance by storm in recent months. Originally from Ghana, Rocky Asante is...'

Faye stared open-mouthed as the camera panned to a close-up of Rocky looking very composed. Almost spilling her wine, she swung round to glare at Caroline.

'You didn't tell me—'

'Shhh!' All three of them chorused; their eyes glued to the screen. Reluctantly, Faye turned back to the TV and took a huge gulp of wine, her heart beating faster as she watched the familiar smile lighting up Rocky's face.

Eliza's questions were insightful and probing. Unlike Clarissa, she used them only as a prompt, giving him the opportunity to talk about his childhood in Ghana, the challenges he had faced in his career and the lessons he could share with the viewers. Rocky spoke fluently about his work, spelling out so clearly what investment banking involved that even Dermot, who struggled to understand his own bank statement, was hooked as Rocky outlined the stages involved in the LaserTech deal right up to the moment of signing.

By the first commercial break, Faye had knocked back most of her wine and her palms were damp from the tension of watching Rocky. After a short break, the programme resumed and Eliza moved straight into questions from viewers and read out a few comments from the texts and tweets coming into the show.

Tossing back what was left in her glass, Faye watched closely as Rocky smiled easily and answered the barrage of questions with confidence. Knowing just how much he disliked public attention, she had to admit that he was giving an impressive performance.

As the interview moved to a close, Eliza looked down at her iPad and giggled. 'We've just had a question sent in to us and I don't want to put you on the spot, Rocky, but Patricia from Southampton wants to know if you are married.'

Rocky's smile vanished and Faye cringed, her heart dropping like a stone as she waited with dread for a re-run of his earlier response to Clarissa's question. Asking Rocky questions about his work was one thing; but as he had made abundantly clear, he would never talk about his private life.

With the camera fixed on him, Rocky uncrossed his legs and leaned forward slightly in his chair.

'Patricia, I'd like to thank you for your question because it gives me a chance to say something very important. I've been accused many times of being too focused on my work and maybe this is a good time to show that I know where my priorities lie.'

Eliza looked at her guest in bewilderment, clearly at a loss as to where the interview was going. She wasn't the only one; Faye stared at the screen in confusion, wondering if Rocky had finally lost his mind and succumbed to his sister's long-predicted breakdown.

However, he appeared sane enough as he smiled in sympathy at the TV host's confusion. 'No, I'm not married, Eliza. But there is someone very special who I'm hoping will help me to change that situation. She's always put me first even when I didn't deserve it and if you'll allow me, I'd like to put that right – and to do it right now.'

Faye's heart was thudding in her chest and she looked around the room wildly to see everyone staring at her.

'What the-?' She was immediately shushed by Caroline who was pointing excitedly at the TV. The camera had pulled in for a close-up of Rocky and his handsome features filled the screen, his voice suddenly serious.

'Faye, I'm hoping you're watching this. Thank you for being everything and more that any man could ask for. Thank you for your patience and for loving me even when I gave you countless reasons not to. You are a far better role model for anyone watching than I could ever be.'

The silence in the room was deafening as Rocky leaned even further forward, his copper-coloured eyes so close to the camera that he could have been standing in the room.

'I love you more than any words can say – and I hope you know that now. Will you marry me?'

The camera pulled back to show Eliza beaming and clapping enthusiastically as the credits started to roll. A loud cheer erupted in the room and a stunned Faye sat immobile as her friends rushed over to her. Caroline was crying and laughing at the same time and her face was almost as red as her hair as she hugged Faye fiercely. Letting out an elated whoop, Dermot gave her a sound kiss on both cheeks and Marcus, grinning broadly, squeezed her by the shoulders with delight. Coco, who had absolutely no idea what was going on, settled for jumping up and down on the spot and drooling with excitement.

Suddenly the door to the living room opened and Rocky walked in. An immediate hush descended and Faye gasped, her heart racing so fast that she could hardly breathe.

'But, how? You were just on TV...' She stammered in shock.

'We recorded the interview earlier this afternoon at a regional studio,' Rocky said softly. His eyes sought out Caroline and he winked at her with a cheeky smile. 'Thanks for your help, Patricia.'

Faye's eyes widened as her friend blushed crimson. Caroline held up her hands helplessly. 'Hey, it wasn't my idea! I just helped to get the message to Eliza. It was all Rocky's doing. Look, we'll leave you two to talk – we'll go ahead and wait for you both at the restaurant. Come on, you lot.'

She scooped Coco up and looked meaningfully at the others. Jumping to attention, the two men hastily gathered their belongings and trooped out of the room, Marcus patting Rocky's shoulder encouragingly on his way out.

Faye was still perched on the arm of the chair, not sure that her legs would hold her up if she stood. Rocky strode across the room and knelt in front of her. He took her hands in his and looked steadily into her eyes.

'You once told me that I'd made you look bad in front of thousands of people by denying you on TV.'

He smiled ruefully and continued. 'I figured that if I was really going to make it up to you and show you how much you matter to me it would also have to be in front of thousands of people. So I asked Caroline to help me out since she was the one who arranged for me to go on the show in the first place.'

Faye stared at him in disbelief, trying to reconcile his words with the Rocky she knew. 'I can't believe you did that for me. I know how much your privacy means to you...' Her voice broke and tears filled her eyes.

'You mean so much more.' He reached up to stroke her hair and gently tugged her down towards him. Still kneeling, he kissed her and she pulled him closer still, her tears spilling onto her cheeks.

'Please, sweetheart, don't cry.' He pulled back and used his thumb to tenderly smudge away the trail of tears from her face.

Then he looked at her quizzically. 'You know I'm still waiting for an answer to my question?' There was more than a hint of anxiety in his voice and her tears forgotten, Faye grinned, feeling happier than she could ever remember.

'Which question?' she asked innocently.

He slid his hand into his jacket pocket and removed a small dark blue box. He opened it and took her hand in his. 'I meant everything I said in that interview, Faye. Marry me. Please?'

She gazed in astonishment at the square cut diamond ring set in a slim platinum band and then looked at Rocky. His face told her everything she needed to know and far more eloquently than any words he could have said.

Suddenly Rose's words came back to her. When it feels right, you'll know. This wasn't a house beside a golf course, but she couldn't imagine a bigger gesture from her privacy-obsessed boyfriend than a marriage proposal on national television. This time it definitely felt right; this time she knew exactly what she wanted.

She cupped his face in her hands. 'Yes, of course I will!'

She kissed him gently and watched him slide the ring onto her finger. 'It's absolutely beautiful! But how did you know...?' She laughed. 'Caroline!'

'I've got a lot to thank her for,' Rocky admitted. He grinned, his eyes alight with mischief. 'I'm so relieved you said yes. My father wouldn't have let me back into the house if I didn't seal this particular deal.'

Laughing, she swatted him on the shoulder and Rocky bounded to his feet and pulled her into his arms. He kissed her again, holding her closely.

'He also reminded me that if you put too much distance between yourself and what's important, it's all too easy to forget what really matters. He loves you like a daughter and he's going to be so happy when he hears our news.'

'I love him too.' Faye's eyes misted over as she thought of how Uncle Fred had once again been instrumental in bringing her and Rocky together. She glanced at her watch and exclaimed.

'Rocky, we'd better go! There's a small crowd of people waiting for us at the restaurant.'

She grabbed her bag and scrabbled to retrieve her phone.

'I forgot to ask Caro where we're eating. She didn't actually say which restaurant she'd booked.'

With a smile, her new fiancé gently plucked the phone from her hand and dropped it back into her bag. His eyes twinkled as he took her hand and they walked towards the door.

'I know exactly where we're going. Caroline's booked a table at Alfredo's. For some reason, she thought you might feel like pasta.'

About the Author

Frances Mensah Williams was born in Ghana, spent her early years in the USA and Austria, and grew up in the UK. After graduating from the University of Reading, she pursued a career in Human Resources Management, Training and Consultancy which spanned the UK and Africa. She is the Chief Executive of Interims for Development Ltd. and the Managing Editor of ReConnectAfrica.com, a careers and business website and online publication for African professionals in the Diaspora.

Frances is the author of the novel *From Pasta to Pigfoot* and the non-fiction titles *Everyday Heroes – Learning from the Careers of Successful Black Professionals* and *I Want to Work in Africa: How to Move Your Career to the World's Most Exciting Continent*. She is the recipient of several awards and, in 2011, was nominated as one of the Top 20 Inspirational Females from the African Diaspora in Europe.

To find out more about Frances Mensah Williams and for regular updates, visit her website and Facebook page.
www.francesmensahwilliams.com
www.facebook.com/FrancesMensahWilliams

Acknowledgements

Writing is a solitary experience but a novel is never produced alone and my special thanks go to my amazing publishers and all the fantastic Jacaranda Books family.

Valerie, thank you for your insightful editing of the manuscript; your suggestions were invaluable and your unfailing encouragement is hugely appreciated. Jazzmine, my publicist par excellence, thank you so much for your tireless efforts to keep me on track; for your positivity and morale boosting support... and your unflagging schedule of promotional events.

My thanks also to Charles Routt for his observations on investment banking (now you know what that conversation was all about), and to Hazel McKinna and Pauline Downie for their insights into the world of interior design. Any errors are the result of my own over-fertile imagination.

My thanks go to my super-wonderful wing women for their continuous support and encouragement, day and night. Simi Belo, Tosin Otubanjo, Karina Bappa, Helen Tucker, Angela Brown, Betty Demby, Lande Belo, Caite Dugan, Mame Gyang, Terhas Berhe, Mallie Kundasamy, Elvina Quaison, Kay Corriette: I'm blessed to have you and I love and appreciate you. Thanks to Chux, my rock, and everyone who keeps me going when I'm ready to tear my hair out.

My love and thanks to my beautiful girls, Seena and Khaya, who bore the brunt of my race against deadlines so generously, and the rest of my wonderful family who I hope will continue to forgive me for disappearing from time to time in this mad quest called writing.

My sincere thanks to everyone who took the time to review this novel – or wrote kind reviews about *From Pasta to Pigfoot* – and to Kate Forrester for another delicious cover design.

Finally, my thanks to Faye and Rocky – it's been an immense joy to peek into your lives and I wish you well on your journey.

Also by Frances Mensah Williams:

From Pasta to Pigfoot, Jacaranda Books, 2015
I want to Work in... Africa, How to Move Your Career to the World's Most Exciting Continent, SKN Publishing, 2014
Everyday Heroes: Learning from the Careers of Successful Black Professionals, SKN Publishing, 2011